Evangeline's Heaven

Evangeline's Heaven

A Novel

Jen Braaksma

Published by SparkPress, a BookSparks imprint,
A division of SparkPoint Studio, LLC
Phoenix, Arizona, USA, 85007
www.gosparkpress.com

Published 2022
Printed in the United States of America
Print ISBN: 978-1-68463-153-7
E-ISBN: 978-1-68463-154-4
Library of Congress Control Number: 2022903757

Formatting by Kiran Spees

To my husband Scott. Soulmates do exist.

CHAPTER 1

Evangeline knows it won't last, but for this one beautiful, fleeting moment, sitting with her sketchbook in hand on the cliff's edge in the Farlands of First Heaven, she feels a sense of peace. The ocean below her, less than peaceful, rages and froths against the white rocks and for that minute, it seems to Evangeline as if the waves have sucked out her anxiety and anger and claimed them as their own. Her fingers, smudged black with charcoal, slide across the ivory cotton-blend paper, her birthday gift from her great-uncle Raziel. She thinks of him now—far from her, in Sixth Heaven—and wonders if her moment of calm is what Uncle Raziel describes as a *thin place*.

"It is anywhere, anytime you sense the veil between God and His angels is at its thinnest, where a touch of the Divine seeps into our world," Uncle Raziel had explained.

Evangeline wishes it were true, that the presence of God in her Heaven could be a blessing of tranquility, and yes, maybe she flirted with Uncle Raziel's charmingly seductive possibility that God is loving and benevolent, but she could not deny her own harsh experiences. In the end, she could come to only one conclusion: that God had long ago forsaken her people.

Still, it would be so nice if Raziel were right . . .

A shadow slips over her and instantly, Evangeline is pulled back into reality, cursing her slip into her uncle's ineffable fallacies. In one

1

swift motion, she drops her sketchbook, jumps to her feet and whirls, her golden sword poised in front of her face. She knew it was foolish to come here, alone and exposed at the farthest edge of the Farlands, but she's not foolish enough to be caught unawares.

The hooded, cloaked figure in front of her steps forward and raises his own gilded sword, and as he brings it towards her, there's a clang of metal, the sound bell-like, echoing above the wind. Evangeline prepares for another strike, a fight, when the man steps back, surrendering.

"Impressive, my sweetness," he says, removing his hood in an easy, languid motion.

"Father!"

Evangeline drops her sword and rushes into his wide embrace, his arms and his thick, black wings enveloping her. This moment now may not have the touch of the Divine, but for Evangeline, being enfolded in her father's strength is better. But then Evangeline remembers herself, remembers the war, and she pulls away.

"What are you *doing* here? It's too dangerous. Gabriel's here in First Heaven, close to the Farlands, you know."

"I know," her father says. He wraps his arm around her shoulder and gently pivots her so they're both staring into the churning sea. "But I wasn't going to miss your eighteenth birthday."

Then, with a theatrical flourish, Lucifer holds out both arms toward her, his left hand cupped in his right, his fingers folded. He bows gallantly, then presents to her a single striking, silky black feather, one from his own wing.

"My dear Evangeline," he says. "I offer you another year of safety and protection."

Evangeline's smile grows as she accepts the feather, then laughs at her father's dramatized formality.

"Are you going to say the blessing like that every year?" she asks, amused. Still, she feels unexpectedly warm, as if the sun, distant in the dreary autumn sky, has found its way under her skin.

"But of course," her father replies, and Evangeline catches a trace of his lips curling in enjoyment. "It is the sacred Commoner tradition. As your only living Commoner relative, it is my responsibility and my *honor* to bestow on you another Naofa feather."

Evangeline wraps her hand around the soft plume, heartened by her growing collection—all black, of course, since she has only her father to bless her. She thinks of the special pile back home in their cozy cottage, the sixteen of them, although, of course, she should have eighteen. It still pains her that she's missing one. But that was her fault. She chose to go to boarding school in a place in Fifth Heaven, where her father was not and would never be welcome. Three years later, she still wishes she'd listened to her father, who warned her against the idea. She should have trusted him, should have remembered her place. She's a Commoner, and a proud one. She should never have tried to hide it, should never have tried to deny her heritage. But then she feels a pang, the same one that drove her toward the school in the first place. *I'm not only a Commoner. I'm also a Dominion.* Is it fair to deny her mother's lineage simply because she died when Evangeline was so young?

But the other angels at school had been so cruel to her. *They* denied her Dominion status. They treated her like a demon djinn, as terribly as if she were a full-blooded Commoner.

"It's because they don't know any other mixed-class angels," her father tried to explain. "You are rare. You are special."

But at fifteen, Evangeline didn't want to be rare. She didn't want to be special. She just wanted to fit in, and the others wouldn't let her. There was constant taunting and spitting and tripping. Her roommate even broke Evangeline's deep violet wings, hobbling her for days. She'd begged her father to let her come home, but he refused.

"I hate to see you suffer," her father had said, "but your instincts were correct. You need to know who you are, who your mother's people are. Harden your heart against them if you must, my sweet Evangeline, but you will not come home. The experience will strengthen you."

He'd been right, of course. Her father is always right.

Now, however, as they settle onto a rock overlooking the ocean, exposed from all angles, the peace she imagined moments ago has disappeared. In its place is fear that her father has misjudged the danger in returning to First Heaven.

"The Archangels have rounded up more than a dozen Commoners, and it's only the first day of the week," Evangeline says. "It's bad, and I can't—" She stops. She looks out at the foamy waves, watching them roll over themselves in a constant, never-ending movement, their power unharnessed. She feels an irrational jolt of envy, wishing she could have the strength of the water instead of this helplessness she feels. A chill runs down her spine, the warmth within her body fading with the crush of reality.

"You can't *what*, Evangeline?"

Her father speaks softly, gently. It's the voice of her childhood. A voice layered with care, with confidence, with reassurance. A voice he reserves for her alone. He's a master of voices—not imitations of others, no, nothing so trite—but of heart. With his tone, his cadence, his inflection, Lucifer could make anyone feel as if he or she was the most astonishing angel in the Heavens. Evangeline has often witnessed it, the light in the eyes of his listeners as they soak up Lucifer's praise, and at first she'd been jealous. She hadn't understood her father's charisma then, hadn't wanted to share him, but with his family voice, his Evangeline voice, he reminded her she was, and always would be, his beloved.

Evangeline sighs. She wishes she'd never said anything. She hates to worry her father; he has enough burdens as it is because of the war. But he persists, and finally Evangeline relents.

"I can't be responsible for your capture or . . . death," she says. She thinks of it often, her father's capture and his death. She fears, with a terror bred in her bones, that one of those two fates is inevitable. She lives and relives her worst nightmare, watching her father die over and over at the Archangels' hands, feeling helpless, feeling hopeless. Her father is their biggest target—he is enemy number one and she is acutely aware that Gabriel, head of the Archangels and once a family friend, will stop at nothing to capture and destroy her father. The *last* thing she can cope with is if something happened to her father because he risked coming back here for her.

He is all she has.

She had thought—hoped, wished, yearned—to build connections with her mother's people when she first begged her father to let her attend Diaga Academy. She was desperate to discover her place in the Heavens, but aside from bonding with her mother's caring, eccentric uncle Raziel, she had failed to find a sense of belonging among the Dominions in her two long years at the school. She therefore shut out all thoughts of Seraphina—who was only a ghost, anyway, considering Evangeline has no memory of her—and refocused her energy on the only person who mattered: her father.

Her father pulls her to him, and she leans into his thick chest, warm in the soft feathers of his wings. She wants them to stay like this—together, the two of them. It's always been the two of them. She wants Lucifer to ditch the Cause and come home. To live a quiet, secluded life in the back corners of the Farlands, away from

Archangels and Dominions and the damn Seraphim, who are trying to obliterate them. She hates them, the seven highest-class Seraphim angels, God's messengers, for their power, their arrogance, but she hates the Cause more. The Seraphim have been ordering all the other classes of angels to abuse Commoners since the beginning of time, but the Cause is the reason for her father's absences. The Cause is why he leaves her to fight the Archangels, to fight the Dominions, to fight the Seraphim and all other classes of angels. She wishes he would quit the Cause, wishes she could quit the Cause, but she can't. Because she understands better than anyone that the Cause *is* Lucifer and Lucifer *is* the Cause. One wouldn't exist without the other. If Lucifer were to give up the Cause, he would shrivel into the shell of the angel he is. If the Cause were to give up Lucifer, it would sputter and die. No, it's Lucifer alone, single-handedly, who is saving them all. It's Lucifer alone who is rising up against their long-suffering oppression, who is inspiring others to follow. And it is Lucifer alone who created his Dragon army, symbolic of the mythical beasts whose strength outstrips all living creatures, and who will win this war, the war Lucifer alone started. Which leaves Evangeline with no choice. She must share her father.

And it is this grudging acknowledgement that engulfs Evangeline in shame. How can she wish for Lucifer all to herself when the Commoners need him? How can she be so selfish?

Her pale cheeks flush in this cold wind, at the thought of her own self-interest. Her father has sacrificed so much to lead their people; should she not do the same?

"Honey," her father squeezes her close. "*No one* will be responsible for my capture or death," he says, "because I *won't* be captured. As for my death, you'll be an old grandmother yourself by the time I'm an ancient, rickety angel nearing the end." Lucifer chuckles softly and Evangeline has to smile because it is impossible to envision her strong, strapping father as anything nearing feebleness.

"But," he says, and as his voice drops, so too does Evangeline's stomach. Whatever he's about to say next, Evangeline assumes she doesn't want to hear it. "We're losing. You know that, too, don't you?"

Evangeline pulls back, shocked at her father's admission. Whatever she feared would cross her father's lips, it wasn't that. Never has she heard her father speak one word of pessimism. Anger, bitterness, yes, but never resignation. Evangeline is worried; but strangely, she's also heartened. She loves that her father has faith enough to confide in her.

"We've been pushed back, you've heard," her father explains. "We lost our momentum in Fifth Heaven," he whispers under his breath. "The Archangels pushed us back to Fourth Heaven—and even then we have only a tenuous grasp. The academics in Third Heaven still refuse to take sides, the cowards." Lucifer's anger colors his cheeks, his expression a familiar flash of her famous father.

"The Dragon army has lost battles before," Evangeline says. She feels unsteady, though, as if these rocks will tremble and toss her into the sea. She can't shake her fear. Does her father believe all is lost?

No. They *can't* lose. Not now. For too many centuries, the Commoners have been pushed out of the higher Heavens—the lands they once shared—and backed into this farthest corner of First Heaven, the farthest from Seventh Heaven. The farthest from God. Well, no more. Lucifer was right to rally their class of angels. He was right to fight for what they once had.

"It's not the battles we've lost," her father explains. "It's the hearts and minds. Our own people have retreated. They don't believe like they once did. They're afraid."

Can you blame them? Evangeline thinks. *Hundreds of young Commoners already killed in battle. How many more need to die?*

But she doesn't say this. She can't. It's not her place, not as the daughter of the rebel leader, Lucifer. But she's felt it, the fear, the sadness, the desperation, the despondency. She's heard the stories, knows the score. She's not out there on the battlefield—Lucifer won't allow her fight, says she's too valuable—but as a sword trainer, she's seen the drop in numbers of recruits, witnesses their pessimism, feels their hopelessness.

Her father stands and straightens, stretching his wings wide. He seems to shake off his torpor, rising, like a phoenix from the ashes, into a newly vibrant Lucifer.

"So we're going to do something about that. *You're* going to do something about that."

A sense of foreboding washes over her. Whatever her father is thinking, she's already apprehensive.

"We're hosting a rally." Lucifer meets her eyes, his smile bright. "*You're* hosting a rally." There's a sense of glee in him, a little boy enamored with his new adventure. It's an expression Evangeline has seen before, one she loved when her father would take them flying off cliffs very much like this one, when he would make them swoop close to the water, the spray of the waves weighing down their wings. Now, though, she is not a frivolous young girl; she's eighteen, an angel who appreciates that the consequences of her father's schemes are much, much worse than an unexpected swim in the whirling ocean.

"No . . . " Evangeline breathes.

"Yes!" Lucifer claps his hands and ruffles his wings. "A large, open-air rally, in Siog Glen. We'll stand tall and proud. Like we used to. Before the war. Our people need to return to that. They need to be reinspired. They need hope."

"It's suicide," she whispers, but even as she says it, she sees her father's rationale. Siog Glen is symbolic, the ground sacred to

Commoners. She pictures her father on the stone, the raised monolith in the valley beside the glassy lake as their people gather below him, rapt with attention, ready to listen. It's the spot where her father, as a young angel, heroically and unexpectedly defeated the irrepressible djinn. It's where, years later, Lucifer first rallied the Commoners to the Cause. It's where Lucifer convinced his people, against the counsel of their Elders, to go to war. Evangeline appreciates her father's strategy in suggesting the rally. His message is clear: *we will not be cowed.*

But it's too dangerous now. Gabriel and his Archangels are hovering and could at any moment capture or kill *all* the Commoners gathered. Why offer him easy pickings?

"Father, it's not safe . . . "

Lucifer rounds on her, his eyes blazing fire. "Safe? *Safe?* When have Commoners *ever* been safe, Evangeline? When the Seraphim pushed us out of the higher Heavens all those centuries ago? When the Archangels refused to protect us from the djinn invading the Farlands a few decades ago? Or how about before the war last year? Were we safe then? Safe from God's plan to exile all of us Commoners to his new planet, Earth, and enslave us as 'guardian angels' to his new human creatures, our 'sister species,' as God calls them? No, we've *never* been safe!"

There would have been a time when Evangeline would have cowered from her father's tirade, but not anymore. She'd heard enough of her father's firebrand speeches, his impassioned rhetoric, to know his diatribe wasn't an attack against her personally. And she knows everything he says to be true, but still, she worries. Why go looking for trouble?

"Honey, let me remind you that we are in a war *not* of our own making." Lucifer softens his tone. "We may have started the fighting, but we had no choice. We *had* to push back. There's risk in that, yes, but ultimately *passivity* is our gravest threat, not God's army. *You* know that. It's what I taught you, and it's what we need to remind our people of. So yes, it may be dangerous to gather so many supporters in one spot, right under Gabriel's damn nose, but I promise you, my sweetness, the risk is worth the reward."

Evangeline wraps her arms and wings around her body against the stiffening wind, feeling dispirited. Her father is right, of course. Firing up the crowd is a smart, simple plan to reengage the Commoners. A few words of inspiration, a reminder that it's always darkest before the dawn . . . yes, Evangeline suspects that will at least partially reinvigorate their movement. Still, she wishes there was another way.

"You won't speak long, though, right?" Evangeline pleads.

Lucifer looks at her, lovingly. "Oh, my sweet Evangeline, I won't be speaking at all. *You* will be."

Evangeline whips her head toward her father. "Me?"

No, no, *she* won't be talking at all. She never has, she never will. Lucifer is the charismatic leader. *He's* the one all the Commoners come to hear. She's just his daughter, a supporting figure in the background, living quietly in his shadow. *She's* not going to inspire anyone.

"Yes, you." Lucifer smiles at her with that confident, charming grin, the one he uses to win over his detractors. "It's about time you took center stage. You're intelligent and articulate and you know the Cause, you know our people better than anyone."

Evangeline shakes her head. "No one will listen to me." She's acutely aware she didn't inherit her father's charisma—and she's okay with it—but there's more to her concern and she wishes her father would finally acknowledge it.

"Nonsense," Lucifer dismisses her concerns with a wave of his hand. The ocean crashes hard against the rocks below, as if to accentuate his point. "You're my daughter. Of course they'll listen to you."

"But I'm not . . . " Evangeline closes her eyes. Her father doesn't understand. Why, after all these years, can't she make him understand? "I'm not a full Commoner," she whispers. Her voice catches on the wind, whipping it away. She's not sure he heard her, but she refuses to repeat herself. There's no end to the argument, anyway. Her father will say it's irrelevant. That she's half Commoner, which is, to him, the same as full Commoner. "Have you only been half discriminated against?" he'd challenge her, and she'd have to shake her head. If anything, she wonders if she's experienced double the prejudice because Commoners don't see her as one of them, but Dominions *only* see her as a Commoner.

"Evangeline." Lucifer turns to face her. He puts his hands on her shoulder and presses hard, as if he were trying to ground her concerns. "You can do this."

No, she can't. She can't speak in public. She remembers the embarrassing disaster of her class presentations at Diaga. All eyes on her, expectant, judging, confident she would stutter, then fail. She won't willingly subject herself to that again.

"Why can't *you* do it?" Evangeline tries to keep the whine out of her voice but she's not sure she succeeded. She doesn't want her father to put himself in danger, but if he expects his people to be reenergized, he's the one to do it.

Lucifer glances into the sky, then gets to his feet, beckoning her to follow. They stroll along the cliff's edge. The winds whips back Evangeline's raven hair, and she feels the cold autumn air flutter through her wing feathers. Her father keeps close to her side, protecting her from the elements.

"I can't stay," he explains. She can barely hear him over the waves below, the wind above, and she leans into him. "I've found the key."

Evangeline stops midstride, shocked. "*The* key?"

She finds it impossible to believe. The Key to the Kingdom, the one that's supposed to be *theirs*, the one that grants Commoners access to power in the Seven Heavens was lost to legend long ago. When her father first united the Commoners in a fight to reclaim it, she knew he was being metaphorical. Lucifer had done an impressive job convincing his followers that it was real, that it existed, that it could be recovered, but Evangeline understood it was only a story. The war would be won, not when Lucifer held up some iron key plucked from the Seraphim secretly guarding God's realm, the land of the departed souls, like the Commoners desperately wanted to believe, but when he brought home a truce from the Seraphim agreeing to stop the Commoners' exile to Earth. The key had always been and would always be a nice, necessary, useful symbol. But now her father says it's actually real and he's found it?

"No one else knows," Lucifer tells her, "and no one must." He wrenches her arm. "You're clear on that, right, Evangeline?" He sounds furtive. "Not Zephon or any of the other generals. They know I'll be on a mission, but not why." Lucifer eases his grip and smiles. "But this is it, honey. Once I have the key in my grasp, we will have everything we've been fighting for."

Evangeline feels stunned, and for a moment she imagines she's been sucked into a book of legends where mythology magically comes to life. That the key is real, that her father found out where it is . . . that her father trusts *her* with the secret. She's been his biggest supporter, obviously, but she can't help asking, "Why are you telling me, then?"

"For the rally, of course." Lucifer's shoulders relax as his wings unfurl. "Until I have the key, we still need to reignite our people. Since I can't be there, *you* have to do it. "But," he adds with a wink, "*you* have to believe."

Evangeline drops her eyes, embarrassed. For all she and her father share, she's never admitted to him her skepticism about the key. She's tried to keep that to herself; she understands how important the symbol is to the Commoners, but she realizes now how much her father sees through her. She squirms under his gaze, but Lucifer pecks her softly on the cheek.

"I've given *you* hope," he says. "Now give our people hope."

He steps back and spreads his wings to their majestic span. "I'll see you soon."

When Lucifer takes flight, Evangeline yearns to grab onto his foot, tug him back to the ground and tell him to stay. Yes, she wants him to find the key—the *key*!—but she needs him here. Despite her father's confidence in her, she is well aware of her limitations: that she can't lead or inspire. And if he must go, she wishes he'd put Zephon in charge of this campaign; he's a seasoned soldier, after all, the best after her father.

But he's not Lucifer.

And the people want Lucifer. Which means only, she, his daughter, comes the closest.

She sighs. She has no interest in organizing the rally. She hates the idea of speaking in public, and she worries about exposing the Commoners to danger out in the open fields of Siog Glen—she'll have to talk to Zephon about security—but more than anything, she's fearful of disappointing her father. It's happened rarely, since Evangeline strives to comply with her father's wishes, but she flushes at the heat of shame as she vividly remembers when she has. And that was for minor infractions, like not returning home for dinner in time or faring poorly in a training exercise. She can't bear to consider Lucifer's deep glare of displeasure if she were to turn her back on him now, at this most fragile time for the Cause.

Which means she'll do as he asks.

She watches her father fly along the rocky coastline, sharp with rugged beauty, as he rises higher into the clouds.

Without warning, four figures shoot up from the cliff's edge and surround her father. Evangeline sees the silhouette of their swords, recognizes the distinctive white of Gabriel's wings among the attackers, and her heart stops.

"No!" she cries, but the wind and the surf eat up the sound. She unsheathes her sword, and leaps into the air. The Archangels encircle her father; she hears the quick, staccato clang of metal on metal as Lucifer deftly, skillfully fights them off. She sees one of them spiral backward through the air and plummet to the ground with an agonizing scream. The other three close in on Lucifer, their attention so focused on Lucifer's dizzying blade that they don't see Evangeline when she dives into the fray, stabbing one of them in the back above the wings. She hears the crunch of bone, and her stomach convulses as she pulls out her sword. For all her skill at sword fighting, she's never had to use it in battle, never had to actually injure someone. It makes her sick. The second Archangel spins, out of control, toward the rocks below.

"Evangeline, *go!*" Lucifer bellows at her.

But shaky or not, Evangeline won't leave her father, not when he's fighting Gabriel, and—

The third Archangel turns to face her.

Michael.

Evangeline hesitates a moment too long at seeing her one-time friend, the only friend she made at school, although she knew he was kind to her only because his father, Gabriel, had made him be.

Michael thrusts his sword at her, cutting into her shoulder. She cries out at the pain, then bites her tongue. The wound burns hot; she feels blood seep onto her skin, but it's not deep. With effort, she refocuses as Michael jabs again. Evangeline parries and attacks. She looks into his silver-gray eyes; she sees recognition and . . .

She can't think. She blocks his cross swipe, and with a swift flick of her wrist she twists his sword away from her. She's desperate to know how her father is doing against Gabriel. They are well matched, the master Gabriel having trained his then-protégé exceedingly well. But Gabriel is older and Lucifer fights with a passion unequaled in all the Heavens, so Evangeline is hopeful, but still, she can't afford to look. Michael abruptly flies to her left, but Evangeline immediately spins to meet his blade. The wind picks up, pushing them past the cliff's edge, out over the rocks frothing with waves. She hears her father's roar.

"No!"

With a gut-wrenching fear, her head snaps toward him as he wrings the tips of Gabriel's snowy wings. Gabriel drops in the air, but he's able to control his descent, injured, as Lucifer launches upward.

"Michael!" Gabriel cries.

Michael rockets after Lucifer, but Evangeline hurls herself at him. She grasps a handful of silver feathers and yanks him back with all her might. They grapple in the air as Michael tries to shake her off, but Evangeline's weight drags them both down. Out of control, they both spiral down, down, down. Michael tries to kick at her, and Evangeline's grip slips, she but holds on. She has to; she has to make sure her father gets away.

They plummet toward the churning ocean. If Evangeline doesn't let go *now*, they will crash into the shallow water together, landing on the jagged rocks. Evangeline calculates. The spray of the water drenches their wings. Another second. But Evangeline jumps away from Michael too late, and the ocean swallows them up. Like a spear, she shoots down through the water. She hits the rocks—the pain is a thousand knife slices—and she rolls, and spins, first her shoulder, then her head cracked against rocks. She feels dizzy, nauseous, disoriented. She spins around and around, unable to find the surface. She feels the current drag her away. Her lungs are bursting. She must breathe. Opening her mouth, she tastes the salt but keeps her throat closed. Air. She needs air. She slows in the water and then sees a pinprick of light.

With the last of her effort, she kicks toward it and bursts above the surface, gasping for breath. Her eyes dim with spots, her head aches, but Evangeline works to orient herself. She sees the ocean has washed her down shore. Where she and Michael crashed into the water, she notices Gabriel pulling Michael from the waves. Michael is crawling, moving. He's alive.

Evangeline scans the skies. The clouds have dissipated, swept away by the strengthening wind, leaving behind a sky of intense clear blue. Her father is fast; Evangeline is convinced he escaped. Weary, aching, Evangeline drags herself toward the beach. She stays low in the water, afraid Gabriel and Michael will spot her. Her wings drenched and heavy, she wants to collapse on the rocks, but instead she creeps toward a narrow cave in the cliff, an underground trench. She needs to rest. And she needs to wait them out. She pulls herself into the mouth of the cavern, crumpling against the cold stone wall. She trembles, soaked and scared.

And wracked with guilt.

She knew it was too dangerous for Lucifer to return to the Farlands. He never should have come for her birthday; that's no doubt how Gabriel found them. He knows Lucifer, knows him better than Lucifer would like to admit, she thinks. Gabriel would know he'd find her for the Naofa feather. It's not a Dominion tradition, but Gabriel has been friends with her father long enough to understand Commoner customs. He could easily have guessed Lucifer would find Evangeline today. And what did she do? Venture out to the most open, vulnerable spot in the Heavens, like a sitting duck. Why didn't she stay at their cottage? No doubt Gabriel would have found them there, too. She should have stayed at their base, protected by Zephon and the others. Gabriel never would have attacked him there.

Evangeline wraps her wet wings around her, shuddering.

But why did Gabriel attack Lucifer at all? The Gabriel she's heard about would never have assassinated an enemy leader. She thought he had too much honor. Enemy that he was, Gabriel remained God's top soldier; they fought within the rules of war.

And Michael . . .

Evangeline closes her eyes. She pictures Michael as he was three years ago, when he first approached her in school. In a dark stairway, when they were alone. Evangeline, always alert, had hurried her steps, but Michael's voice from the shadow stopped her.

"You can ignore Abdiel, but you'll have to stand up to Uriel. The torment will only get worse if you don't."

Evangeline paused. It was the first time someone at the school had acknowledged she existed. The direct contact alone, addressed to only her, made her at once desperate for more interaction but also incredibly wary. She didn't know who he was; she didn't know if he was playing her. But her distressed need to connect with *somebody* made her stop to listen nonetheless.

"Remind Uriel that his father ran, like the coward he is, from a battle during the Djinn War. He'll explode at first, but that'll tell him you have inside information. He'll be afraid about what else you know, so he'll leave you alone."

"What else do you know?" Evangeline asked. She clung to the idea that there was actually a way she might survive this school yet, but still she was cautious.

"How to help you," he said in a surprisingly soft tone.

Evangeline narrowed her eyes, glaring at him, suspicious. "Why would you help me?"

"My father is making me."

He was honest, direct, forthright. She liked that. "Who's your father?"

"Gabriel. And with your father being Lucifer, you're going to need all the help you can get. You know what they call him?"

"Of course," she said, drawing back her shoulders, standing straight. "Leader of the Cause. Savior of the People."

Michael laughed, then. "Open your eyes, Evangeline. Your father is nothing more than a power-hungry thug. A devil worse than the demon djinn."

It shouldn't surprise her now that Michael is fighting alongside his father; she was doing the same, after all, for hers, but still she feels sad, disappointed. She liked Michael, even if they had rarely spent time together. She understood he, the son of God's top Archangel general, couldn't be seen with her, a mixed-class nobody, but still, she valued his concern, no matter his motives.

Evangeline hears the scrape of rocks outside her cave. She stops breathing. She pulls herself up flat against the wall, willing herself to become invisible.

"Where did she go?" Evangeline hears Gabriel's sharp voice. It sounds full of confidence, authority and a grating sense of righteousness.

"I don't know," Michael replies. He sounds weak, shaky, and Evangeline wonders, worries, how injured he is. "She could be anywhere."

"Dammit," Gabriel cries out. "We were so close. Now we have to find Lucifer before he gets the key."

Evangeline's blood runs cold. How does Gabriel know about the key? And how does he know Lucifer is after it?

"What about Evangeline?" Michael asks.

"Not our concern. Finding Lucifer has to be our only priority."

"But we have no idea where he's going. We don't know where the key is."

"So we'd better damn well find the key before Lucifer and then wait."

"An ambush?" Michael asks.

"Precisely. It's the only way we can end him."

Evangeline's heart stops. Her vision blurs, her mind reels. Her worst fear: her father's death is being plotted right in front of her.

"Do we send out scouts?" Michael asks his father.

"No." Gabriel is vehement. "No, we can't risk Lucifer catching on to us. If he gets his hand on that key before we do, the consequences are unfathomable. No, until we locate him, it has to be only you and me."

Evangeline wants to jump out of the cave and plunge her sword into both of them before they can harm her father, but she lost her blade in the swirling ocean. Instead, she listens, helplessly, as her father's would-be assassins scramble away over the rocks. Finally, she lets out a slow, deep breath, and presses her hands together to stop them from shaking.

Gabriel and Michael know about Lucifer's mission.

How? Lucifer was adamant no one else knew.

But Evangeline realizes the "how" is irrelevant now. The only thing that matters is her father.

She has to find him and warn him that he's walking into a trap.

If she can find him.

And find him first.

CHAPTER 2

Hidden in the cave, Evangeline frets impatiently, waiting for Michael and Gabriel to leave the beach. She feels herself vibrating, her muscles taut, a band ready to snap. She's hyperaware that every second she delays going after her father will exponentially increase her challenge of finding him. Already she feels a surge of panic. Her father could be anywhere. He is cunning and resourceful and knows these Heavens like the back of his hand. As leader of the Cause, he is always in danger, so he has cultivated an incredible ability to disappear. He is often gone for weeks at a time, and Evangeline never knows where.

The thought actually calms her. Her father excels at being a phantom, so maybe she has nothing to fear. Maybe Gabriel and Michael will never be able to find him anyway.

But she can't take that risk. She can't sit back here in the Farlands, waiting, wondering, hoping her father can escape an ambush by the Archangels, not if there's the slightest possibility she could warn him. And of course she has the advantage: she understands her father better than any angel alive. As long as she tries to think like him, she stands a good chance of finding him first.

Michael and Gabriel finally fly off. Thin cirrus clouds have rolled back in, streaking the azure blue sky with long, streaking patterns of white, like the tail of a sky horse. Evangeline watches as the two

Archangels head into the cloudy wisps, in the direction opposite from Lucifer, a gift to her, and she exhales a breath she didn't realize she'd been holding. She suspects they're going to plan and strategize and that will take time, which means she'll have a head start. There's no way she's going to waste it.

She slides along the slick rock wall to the mouth of the cave, carefully peering out. Simply because the two Archangels flew off doesn't mean it's safe. She never saw what happened to the other two angels who attacked Lucifer, but she tells herself she won't take any stupid chances. She may not have fought in any formal battles, but she is well trained.

Evangeline sees that the skies are empty and the long rocky beach, a thick pile of pebbles and stones, is deserted. She listens for sounds of footsteps or the flutter of wings, but she hears only the incessant crashing waves, a steady, consistent drumbeat that refuses to keep pace with the rapid hammering of her heart. She satisfies herself that she is alone before she probably should, and then leaps into the air to fly after her father. The autumn wind on her face, strong and cold, feels like a blast of winter. It drives her backwards, but Evangeline redoubles her effort and flaps harder. Her shoulder throbs from where Michael grazed her, and her body aches from where the rocks pummeled her, but she shakes off the pain. It's not the first time she's been bruised in a fight; Lucifer ensures their training is realistic, so Evangeline is confident she can manage.

Now to figure out where her father is going. Since she never believed in the existence of the key before today, she can't possibly imagine where Lucifer thinks it's hidden. Instead, she tries the process of elimination. Since Seventh Heaven is accessible only to the seven Seraphim, there is no possibility Lucifer will go there. Sixth Heaven, home to the ten Cherubim, the Divine Record Keepers, is also protected. But Evangeline still must consider this. Other angels can get into Sixth Heaven if they're accompanied by a Cherubim—and there happens to be a Cherubim in their family. Her great-uncle Raziel, her mother's uncle, often invites Evangeline to his home. But Raziel always said she was an exception. The other Cherubim dissuade visitors and she finds it hard to imagine Raziel would flaunt his colleagues' rule for Lucifer. She knows her uncle and her father are friendly; she'd heard that Raziel was the only member of her mother's family to support Lucifer's marriage to Seraphina, but Raziel is also a discreet angel. It's one thing for Raziel, a scholar, her tutor, to sneak his great-niece into Sixth Heaven to study; it's another for him to invite in the leader of the rebels, no matter how sympathetic Raziel may be to their Cause.

So if not Sixth Heaven, then Fifth Heaven? Here is a real possibility. Lucifer once lived there, when he was stationed as an Archangel in his former life. It's where he met Seraphina and where Evangeline was born, but Lucifer has harbored a vicious hatred for the place since Seraphina's parents tried to steal Evangeline away from Lucifer after her mother died. It's why she was initially afraid to ask him about attending Diaga Academy in Fifth Heaven, and it's also why he never visited her there. But maybe his loathing was reason enough to suspect Lucifer would look for the key there. He's been all over First Heaven in his drive to recruit Commoners to the Cause, and he's lived and trained in Second Heaven as an Archangel, so if the key had been in one of those two Heavens, he might have already stumbled on it. But since he rarely ventured into Fifth Heaven, he might expect to find the key there.

Evangeline briefly considers Third and Fourth Heaven, but quickly dismisses them. The angels in Third Heaven are faithfully neutral in the war; she can't picture a key that rightfully belongs to the Commoners to have landed in that Heaven. Fourth Heaven is vast, but sparsely populated. Nature reigns, so it's unlikely that a key that grants powers to angels would be hidden among rocks and trees.

Of course she could be wrong. Lucifer was never looking for the key before. So maybe it is right here in First Heaven. Or Second. Or Third or Fourth. Her mind spirals with possibilities, one as likely as the last, and she feels the flutters of panic again. But she has to make a decision, so she reminds herself to think like her father.

Fifth Heaven.

She thinks he'd like the delicious irony of finding the key to reclaiming the rights of his people under the very noses of the angels who have discriminated against them for so long.

But as Evangeline flies on through the cold afternoon, she begins to tire. She'd been clinging to the faint hope that she'd catch up to her father before long, but with every passing hour, she realizes how slight those chances are. Instead, she needs to refocus. Plan on getting to Fifth Heaven, then look for her father. If she encounters him before, well, all the better. The difficulty, though, is that it's a three-day journey to Fifth Heaven at the best of times, yet she's now weakened from her injuries, she has no food and no warm clothing for the coming night. As much as she needs to hurry, to ensure she beats Michael and Gabriel to her father, she needs more supplies.

And she knows exactly where to go.

Sophia's.

Well, Sophia's parents'. Evangeline's heart squeezes in sorrow at the thought of her only childhood friend. She died in battle six months ago, fighting side-by-side with Lucifer.

"She was extraordinarily brave," Lucifer said when he broke the news. "A true warrior."

The battle had been at the border of Second Heaven, not far from

Sophia's village. Evangeline ached to think how close to home Sophia had been when she died.

"I should have been there, Father," Evangeline whispered, her throat almost too tight to speak. Her heart burned with remorse and regret. She and Sophia had trained together; they worked so well as a team, always having each other's backs. Evangeline couldn't explain it, had never experienced it with another soldier, but it's as if she could anticipate Sophia's moves and Sophia instinctively understood hers. They were on fire in training, unbeatable. It's one reason her father called Sophia up; she'd proven herself so well. But Lucifer, as always, refused to allow Evangeline to fight.

"As my daughter, you're too valuable," Lucifer insisted. She heard his logic: she was a symbol of their fight, of the Cause, a shining light that glowed no matter the outcome of any battle, and she knew she was also his backup. If anything did happen to Lucifer, then she'd be there to lead the struggle. But she also knew what Lucifer refused to admit: he was just plain scared of losing her.

It rankled Evangeline. It smacked of nepotism, of preferential treatment. Lucifer would persuade hundreds of other angels to give up their sons and daughters to the Cause, but he refused to do the same. She was as good as the other soldiers—better—yet her father would never let her prove her worth on the battlefield. It's not that she wanted to die—it's not that she wanted to fight. But since she was, through no choice of her own, burdened with a legacy to lead the Cause by her father's side, how could she earn the respect of the Commoners and her father's army, the Dragons—who were already suspicious of her mixed-class status—if she never ventured into danger?

Evangeline has convinced herself that if she'd been in battle with Sophia, Sophia would have lived. She still feels the shame of a coward;

she should have insisted harder, maybe defied her father. She should have shown up on the battlefield. She should have protected Sophia. But she didn't argue with her father, not once. She asked, he said no, and she dropped it, secretly relieved. It's so easy to say she wants to prove her mettle when she knows she'll never have to.

Evangeline nears Sophia's village around dusk. Although splashed in lengthening shadows that obscure the community, Evangeline pictures its beauty in her mind's eye, and her spirits immediately lift. The land is a lush spread of rolling green hills, with cozy cottages nestled on expansive homesteads. A small market sits in the center, surrounded by a few clusters of houses, one of whose is Sophia's. Of all the houses and of all the hosts Evangeline had to endure during her nomadic childhood, during her father's interminable trek through First Heaven to gather supporters for the Cause, this was her favorite.

All because of Sophia, the closest angel Evangeline had to a sister.

Evangeline never wanted a sibling. She loved that it was only her and her father, the two of them against the world. But then Lucifer began recruiting Commoners, began dragging her to strangers' homes where she was thrown in the viper's pit of children's cruelty. She'd never gone to school—Lucifer insisted on complete control of her education, so he taught her himself. He was thorough, a harder taskmaster, Evangeline suspects, than a real schoolteacher, and she learned a lot—except how to interact with hostile little angels. Evangeline remembers enduring taunts and insults, but more than anything, she remembers the stinging isolation. It never bothered her to be alone when they'd been at home, but the hurt cut deep when the other kids purposely excluded her.

Until she met Sophia when she was twelve. Evangeline had lost count of the number of host families she'd stayed with, had long since gone numb from the alienation, but to Evangeline's great surprise,

Sophia didn't ignore her. In fact, Sophia, the oldest of seven and the only girl, clung excitedly to Evangeline.

"You have the most *thrilling* life," she gushed, her arm wrapped in Evangeline's as they sauntered over the green meadows. "Imagine seeing all of First Heaven!"

Evangeline remembers shrugging, trying to act nonchalant, but inside she was giddy with joy. She understood her life was an anomaly, but she never suspected it could be one of envy.

Still to this day, Evangeline misses the lightness Sophia brought to her life. She'd never before jumped in puddles, or swung on a rope swing tied to the tallest tree. She'd never before laughed at silly gossip—*Did you see Hemah cut off part of Auriel's braid in the schoolhouse yesterday?*—or play childish pranks, like the time she and Sophia glued the pages of Azael's textbook together and giggled at his puzzled expression when he tried to open it.

Evangeline smiles at the nostalgia. She loves that Sophia reminded her how carefree life could be. She wishes her days could be filled with fun like that again.

Evangeline lands on a nearby hilltop, the surrounding landscape now cloaked in the chalky gray of early night. She's apprehensive suddenly. She hasn't seen Sophia's parents since her funeral and she worries how awkward the reunion will be. She berates herself now; she should have written, should have kept in touch. She should have told them how much their daughter meant to her.

Evangeline makes her way to the bottom of the hill, toward the town square. She feels her skin prickle and casts a furtive look around. Her sense of unease escalates. The farmhouse near where she landed, where she and Sophia cuddled with barn cats, is dark. Troubled, Evangeline approaches it. She expected warm candlelight in the windows; there always was, and she should smell smoke billowing from the brick chimney. But the dark windows stare back at her, the blank, empty eyes of an abandoned house. Evangeline circles the property and lets out a small cry when she sees the back.

Instead of a wall, there is only a pile of bricks and stones flowing incongruously onto the weather-beaten hearth rug.

What *happened* here? She knew there'd been fighting nearby, but that had been months ago. And when she'd heard about the battle so near the village she loved, she'd begged her father for details. He'd put a hand on her shoulder and squeezed gently.

"All is well, Evangeline."

But this is only one farmhouse, and maybe something else happened to it. Structural damage, or a horrific windstorm.

But even as Evangeline approaches the rest of the village, she doesn't believe it. She may not have fought in battles, but she's seen plenty of their aftermath. The lands are scorched, trees torn down, buildings plundered for material . . . this village has all the hallmarks of a ruined town.

Evangeline weaves through the market square, empty at this time of night. But still an unnatural silence hangs heavily in the air. She sees no one, not a single angel stumbling merrily from the local pub. The homes, Evangeline notes, are intact, unlike the farmhouses she passed, but they are all cold and dark.

With a trembling feeling of foreboding, as if eyes watch her behind the darkness, Evangeline approaches Sophia's house. This is not the warm, lovely home she remembers. Weeds trample the small garden path, the paint on the front door, once a welcoming sky blue, bubbles and peels, and instead of glass, dark curtains drape like mourning cloths in the empty windows.

Evangeline hesitates. For a moment she thinks about running. The place scares her and she doesn't want to find out why. But she steels herself. Her father's life is at stake. She has to find him and to do that she needs supplies, so she knocks.

No one comes to the door, but she hears furtive movement inside. She feels her pulse rise, her heart quicken. She wishes she had her sword. She wishes she'd gone back to her cottage to replace the one lost at sea, but she'd been too impatient to follow her father. She'll have to ask for a weapon here.

She knocks again, this time more insistently. Again, she hears the scuffling of feet.

"Christie, Sidriel," she calls softly to Sophia's parents. "It's Evangeline."

The shuffling stops. For a long, tense moment, there is no sound, not even the crickets of the evening. Evangeline worries about what she should do. Given their longstanding support of the Cause, she's sure that once they hear about Lucifer's plight, they'll be eager to help, but how to get their attention? Should she barge in? Come back in the daylight? While she vacillates between aggression and retreat, the door creaks open. Evangeline sighs, relieved she doesn't have to decide.

Christie stands in the sliver of the doorway. Evangeline can't see beyond her, except to notice darkness. There seem to be no candles, no fire to light the home.

"Why are you here, Evangeline?" Christie asks. Her voice is cold, like that of the winter wind.

Evangeline shivers, taken aback. Christie was always a warm, caring angel. Busy, yes, and distracted, overworked with seven children as well as her role organizing the community for the Cause, but always pleasant. She was the type of mother Evangeline always envisioned her own mom would have been: smart, strategic, strong, yet soft and gentle.

"I need your help," she says. Before the words have left her mouth, however, she feels the creeping heat of shame. She hasn't contacted the family in all the months since Sophia died, and now, abruptly, she lands on their doorstep and the first thing she demands is their help? "Please," she tries to soften her tone.

Christie slams the door in Evangeline's face.

Evangeline stumbles back, shocked, baffled. She appreciate it can't have been easy for them to lose Sophia, but they'd never been rude to her before. Is she too much of a reminder of their daughter? Or maybe they blame her for Sophia's death, the way she blames herself. The coddled daughter of the fierce leader safely ensconced on the sidelines while they had to sacrifice their own child.

The guilt, which has festered quietly for so long, thrums to life.

"I'm sorry," she says to the closed door. Her voice is quiet, shaking. "I'm so sorry . . . "

The door abruptly flies open. A strong hand grasps her arm and before Evangeline can fight off the grip, she's pulled inside. The entryway is dark; she can see only the outline of shadows. Abruptly, the hand releases her.

"Sidriel?" Evangeline asks hesitantly. She feels as if she's entered a strange reality. This dark, dank house is nothing like the welcoming warmth she remembers.

"What do you want, Evangeline?" Sophia's father's tone is as gruff as Christie's voice was cold.

She feels off-kilter, as if she's balancing on a river log. She hasn't yet fallen, but her heart races at the possibility.

"My father's in danger."

Saying the words aloud embolden her. She lets go of the guilt swallowing her. She's sorry Christie and Sidriel lost a daughter and she's sorry she wasn't there to help save her. But this goes beyond

Sophia now. This is about her father, about the Cause, so she can't be afraid to ask for help from loyal supporters, no matter their personal losses. It's what her father would do.

"Good," Sidriel spits out.

Evangeline blinks in surprise. She must have misheard.

"Gabriel is after him," Evangeline starts to say, but Sidriel interrupts.

"I hope he finds him."

Evangeline frowns, puzzled. Christie and Sidriel are one of the strongest supporters of Lucifer and the Cause in this part of First Heaven. Lucifer told Evangeline it was a coup to gain their support. So many Commoners were pushed to the Farlands, but Christie and Sidriel held out in their part of First Heaven. They are quiet heroes, Lucifer boasted about them, surviving in a minority community surrounded by Principalities, who, despite being only one rung up on the class hierarchy, spit on Commoners. Christie and Sidriel's endorsement of the Cause made all the difference in recruiting Commoners beyond the confines of the Farlands.

"Is this because of Sophia?" Evangeline ventures a guess. It pains Evangeline to bring up her name in this house; she can imagine how much it must hurt Sophia's parents, but she feels she has no choice. She has to get past their suffering to get what she needs.

Sidriel snorts. "Sophia? My daughter who died for nothing?" The bitterness runs deep beneath the words, startling Evangeline.

"I know it's hard," Evangeline tries again. To be frank, though, she's losing patience. She understands their pain; she feels it, too, even if her grief is incomparable to that of a parent's, but she has to make them see she's trying to prevent further catastrophes, because she fears if her father dies, so too does the Cause.

"You don't know hard," Sidriel says. "You have some nerve, showing up here, demanding help for Lucifer—"

Christie appears in the shadows beside her husband. Evangeline didn't hear her approach, and now she wonders why she doesn't hear anything else. This house was never silent, not with so many little ones around. It makes Evangeline worry. Where are Sophia's six brothers?

Christie speaks up. "You don't know, do you, Evangeline?" Her tone has shifted, no longer cold, but soft, gentle.

Yet Evangeline remains on edge, grated by the hint of pity in Christie's voice.

"Know what?"

Evangeline hears Christie sigh, then the older woman tugs her husband's arm. "The poor child," she says.

Evangeline clenches her fists, her nails digging into her palms. She's normally slow to anger and slower to explode, but Christie's insulting condescension is too much to bear.

Christie takes in a deep, slow breath and when she speaks again, her voice nearly matches the motherly tone Evangeline remembers. "Come in, please, Evangeline. We need to talk."

Evangeline hesitates. She came here for help, but she's still put off by their initial reaction. She doesn't understand their attitude. Still, she reminds herself that her father needs her, so it's her duty to put aside her own discomfort. Christie and Sidriel are willing to talk, which means they may be willing to help, so of course she should follow them in.

Christie leads her to the kitchen at the back of the house. A low fire smolders in the grate, throwing barely a glimmer into the room. Evangeline stops at the door, saddened by the gloom in a house that always held cheer. She remembers the house as vivid and shining. With nine angels living in the cottage, and each with wings a different color, the place felt like a summer garden always in bloom. Sophia, with sky blue eyes and wings, insisted she envied Evangeline's deep violet irises and feathers, but Sophia didn't know envy as strong as Evangeline's. When she saw Sophia's impressive collection of Naofa feathers, dozens and dozens, given to her by each family member on every birthday as a blessing, Evangeline felt a visceral bitterness at the riot of color she could never have. Rose for unconditional love, red for courage, green for health, blue for peace, and so, so many more. Evangeline was grateful for her father's singular blessing of protection from his black feathers, but she could never stop herself from wondering, irrational as her worry may have been, that she always struggled not because she was half Commoner but because she was never honored with the variety of blessings most Commoners had bestowed on them.

Then again, Sophia is dead. And Evangeline is very much alive, as is her father—unless she stalls even more.

Christie ushers her to the wooden table, once scrubbed and clean, now covered in grime, something Christie would never have allowed to happen before. Awkwardly, Evangeline sits, straight and tall, now a stranger in a place that had once felt like home. She notes the silence in the drafty house and it is deafening, a sharp, discomforting contrast to the rambunctious racket such a large family always created. Evangeline wonders, worries, where Sophia's brothers are.

Christie bustles to the pantry, pulls out a small loaf of bread, and cuts a thin slice. She places it on a chipped plate—something Evangeline has never before seen here—and thrusts it toward Evangeline.

"I'm sorry we have no butter for you," she says. "We ran out months ago."

Evangeline feels a chill travel up her spine. "I don't understand."

Christie settles into a chair across from Evangeline, but Sidriel stands, as if on guard, hovering over her.

"The blockade is extraordinarily effective," Christie explains ruefully.

Evangeline is now thoroughly confused. "There's no Archangel blockade," she explains, shaking her head. "My father crushed that a long time ago."

From his position standing guard, Sidriel laughs bitterly. He waves his arm around the small stone kitchen, once the setting of so many chaotic dinners. Now Sidriel's abrasive laughter echoes as if in an empty tomb. "Who said anything about an *Archangel* blockade?"

Evangeline stares at him, uncomprehending.

"Lucifer is starving us out," Christie explains.

Now it's Evangeline's turn to laugh. "That's crazy," she says, and she's relieved. If Christie and Sidriel are working from false information, all she has to do is correct them. Then they'll understand and be willing to help her. "My father told me all about his visits to the stranded communities after he defeated the Archangels and reopened the supply routes."

Evangeline barely remembers the conversation. It was so long ago. She vaguely recalls being pleased that Lucifer managed to save the outposts. It's hard enough for Commoners to exist in First Heaven outside the Farlands; she can't imagine having also to worry about sourcing food.

And she doesn't recall him saying anything about this village. Surely Lucifer would have told her, since he understands how important this place is to her.

But Evangeline can't deny the dire conditions. The house, damp and cold, despite the small fire, smells musty, old. She thinks about the ruined farmhouses, the empty streets.

"Even if there was a blockade," Evangeline concedes, "it would be the Archangels' fault, not my father's."

But a worrying thought begins to gnaw at her. *Why wouldn't Lucifer have sent in his army, a platoon of Dragons, to break the Archangels' stranglehold like he did in the other villages?*

"It's not the Archangels, it's your father," Christie says warily. "He needs martyrs. Deaths of Commoners blamed on Archangels to further the fury of his followers."

Evangeline goggles at the two of them. "You are insane," she says, and she no longer cares whether she insults them. It's abhorrent that they'd accuse her father, their leader, of such despicable behavior. There is no *way* Lucifer would starve his own people for propaganda.

Her mind flashes back to this afternoon, to her father's confession on the cliff that he feels they're losing. Could Lucifer have thought that hurting his people—?

No! What is she *thinking*? It's beyond absurd to think he'd starve his own people. Evangeline snaps her head up. She thinks she hears a scuffle of footsteps outside. Christie and Sidriel also freeze at the sound. Then they hear voices, low at first, then growing, loud and angry.

"Sidriel!" One voice from outside rises above the rest. "Give us Lucifer's daughter! We saw her come in."

A cold sweep of panic runs down Evangeline's spine. Christie's expression, too, widens in fear. Quickly, she jumps from her chair, and with quiet efficiency, rummages around the kitchen and pantry. She shoves a bundle in Evangeline's arms. A blanket, a heel of bread, a chunk of cheese.

"*Go,*" she whispers urgently, guiding Evangeline to the back door. "Head to Duma's barn across the field. Hide there until you hear that all is quiet, but then you must leave before daylight. If they catch you here, they'll string you up alive."

"But . . . " Evangeline's mind whirls in dizzying confusion. These are Commoners; they're all on the same side. If she could talk to them, she could make them see reason.

Christie puts her hand to Evangeline's cheek, and despite the chill in the house, her touch feels warm. Evangeline finds herself leaning into the motherly caress.

"It's not fair to you, I know," Christie says.

Evangeline wants to object. It's not about being fair to her, it's about not being fair to her father.

"Sidriel, get Sophia's sword," Christie says to her husband. "She must be able to defend herself."

Without hesitation, Sidriel hurries into another part of the house and quickly reappears, holding out her best friend's sword.

Evangeline takes it, although she feels like she's in a daze. This is all too surreal. The ruined village, the darkened house, Christie and Sidriel, accusations against her father . . . but she's not an idiot. She hears the rage in the voices outside. Rational or not, reasonable or not, the mob on the doorstep is out for blood.

"Go," Christie repeats, softly this time, reluctantly.

Sidriel eases open the door and scans the back garden. He nods at her then ushers her out.

Evangeline slips quietly into the night. The moon has risen, casting a bluish hue across the land. She stays to the shadows as she creeps along the side of the house. She hears the angry shouts of the villagers at Christie and Sidriel's door and she feels a twinge of remorse for putting them in harm's way. But she didn't know—how could she have known? She's sad to see how little the village has; it *is* a shock, considering her father told her everything here was fine. But to blame Lucifer? To accuse him of starving them out? She doesn't know what sick game the Archangels are playing, but it's despicable they'd malign her father like that. She'd always heard that Gabriel was honorable, that he fought clean and fair, but these falsehoods are beyond the pale.

Evangeline makes her way to the end of the row of house and sees the field she needs to cross to reach the safety of the neighbor's barn. She'll be exposed for sure, but it's not terribly far. She thinks about flying, which would be faster, but reasons the risk of being seen is greater than on foot and there's no need to look for trouble. She listens for the voices of the mob, but Christie and Sidriel must have appeased them, because she hears nothing. The night is quiet. Evangeline checks around her; she's alone.

She darts out, sprinting across the meadow. She'd run this way dozens of times with Sophia, skipping and laughing and tumbling as a twelve-year-old but now she runs fast and hard, an alert soldier. The silhouette of the barn comes into view; she's almost there.

She hears a shout. "Hey! Over here! She's running!"

Evangeline instinctively whirls toward the high-pitched squeal. She sees a shape, a figure at the window of the last house waving frantically, calling to the mob on the street. Evangeline slows, then curses herself for getting distracted. She's been trained better than that. Be aware of danger surrounding you, but never lose your focus. She turns again, the barn in sight, but she hears the thundering of feet, on the hard ground, the whip of wings in the cool air. Now Evangeline must pause; she needs to know what she's up against. She appraises her attackers. A dozen, she counts, at *least*. More could be obscured in the shadows. But they are farmers, merchants, not soldiers, and while Evangeline has no doubt they're strong, she also hears in their cries their emotional rage. It could make them dangerous, unpredictable, but more likely Evangeline calculates that their anger will make them irrational. They will not think clearly, which means, to outsmart them, all *she* has to do is think clearly.

She makes a beeline for the barn. They think, of course, that's where she'll hide. But she can't. Not now. She'd be trapped—they'd rip the place apart until they found her. Still, she needs them to believe she's gone in, and she suspects that won't be hard to do. They'll see what they want to see, so when Evangeline reaches the door to the barn, she yanks it open then drops immediately onto the grass. She slithers away from the door on her belly, clutching tight to the blanket, food, and sword Christie and Sidriel gave her. She hears the clatter of the barn door as it bangs shut, the sound echoing across the field. Evangeline continues to slide through the cold grass, around the corner of the barn. She's anxious to spring up and run, but she stays on the ground until she's around back. Then, with the thick, solid barn between her and her pursuers, she jumps to her feet and flees. This time she doesn't let the angry shouts of the mob distract her. She sets her sights on the black line of trees and with a burst of speed, delves into the forest. The thick branches block out the light of the moon and Evangeline has to slow before she trips. She can't afford to be careless, not now.

Evangeline's heart pounds from exertion, but her fear is minimal. She has a plan, she's figured out where she'll be safe. Evangeline picks her way cautiously through the trees until she finally finds what she's looking for: a large hollow in a tree. She glances furtively around her, but she's alone. She crouches low and crawls into the wooden cave. There's room; it fit both her and Sophia comfortably when they were twelve, but still Evangeline feels the space close in on her. She thinks of the peace she felt for a fleeting moment earlier today, on the cliff, her dissipating sensation of a thin place. If the veil between God and angels was at its thinnest then, she now believes the barrier between them is at its iron and steel thickest. She was a fool to lapse into her uncle's foolish ways. She folds in her wings, wraps Christie's blanket around her, and pulls her knees up to her chest. She stuffs the bread and cheese deep in her pocket—she's not hungry, not anymore, and then finally she breathes out.

But she finds herself trembling. Her whole body starts to shiver, and she can't stop. What *happened*? Being chased by a mob that believes—wrongly—that her father is purposely starving them out to create martyrs for the Cause? It's insane. This whole day has been insane. First her father shows up at the most dangerous time, announces he's discovered the mythical key, which will end this war and restore the Commoners to their rightful place in the Heavens, and then he gets attacked by Gabriel. Evangeline fights off Michael, her once-friend from school, flies after her father, only to land in a strange, inverted world where her very own people believe she is now their enemy.

Her head pounds. She can't make sense of any of it. Evangeline leans back against the damp wood and closes her eyes.

Happy birthday to me.

CHAPTER 3

Evangeline gradually becomes aware of a stream of light behind her eyelids, a hue of reddish orange, and she snaps open her eyes. She gasps. Weak sunlight trickles into the hollow of her tree. Beyond its opening, she can see the trees of the forest are already painted pink with the rising sun. With sinking dread, Evangeline shakes herself fully awake. *Stupid, stupid, stupid.* She meant to rest for only a few minutes and escape before dawn the way Christie and Sidriel warned her, but she'd been so tired, not only her body, but her mind. She wanted to stop the swirling madness in her head—the false accusations against her father, the reasons why Sophia's parents betrayed Lucifer's Dragon army—and the best way to do that, she discovered, was simply being unconscious.

It worked. She didn't dream once.

No, her nightmare exists in her waking hours.

She slides cautiously from her hiding spot, looking and listening intently for her pursuers, but the woods are quiet. She hears the trill of birdsong, and gently rustling leaves, but no pounding footsteps or angry cries. She guesses the passion of the crowd lost its heat when they couldn't immediately find her. Regardless, she needs to leave. She needs to find her father.

She weaves her way through the woods, familiar to her only in her vague memory from six years ago. She can remember details

of Sophia's thick hairstyle (plaited fishtail with a red ribbon running through it) and the contents of their shared journal (a length
of parchment dedicated solely to Azael, the boy with the textbook
whose golden wings matched his glowing auburn eyes), or their
secret handshake (two pumps of the hands, then slide the fingers
back till the tips touch, spreading them into a fan, mirror-like), but
she could not recall the location of the path she sought. She knew the
tree hollow well because she had often found her way there alone to
wait for Sophia, but she'd never ventured by herself on the winding
trail that led to the forbidden edge of First Heaven.

Lucifer would have killed her if he'd discovered she'd even
approached Second Heaven, let alone crossed into it. But that was the
thrill, of course. And, really, it wasn't much of a daring feat. There
are no borders or barriers between the lower Heavens—where Sophia
led her had only a low, wooden fence marking the line between one
First-Heaven farmer's property and his Second-Heaven neighbor.
Still, Evangeline remembers the excitement she felt straddling the
wooden posts, one foot in her own land and one in foreign territory.

Evangeline now circles the forest, searching for the rocky path.
She wants to dart out into the clearing, to assess her direction from
a distance, but there's no point in unnecessary exposure. If she concentrates, she trusts she'll find it.

Her patience pays off. She finally locates the right trail and
takes off toward Second Heaven. When she gets to the dip in the
land where the fence is the lowest, Evangeline easily hops over and
sprints across the field. She thinks, for a moment, that stalks of wheat
should be rising high around her on both sides of the border, but
the ground in every direction is scorched, blackened, and dusty. It
surprises Evangeline, although she doesn't know why it should. It's
true that she hasn't flown through Second Heaven since she returned

from school over a year ago, but she's well informed about the battles Lucifer has pushed into Archangel territory. And it's no different than the destruction wrought by their enemies in the battles in First Heaven.

Still, it unsettles Evangeline.

She takes to the air, confident she's far enough from Sophia's village that she won't be seen. She feels better, rested, in less pain. While her muscles ache, it's more like the strain after a grueling training session, a sensation that's always left her feeling stronger, more alive. Maybe it was worth spending the night curled in the hollow; maybe she'll make better time now that she's alert and energetic.

Which is why Evangeline decides to take the shortest route to Third Heaven. It's more dangerous; she'll need to fly right by the Archangels' training grounds, but given the stakes—her father's *life*—she's willing to take the chance. The threat to her is still minimal, she reasons, because she is but one angel. Obviously if she were here with a battalion of Dragons, that would be a different story. But she's not trying to attack; she's simply passing through.

Besides, delivery angels, who are civilians, often come and go from the training ground. Evangeline expects enough company in the skies that she'll be able to blend in. She won't be recognized, she's sure. While she may be well known as Lucifer's daughter at home, she hasn't ventured out of First Heaven since the war began. Since she hasn't been in battle, none of the Archangels will know her. Except Michael and Gabriel, of course, but they're too busy plotting the ambush of her father to worry about her. It's why she believes she's the only chance her father has. She can slip quickly and quietly through the Heavens before the Archangels realize she's a threat.

Evangeline glides on the misty morning air. Wisps of fog begin to swirl as the darkening clouds overhead swell with rain. Inwardly she groans, hoping the sky won't crack open. Damp feathers make flight more difficult; there are times she feels more like she's swimming than flying when the storms are bad.

The first raindrop lands on her nose, a cold splash. Then another, and another. The rain thickens, first into a hazy veil, then into a dense curtain of water. Evangeline feels the weight of her wings, as if an invisible hand tugs her back. Her progress slows. She thinks about landing, taking cover and waiting out the storm, at least the worst of it, but she can't imagine she'd have the patience. No, she decides, it's better to keep moving forward, even at a slower, soggier pace.

She nears the training base, invisible behind an impenetrable stone wall. She's never seen the vast lands on the other side. Her father has, when he trained there as an Archangel decades ago, but he never talks about it. Evangeline now understands why he never did. She learned, after her time at school in Fifth Heaven, just how hard it is to be a Commoner among higher classes of angels—and unlike Lucifer, she's half Dominion—so she can finally appreciate the odds her father had to surmount in such a hostile environment.

The wall, miles long, appears out of the fog. She feels her stomach churn, as it always does when she has to pass near the base. She hates them, the Archangels, more than any other class of angels. They not only perpetuate the toxic status quo in the Heavens, they actively seek out Commoners to destroy them. It is the Archangels who are rounding up Commoners and expelling them to God's new Earth to become slaves to angels' new "sister species," the humans.

She understands that some Commoners, like Sophia, always blamed God for their plight instead, arguing the Archangels are simply following orders. It's a conversation—an argument—the two of them had time and again.

"God is not worth my time hating," Evangeline would respond. He is worth only disdain, as her father always said. He was an ineffable enemy, ephemeral and evanescent, an impossible target, one never seen by any mortal angel except the seven Seraphim. It's impossible to fight against an invisible foe and Lucifer was much too smart to waste his energy on something impractical. No, better to attack the spineless cowards who claim to do God's bidding.

"But *God's* the one banishing us," Sophia would retort.

"And if the Archangels stood up for what is right, what is decent, they'd defy God's callous commands and we'd be safe," Evangeline always countered.

They never agreed and Evangeline continued to take out her hatred of their injustice on God's army instead of God Himself.

But as she flies closer to the Archangels' training ground, a prickle of anxiety, separate from the low-grade burn of her animosity, tingles her skin. Something isn't right. The sodden skies are empty. She sees no fast-flying messengers in the air, nor fleets of hayyot-driven chariots on the ground. The traffic in which she was planning to camouflage herself simply isn't there.

Because, Evangeline realizes with a sudden slap of stupidity, it's raining.

Of course no one is about, not if they don't have to be. She's the only fool dumb enough to fly in this wet weather. Evangeline dives to the ground, landing hard, but already she's shaking her head, angry at her own folly. No doubt every guard from every watchtower would have noted her approach. She couldn't have been more visible if she'd lit the sky on fire. She's done nothing wrong; simply flying by the gates is not a crime, but with a war going on, she expects the Archangels to be on high alert.

Evangeline walks away from the wall, thinking only about gaining as much distance as she can from her enemy. But she's on flat prairie land; there is nothing but empty space in every direction. A great vantage for the security of the Training Base, of course, but that's a benefit to the wrong side. Evangeline feels eyes on her back, a target for the likely point of an arrow. She slows her pace, trying to demonstrate through body language that she is no threat. A lost angel is all. A silly creature, caught out in the rain.

Evangeline shivers from a chill. The water has long since soaked into her bones, drowning the high spirits with which she awoke. She should have taken shelter when the rain came; she could have stayed warm with Christie's blanket; she could have stayed dry. Now she's no further ahead. In fact, she's behind, given that she'll need her wings to dry out if she plans to fly hard and fast to make up time in the air.

Evangeline keeps trudging, looking for cover, but in this mist, she can see very little in any direction. She remembers there's a slope to her left, not far from the main gates that have become an unofficial market of sorts. Traders and caravans, hoping to do business with the wealthy Archangels, will make camp for a while, eager to sell their wares. They often have tent or tarps and the regulars have makeshift lean-tos. She's never actually stopped since Lucifer never wanted her to linger too close to his enemies, but surely, in this weather, someone would let her huddle under their covering until the rain lets up.

As she gets closer, the fog seems to dissipate—except for a thick column ahead of her. At first Evangeline believes her eyes are playing tricks on her since mist does not hold together in the shape of a pillar, but then she smells the air, heavy with the wet scent of charred wood.

Smoke.

The thick, grayish column is smoke.

Evangeline quickens her pace. She wonders if lightning struck the makeshift market, or maybe an unattended candle turned over in the wind.

She comes to the crest of the small rise, below which should sit the market.

Only it doesn't.

In front of her, visible through the easing rain, are the charred remains of the market, much, much larger than when she was last here. In front of her, all the way to the horizon is a mass of ruined tents and shacks, blackened and burned, like a town incinerated.

Evangeline coughs and covers her mouth with her sleeve. Dust, smoke, cinders swirl in the air around her. She notices a level of heat trapped in the atmosphere, as if the fire still smolders. She sees no flames but suspects embers may still burn beneath the rubble. Whatever destruction happened here, it happened recently.

Evangeline is surprised not only at the destruction, but at its size. This was obviously more than a market; the shape and struc-tures remind her of the refugee camps back home. But she's con-fused because she's never heard of the need for camps in Second Heaven. Lucifer's Dragon army may be effective in battle, but they're never cruel enough to drive people out of their homes the way the Archangels do to Commoners.

And how did it burn to the ground? Did the Archangels attack? Did they catapult fiery arsenal onto the camp? And if so, *why*?

Evangeline descends slowly, reluctantly drawn to the ruin in search of answers. She should fly past this horror and find her father, but she aches with curiosity. What happened here to make the area resemble the remnants of a battlefield?

As she nears the perimeter, she sees through the haze what she'd missed before. Slow, tired movements. Angels, smeared with soot, covered in ash, shuffle around the wreckage, picking up dark bun-dles, heavy, by the looks of the effort it takes to carry them. For a fleeting moment, Evangeline is pleased these victims seem to be able to salvage a hefty load—until, with a horrified start, she realizes the bundles are not goods.

They're bodies.

Evangeline's heart catches in her throat. In one angel's arms, she sees a figure whose long blond hair, streaked with cinders, sweeps the ground. In another, she sees the small shape of a tiny child. Her chest squeezes in sorrow. She's seen death before; she's walked the bloody battlefields after the fighting, has buried more of her father's Dragon soldiers than she cares to remember. But this scene eats at her in a different way. These angels are her enemies, but they're civilians. She should rejoice in their sorrow, but she can't. They wear no armor, wield no swords. It's not right they were attacked.

Evangeline ventures into the charred camp, with a vague notion that maybe she can help. She steps hesitantly among the ruins and sees an old woman leaning against the blackened half-wall of a hut. She cradles a young angel, a child of maybe eight or nine. The little girl stares ahead, as if she's unaware of the protective arm around her. Their clothes are ripped, burned, and they tremble in the spit of rain.

Evangeline notices a glint of gold on the ground, a lost coin mostly buried in the ashes. She picks it up, with the thought to give it to the woman in obvious need, but first she unwraps the blanket Christie gave her and holds it out to the old angel. The wool is soaked through; it will provide no immediate warmth, but at least it's whole and will keep the wind's chill off their skin. The grandmother accepts it with a weak nod of thanks.

"What happened here?" Evangeline asks. She leans down, keeping her voice low, as befits the solemnity of the scene.

"Lucifer happened," the old woman spits out with unexpected vehemence.

Evangeline stumbles backwards, knocked off her heels, shocked. Never in a million years did she expect that answer.

"*Lucifer?*" she repeats.

"His Dragon army, anyway," the old woman sighs, the prick of her venom dissipating.

"Dragons," Evangeline again repeats.

But there is no logic to the angel's words. Dragons don't attack civilians. Does the old woman mean that the Dragons were fighting the Archangels here and the poor community got caught in the crossfire? But still, that's absurd. Lucifer never warned her of an impending Dragon attack on Second Heaven. He would have told her yesterday. Were the *Dragons* attacked, then? Surprised by the Archangels on their way through Second Heaven? But again, Evangeline didn't know about *any* Dragons in Second Heaven. The Archangels had pushed them back to First Heaven; it's why Lucifer was so afraid they were losing.

"Came in the middle of the night, the spineless cowards," the old angel seethes. "Surrounded the whole refugee camp, then set it ablaze."

So it *is* a refugee camp . . .

"We came from the Midlands," the angel explains. Evangeline hears the sad note of resignation. "The Dragon army burned our village to the ground there; we thought we'd be safe from them close to the Archangels. We were wrong."

Burned her village? Dragons? That's not possible. Her people don't *burn* villages. And they certainly don't go around burning refugee camps. Especially not on the Archangels' doorstep.

This old angel must be wrong. She must have thought she'd seen something or someone who looked like a Dragon soldier—like an Archangel pretending to be a Dragon. Yes, that's the only way this makes sense. Like the rumors in Sophia's village blaming Lucifer for the food blockade, the Archangels must have torched their own people's camp and then accused her father.

Evangeline's stomach churns in disgust at the lengths to which the Archangels will go. Burning their own people alive for the sake of propaganda is the depths of depravity. She understands that the sooner her father finds the key, the better. This war *has* to end.

Evangeline wants to tell the old angel how wrong she is, how the cruelty of the Archangels is actually to blame, but instead she sighs. There's no point. She expects the old angel wouldn't listen to reason, poisoned as she's been by the Archangels' lies. All she can do to make this right is help her father. After they win the war, after they've reclaimed the rights for the Commoners in the Heavens, they'll be able to counteract the vicious rumors against them.

She smiles weakly at the old angel and the little angel, then turns to go, the coin she meant to give all but forgotten. She's taken no more than two steps when the sharp pitch of the old angel's voice stops her.

"Where did you get that sword?" Her words crackle with a ferocity that belies her age and her condition.

Startled, Evangeline spins around, her hand on the hilt of Sophia's sword.

The angel releases the child from her arms, sits her gently against the wall, then struggles to stand. Evangeline looks at her, confused, but something in the grandmother's eye, a hardened glint, a flash of ice, makes Evangeline wary. She grips her sword tighter, pressing her palm into the grooves of the hilt, feeling its familiar, intricate design. The sword may have been Sophia's, but holding it gives Evangeline a familiar comfort. The weapon, like all those wielded by Dragons, is identical to her own, and she always feels a special ownership in the swords because they were designed by her father, who few younger angels remember is also an accomplished blacksmith. His design, Evangeline always thought, was inspired: a hilt made to look like the head of a dragon, out of whose mouth steel flames shot down the grip toward the blade.

Dragon.

Evangeline takes a slow step backward.

The grandmother tugs the blanket Evangeline gave her off her shoulders, then throws it to the ground.

"*You,*" the old angel seethes. "*You* did this!"

Evangeline shakes her head. "No, *no.*" She takes another step backward as the old angel advances. "No Dragon soldier did this."

"Dragon!" The old angel's piercing cry rings through the quiet solemnity. Evangeline is in the air before the last echo of the word fades. Her wings still feel heavy, wet, but the rain has eased into a light drizzle.

A dark mass near the center of the camp, the original market, lifts into the air in response to the grandmother's alarm. Shouts, cries, cross over Evangeline's head, but she doesn't listen for words. She hears only their irrational anger—very much, she thinks, like the mob last night at Christie and Sidriel's. Evangeline is on guard; logic is useless. They will not listen to reason. And, like last night, she recognizes the best thing for her is simply to slip away.

She flies steady as the group of five angels approaches. They look thuggish, in their tattered clothes and soot-stained faces, ragged wings, ugly and mean. She lets them think they're gaining, lets them believe that in the next second they'll grab hold of her and drag her down. She flashes onto her face an expression of fear—not entirely false, she admits—but exaggerated, so the goons will believe they've intimidated her. She sees a tight grimace on one angel's face, a look of plain hatred.

"You die now, Dragon." The leader lunges.

But Evangeline drops low, feints right, and is out of arms' reach before the lumbering fools know what's happening. She sucks in the temptation to smirk—she cannot afford the millisecond to gloat—but she does twist back to assess where they are. They're turning, clumsily, and are slow to accelerate. It's all the lead Evangeline needs. She flies faster, pushing her herself harder. She has to exert more energy because her wings are drenched, but she reasons so, too, are her pursuers'. There's no place to hide, not like last night, so she'll have to count on her stamina, which makes her grateful for the longer sleep she had.

She turns again, as a matter of strategy, to ensure she's outflying the refugee angels, but then she spins forward and—

Bam!

She wallops, hard, into the chest of another angel. She bounces off the metal breastplate, realizing in a frantic instant that she's up against an Archangel. She reacts instinctively and draws her sword. She doesn't know how the Archangel got the drop on her; she'd seen none in the skies a minute ago, but she won't let herself think about that.

In training, whenever a scenario caught them by surprise, her father would say, "React to what is, not what you want it to be."

Evangeline raises her sword, blocking the Archangel's first downward blow. Her enemy, a girl not much older than her, seems surprised, and Evangeline presses her advantage. She slices up and over her enemy's head, skimming the tip of the Archangel's helmet. It's a trick of offense: the opponent thinks Evangeline is going for her head and impulsively raises her hands to protect herself, when in reality, Evangeline arcs her leg in round kick to the Archangel's midsection. Evangeline can hear the air seep from her enemy's lungs, as she flaps backward, out of sword range.

But the Archangel recovers faster than Evangeline expected. She's back at Evangeline with such intensity, it's all Evangeline can do to cross her sword over her chest. She rallies and attacks again, but this Archangel is strong. There's no heated emotion, passion, anger, or madness in her strokes, not like the mob from last night or the refugees chasing her. This, Evangeline realizes, makes her opponent very, very dangerous. This Archangel is doing her job; she has nothing at stake.

A slice of sword whizzes by her ear.

Goddammit.

She swings her blade but misses the Archangel. Her enemy easily pushes back her sword. Evangeline feels a sudden terror rising up the back of her spine. She's rattled. It's as if all her training disappeared. She feels as if she's a child, the sword heavy and foreign in her hand. She's better than this—yet the evidence indicates otherwise. Her father would be so disappointed in her. It's only the second battle she's sucked into, after Michael and Gabriel's attack yesterday, and she can't manage to fend off one simple opponent? What kind of Dragon soldier is she? How can she call herself Lucifer's daughter? The panicked thoughts spiral onto one another.

Another Archangel appears out of the mist and it's ironic, because the sight of a second enemy pulls Evangeline out of her tailspin. She feels like she's got this. She's trained for two-on-one combat, and this time, she won't let her father down.

The second Archangel advances from her side, but Evangeline is too smart to be distracted. She whips her sword first to her left, grazing the new Archangel on the arm, and then flashes back toward her first opponent who leaps away with a hair's breadth between her chest and Evangeline's sword.

Evangeline feels better now. She's regained control—of herself, of the fight. She's not letting them inside her head. If they fight cold and calculating, then Evangeline will do the same.

She does well. She's holding her own. It's tiring, battling two at a time. She's not yet winning, but she's far from losing. Yet after a few minutes, she realizes she has to end this stalemate—otherwise, she fears she'll weaken, make a mistake and succumb.

And *that* can't happen.

But it does.

Two more Archangels fly into the fight, and as hard as Evangeline tries, she can't hold off four of them. Within minutes, they've torn her sword from her grip, bound her hands behind her, and dragged her to the ground.

Evangeline's heart is in her throat, she's so afraid. The Archangels, mute and silent, nudge her roughly toward the gate of the training ground. She tries to rearrange her face to express disdain, but still, she's sure they can smell her fear.

The thugs, her original pursuers, the ones she outsmarted, sally up to her, smug and self-righteous, as if they brought her down. One of them spits in her face and Evangeline is so shocked by the unexpected affront that she can do nothing but gape.

The Archangels immediately surround her—protect her—and push back the refugees.

"Get back, you morons." The first Archangel, the one Evangeline almost beat, shoves the spitting goon. She yanks a cloth from her uniform pocket and dabs gently at Evangeline's cheek where the gob of saliva drips off.

Evangeline is unexpectedly grateful. She's had to endure a lot of taunts in her life, both in Commoner territory and at the Dominion school, but no bystander before now has ever come to her defense.

But then Evangeline remembers she hates the Archangels. They are cruel and vicious and they rip her people from their homes, casting them out of the Heavens into a strange new place called Earth. And then she is embarrassed and angry and riddled with guilt all at once.

But she shoves all her emotions deep down inside, in the part of her soul reserved for her hurts. She's learned. Her sharp feelings did her no good in school; they cannot help her now. Instead, Evangeline raises her chin and walks, head held high, a step ahead of her captors.

Chapter 4

Evangeline paces back and forth across the tiny room, four steps in one direction, four in the other. The space is small like a cell and she's *trying* to think of it like a cell. She is a prisoner, after all. She cannot walk out on her own or leave when she wants. The thick wooden door is locked from the outside and there is but one small window, much too narrow to crawl through. Yet still Evangeline catches herself sighing as the warmth from the crackling fire in the snug hearth seeps into her bones. She can't help it. This is the warmest and driest she's been in the day and a half since she left home. She knows she's trapped, a prisoner in a cell, but she can't help feeling it's more like a cozy cottage. And much to her shame, she devoured the piping hot mutton stew a guard delivered to her. She wanted to resist; she tried to resist. She sat, straight and rigid in the sturdy wooden chair, staring determinedly past the guard as he placed the steaming bowl on the table in front of her. After he left, she didn't move for a long minute while her physical needs, loudly argued by her growling stomach, battered it out with her psychological need to reject any and all aid from her enemy.

But it smelled so good.

And she was so hungry.

And, she reasoned, she still had a long journey. She'd been counting on Christie and Sidriel to supply her with food. She has so little money on her—when she left for her quiet cliffside meditation yesterday, her birthday, she never expected to be in need of money to travel the Heavens. She therefore must conserve what she has. So maybe a free meal on her enemy's coin is justified. She'd do her father no good if she fainted away from hunger because she was too proud to eat the Archangels' food.

If anything, she decides, she's exploiting them. The Archangels are strengthening her, and that, she determines, will ultimately lead to their ruin. She'll revive on their watch, find a way to escape, track down Lucifer and his key, then return to tear them apart.

But the meal had been hours ago—longer since she'd been captured—and she sees no opportunity for escape. Through the tiny window, Evangeline can see the sky darken, can see the night descend, filling the room with flickering, firelit shadows.

Evangeline walks, turns, then walks again. She's agitated, restless. She thought she could talk her way out of her predicament, but except for the silent guard, no one has come. She expected to be questioned, and since she knew from her father's stories how ruthless the Archangels' interrogations could be, she had steeled herself for it. Instead, the torture came from not knowing. Not knowing how long she'd have to wait, nor what, exactly, she was waiting for. Scenarios played out in her mind—they'd assault her with their bare hands, or lock her up in irons, or put a knife to her throat and threaten to kill her—but Evangeline knew that no matter what they threw at her, or how, she'd never break. She'd rather *die* than betray the Cause.

But then she remembers that if she dies, no one will warn her father. As it is, she's terrified that this delay—her mistake with Sophia's sword—will cost him his life. Michael and Gabriel could have long since leap-frogged over her and be well on their way to Fifth Heaven. She'd love to comfort herself by thinking they won't find Lucifer, and that's of course, absolutely, a real possibility, but Gabriel's smart. Gabriel's cunning. And Gabriel, as her father's former commanding officer and once best friend, would be the one angel capable of divining what's in Lucifer's head.

"The greatest sin," her father always taught her, "is to underestimate your enemy."

But *dammit*, the enemy won't appear.

Unless that's the very mind game the Archangels are playing. Wait her out, watch her get rattled, mess with her head, then attack.

Evangeline drops into the chair. Well, if that's their plan, she isn't going to let them win. She crosses her ankles, folds her hands, and takes a deep breath.

Evangeline is still, her body unmoving, but she finds she cannot quiet her mind. Surprisingly, unexpectedly, her thoughts turn to her mother. After Evangeline's return from Diaga, where she had, with bitter disappointment, failed to feel closer to her mother's spirit, Evangeline locked away all thoughts of Seraphina. She stopped asking Lucifer and her uncle questions about her, no longer able to cope with the way they compared her to her mother. Seraphina was a heroine, a holy soul who sacrificed *everything*—her family, her high social status, her future as a healer—all to forge a new and difficult life with the Commoner Lucifer, her greatest love. How could Evangeline, an epic failure at forging her own way in the world on her own terms, live up to such a paragon of virtue?

But now with so much motionless time in this little cottage cell in Second Heaven, Evangeline's mind drifts toward Seraphina. She's a ghost, a phantom who exists only in stories. But still, Evangeline wishes she knew what her mother would think of her. Would she be angry that Evangeline has so far botched her mission to keep Lucifer safe? Would Seraphina hang her head in shame at Evangeline's incompetence? Or would she pull Evangeline into a warm embrace and reassure her she did her best? They say that souls, the spirits of departed angels who live behind the veil in God's Realm of Seventh Heaven, can look upon mortal angels. Does Seraphina watch Evangeline? Or has she long ago abandoned her daughter in spirit as she did in life? Evangeline understands logically, of course, that it was not Seraphina's choice to die, that she could not escape the cowardly Dominions who burned down their Fifth Heaven cottage, expecting to assassinate Lucifer, but Evangeline cannot shake the blame she assigns to her mother nonetheless. Seraphina could have traveled with her and Lucifer to visit his parents in First Heaven; she could have chosen to be with her family, and if she had, she would have lived.

But the pain of the possibility is acute, so Evangeline again tries to shut Seraphina out of her head. Her mother did not accompany them on their sojourn, so therefore she did not live. There is no point, no purpose in wallowing in "what-ifs."

Instead, she refocuses on her father, the parent who has always been present in her life, and is still thinking about him when an hour—or more?—later, the door creaks open on its hinges.

Two Archangels enter. One is a young private. A minion, most likely. He's lanky, with long, thin wings, folded and hunched. But it's the second angel who stops Evangeline's heart.

It's Danielle.

Michael's older sister, Gabriel's oldest daughter. Evangeline's never actually spoken to her. Danielle is about ten years older, but Evangeline has seen her at family days at Diaga Academy. She's a petite angel with snowy-silver wings, similar to her father's, but she's a powerhouse, Evangeline has heard. Danielle is strong and smart and according to Michael, who once confided in Evangeline back at school, his sister is perfect.

But then Evangeline's heart settles because she thinks there's a good chance Danielle doesn't know her, won't recognize her. Evangeline was always slinking into the shadows at school, even more so when families arrived. Lucifer, of course, never attended any events at the Fifth Heaven school, so there was no reason for her to show up.

Evangeline looks closely at Danielle's face, searching for a spark of recognition. She sees none, and this gives Evangeline an idea. In fact, her spirits rise enough that she thinks she may actually be able to get out of here.

Evangeline scrapes back her chair and jumps up.

"It's about time," she spits at Danielle and then strides toward the door with a dismissive flip of her raven-dark hair and an impatient bristle of her deep violet wings. She ignores the other Archangel entirely.

Danielle immediately slides in front of her, a move graceful in its execution, yet strong as steel. She's shorter than Evangeline, but still Evangeline feels her intimidating authority. Even as her face breaks into an amused smile, her body is nonetheless rigid and alert.

"Going somewhere?"

"Yeah," Evangeline answers. Her tone is cocky and sure, although her stomach clenches at her ruse. "Out of here."

"Before we've had a chance to chat?" Danielle asks smoothly. The smile remains, but Evangeline notes it never reaches her eyes.

"I'm not much of a talker," Evangeline scoffs.

The smile falls from Danielle's face and Evangeline can see she hates the sass.

"Sit."

Evangeline raises an eyebrow. "Am I a dog?"

Danielle narrows her eyes, her face darkening, and Evangeline fears she's taken her attitude a bit too far. Submissively, she sits. She feels tears burning at the back of her eyes.

"Please let me go," Evangeline says, shifting to meek and scared.

Danielle seems satisfied with Evangeline's abrupt shift in manner.

"What's your name?" she asks Evangeline.

"Alina." Evangeline holds her breath. She hopes against hope that Danielle doesn't remember her roommate from Diaga. Her whole gamble is lost if Danielle recognizes the name. But Evangeline sees no flicker of reaction.

"Where are you from?"

"The Highlands, in Fifth Heaven." Lies are so much easier when they're the truth—somebody else's truth.

Danielle frowns. "You're a Dominion?"

A millisecond of hesitation. Yes, Alina is a Dominion, and yes, Evangeline needs to pretend to be a Dominion for her plan to work—but then, Evangeline reminds herself that she is, in truth, *half* Dominion. She never liked to think of it like that because it made her feel guilty, like she's betraying her Cause by denying who she truly is. Still, Evangeline nods.

Danielle looks puzzled. "What are you doing here in Second Heaven?"

"Penance," Evangeline answers ruefully.

She sees a small, wry little smile tug at Danielle's lips.

"For what sins do you require penance?" Danielle asks, and Evangeline can hear the hint of laughter, of lightness in her voice. Danielle's shoulders drop; she seems to relax.

"For breaking a Commoner's wing," Evangeline says.

Her answer is like a wish fulfillment. She wishes Alina *had* been punished when she'd broken Evangeline's wing. It happened a few weeks after Evangeline arrived at school, more than three years ago.

Evangeline came back to their room, saw that Alina's friends were sprawled on her bed and asked, politely, deferentially, for them to move.

Alina rose from her own bed, came over to Evangeline and stared at her with a look of pure loathing.

"The day a *Commoner* orders a Dominion around is the day the Heavens fall," Alina jeered, and her friends clucked loudly beside her.

Evangeline remembers the words sliced through her like a knife. She's not sure why they hurt so much more in that moment; she'd been verbally taunted since she arrived, but still Evangeline felt crushed. Maybe it's because she finally had to admit that Diaga was not the safe haven she imagined, nor would it bring her closer to the spirit of her mother as she had so desperately wanted. Beaten, humiliated, she turned to go. That's when Alina lunged, like a cat clawing at Evangeline's wings. Alina twisted Evangeline's deep purple feathers as if they were a dishrag, then yanked her backward, toppling her to the floor.

Evangeline cowered, in real physical pain, as Alina stood and straightened her clothes. Without a word to Evangeline, Alina nodded to her friends, who rose from Evangeline's bed, and the three of them floated into the hall.

Her father would say that was a victory—she got her bed back, after all—but with an injured wing and wounded pride, Evangeline felt she had yet again thrown herself into the viper's pit by insisting to her father that she be allowed to attend Diaga. On her bed, Evangeline drew up her knees and buried her head, cursing her father for not letting her leave and cursing her mother's spirit for not showing up.

Still, she remembers wishing that she knew what her mother would say. Would Seraphina have let her come home? Would Seraphina have let her attend in the first place? Maybe Evangeline wouldn't have felt the need to enroll in Diaga if her mother had still been alive. She'd have known her place, mixed race that she is. Her mother would have ensured she'd be welcomed into the Dominion world.

Right?

But that's just it. Evangeline, to this day, remains terrified that her mother would not have protected her. Her old antagonism against Seraphina rears up. What did she think she was doing, marrying a Commoner and having a child? Did she ever think of her daughter's well-being? Her future as a half-breed? Funny how Evangeline doesn't blame Lucifer for the same sins, but then, Lucifer raised her with love and passion. To Evangeline, Seraphina remains a phantom upon which she can paste any number of hurts. It is much easier to blame the dead than to condemn the living.

"How did you come across a Commoner?" Danielle asks suspiciously.

Evangeline's insides swoop in fear. Of course a Dominion like Alina wouldn't normally come into contact with a Commoner.

"There was one at my school," Evangeline answers, sticking to Alina's truth.

She sees Danielle's eyes widen. "You know Lucifer's daughter?"

Evangeline scoffs. "Yeah, the bitch. Thought she was as good as us."

The words, necessary for her ploy, nonetheless sting as they cross her lips. Evangeline clenches her hands trying to keep control.

"But she left the school over a year ago. If you broke her wing, why are you here only now?"

Evangeline thinks quickly. "My parents just found out about it," she sighs. "They say I'm better than that and made me come here to help the refugees as punishment."

Evangeline knows nothing about the refugee camp outside the Archangels' door. She has no idea how long it's been here, or who is running it, or whether they'd take volunteers. It's a risk, but it's the only story she can think of.

Danielle doesn't seem to question it, though, and Evangeline breathes out quietly.

The Archangel again offers up a wry little smile. "Helping fellow angels who have lost everything in this war is punishment?"

Evangeline frowns and shakes her head as if it's obvious. It would absolutely be obvious for Alina. "Uh, *yeah.*"

Danielle sighs, but Evangeline can't figure out if that means Danielle is buying her cover. She is so well aware that she's not yet in the clear.

The Archangel then withdraws Sophia's sword from her cloak. Evangeline steadies herself, trying to contain her reaction. She tries to look bored, but inside she's seething that an angel like Danielle has the gall to believe she's worthy enough to hold Sophia's sword—a Dragon's sword.

"How did you get this?" Danielle thumps the sword on the table in front of her. Evangeline longs to swipe it up and injure Danielle with it, but it's clear the young guard behind Danielle would take her out before she got to the door.

Evangeline takes a long, deep breath. "Found it."

Danielle responds with only a raised eyebrow.

Evangeline squirms, realizing how lame that sounds. Of course no Dragon would willingly part with his or her sword.

"I *did*," Evangeline-as-Alina answers defensively. "I was at the inn last night and only heard about the fire this morning. The sword was near the . . . " Evangeline tries to think quickly. Near the what? " . . . the woodshed."

She's only guessing there *is* a woodshed in the camp, but woodsheds exist in camps back home in First Heaven, so she goes with it.

"Why pick it up?"

Evangeline glances up at Danielle, feigning surprise. "You don't know how much those will go for on the black market?"

Evangeline is well aware of the black market in the higher Heavens—her father runs it. When she questioned her father's shady involvement, he said, "We do what we have to do to earn money for our Cause. Better we're in control than cutthroat thieves." And she's seen swords and helmets and other Dragon trinkets make their way back home through this illegal network, so it's not unheard of to think a Dominion would sell a lost or pilfered Commoner item. The Dominions are always willing to exploit the Commoners whenever they can.

"What's the name of the inn?" Danielle asks abruptly.

Evangeline is thrown for a second by the change in the questioning, but she recovers quickly.

"The Ostan."

Evangeline has seen it, passed it many times, and she's been in the pub once with her father, who had business there, years ago. But Evangeline also guesses Danielle's direction with her questioning.

No Commoners are allowed to stay there.

"What room are you in?"

Evangeline stares defiantly into Danielle's gray eyes, so similar to her brother's, hoping she looks indignant enough at these questions. "The attic room, the only one with two windows. It's got the best cross-breeze."

Evangeline exhales at her answer. It's what Lucifer's contact said in the pub all those years ago. She hopes the rooms haven't changed.

Danielle nods, as if she's satisfied, but Evangeline fears her story will hold only until Danielle checks it out. One question to the innkeeper or Alina's parents will ensure her imprisonment.

But how to get out of here before Danielle tries to corroborate her account?

She can think of nothing.

Danielle rises, and Evangeline feels a rush of panic. Maybe this Alina ruse wasn't smart. All she's done is postpone the inevitable. It won't be long before Danielle discovers she's not Alina, before she discovers she's actually Evangeline, Lucifer's daughter. And what a coup for Danielle, to nab such a valuable commodity.

Because, Evangeline realizes, she *is* a valuable commodity.

Danielle reaches the door, her hand on the latch.

"Wait!" Evangeline calls to her, the panic plain in her voice. "If you let me go and don't tell my parents, I'll dish dirt on Evangeline."

Danielle pauses. She straightens her shoulders, her perfect silver wings fluttering slightly. Slowly, she turns, but now she seems wary. She drops her chin, closes her eyes and shakes her head. Evangeline isn't sure if her demeanor is a negotiating tactic, if Danielle is trying to hide her interest, or if she doesn't believe "Alina" has anything to offer.

"What about Evangeline?" Danielle asks, sighing.

"She was my roommate," Evangeline responds.

She's stalling, of course. She has less than a second to determine a piece of valuable intelligence about herself that will satisfy Danielle but also not actually compromise anything about herself, her father or their Cause.

"Yes, and . . . ?" Danielle sighs.

"I know . . . "

Danielle presses her lips together, obviously annoyed.

"I can tell you about Evangeline's secret cottage."

The words are out of her mouth before she's thought it all the way through, but as she's talking, her mind whirls with strategy.

Evangeline is aware Gabriel and Michael are after Lucifer, but no one else should be aware of their mission, Danielle included, she suspects. But if she plants misleading information, maybe Danielle will pass it on to Gabriel and divert him from where Evangeline believes Lucifer truly is.

"A secret cottage?" Danielle is doubtful. "Evangeline, whose wing you broke, told you about a secret cottage."

Think fast, Evangeline, she tells herself.

She rolls her eyes. "No, obviously Evangeline didn't *tell* me," she says. "I read her journal."

Evangeline is pleased with herself. It sounds wholly plausible, something a teen angel would do. It's also the exact reason why Evangeline would never have *kept* a journal in the first place. Then, as now, she doesn't trust a single Dominion.

"And what . . . " Danielle draws out her question, "did you read in Evangeline's journal about this supposedly secret cottage?"

Danielle still has the same bored expression, but Evangeline catches the tiniest crack in her voice, a betrayal of her true interest. She's intrigued.

Evangeline hides a fragment of a smile. Her crazy plan may actually work.

"It's in the Farlands, near the Draiochta river. Used to be her grandparents' cottage," Evangeline explains.

Danielle shakes her head, again wary. "Nice try, Alina. That burned down years ago."

Evangeline knows this, obviously. It's how her father's parents died, after their chimney got stopped up. Smoke poured back into the little shack while they were sleeping; they never tried to make it out. But what Danielle doesn't know—*no one* knows—is what happened to it after that.

"Lucifer rebuilt it," Evangeline explains.

She hates that she has to reveal this family secret to her enemies, hates to give up a space that was hers and her father's alone—not even Lucifer's generals know about it—but the cottage is worthless if she doesn't *have* her father, and that's precisely the outcome if she doesn't get out of here. She determines the sacrifice of a cottage is worth his life. Besides, Lucifer always hated the cottage, reminders of his miserable childhood. He only rebuilt it as a backup, a place to go if they ever needed it. There's nothing there, no Commoner secrets, no Dragon strategies. Danielle—and then Gabriel—will think this news is vitally important, but in reality, they'll find nothing. She hopes.

Danielle is silent for a long moment. Her face is inscrutable. Evangeline's heart races as she awaits the verdict. Did she sell her secret well enough to convince Danielle to let her go?

"Your information is old," Danielle counters.

Now Evangeline is annoyed.

"Your reaction tells me you *didn't* know about the cottage before," Evangeline dares to contradict her. "Imagine what else I might remember from that journal."

"All the more reason to keep you here."

"You think I'd talk against my will?"

"We have ways."

Evangeline shivers, but she won't let Danielle see she's rattled. At least not any more than Alina would be.

"Look, I'm sorry I took the sword," Evangeline tells her. "I wish to God I hadn't. But I'm not a Dragon." Here, Evangeline spits out that word, *Dragon*, as if it burns in her mouth. "Please believe me."

It kills Evangeline inside to deny who she is. She wants to shout from the rooftops that she's a proud Dragon, Lucifer's daughter, a Commoner who would *never* reject her pedigree.

Only you did, Evangeline thinks. When she was fifteen. When she insisted her father send her to Diaga Academy. She hated being a Commoner, hated the discrimination and disdain, and thought she could escape it by focusing on her other half, her mother's half, the half she never knew growing up.

She wonders now how much of her decision was to escape her father's heritage and how much was to learn about her mother's. At first, she thought it was only about fleeing the torment of a Commoner, but as the taunts continued at Diaga, she realized her resolve to attend the school was as much a part of desire to connect with her long-dead mother as it was about denying her Commoner status.

So who is she? All these years later, Evangeline still feels lost.

Danielle stands abruptly, signals to the minion, and they both sweep out of the room. Evangeline hears the bolt click behind them before she has a chance to plead more. Her heart sinks; it didn't work. She thinks, ruefully, how ironic it is that her very own information about *herself* isn't enough to free her.

Darkness seeps into the little cabin. Evangeline sits on the stone hearth and stokes the fire, grateful still for the light, for the heat.

A long time later, a new guard comes in and deposits a bedroll, a thin hay mattress, and a thick woolen blanket. Evangeline inwardly groans. That means she's trapped for the night. She unrolls the mattress and slides under the blanket. She tries to convince herself that every passing hour without being caught out by Danielle is positive, but then every passing hour means Gabriel and Michael may gain on Lucifer.

Unless Danielle shares her information about the secret cottage, and the Archangels set out to find Lucifer there.

Evangeline prays to God she's been convincing enough.

No, what is she *thinking*? She doesn't pray to God. God long ago abandoned her people. Now God is exiling her people, turning them into slaves for his new human creatures. No, she will *not* petition God. She will only depend on her own powers, her own strength.

But then she thinks of Uncle Raziel, of his faith in God's benevolence, of his calm, of his quiet hope for a compassionate future. As a Cherubim, a Divine Record Keeper, it is no surprise that he would put his faith in God's goodness, but it was always a source of distance between them. Evangeline, growing up with little respect for the Divine, would not only dismiss her uncle's conviction, she would vehemently try to convince him of her own rightness. Uncle Raziel always listened to her patiently and never belittled her beliefs. Instead, he empathized with her struggles, understood why she blamed God. And while he never tried to coerce her into his way of thinking, he did start to teach her more about the history of his world, the history of *their* world, the history of God. He would often speak of a treasured book, lost long ago to legend, in which an assembly of disparate angels came together to write about the virtues of God they themselves personified: Wisdom, Truth, Justice, Mercy, Peace, Love, and Hope.

"They teach us that having faith in the goodness of God offers us a connection to something larger than ourselves," Raziel would explain. "That connection gives us hope—and hope, my dear, is what we all need to keep going."

It was such a pleasantly optimistic thought that Evangeline soon found herself pondering. She envied her uncle's serenity, which he attributed, in part, to his absolute faith in God's love. She could never go that far, but was there merit to his idea? Was a sense of peace, of tranquility, possible with a faith in the benevolence of God? The idea goes against every value with which she was raised, but the possibility seems so restful.

But Evangeline shakes her head. She cannot be distracted. Instead, she drifts off, choosing to focus on the reality around her instead of her tormented philosophical musings. She listens for a creak in the latch, the squeal of the door.

It never comes.

The third morning of the week. Evangeline awakens with a sense of despair and anguish. She's frustrated she's still stuck here, in the Archangels' locked little cabin whose fire has dwindled to ash, petrified her father has been found in the meantime, and humiliated she got caught. She thought she'd been so clever with the Alina story, but now she fears the only thing she's been able to accomplish since she left the Farlands is to give away to her enemy sensitive secrets.

Lucifer would be so ashamed.

Evangeline pulls out her father's Naofa feather and runs her fingers over the soft plume. Black, meant to keep her safe and protected. It's symbolic, she knows, but she suspects, wryly, it would work better if she didn't keep getting herself in trouble. She thinks of her own annual gift to her father on his birthday, one of her violet feathers. She's always scoffed at the idea that her Naofa feather would bestow deep, spiritual insight onto the receiver, a blessing she and her father had dismissed since they saw no purpose to spirituality. Instead, Lucifer suggested a variation on the symbolism of the color purple.

"You offer me the blessing of deep, passionate feelings and profound insight," he said.

She just wishes she had actual insight to bestow.

Sighing, Evangeline tucks the black feather back in her pocket, feeling remarkably sad.

When first breakfast and then lunch get delivered—without so much as a message from Danielle—Evangeline doesn't eat.

She can't eat.

Instead she lies despondent on the mattress, the blanket over her head. The guard has built up the fire again, but she doesn't care. Two days into her rescue mission, and she's screwed up. She deserves her fate. She still doesn't know what her fate is here among the Archangels, and she can't bring herself to actually imagine it.

By evening, a full day after Danielle first appeared, she returns. She waltzes into the cabin, her stride purposeful, and confronts Evangeline.

"We've found the cabin," she announces, her expression flecked with a tinge of impatience.

Evangeline grimaces, both grateful and resentful. The image of Archangels pawing through her father's cottage makes her skin crawl, but now, at least, she can leave.

Unless Danielle thinks she can get more out of her?

The sudden thought terrorizes Evangeline. Her face flushes with anger at herself, for not recognizing, and planning for, all possible outcomes of her Alina strategy. It's a mistake her father never would have made, and she burns with shame that her focus was too narrow. Not only that, she feels like if she stays a moment more in this infernal cabin, she'll suffocate.

"Your information is invaluable," Danielle tells her with the trace of a smile, indecipherable to Evangeline. Is she trapped or is she free? "So we'll let the issue with the sword drop," Danielle continues.

Evangeline feels a rush of muted relief, but she's still afraid. She appreciates now how terribly she thought through her ruse. She worries if Danielle has talked to the real Alina's parents.

"And my parents?" Evangeline holds her breath. Why did she think she was so brilliant?

Danielle stares at her for a long moment, as if she is contemplating. Finally, Danielle exclaims crisply, "I see no reason to involve them."

Evangeline exhales.

Danielle strides to the door, the casual saunter of a victor, and holds it open. She then indicates the guard. "Ansiel will show you to the Training Ground entrance."

Yet Evangeline hesitates. She's pressing her luck, but she can't leave yet.

"My sword?"

She can't bear to think of Sophia's sword in the Archangels' hands, but more than that, she'll need a weapon on her travels.

Danielle narrows her eyes, her expression again inscrutable, and the moment stretches to infinity. The door stands open, blowing in the blustering night, but then she seems to make a decision. She withdraws the blade and hands it to Evangeline.

Surprised—she truly thought asking for it was a long shot—Evangeline grips the hilt, then makes for the door.

"See you around," Danielle calls after her in with a wisp of sing-song lilt. "Alina."

The pause before her "name" momentarily slows Evangeline, but then she hurries out faster after the guard, Ansiel. Whatever Danielle is thinking, Evangeline doesn't care to find out. It's enough she's getting out of here. But a small, intrusive image creeps into her mind. She pictures Danielle appearing on the real Alina's doorstep, demanding information about Evangeline's nonexistent journal, and the trouble and confusion it'll cause for Alina brings to Evangeline's lips a smug little self-righteous smile.

But she wipes it off immediately. She can't wallow in vengeful fantasies. She has more important worries now. She has so much time to make up if she expects to find her father before Gabriel. She hopes that her ploy to send him on a wild goose chase will at least slow him down.

CHAPTER 5

Evangeline stops behind a small, darkened cottage at the edge of a tiny Third Heaven village on the shores of Lake Neam. Daylight is fading, the sky muted with a pallet of pastel pink and purple. She keeps to the shadows, her senses alert to noise, to movement. This is the riskiest part of her journey through Third Heaven. If she doesn't want to waste precious time circling the great lake to cross into Fourth Heaven, she has to steal a boat from the village harbor. She wonders again if maybe she should risk flying—she could wait till dark where her silhouette wouldn't be seen in the sky, but she remembers from her travels back and forth to school in Fifth Heaven that the nights here are black as ink. Without a pinprick of light by which to guide her, she fears she'd easily swerve off course. She can't afford the delay.

Evangeline peers around the corner down the main street—the only street. Squares of light start to flicker on in the windows of the thatched-roof homes, so different from Sophia's cold, lonely village. She hears a gale of laughter from a trio of Virtues, the Third Heaven class of angels, and she sees them heading toward the pub, its wooden sign creaking gently in the wind. One of them, a short, thin angel, turns in her direction and Evangeline flings herself back against the wall, out of sight. She takes in a sharp breath, although she's pretty sure he didn't see her.

But pretty sure isn't good enough. She has to do better. She has to make sure *no one* sees her, not after what happened both at Sophia's house and in Second Heaven.

Both incidents still make her shiver, but it's not the accusations about her father themselves that bother her. No, what chills her is a thought that's snuck into her mind. *What if they're right?*

She reaches into her pocket and withdraws the piece of gold she picked up in Second Heaven. She'd forgotten about it until after she'd left the Archangels' training ground, and that's when she notices it's not a coin at all. It's a button.

From a Dragon uniform.

She fingers the raised ridges on the surface, the image of a dragon, trying to imagine *any* scenario to explain the button's presence in the charred remains of a Second Heaven refugee camp.

Any scenario other than the old woman's assertion that Dragons burned down the camp.

She can think of none.

Evangeline feels more of an anxious urgency to get to her father, one separate from the threat to his life. She wants to reach him to confront him with her venomous thoughts, to have him deny it, to have him chuckle at her overwrought imagination and then have him pull her into a smothering embrace and reassure her, like he always did, that everything will be okay in the end.

"If it's not okay, it's not the end," he'd always say.

Evangeline slows her breathing. She regains control. She reminds herself that she's in Third Heaven, that the Virtues are the closest thing to neutral in this war. If she does encounter a local, if they do recognize her, she may still be all right. The Virtues are scholarly people, interested more in the philosophy of the cosmos than the practicalities of governance. In fact, the village itself remains unscarred from battle; it appears an anachronism—a cozy, homey place nestled on the clear lake far removed from the destruction her own Heaven has seen. Evangeline tastes the bitterness in her mouth, envious these people have escaped the ravages of war, but that's because they kept to themselves throughout the war, ignoring the Commoners' desperate plight, as they—as every higher class of angel—have always done. Evangeline expects they'll still keep to themselves, even if someone sees her—but she'd prefer not to chance it. After all, she thought her fellow Commoners would support her and she'd been disastrously wrong.

The harbor is at the end of the main street, but Evangeline doesn't want to stroll through the center of town, so she'll skirt around the village and approach the docks by the water's edge. She'll wait for full darkness to descend, then trust that there will be enough light from the lamps on the wharf by which to steal a boat. She doesn't relish the idea of theft, but she can justify it because her needs are greater. If her father dies, the Cause dies. Commoners die. And those who don't die will be exiles from the Heavens, banished to Earth.

She again peers around the corner of the little cottage. The street is empty now, but she hears the clomp of a hayyot's hooves and the clatter of wheels on the cobblestone up around the bend. She scurries across the street before it comes into view, but she doesn't reach the other side before she stops dead. Forgetting she is trying to remain hidden, Evangeline stares at the mouth of a narrow alley, at the retreating shadow disappearing down it.

Father.

Evangeline's heart pounds.

Father! She's found her father. He's alive! And he's alone. Gabriel hasn't gotten to him yet.

But then her skin prickles. She frowns, confused. What's her father doing in this backwater village in Third Heaven? The key couldn't possibly be here. It's a small Heaven, populated with people who have no interest in power. They show no concern for the well-being of other classes; how could *they* have the key to righteousness and justice? The irony stings, but Evangeline shoves aside her doubts. The key, if it does exist as her father insists, has been lost for centuries. A millennium. Of course it's possible it wound up here.

It's just she never imagined it. Not after all of Uncle Raziel's lessons. As the Heavens' preeminent expert on angelic history, he should know, and he never once spoke of the Third Heaven as a place of importance, of consequence. It's a stepping stone, a path through which one must travel to reach the power centers of their world. But, upon reflection, Evangeline guesses it's possible to hide a key along the way. Maybe an unknown angel, determined to bring the key back to its rightful owners, the Commoners, smuggled it from the higher Heavens where it had languished in stolen hands for so long, but had to abandon it here before she was captured. Evangeline wonders if that could be true, but then she wonders how that scenario is any less realistic than believing in the existence of the key in the first place.

No longer concerned about being seen and immensely relieved that her journey is nearly over, Evangeline hurries down the street toward the alley into which her father disappeared. The cart clatters past, an angel on its seat trying to rein in a playful hayyot trotting too quickly. A few Virtues spill onto the road, a couple coming from their home, a family leaving the baker's with a sweet-smelling loaf of honey bread, but they take as little notice of a stranger in their midst as she does of them. Her whole focus is on her father.

She veers the corner; it's dark here in the shadows and she slows until her eyes adjust. The alley is narrow, dank, and has the stale odor of day-old fish. Evangeline wrinkles her nose but plunges ahead, determined to finally end this nightmare.

She sees her father's figure sweep ahead of her, then he disappears. Evangeline blinks, unnerved. Where did he go? She hastens down the path, glancing left and right for her father to emerge, but when she reaches the spot where she last saw him, she is alone.

"Damn," she mutters, circling on the spot, but then she sees a streak to her right.

She catches it, barely, with her peripheral vision.

With a prick of anticipation, Evangeline pulls open the thin wooden door and steps inside. She finds herself in a tidy little kitchen beside a simple stone hearth. There's a small fire in the grate, not much more than embers, but the orange glow lets off a modicum of light. And in its spark, Evangeline sees her father. Lucifer stands tall, menacing. In profile, the shadows sharpen his jaw and cut into his cheekbones. He turns toward her, and Evangeline shrieks in fright.

It's not her father.

It is a grotesque caricature of her father. Taller, darker, wingless, with features more severe: an angular chin, chiseled cheeks, square face, pointed ears pressed so close to its scalp that they resemble horns.

Evangeline shudders. She thinks, at first, it's her imagination—she sees in front of her what she's seen a thousand times in Uncle Raziel's history books: a djinni.

But it's impossible. They cannot penetrate into the Heavens, not after her father sealed their last portal at the end of the Djinn War decades ago. Yet how else to explain the creature in front of her?

Blood pounds through Evangeline's head. She stops trying to understand and starts trying to get out. She steps back toward the door, reaching instinctively for the handle. She has Sophia's sword but fears she won't have time to use it—not if what she's truly seeing is, in fact, a djinni. She'd rather run—fly—far, far away.

As she feels the cold metal latch against her skin, she spins around and yanks open the door, but instantaneously she senses a rustle in the air beside her, sees a white haze and hears the thud of the door slamming shut. Suddenly the djinni is between her and the door, a space so narrow, Evangeline recoils from the stench of brimstone wafting from the creature's mouth. A clawlike hand shoots out and long, pointed fingers close around her throat. Instinctively, Evangeline's hands fly up and scrape at the arm, but sharp, talonlike nails only dig deeper into her skin.

"How did you get in here?" the djinni demands. His voice is raw, rough, a discordant sound to her ear.

Evangeline struggles to breathe. She feels the pressure tighten on her windpipe. A ring of black seeps into her vision.

"Who *are* you, angel?" He shakes her for added emphasis.

Evangeline tries to focus, tries to think. She cannot rip his arm from her throat—if he is a djinni, he is inherently stronger than any angel—so she must find a way to make him loosen his grip. He needs an answer, an explanation, from her so she has to convince him to allow her to talk. And breathe.

She sucks in as much air as she can as his dark face swims in front of her eyes, then tries to push a sound out through her vocal cords.

"Uh," she gasps. It's barely a whisper, more air than sound, but the djinni relaxes his hold the tiniest bit. His strong fingers still circle her throat; she can feel her skin bruising under his punishing grip, but it's enough. Evangeline drinks in the air with a long inhale. Her vision clears.

And for a hallucinogenic moment, Evangeline feels as if she's staring into her father's eyes—the same black-brown color, the same narrow shape. But she blinks and sees what's actually in front of her: eyes that are dark, cold, bitter, filled with hate.

"Dohh," Evangeline tries to squeak out. She's answering his question—how she got in—but she senses it's not that simple. Since his first question was *how did you get in?* not *who are you?* she suspects that her entry, for reasons unfathomable to her, is significant.

The djinni frowns. Still trapped by his clasp, Evangeline tries to nod her head toward the door behind him. A slow look of understanding seems to spread across his face, then his expression turns into a storm of anger. With an unexpected flick of his wrist, the djinni hurls her backward. Evangeline gasps in surprise as she soars in the air and lands hard against the stone hearth. The impact knocks the wind out of her; she's left breathless long enough she's scared she might die. When she can swallow air again, she feels the sharp stab of the rock against her back, the hammering thud from where her head hit the stone. The fire in the grate, so close to where she lies, threatens to singe her wings. Evangeline folds them in, then tries to rise to her feet. Her knees wobble; she loses her balance and sinks back to the floor. She closes her eyes, the sting of tears hot inside her lids.

"You are Lucifer's spawn," the djinni snarls, his voice dripping with contempt.

Evangeline looks up, terrified. If her own people in First Heaven are willing to mob her for being Lucifer's daughter, what will this *thing*, this djinni, a member of the enemy race destroyed by her father, do to her? But she says nothing. She will not give him the flint by which to burn her.

She remembers what her father once told her about the djinn. "They are heartless creatures. They have no honor, no loyalty. They fight dirty and are praised for it."

"How did you beat them, Papa?" Evangeline had asked.

Lucifer patted her cheek, then let his palm rest against her smooth, angelic face. "You fight fire with fire," he winked.

Only when she was older did Evangeline realize that her father had been speaking metaphorically—that he hadn't literally burned every single djinni as a way to drive them back into the UnderRealm.

Think like your enemy is what he meant.

Evangeline wishes she knew how to do that. She feels like all of Uncle Raziel's stories and legends of these UnderRealm creatures, and all her father's tales of the djinn are wholly immaterial, like they were all fairy stories, told to children only to frighten them into obedience. Nothing from her memory seems relevant.

"I have heard of you, *child*," the djinni hisses, his voice low and long, like the sound of a serpent. "Lucifer said you were . . . special."

Evangeline freezes. She must have misheard. She thought he said Lucifer has talked to him about her, but . . . but . . . that's ridiculous. Her father last had contact with the djinn more than twenty years ago—when he was a single, *childless* young angel. And if all their portals were sealed, how did this djinni even *hear* about her?

No, he's messing with her. He knows, somehow, that she's Lucifer's daughter. It would make sense that he'd screw with her, the child of their enemy.

But how did he even *get* here, in this Heaven? In *any* Heaven?

"Neecy, Neecy, *Neecy*," the djinni drawls, gliding forward slowly, with a deliberate menace. His bulk fills the little space in the kitchen. Evangeline scrambles to her feet, pressing herself into the wall. She doesn't know what he's saying, but she doesn't try to understand. He's almost on her now; Evangeline waits another heartbeat, then with the advantage of surprise, she launches herself from the wall, ducks under his outstretched arm, and flings herself toward the door. She manages to grasp the latch and tug the door open before the djinni grabs her from behind and pulls her back. Evangeline shrieks in terror, and now she flails and kicks and screeches at the djinni, who tries to drag her away. She loses all control; there is no thought, no strategy, no plan. She lashes out as the djinni wraps his hands around her arm, around her waist, pulling her back. She cries out again, kicks out again, and feels, for the sliver of a second, his grip slacken. She bolts out of his grasp, flings open the door—if only she can get *out* of here—and she makes it partway through the doorway. He tackles her, and again leaps for her throat, but then Evangeline feels a crazy surge of irrepressible anger. She doesn't want to just escape anymore; she wants to rip this djinni's throat out, gouge his eyes out, tear his heart out. She wants to *destroy* him. Her fear diminishes, replaced by a rage so intense she gains a strength she never knew she had. She pummels him with her fists, claws at his skin with her nails and sinks her teeth into his arm, a wild animal unleashed.

Locked together in their fight, they tumble outside the cottage into the alley. All of a sudden, Evangeline feels a sharp, burning pain in her side; she gasps as she wrenches away, and doubles over. She presses her hand to her waist. She feels hot, sticky blood pool onto her skin.

The djinni grabs her by the hair and yanks. Her head snaps back and with it comes her fear again.

Get away! she tells herself. She can't let him drag her back into the cottage. She shrieks again, but her strength is fading. Of course he's going to win; he's a djinni. Why did she ever think she could escape?

And then, improbably, she hears her name.

"*Evangeline!*" Instinctively, she tries to turn, and so, too, does the djinni; he is distracted enough that she frees her hair from his grip.

A figure emerges from the dusk-filled sky, a silhouette with expansive wings. For a half-second, Evangeline thinks it's her father, but then she sees the angel's wings are a charcoal gray, not the midnight black of her father's. The angel swoops at the djinni's head with his sword, but in a flash, the djinni dissipates. As he turns to vapor, he releases Evangeline and the heavy sword crashes down a hair's width from Evangeline's face. She whirls toward her rescuer—and her mouth falls open.

It's Michael.

Evangeline watches, stunned, as Michael spins with lightning-quick reflexes and blocks a blow from behind, where the djinni reappeared. Michael parries another attack by the djinni's sword, but the djinni wields his weapon with ease. Michael is pushed back, toward the stone wall of the cabin.

"Will you *help*?" he cries to Evangeline and immediately she shakes off her stupor. She can't understand where Michael came from, but she can't afford to guess. She tries to shake the fog from her mind, to focus on the fight in front of her. She's sparred many, many times; she's taken on more than one opponent, and she's fought with more than one partner, but never a djinni . . .

Never with this thirst for blood that she now feels . . .

Evangeline cuts off her thoughts. Instead, she takes action. She unsheathes Sophia's sword and swings at the djinni's shoulders. She misses and the djinni dances closer to Michael. She raises her sword to fight again as her temper flares again—the bastard will *not* win—but it's as if the djinni has eyes everywhere. He pivots and slashes in her direction, then fends off Michael an instant later.

No. This is not how it's going to end.

Evangeline reacts. She lunges forward, closing the space between them, and this time, she nicks his shoulder.

Yes!

The djinni howls.

Evangeline smiles. It's a wicked smile.

The djinni staggers back, and for a moment the three of them are frozen in an ugly tableau: Michael with his sword raised midway, his forearm in front of his face; Evangeline with the tip of her blade still pointed up; the djinni with his hand across his shoulder.

"*Fly!*" Michael breaks the spell and grabs Evangeline's arm as he pulls her into the sky.

Evangeline doesn't unfurl her wings. She's trapped in her anger, her revenge. Michael flaps hard, drawing them both up higher, out of djinni's flightless reach. It takes her a moment to come back to herself, and then, finally, with a ferocious beat of her wings, she ascends above the rooftops. The cold night air stings her burning cheeks and her arms ache from the djinni's attack. Evangeline's whole body feels heavy, and without warning, she drops like a stone.

Michael sees her, catches her and gently wraps his arms around her waist. She yelps when he touches her stab wound, a wave of pain washing over her.

"Let me lead," Michael says to her, and Evangeline can't argue. She can't think. She can't figure out why Michael is here or where he came from. She last saw him with his father, by the cave in the Farlands, preparing to chase after her father. So how is he here? The questions hurt her head; she has to stop.

"Hold on, Evangeline," Michael tells her.

She grips Michael's arm as she leans into his shoulder. She lets her wings droop. She lets Michael carry her away.

CHAPTER 6

Evangeline is well aware how much it is *not* a good idea to be here, in a guestroom above the pub in the very village where, an alley away, lives a djinni.

A djinni, for God's sake.

Besides, there are other travelers next door, and locals merrily drinking downstairs. She meant to stay *away* from angels; not frolic with them in their midst. But she is secluded, she reminds herself, hidden behind closed doors, and it's true no one recognized her when Michael led her in, but maybe that's because Michael told the innkeeper that his "wife" was injured in a clumsy flying accident.

Wife.

She understands why he had to say it. Etiquette would otherwise demand they take separate rooms. But still, it's strange to hear.

Evangeline leans against the iron headboard in the clean, simple room. She's washed up, thanks to the buckets of hot water the clucking innkeeper delivered, and her wound is bandaged, thanks to Michael's efficient skill.

Her skin, raw and bruised, still tingles, though, from Michael's touch. She still feels the warmth of his skin on hers.

Michael wraps an extra quilt around her shoulders, as if he actually is her nurturing husband, and Evangeline feels his hand rest for a second longer on her shoulder.

Or she imagined it.

She closes her eyes, then opens them. The room is still there. Michael is still there. Her enemy. The angel meant to find and kill her father. He hasn't yet cleaned himself up from their battle with the djinni. His face is streaked with dirt, his shirt is ripped, but Evangeline's eyes play tricks on her and she finds that she can only see the boy she once knew. The angel who befriended her in secret, who helped her survive Diaga.

With a squeak of the mattress, Michael settles on the end of the bed. He looks older, Evangeline observes. She had in her mind the sixteen-year-old kid she'd met that first term at Diaga, the tall, lanky boy who hid in the shadows to teach her the social survival skills she so desperately needed. But now, in front of her, is a young man, about twenty, a warrior, a soldier, a veteran of more than a year's worth of battles.

Against her people.

Against her father.

Against her.

Evangeline stiffens, feeling like she's betraying her father. She knows she should be grateful to Michael—he saved her life, after all—but the air around them thickens.

She can't be here. She shrugs off the quilt and swings her legs over the bed, but a wave of nausea rolls over her. The stab wound in her side throbs and she's tired, tired, tired . . .

She lies back with an air of defeat. For the second time, she's been caught by the enemy.

A heavy silence falls in the room. Evangeline closes her eyes, wishing Michael would go, leave her alone with her own misery. She had one job to do. *One.* She was supposed to rally their people on her father's behalf, but instead, she flew off, half-cocked on a crazy rescue mission. Who in the Heavens did she think she was? Her father?

Michael pops up off the bed, breaking the icy silence. "Why did that djinni look like Lucifer?"

Evangeline's eyes fly open; Michael's words send a shockwave through her. He saw the resemblance, too? She'd convinced herself it had been her imagination, that because she'd been looking for her father, she saw what she wanted to see. Her warped mind must have unconsciously pasted her father's image onto the vile djinni. But Michael's comment would suggest otherwise . . .

Instantly, Evangeline regrets her dramatic reaction. She struggles to neutralize her expression; like with the djinni in the cabin, she will reveal nothing to her enemy.

"You're going to freeze me out?" Michael presses her.

He's standing with his back to the little window, his arms folded across his chest in a posture of entitlement. It's like he's saying, *I own this place. You* will *answer me.* But Evangeline is so tired of their— Michael's people's—privilege. Who are *they* to determine what happens? They're not better than Evangeline. If there's one thing her father taught her, it's to *never* concede her right to equality. Michael and his father may have grown up in Fifth Heaven as Dominions before they became indispensable as Archangels in God's army, but that by no means give them the right to think they can order her around.

So she says nothing.

"*God!*" Michael exhales. "You are exasperating, Evie! I am trying to *help* you!"

Evangeline is drawn up short.

Evie.

No one ever calls her that.

She remembers the first time Michael used it. It was their second meeting, both of them hidden in the stairwell before class.

She'd squeezed into the tiny space Michael had insisted on, expecting to be attacked, of course. Such a secluded location? There was no doubt. But she had no choice. At least a private assault by one angel would be better than the public humiliation she'd endured up to this point.

Michael had come furtively. No one wanted to be seen with the half-breed, not the least of which was the son of the great Archangel Gabriel.

But he had come.

"Hey Evie," he'd said, as if that was her name. She was about to correct him—*Evangeline, thank you very much*—because no matter how much her peers tormented her, she couldn't shake the feeling that she *shouldn't give in.*

Lucifer called it pride.

Uncle Raziel called it strength.

She called it foolishness in the extreme, but she knew no other way.

Yet she liked the sound of her shortened name. She liked the ease with which he used it, the informality, the implied closeness.

Michael now throws his hands up and starts pacing in front of the bed.

"What is your father up to?" He stops to face her.

Evangeline's eyes flare with fire. What is her father *up to*? Her father is up to winning this war so they can reclaim their rights as Commoners.

"This is bad, Evie," he says, gripping the footboard. He stares hard at her, but Evangeline returns his fierce gaze. "If Lucifer has reopened a djinn portal . . . "

"Oh, so you automatically assume it was my father?" Evangeline snaps.

Michael pauses at that—as if he never thought there was another option.

"One djinni, in *Third* Heaven," she continues, "far away from any Commoner, nowhere close to my father and you blame *him*?"

Evangeline's voice has all the indignation she can muster, but even as she says it she feels removed from her own words.

Lucifer said you were . . . special.

Her father is involved. She can feel it. There's a connection between a djinni that strangely looks like Lucifer and Lucifer himself. Evangeline can't fathom what it could be—and that unnerves her. She'd love to talk it out with Michael, since he saw the djinni with his own eyes. She'd love to voice her worry and confusion, and have him help her work out what it all means, but that's impossible. If she were to open up to him about her unsettling doubts, Michael would immediately exploit her vulnerability.

"Your father is about to destroy our world as we know it," Michael tells her.

"Yes," Evangeline retorts, harsh and bitter. "That's the point. No longer will we accept your world as we know it."

Michael shakes his head, then sits on the edge of the bed at her feet. "I mean the key will be the death of us all—*including* the Commoners."

"The *key* is our birthright," Evangeline replies. "Once my father finds it, we will gain our rightful power and glory in the Heavens."

"Oh, spare me the rhetoric, Evie," Michael sneers. "Your father is dangerous and you know it."

Evangeline thinks she should feel as if she's been slapped—that he would have the *nerve* to question her loyalty like that—but instead she feels like Michael has glimpsed inside her head. For the first time, she fears that maybe Michael is right; maybe her father *is* dangerous. She thinks of Christie and Sidriel's bare cupboard, the anger of the

Commoner mob, the Dragon button in her pocket, and she's afraid. Afraid she can no longer ignore the evidence she witnessed in First and Second Heaven.

But there's a good reason for it all. Of that she is certain. If her father *has* had to resort to violence, it's because he had no choice.

Fight fire with fire, he used to tell her, so that must be what he's doing. The Archangels and the Seraphim are powerful, devious enemies. If that one djinni *is* involved, it's most likely Lucifer's way to even the playing field. Lucifer did confide in her that their side was on the verge of defeat, so this djinni must be a scare tactic, a warning. If Lucifer did know how to access a portal, if he *did* call forth this strange djinni, then it was mostly likely to threaten the Archangels. Her father would never *do* anything with the djinni, of course. And even if he could find a way to bring through a djinn army—an impossible "if"—he never would. Her father, of all angels, appreciates first-hand the horror and destruction of the djinn. There are countless reasons why he'd never unleash such terror on the Heavens. Not the least of which is because then his own people, the Commoners, would also be at risk. Since Lucifer almost *died* trying to protect his people from the djinn all those years ago when no one else would, he would never endanger them now.

Evangeline feels some strength seep back into her bones. Her mind settles. It's difficult, true, to not know the details of her father's plans, but she's always trusted him before, so there's no reason to stop now. And the more she thinks about it, the more it makes sense why he wouldn't tell her about summoning a djinni—*if* indeed, he was the one who did. He was trying to protect her. He didn't want her to worry, as she would *absolutely* have worried if he'd even hinted he planned to use a dangerous former foe to conquer their current enemy. Her father is nothing if not strategic and she's always admired him for it. Whatever is going on, then, must be part of his design and if she doesn't have the skills to see it, then that's on her, not her father.

Emboldened by her rationalization, Evangeline goes on the offensive.

"Why are *you* here?" she demands. "Won't your father be angry you're not following orders to find my father?"

"I am," Michael snaps. He jumps off the bed, then strides to the window, his back to her.

Evangeline now feels as if she has been slapped.

Danielle. His sister told him about her, knew all along she wasn't Alina. It's why Danielle let her go, why she returned the sword to her. Evangeline's face reddens as her stomach contracts in humiliation. How could she be so *stupid*? She'd avoided Lucifer's soldiers, afraid they'd question her about her disappearance, and she'd learned to stay away from regular angels after she was released from the Archangels. But she never dreamed that she'd actually been leading her father's killers right to him.

Michael's shoulders slump, and Evangeline thinks he *should* have the decency to be ashamed. But then he whirls back on her.

"Your uncle found the lost book," Michael recounts, defiantly. "The one from the Assembly of Angels."

Evangeline blinks in surprise.

The book? *The* book? The one that was lost for a millennium? The one Uncle Raziel feared didn't actually exist, considering his exhaustive search for it throughout his whole life?

Her mind is drawn back to her uncle's teachings about the long-ago gathering of Singular Angels, where one angel was chosen by God from each Heaven to join together in an effort to unite the classes. Each was tasked with defining a different virtue, and the seven, the Angels of Wisdom, Truth, Justice, Mercy, Peace, Love, and Hope became known as the Assembly. But this is ancient history, barely remembered by angels today, so Evangeline cannot fathom the connection to Gabriel hunting down her father.

"It's not actually called *The Assembly Book*, did you know that?" Michael's voice contains a hint of bitterness Evangeline doesn't understand. "You know what it's called?" Michael doesn't give her an opportunity to answer. "It's called *The Keys to the Kingdom*."

Evangeline draws in a sharp breath.

The Keys to the Kingdom. The key.

The key is a *book*? Uncle Raziel's missing, mysterious *book* is the key?

The key . . . the legends . . . the sketches she drew back in school based on the images of the lost book . . . were keys . . .

Keys her father took great interest in.

Evangeline feels as if she's been punched in the gut. Could all this be true? Could her father have known all this time that the book was the *key*? He always believed the key was real, but *everyone* who believed the key was real thought the key was a *real* key, thick and heavy, made of iron. Did her cunning, strategic, intelligent father know differently?

Is that what he's been after all this time? A *book*? *The* book? Her uncle's book?

And now, after all this time, he's found it?

Unbelievable.

Yes, actually, it *is* unbelievable.

Evangeline shakes her head. Michael is messing with her. How low can he sink, using her sweet, eccentric uncle against her?

"You're lying," she says. A statement, not a question.

But Michael meets her eyes; he doesn't drop his gaze.

"I'm not. Your uncle discovered it wrapped in another cover in the Ancient Archives. It's been hiding in plain sight for centuries."

"No . . . " Evangeline breathes, but she can picture it. She can see her uncle, in the cavernous hall, filled to overflowing with ancient texts, meticulously removing each and every book, scanning, searching. The man is a virtue of patience; he would have spent the last of his waking minutes in hell if he felt his long search might finally bear fruit. She can still smell old, brittle pages, the dried ink, the intoxicating smell of history. It was her uncle's life, and until her father recalled her for his war, Evangeline had hoped maybe someday it could be hers, too. No Commoner had ever been appointed a Cherubim, a Divine Record Keeper, but she was half Dominion, and Uncle Raziel encouraged her to hold out hope.

"How do you know?"

It's not Evangeline's question. Her question is how does *Michael* know before her? How does *he* know about her family's discoveries and not her? She feels a sharp pain of betrayal; she was her uncle's favorite; she was his legacy, a living vessel into which he could pour his passions so they would live on in her—and they would. Evangeline adores her uncle; she loves his work studying the ancient world. History is like a puzzle. She loves piecing together the past.

And then there's her father.

She understands if her father hadn't informed her of his plans to use a djinni—that is tactical—but to keep from her that he learned the key is a *book*? Why didn't he trust her with that? Because she was skeptical the key existed at all? She would have believed him—in fact, she thinks it's likelier she would have believed a book could be the key than some magical iron instrument.

But it's not only that. It's not that her father kept from her the biggest secret. It's that he was secretly colluding with Uncle Raziel. She doesn't know if Uncle Raziel discovered the connection between the book and the key and then told Lucifer, or if Lucifer made the extraordinary leap in logic, but either way, they shut her out. The only family she has ever known, her beloved father and her adored uncle, lied to her.

Evangeline shrinks into herself, wishing she were alone in the room. She feels raw, exposed, as if Michael has cut her open.

"Yesterday, your uncle removed the book, an invaluable artifact from the Ancient Archives, might I add. He may be an outstanding scholar, but he makes for a lousy spy," Michael smiles ruefully.

Evangeline wants to smack him hard across the face. *No one* insults her uncle. He's ostracized from the other Cherubim enough as it is for his obsession with researching the history and impact of the Assembly of Angels; she won't stand for a hard-mouth enemy to slag him. Her palm tingles in anticipation, but with great effort, Evangeline reins in her anger, and she clenches her hand into a fist.

"The Cherubim alerted my father to the theft," Michael continues. "They heard rumblings your uncle is on his way to meet Lucifer."

Evangeline feels light-headed; her nausea returns. "It's why you were in the Farlands; Gabriel knew my father would find me on my birthday. He always does."

Michael nods heavily.

"But you lost him," Evangeline smiles defiantly. "And you lost a tottering old angel, too."

Again, Michael nods, sheepishly.

"And you want to intercept them before my father can get his hands on the key because you know that if he has it, he wins. *We* win. The Commoners win and you won't be able to banish us to Earth or bully us in the Heavens anymore."

"*No*," Michael insists. "The book is dangerous. In Lucifer's hands, the existence of the very Heavens is at stake."

Evangeline laughs cruelly, bitterly. There's a dark joy in the sound, and it reminds her of the wicked sense of glee she felt attacking the djinni. "Your father told you that? Your father, the hypocrite? The one who speaks of peace and harmony among all angels, but then upholds the Seraphim's orders to destroy us? And you believe him?"

She sees Michael stiffen, but she doesn't care. The bastard. Whisking her to this inn, tending to her wounds, pretending to care, all the while setting up a trap for her father based on their fear that Lucifer might actually be able to end this war and with it the injustice against Commoners.

"You are so gullible," Evangeline scoffs, "if you think a book written by the Assembly of Angels a millennium ago for the *express* purpose of helping angels live in harmony can actually destroy the Heavens. Don't you know your history, Michael?" She relishes in her contempt. "God was so concerned about the divisions the angels were creating among themselves that he appointed to each class a Singular Angel who would become a member of the Assembly. Each leader would represent a specific virtue: wisdom, truth, justice, mercy, love, peace, and hope." Evangeline continues to revel in her knowledge, pleased she can correct Michael's poor grasp of history. "The Assembly gathered to share their virtues with the others so goodness and morality could spread. As part of their work, they created a book to which each Singular Angel contributed a treatise on how best to enlighten angels based on their virtue. The book was conceived as a work of unity, so no, Michael, you are entirely wrong; it cannot ruin the Heavens."

But Michael shrugs off her history lesson as if it were irrelevant. "Help me find your father, Evie. For all our sakes."

Evangeline is about to refuse with a vehemence born of righteousness, but then another thought strikes her. An ingenious, strategic idea.

"Fine," she says. "I'll help you find him, but on two conditions. You guarantee me a chance to prove his innocence. And two . . . " Here, she pauses for effect. "You swear to God that neither you nor your goonish Archangels, including your father, kill him."

Evangeline sits up, feeling confident for the first time since Sophia's village. She realizes she holds all the cards. It's true she doesn't yet know where her father is, but Michael is right, she has a much better chance of finding him than anyone else.

And she can't do that stuck here as Michael's prisoner.

But it's less about saving his life, she realizes abruptly. Now, she needs to find him to confront him.

She has to find out why he lied to her.

"You know you need me," Evangeline presses Michael.

Michael considers her proposal. "Yes," he finally says, in a soft, mellifluous voice. "I need you."

CHAPTER 7

The air of the fourth morning of the week blows cool on Evangeline's face. She likes the wind swirling off the lake wafting against her skin; it's a sign of movement, of motion, of going forward. Finally. Last night in the inn had been long, too long. To her dismay and despite her utter exhaustion, physical and mental, Evangeline hadn't been able to sleep. She had so desperately wanted to count on the sublime fantasy that the unconsciousness of sleep would erase her mind, but to no avail. Whenever she closed her eyes, she saw the djinni. The harsh, sharp face that resembled her father's. Then she heard Michael's voice. *Your uncle found the lost book, the one from the Assembly of Angels.* None of it makes sense. How can a djinni be in their world, let alone look like her father, and how can Uncle Raziel have found a book that had been lost for a thousand years? And how had those two most improbable events happened at the same time?

"Coincidences are simply two pieces of the same puzzle," her father always told her. "Simply because you don't know how they fit together doesn't mean they don't belong."

Evangeline wonders what possible connection there could be between her uncle miraculously finding his lifelong grail and her strange, impossible encounter with a djinni.

She'd lain awake, her side throbbing from the stab wound, her throat still raw from the djinni's stranglehold, trying to answer the unanswerable. She felt restless, but she dared not move. Michael lay beside her, sharing the bed, as they had agreed, so both could restore their strength with a solid night's sleep. It seemed to be working for Michael. He snored softly, as if the Heavens themselves were paradise, while she bristled with irritation. She was annoyed he could sleep so soundly when so much was wrong. She wanted to pummel him awake, so he would have to suffer her torment with her.

Or so she could again feel her skin on his.

God! What was she thinking? She shook her head, flipped over onto her side, and yanked the soft wool blanket over her. She lay, staring at the shifting patch of moonlight on the hearth rug for a long, long time.

Which is why Evangeline is now so relieved to be out here on the water of Lake Neam, bobbing on the waves in the small rowboat Michael rented, on their way to Fourth Heaven. Michael concurred with Evangeline's original plan to search for Lucifer in Fifth Heaven, so they're continuing on her path. Michael has the oars, while she sits in the stern, wrapped tightly in her cloak, her body still too injured to fly. Their progress is swift; Michael rows steady and strong.

She watches his strokes, lulled by the rhythm. She sees him better now, in the daylight, sees how wrong she was to think of him still as a boy. He now moves with a flourishing confidence, an assurance born of righteousness. She recognizes it; her father carries himself like that, too. Michael's tilt of his head, his crooked smile, are smaller, subtler, than Lucifer's bold movements, but the two men share the same regal posture, as if they wear an invisible cloak of authority. Evangeline wonders how Michael learned it—Gabriel is more languid, more fluid in the way he moves—but, then, she doesn't know what experiences in the war Michael lived through. Perhaps, by dint of association, he was made commander. Evangeline has learned throughout her own life that age has nothing to do with authority; Commoners often fawn over her, ask her for advice, expect direction from her simply because she is her father's daughter. Her father's surrogate. Is Michael the same? She wonders if Archangels treat him deferentially because Gabriel is so revered. Or maybe not, because they are a fine-tuned military meritocracy. In which case, Michael must have earned the respect he wears comfortably on his shoulders. She tries to think back over all the battles her father has recounted this past year, tries to remember if he, or any of their soldiers, ever mentioned Michael. Gabriel, yes. Gabriel is always on Lucifer's lips. The once-great general long past his prime, the sad soldier, desperate in defeat. Evangeline knows, of course, that it's all rhetoric for the Commoners; Lucifer is a master of propaganda and persuasion, convincing his people how weak their enemy is, but she wonders if that's why she never heard about Michael. Ignore the enemy, deny his existence, and his threat is diminished.

But Evangeline saw how Michael attacked the djinni. Whatever his training, whatever his battles, he's skilled.

Almost as skilled as she is.

Evangeline notices the slowing rhythm of the boat. She realizes that Michael has stopped, the oars resting on the gunwale. The morning is crisp and fresh, as if she can smell a hint of mint on the breeze, but she notices a thin sheen of sweat on Michael's forehead, and she shifts uncomfortably. Here she's sat, allowing him to do all the work, while she, like a princess, lounges in the boat. That's not what her father taught her; she knows to be self-sufficient, even if she's in pain. She knows the sting of sword wounds and combat bruises, and she knows to press on.

"I'll row," she says, shifting forward.

Michael laughs, and Evangeline scowls at the discordant sound. For a moment, she's carried back to school, when the bitter hilarity around her was always at her expense. She would walk down the hall, and an angel at random would bump into her, knocking her against the stone wall.

"Watch where you're going," he—or she, because cruelty knows no gender—would say, and then cackle.

When she'd told her father in hopes of building her case to leave, Lucifer had also laughed. But his laugh was a welcoming chime.

"You've been dragged through the mud by Dominions long before attending this school, my darling. You're usually so feisty in your retaliation. I can't imagine a trivial shove would leave you cowering."

But it did. The taunts at school stung more than they had before. Naïvely, foolishly, she had believed she was one of them. Her mother had been one of them, and she is, in part, her mother, but when she discovered that Seraphina's spirit did not protect her the way she had imagined, she felt stripped bare in a way she had never before experienced. She felt vulnerable, exposed and very, very alone.

"What?" Michael is asking, amused, which irritates Evangeline all the more. She grabs for the oars, but Michael pulls them back out reach. He chuckles, he smiles.

She grimaces. He doesn't get it.

"Evie, it's okay, I got this."

Evangeline tries again. This time she gets her hand on one of the wooden paddles, but the effort to reach across a half-length of the boat makes her wince.

"Evie," Michael puts his hands on hers. His warm skin on hers. "Let me help you," he says quietly, the laughter gone from his voice.

Evangeline thinks about resisting, but instead, she drops her hands from Michael's and leans back. Her father would be appalled;

not only has she allied with the son of his worst enemy, now she is beholden to him, too. But Evangeline likes it. She's ashamed to admit it, but she likes the relief that courses through her body. She likes that, at least for the length of the lake, she'll be taken care of.

Michael dips the oars into the water and again begins to row. They glide across the smooth, dark water in silence. Evangeline thinks of the dagiel, the merpeople who live beneath them. There aren't many of them, spread across the Heavens' waters—far, far fewer of them than the dominant angels—but what she's learned from her uncle's ancient texts is how they have never, throughout history, fought each other. There have been skirmishes, usually territorial in nature, but never outright war.

"Then why do angels fight so much?" she has asked.

"Because, my child," Uncle Raziel smiled sadly, "angels always have to be right."

She thinks of her father, whose whole life has been based on the righteousness of their Cause. Uncle Raziel made it sound like being right was a bad thing, but how could their fight for equality, for justice, for dignity be bad?

"War begets peace," Evangeline told him, quoting her father.

"Oh, my sweet angel," Uncle Raziel said, "*Peace* begets peace."

This, from an angel who grew up privileged as the child of a Dominion governor, in the riches of Fifth Heaven, then honored with the quiet, prestigious life of a Cherubim, one of only ten divine scholars handpicked by the Seraphim. Raziel knew nothing about being spat on by angels who believed they were better. Or about foraging for wild mushrooms because food and jobs were scarce for their kind. Or about listening to incessant insults about her filth staining the hallowed halls of their academy. No, Evangeline knew her father was right. The only way to win against these Dominions—the ones bullying her at school as well as the ones bullying her people in the rest of the Heavens—was to fight back.

"Did you know dagiels can breathe air as well as they breathe water?" Evangeline asks absently, reaching over the side and running her fingers across the shimmering surface of the lake. "They choose to stay away from us."

"No," Michael answers, with a hint of wonder. "How do you know that?"

"My uncle Raziel taught me."

"The Cherubim who always came to visit you?"

Evangeline nods.

"That made all the difference, you know," Michael says.

Evangeline looks up, confused. "What do you mean?"

"Having a Cherubim as an uncle."

"What are you talking about?"

"The parent council were about to have your head—or at least your father's," Michael says. He pauses, then adding as an afterthought, "And my father's head, too, since he vouched for you."

Evangeline's stomach clenches, the injustice churning her insides as if it were happening here and now.

"But I am a *Dominion*," she seethes. It's not true. Not true enough, but still, she clings to the morality of it. "And even if I wasn't, why couldn't *any* angel attend the school?"

"Hey, you don't have to lecture *me*," Michael exclaims.

Evangeline shakes her head at him in disbelief. "Are you *kidding*? You've been fighting my people for a *year*!"

"Because of a war *your* father started," Michael shoots back, his voice dripping with accusations.

"Because *your* people deny us basic angel rights!"

"I know they do!" Michael cries.

That stops Evangeline. She thinks she misheard. "You *know* we're discriminated against and yet you still fight us?" The hypocrisy rankles her more than she expects. In fact, she thinks she held more respect for him only a minute before when she thought he actually believed in his misguided reality. But to hear he *knows* his people have wronged hers and *still* he fights for the status quo? She feels a hurt, deep under her skin, which she can't explain.

Michael stops rowing. He faces her straight on, his eyes burrowing into her. "Evie, the war isn't about stopping the Commoners from rising up. It's about stopping your *father* from rising up."

Evangeline clamps her mouth shut. She's been in this situation before, feeling a visceral, primitive instinct to defend her father. She's felt the burn of hatred roil through her blood, the anger rising in her gorge, but she's also been well trained to restrain herself. "Do not engage, Evangeline," Lucifer always told her with a light touch, spoken from the moral high ground. "True believers have faith in me, and anyone else is beneath us. The time will come when they will recognize their true place, but until then, bide your time, sweetheart."

But there's a strange shift in Evangeline's reaction to Michael's accusation, like a joint knocked out of alignment.

What if he's right? She thinks back to Christie and Sidriel in First Heaven, the accusations of the old angel in Second Heaven, the djinni in Third Heaven who looks like Lucifer . . . the evidence is mounting against her father and, minute by minute, she feels her certainty, her trust in him, ebb away. She feels wretched, doubting her father, after all they've been through together. He's been her rock her whole life, the one constant in their nomadic life. She may have been lonely for friends her own age, as they traveled through First Heaven rallying for the Cause, but she'd never trade it in for another existence. She loves Lucifer. He's been her hero, her mentor, her guide, her compass; she is a horrible daughter to turn on him now.

She feels bewitched, as if a current stronger than her own faith is pulling her away from her father. She blames Michael. He's the one poisoning her against Lucifer.

Or merely giving name to the poison that has already leeched into her mind.

No, she should never have trusted him. Now she feels trapped here in the boat with Michael. She wonders if she's strong enough now to fly, but even if she were, she could never outfly Michael—not injured—so she has to figure out a way to escape Michael once they're on shore. The woods are pretty dense; maybe she can lose him in the trees.

Michael, too, seems to retreat into himself, and the air between them turns frosty. They say nothing to each other as Michael pulls hard on the oars. Evangeline isn't surprised when their speed increases; anger gives you strength. Evangeline thinks back to the djinni, to the joy of the rage she felt inside. Yes, she's learned that lesson well.

Not long afterward, they sight the Fourth Heaven shoreline. Evangeline notices Michael veering away from the village harbor, toward a secluded inlet among the dense, evergreen forest. That works well into Evangeline's plan. As soon as they beach, when Michael draws the boat out of the water, Evangeline will slip away into the trees. The thick canopy of boughs and needles will camouflage her path from the air and the autumn leaves on the ground will mask her footprints.

But as they approach the rocky beach, Evangeline's heart skips and then sinks. She sees shapes, forms, silhouettes on the beach, two angels, their wings spread wide. From their posture, she senses they are alert, on guard, and Evangeline senses they are there for her.

The *bastard*, Evangeline thinks of Michael, feeling a deep cut of betrayal. She can tell the angels on the beach are Archangels; Evangeline can see from the glint of sun off their armor. Michael must have contacted them when he left to secure the boat.

Evangeline curses herself. She assumed her alliance with Michael would be secret, but now she realizes her mistake.

Trust no one.

Yet Gabriel had told Michael back in the Farlands not to breathe a word of their mission. So why would Michael arrange a welcoming party?

Unless the mission is no longer secret because Gabriel has already caught Lucifer . . .

The thought stops her heart.

Is her father already dead?

Evangeline has trouble breathing, thinking she may be too late to save her father. She clenches her fist, her nails digging half-moons into her palms. She is wound up with too much emotion, too many jagged feelings—terror, betrayal, guilt—that she is on the brink of exploding. But she contains herself. Her father always praised her stoicism, and she will not disappoint him.

Michael rows the boat to the shallows, where the Archangels wade into the water to tug it to shore. Michael clambers over the side and holds out his hand toward Evangeline, but she climbs out herself. Never again will she accept anything from him.

"Michael, we've got him, but it's bad, and he'll only talk to her." The Archangel, scrawny and skinny, like a child dressed up as a soldier, nods his head in Evangeline's direction.

Evangeline's heart wrenches open. Relief floods through her—her father's alive—but then cold, paralyzing fear. *It's bad.* What does that mean? What did they do to him? She's afraid and she wishes she could react the way she did as a child, in the early days, before they began traveling for the Cause, when it was only the two of them nestled in their little wooden cabin, built by Lucifer. If she had a bad dream, for example, she'd clamor onto her father's lap in front of the fire and bury her head in his chest, smelling the fresh sawdust on his clothes and the scent of lemon on his skin. He would wrap his arms around her, and she'd be safe.

"Where is he?" Michael demands. He morphs easily, seamlessly, into the regal leader Evangeline glimpsed on their crossing.

"Your father has him in an abandoned cabin nearby," the skinny kid-soldier explains. "Raphael is with him, but your uncle is doubtful he'll survive."

Evangeline's legs quiver, but she strains to keep her balance. This is bad if Raphael, the founder of modern medicine, renowned throughout the Heavens for his miracles, can do nothing for her father.

She concentrates on keeping a calm, outward appearance. "Take me to my father now," she demands.

The Archangel blinks at her. "No, Evangeline, you misunderstand. It's not your father we have. It's your uncle Raziel."

CHAPTER 8

E vangeline's mind is reeling as she rushes after the Archangels through the dense forest. They follow no path she can identify, and they are fast on their feet. Still recovering from her injuries, Evangeline strains to keep up. Michael remains behind her—to keep her captive, she thinks.

Or to keep her safe.

Evangeline doesn't know what she's thinking. Her thoughts swirl around in a fog without meaning. Michael told her that Archangels had followed Uncle Raziel from the Archives soon after they were alerted to the theft of the Assembly book, the supposed "key," but that the soldiers lost the trail of the frail old man, whom they believed to be on his way to offer the priceless treasure to Lucifer. But that was days ago; Evangeline has been searching for her father for three days already, and since Michael was still on her tail as of last night, it must have meant that neither Lucifer, nor Raziel, had been found.

So what changed overnight? Where and how had the Archangels found Uncle Raziel? Why was he hurt? What did they *do* to him? And what did this all mean for her father?

With their pace brisk, the walk to the cabin isn't far from the lakeshore. It's hidden, well concealed among the dense pine, spruce, and fir trees. The walls, logs made of cedar, slump against themselves, a tired little cottage, burdened under its own weight. Evangeline guesses it was an old hunting cabin, but it doesn't matter; she only cares about who is inside.

The Archangels step back at the edge of the sagging porch to let Evangeline pass. She rushes up the wooden steps, ignoring their ominous creek, and pushes her way through the warping door.

Inside, faint rays of daylight filter in through the small, grime-covered windows. Despite the mid-morning hour, candles burn on a deeply scarred wooden table, plunging the whole eerie room into dusklike shadows. Evangeline's eyes leap to the bed in the corner. She can see a figure, buried under a faded quilt, but cannot make out her uncle's face. Beside him stands Gabriel, with his usual aura of benevolence, which, at this moment makes Evangeline want to scream. The snow white of Gabriel's wings glint in the flickering candlelight, his ice-blue eyes reflect the flame. In them, Evangeline sees concern, but she also catches a steely coldness. However admired Gabriel is by the rest of the Archangels, he is actually more like her father than he'll admit. Lucifer says that often—to her, at least.

"A soul cannot lie and the eyes are its only mirror," Lucifer told her.

If that's the case, then today, right now, Gabriel's soul is speckled with darkness.

On the edge of the bed is another formidable angel. Evangeline has never met Raphael, but she's sure it's him; he shares his brother Gabriel's light coloring and imperious attitude. Evangeline wants to glare into his eyes, to see into his soul and know he will not lie about trying save her uncle, but his back is to her; she can see only his gray-white feathers trembling with intensity.

Evangeline ignores Gabriel and settles herself on the other side of the bed. She ignores Raphael too, who seems not to have registered her presence.

Finally, she sees Raziel's face, and she chokes back a sob. He is unrecognizable. His left eye, swollen shut, is bruised black, matching the color of the surrounding shadows, and his right is a slit, crisscrossed with jagged red lines, like claw marks. His cheeks look sunken, like a man who has breathed out his life, his soul, and has nothing left inside. His breath rattles; it's a fearsome, haunting noise that is all the scarier when it momentarily stops.

Evangeline tugs down the quilt to take her uncle's hand and then she sees the blood-soaked bandage around his throat. Evangeline's hands fly to her own; she can feel the scratch marks left by the djinni, but these wounds on her uncle's neck look nothing like cuts from a struggle.

"His throat was sliced open," Raphael says, his tone detached. "The incisions cut the arteries on both the left and right side of his neck. Raziel seems to have been able to stem the flow of blood, because the bleeding had slowed by the time he was found. But hear me clearly, Evangeline, your uncle is near death. I cannot reverse God's will."

God's will . . . the phrase buzzes in her head, a swarm of nasty gnats. In her world, invoking "God's will" only serves to demonstrate you are a contemptuous coward; it means you cannot stave off defeat, so you blame someone else.

Evangeline bristles, wishing she could be alone with her uncle. He deserves his privacy, his dignity. But Raphael doesn't move from the bed and Gabriel remains still as a statue behind her.

Evangeline bends over to kiss her uncle's cheek. Her lips touch paper-thin skin, dry and cold. At the same time, she presses his ice-like hand in hers, trying to keep control.

Uncle Raziel's eye flutters open and Evangeline sees a speck of blue-gold.

"Uncle," she says. Her voice quivers; she holds her breath to steady it, and tries again. "Uncle, I'm here."

His lips try to curl; she sees the muscles twitch, although no smile appears.

"You'll be okay. Raphael is here." She doesn't want to believe Raphael's own warnings about her uncle's deteriorating condition. She wants instead to believe in his legend, in the magic of his miracles.

Raphael turns to her as if noticing her for the first time. Evangeline feels exposed, as his eyes scan over her.

"You're injured," Raphael says to her, as if she weren't already aware of the fact. "Let me help you."

The healer reaches toward her, but instinctively she pulls away.

"Help *him*," she points to her uncle.

Raphael's look softens into sadness. "I can do no more for Raziel."

Evangeline twists away from the healer, refusing to believe him. Raziel has to be okay. He and Lucifer are the only family she has; she can't lose him.

Uncle Raziel blinks at her, the circle of blue iris bright, expressive. Evangeline sees in them his beautiful soul. With an effort that Evangeline attempts to discourage, Raziel opens his mouth. His lips part, a slit, but he tries to speak; a breath of air escapes. Evangeline leans in, her ear against his mouth. She smells the metallic tang of blood, the sour odor of death. She squeezes her eyes shut, wishing she weren't here, wishing they were back in her uncle's coveted chambers in Sixth Heaven. She was lucky, she'd always known that; most Dominions—forget about Commoners—were never allowed to set foot in Sixth Heaven, reserved only for the Archivists, Divine Record Keepers and their staff. But she was special, Raziel proclaimed proudly. She had all the markings of a future Cherubim, he said. He said she belonged there.

Raziel breathes out. The air is barely a ripple on Evangeline's cheek, and she has to bite her tongue to keep from crying out.

"Lu . . . ci . . . fer," he murmurs. He is so quiet, barely audible, that at first she imagines he said her father's name, but then he repeats himself. The effort drains him, and Evangeline wants him to stop, but he squeezes her hand with a weak urgency that terrifies her. "Lu . . . cifer . . . did . . . this . . . "

Evangeline's head springs up, as if by an invisible force. She stares into her uncle's one good eye, searching for the delusion that must be in his words. She thought he said her father did this. That is lunacy. Her father loved Uncle Raziel—*loves* Uncle Raziel. He is all the family they've got.

But Raziel squeezes her hand once more. The pressure is light, but the intent unmistakable. Evangeline doesn't want to hear any more nonsense, but she again bends close to his lips.

"Six, six . . . " Raziel takes a shallow breath. " . . . six . . . "

Evangeline is bewildered. She doesn't understand. She looks to Raphael, who shrugs unhelpfully.

Gabriel steps over to her, his movement swift, clipped. "Ask him about the book, Evangeline," he says.

The book? *Now*? In the shape he's in? She refuses to answer. She doesn't move.

"Evangeline," Gabriel speaks in a soft lilt that makes her shudder. "The book is dangerous. For the sake of all the Heavens, we need it returned."

Dangerous . . .

Lucifer did this . . .

Evangeline's head swirls in confusion. Nothing makes sense anymore. Her uncle *attacked* by her father? A mysterious lost treasure, dangerous in his hands?

Six, six, six.

What does her uncle mean?

Evangeline has to ask, despite the effort it will cost him. But then she realizes, with a clenching heart, the old man's hand in hers has gone still. She lifts her gaze to his face.

The light behind his eyes fades. She blinks, and it is gone.

He is gone.

Her beloved uncle is dead.

At the hands of her own father, if Raziel himself is to be believed.

Evangeline grows cold from shock.

Dear God, could it be true?

CHAPTER 9

Evangeline walks out of the cabin. She leaves her uncle's body in the bed. It's not him, her surrogate grandfather, not anymore. Uncle Raziel is gone. His soul has already traveled to God's Realm, the one place in all the Heavens inaccessible to any living angel, even the powerful Seraphim. She hopes Uncle Raziel will be reunited with her mother. She doesn't know if souls can talk, but she likes to think her uncle will regale Seraphina with all sorts of stories about their time together. She regrets now that she stopped prodding Raziel about her mother's life. In her uncle's telling, Seraphina was flawless, well-loved, and talented, everything Evangeline wasn't, so she discouraged any reminiscence on his part. If he brought up Seraphina, Evangeline would quickly change the subject. Now she laments how childish she'd been. Now she'll never learn about her mother, about why she wanted to become a healer, about how she felt when her parents disowned her, about whether Seraphina regretted her choices in life.

About whether Seraphina regretted having her.

Evangeline wonders if souls can ache with longing, like hers does now. Does her mother's soul miss her? Will Uncle Raziel's? Or are they happy? Content without the excruciating pain of grief, of betrayal, of hurt? She'd like to think so, if only to be assured they are at peace, but then, it hurts even more to think that she is suffering alone.

Gabriel calls after her. She hears his voice, but it sounds like an echo across a valley, distant and indistinct. She doesn't listen, though, doesn't know what he says. It's irrelevant, whatever he wants. The book, her father . . . it's all irrelevant because Uncle Raziel is dead.

She sees Michael at the edge of the porch, his face etched with questions, but she brushes past him without a word. Her body still aches from her injuries yesterday, but her physical pain is insignificant. She didn't know a heart could be crushed so vehemently. She's seen death before, yes. She's suffered watching her people's bodies return from the horrors of the battlefield. She's sung the Lament of Death at funerals more times than she can count, and every time, her heart has been full, a heavy sadness weighing her down. She thought she knew grief. When Sophia died, it was like losing a sister. The hole in Evangeline's heart was real.

But this . . .

Evangeline walks among the trees, unaware of her direction. When there is a tree in her path, she veers around it. When there is another, she turns again. She doesn't know where she's going, and she doesn't care. All she wants is to run away, to escape her crushing torment, because she can't live like this. She is only grief, her whole identity, heart and soul, one of unbearable sorrow. She wonders if this is how she felt when her mother died. She doesn't remember. She'd only been three. In fact, she doesn't have a single memory of Seraphina that she's sure is her own. She has her father's stories, and Uncle Raziel's tales, too, and over the years, she's pieced together a composite of what she came to believe was her mother, but she's not fool enough to believe it was reality. Her father loved her mother with an unbridled passion that seems both impossible to experience, it was so intense, and at the same time, the ultimate goal for which one must strive. And Uncle Raziel, the old, childless bachelor, doted on

Seraphina like a daughter, so of course the two angels' stories were undoubtedly rose-tinted.

Evangeline wonders now, as she stumbles through the forest, tripping over tree roots, if how she feels now is how they felt when her mother died. Was it possible? Not that they felt such grief, but that they survived it?

Evangeline doesn't believe that she can. Not only because Uncle Raziel died, but because of the *way* he died. If she puts aside his accusation that Lucifer is to blame—and she *has* to put that aside, because she has no way to process that—the violent way he died is enough to suffocate her. He should have died in his own bed of a slow, gentle decline, his life gradually slipping away in stages both he and she could learn to accept. Uncle Raziel would lie comfortably, with a thick blanket tucked under his chin, and Evangeline would sit at his side, holding his hand in companionable silence. Then he'd speak, softly, of course, but steady and strong, to reassure her it was simply his time to go, that God had other plans for his soul, and it would be okay, that he would be fine, and so would she. And then Evangeline would let slip a few tears, but she'd nod her head, stoically accepting the inevitable. She'd never imagined his death before, but if she had, that's how it should have been.

Not the brutal, angry, violence of a sword or a knife across his throat.

She thinks of her father, as their Cause grew in power, as the threats against him also grew, when she worried for his safety and he calmed her fears.

"You'd know what I'd do before anyone had a chance to kill me?" Lucifer would joke. "I'd . . . " and then he'd drag his fingers across his throat.

It was nothing. A stupid sign. It was Lucifer reacting to the innumerable threats on his life in an exaggerated, childish way simply to alleviate her fears. Of course he'd never slit someone's throat. That would be gruesome, barbaric, unthinkable. No, Lucifer meant that he'd vigorously defend himself, no matter the threat.

So had Uncle Raziel threatened her father? If what Raziel said was true—and how much could you rely on emotionally wrought deathbed testimony?—then did *Raziel* threaten her father? If Lucifer *did* inflict such cruelty, was it because he felt it was his life or her uncle's? Could Raziel have set up her father? Betrayed him to Gabriel, and *that's* why Lucifer had no choice but to kill him? His life or her uncle's?

Evangeline tries to imagine that scenario. She finds it impossible. Her father, a seasoned war hero with an innate sense of self-preservation, an angel with prodigious swordsmanship, up against an eccentric bookworm whose physical movements never exceeded the reaching for a book on a top shelf? It seems ridiculous that Raziel could have threatened her father in such a way as to cause such a vehement reaction—if only because Lucifer *knows* how much Uncle Raziel means to her. She'll reluctantly concede that maybe her father *could* harbor such violent capabilities in the act of war, on the battlefield, and only because he has to, but no, never could she accept that he'd go to such extremes against Raziel. If anything, Evangeline believes Lucifer would have put *himself* in danger to ensure Raziel's safety. It's true they weren't blood-related, but her father always said that Uncle Raziel was the only family he had—that of anyone on both sides of either Seraphina's family or his own, Raziel was the *only* one who supported their marriage, who was kind to Lucifer as a new bridegroom living in the strange Fifth Heaven.

Evangeline's mind cycles over and over, like she's rewatching, reexperiencing special moments. She thinks that if she ruminates long enough, then her world will right itself. Her father will appear at her side—any minute now—and will, with regret and longing, reflect on the tragedy of war.

"Your uncle Raziel was an innocent victim in this horrid conflict," he'd say, wrapping his arms, his wings, securely around her. And she'd feel safe, even as she'd feel grief. She'd be convinced her father was not responsible; instead, he'd comfort her for her loss. He knows how much Raziel meant to her—and, if it weren't for Lucifer in the first place, she never would have known him.

Evangeline comes to the lake. She doesn't remember how she arrived; she's not at the same shallow cove where she and Michael came ashore, and while she can imagine Third Heaven across the water, she can see nothing but steel-gray water. She feels like she's arrived on another world—the new Earth, maybe—where the dappling sunlight seems alien and unfamiliar.

She crumples to the ground, weary, frightened, alone. She senses her body, the physical discomfort of her muscles, the effort to get air into her lungs, but she feels removed from it, as if her flesh and blood were not her own.

She doesn't know how long she's been there—a minute? An hour? A day?—when she registers footsteps, soft and tentative behind her. She doesn't turn. If it's an enemy, let them kill her.

Michael drops beside her, and she scowls.

"Go away."

"No," Michael responds quietly.

Evangeline turns. Michael sits a few feet from her, his hands hanging over his tented knees, staring at the distant horizon.

"You killed my uncle; go away," Evangeline spits out.

She senses, rather than sees, that Michael's eyebrow arch high.

Am I the one who slit his throat? She imagines him saying.

Evangeline hears herself, hears that she's wrong, obviously, since Michael has been with her this whole time.

"Your father, then," she snaps, again knowing she is very, very wrong.

"Is that what your uncle said?" he asks softly.

Evangeline whirls on him, as if he lit her wings on fire.

"What did you *hear*?" she demands.

Michael raises his arms in surrender, but his voice is ice cold. "My father recognizes a Lucifer attack when he sees one."

Evangeline's blood boils; she feels the white-hot lick of anger and she lunges. She screams as her hands land on his face, her nails viciously scratching his skin. Michael recoils, startled, but then he swiftly grasps her wrists in a painful grip. With all her strength, she twists her arms in his clenched fist and flails her body against his. She hears a cry, a wail, high and piercing, and it takes her a long minute to understand it's her own voice. Michael sits, unmoving as she rails against him, but she is nothing compared to his strength. She is a rag doll, limp and motionless compared to his power. Whimpering, Evangeline stops, the fight seeping out of her. She collapses against Michael's chest, her sobs, silent and intense, shaking her whole body.

Michael wraps his arms around her, the way he did the one time— only one time—at school, when Uriel had been extraordinarily cruel to her. Evangeline remembers she'd followed Michael's advice to ignore his taunts; he said a nonresponse would drive Uriel crazier, and he'd been right. She'd proven him right with a broken wrist and two bruised ribs.

Michael had been the one to find her after Uriel's attack, cowering near the waterfall. She'd slunk away from Uriel, mortified by her weakness, but Michael curled himself around her as he led her to the healing ward, clucking soft apologies.

Evangeline wanted then, wants now, to blame her victimhood on Michael, on his Dominion cronies, but she remembers why she begged her father to send her to Diaga. She hated the prejudice against her because she was a Commoner—worse, because she was mixed-class angel—and, at fifteen, Evangeline thought she'd out-smarted everyone. Whereas her fellow Commoners would forever have to subject themselves to humiliation and torment at the hands of angels who believed they were superior, Evangeline realized she'd never again need to suffer their fate. She was, after all, half Dominion. She thought her half-class status would be her salvation, that she could, forever after, forgo the disgrace and mortification of being a Commoner, that she, alone, embodied the secret her people could never breech.

I am a Dominion, *she sputtered at her father, shaking with rage at yet another injustice against their kind.*

You are a Commoner! *her father roared.*

His anger was intense, which was why, a month after her request, she was beyond shocked when her father agreed she could attend Diaga Academy.

"I had to call in a favor." Her father came into her little bedroom in their tidy little cottage on one of the few days they weren't traveling. "Gabriel got you in," he said.

"You went to Gabriel?" Evangeline asked, surprised, and touched that her father would set aside his pride and ask his one-time friend for help. She threw her arms around him and hugged him hard, giddy with excitement at the idea of starting a new life.

How did she *not* realize the Dominions at school would never see her as one of them?

Now, Evangeline sinks to the ground, still in Michael's arms. He eases her against the bark of a fallen tree.

"I'm sorry about your uncle," he says quietly. "I understand he was special to you."

Special . . . special . . . it's the right word, but it doesn't do justice to her relationship to her uncle. She thinks back to the first time they met, in her dorm room at Diaga. She'd been on her bed, tucked into the corner a few days after Alina broke her wing. Her roommate wasn't there, but Evangeline found no comfort in the quiet of their small quarters.

Her wing, although healing, still ached. She had told the healer in the infirmary that she tripped and fell down the stairs, never revealing Alina's part, knowing such an accusation would bring her more misery.

And since her father refused to let her quit—*the experience will harden you for the better*, he'd said—her only wish was to become invisible. She wondered again why she thought she could belong. Because her mother once lived in these aged stone halls? Because, according to her tutors, Seraphina once owned this school with her charm the way her father now owned the Farlands with his?

But she was neither her mother nor her father. Not Dominion, not Commoner. Pretending to be one or the other, it seemed, was a privilege no one would extend to her.

She heard an unexpected knock on her door. Startled, worried, she quickly wiped the sadness off her face, suppressing it deep into her soul, and walked across the room. The door opened before she reached it and Headmistress Hariel strode in. Evangeline retreated a step or two at Madame Hariel's regal posture, her ice-blue wings folded straight and sharp against her back. The woman was intimidating, with her grim mouth and cold eyes, but Evangeline felt it was practiced, as if Madame Hariel had consciously determined this is how a headmistress should look.

"Evangeline," Madame Hariel spoke in a crisp, clipped tone. She paused, as her eyes fell on Evangeline's bandaged wing. A look of surprise—and softness?—flickered across her face and for a crazy, fleeting moment, she imagined throwing herself into Madame Hariel's arms, crumbling under the weight of her anguish and having the old woman's arms encircle her. "There, there, my girl," she would say in soft comfort and Evangeline would feel the warmth in her words and her touch.

Instead, Evangeline stood, straight and rigid, her stomach contracting into knots. Since the headmistress didn't normally drop by the girls' quarters, Evangeline knew she was in trouble, but she wasn't sure why.

"Evangeline, I'd like you to meet Lord Raziel," Madame Hariel said formally, with a studied nod toward the door.

An old angel stepped hesitantly into the room. He was stooped, as if his blue-gold wings weighed him down. His face, wrinkled and lined, indicated long wisened experience, but his blue eyes shone with a child's excitement. Lord Raziel clasped his hands and raised them to his chest as if in prayer.

"Evangeline," he said, and Evangeline sensed a tenderness in his tone she couldn't understand. Was she supposed to know this man? Quickly, she sifted through her memories since she arrived at the school three weeks before but could find no match to this old angel in front of her.

"Lord Raziel is a Cherubim," Madame Hariel explained with a hint of pride.

Evangeline's eyes widened, although she tried to keep her surprise discreet. She was still learning the Dominion ways. As a Commoner she was shocked and honored that such a distinguished angel belonging to the second highest class, under the Seraphim and almost as revered, would be standing in her room. But she didn't know if Dominions, one class lower, would be impressed. Were Cherubim visits to this school common? They were academics and scholars, of course, and the school did have a prestigious reputation, but the students here were young, only teen learners, not apprentice intellectuals at the universities. What would draw a Cherubim away from the Divine Archives and into her small quarters?

Evangeline worried that Lord Raziel was here to study her. She was a rare species, after all, a half-class angel living among the Dominions, but then she realized her own arrogance. Of course no one, let alone an important Divine Record Keeper, would bother with her.

"Lord Raziel," Madame Hariel continued, "is your great-uncle."

Evangeline's mouth dropped open; no amount of good manners or etiquette could stop it.

"Your mother's uncle," Madame Hariel added, although it was entirely unnecessary. Evangeline knew about her father's family—his cold mother and distant father, grandparents she had met only once as a young angel before they died in the cottage fire. Foolish, careless people, her father had described them. And there was no other family, not like her friend Sophia, whose family tree overflowed with cousins and aunts and distant relations.

And she thought she knew about her mother's family. Her father had never kept secrets from her; if she asked about Seraphina, Lucifer would answer. She knew all too well the hubris of her mother's parents, the ones who hastily buried their daughter before her husband and little girl could return to Fifth Heaven for the funeral; the ones who tried to steal her away from Lucifer; the ones who forced her and her father out of their home and sent them on the run to the Farlands.

But Evangeline didn't remember hearing about other members of her mother's family and now she wondered if it's because she never asked. She knew speaking of Seraphina was difficult for her father; she saw the pain in his eyes when he talked about her, and she hated to be the cause of that sorrow, so maybe she never asked.

"I will leave you," Madame Hariel announced and then she swept out of the room with a respectful nod to Lord Raziel.

"Yes, well, uh . . . " Raziel's eyes darted around. He looked as lost as she felt. A piece of her history, one she didn't know existed, had strolled into her room and Evangeline didn't know how respond. She felt she was looking into the vague fog of her past, never knowing until now that shapes existed among the mist. It unnerved her, she had to admit; if Raziel could stroll out of the mist, what other elements in that fog could turn corporeal?

"Lord Raziel," Evangeline finally recovered her manners and offered him a small curtsy.

The old angel waved away her formality in a fluster. "Oh, no, my goodness," he exclaimed. "I am merely Uncle. Although you used to call me 'Uncue' when you were tiny, since you had trouble with the 'cl' sound."

Evangeline reeled. She felt herself take in a short breath. "I knew you?"

Lord Raziel—Uncle—smiled sadly. "I feared you wouldn't remember. You were so young when you left."

"My father—" Evangeline stopped herself. She couldn't be so rude as to say her father never mentioned him. But she also felt a stab of anger, of hurt. *Why* had her father never mentioned Uncle Raziel if she had actually met him and he would be here at the school?

"Your father thought it best," Raziel interjected. "And as much as it broke my heart, I couldn't blame him. There was no way for me to safely travel to First Heaven to see you and much too dangerous for your father to bring you to visit me in Sixth Heaven."

"You are my mother's uncle . . . " The fog of her past has taken over her mind. She was finding it difficult to process all this new information, as if her own history were being rewritten right in front of her.

"Seraphina's mother, Laila, was my sister," Raziel explained, and as he talked, Evangeline noticed his expression sour. "I suppose I loved her, as dutiful brothers ought to, but I assure you, I never supported her poor treatment of your father."

Raziel paused. A heavy wave of sadness rolled across his face. "Lucifer and Seraphina were so much in love," he said quietly, and Evangeline felt for a moment like he wasn't talking to her, like he had disappeared in time. It was strange for her to hear about her parents as young angels—actually it was disconcerting to hear about her parents from anyone but her father. She tried to remember if anyone else had ever talked about them, but no, of course not. No one in her life, no one in First Heaven had ever met her mother.

"Your mother was incredibly brave," Raziel continued. "Oh, of course your father was, too," he added as if Evangeline had objected. "That, however, had been well established, yes? His heroic deeds in the Djinn War and all. But Seraphina," he said her name with the same tenderness Evangeline heard him say her own. "Seraphina was bright and ambitious and could have had a charmed life, but instead, she chose the difficult, stony path and married your father."

Raziel stopped again and Evangeline became aware she was hanging on his every word, desperate to hear more. Except for her father, no one she knew had ever met Seraphina. Hearing Raziel speak with such confidence, such authority about the phantom that had lived at the edge of Evangeline's consciousness made her feel like the blurred lines of that ephemeral being were hardening into the concrete shape of a real angel.

"No, I rescind that," Raziel smiled at Evangeline, as if seeing her for the first time. "Your mother did have a charmed life. She had love. She had your father and she had you."

Evangeline's chest felt heavy, as if a rock had settled on it. Her throat ached and her eyes burned at the affection Raziel infused into her history. She'd always known how much her parents had loved each other—Lucifer was abundantly clear on that—but to hear an old man, an outside observer, say it meant more to her than she could explain. It was as if her existence had been validated.

Half Commoner, half Dominion.

Abruptly the door flung open and Alina glided in. She stopped, shocked to see Raziel. Flustered, she tried to rearrange her expression into one of deference. Evangeline didn't know if she recognized Raziel, if Alina recognized he was a respected Cherubim, but she took her moment.

"Alina, may I present my great-uncle Raziel, a Cherubim from Sixth Heaven who came specifically to visit me." Evangeline didn't know if this was true—she still didn't know *why* Raziel was here, but she liked how it sounded, and as importantly, she liked how it sounded to Alina. Her roommate blinked in surprise and glanced sharply to Evangeline, then back to Raziel. "Uncle, this is Alina, from the Mitzvael family."

Raziel nodded to Alina absently. "A pleasure," he said, then refocused on Evangeline, and Evangeline did little to hide her smile.

"My dear, will you come for a stroll with me?" Raziel offered her his arm.

Regally, trying to imitate Madame Hariel, Evangeline strode past Alina to accept her uncle's embrace.

For a moment—only one—Evangeline felt like she'd finally found her place among her mother's people.

And now, a few scant years later, her one, true connection to her other half was gone. It didn't seem real, no matter how many times Evangeline rolled the word around in her head. *Gone. Gone. Gone.*

Abruptly, she becomes aware of her surroundings. The sun high overhead, above the tall canopy of trees, the cool breeze wafting in from the lake, the clouds in the distance rolling across the water from Third Heaven, the rough bark against her wings, the warmth of Michael's arms around her waist . . .

Evangeline struggles to her feet, embarrassed. She shrugs off her nostalgia, returning to the present.

Trying to understand the insanity that is the present.

She starts by grounding herself with what she knows. Archangels want her father dead. Commoners want her dead. Uncle Raziel *is* dead.

At the hands of her father, if he is to be believed.

And what did Raziel mean by *six, six, six*?

She stretches, then paces as if she can shake out the sorrow burrowed deep into her bones. She rolls the numbers around in her head, trying to wrest meaning from them, but they remain an enigma. Did her uncle mean six hundred and sixty-six? But that number makes as little sense to her as three sixes.

Evangeline sighs, tired and overwhelmed. She can't deal with this. She doesn't want to deal with this. Any of it. Her uncle's brutal murder, her father's quest, the mysterious book . . .

All she wants to do is go home.

She imagines herself curling up in her own bed, tucked underneath her mother's old quilt, and closing her eyes to shut out the world. The sense of relief she imagines she'll feel is enough for her to make her decision.

She *will* go home. She was foolish to think she could find Lucifer.

She finally recognizes she's out of her depth—far, *far* out of her depth and she's learned her limitations.

So, keys, books, numbers, none of it means anything to her.

She brushes off the dirt from her clothes, already relieved about her choice.

"Goodbye, Michael," she says, more formally than she meant to.

Michael looks at her with a puzzled expression. "What are you doing?"

"Going home."

"No, you're not," Michael says firmly.

Evangeline sighs warily. "I assure you I am."

"We need to find your father. We need to find the book."

Evangeline shakes her head with a tinge of irritation. "My father is untraceable, even to me. I know that now. And if there is a book and my uncle had it, then how am *I* supposed to find it?"

"We have to try," Michael insists.

"No, *we* don't."

"Evie, you *know* what's at stake."

Evangeline laughs bitterly. "A book that is mere legend can destroy the Heavens? I told you, that's impossible."

"Your father doesn't believe that. I'm sure it's why he killed your uncle."

A sharp pain cuts up her insides. She hates that Michael speaks so cavalierly about her father. Her uncle. His last hours.

"We know Raziel left the Divine Archives with the book," Michael continues. "We suspect he was meeting your father to give it to him. But when my father found Raziel, he had no book. One of two things must have happened: Raziel didn't give Lucifer the book and he became so enraged he killed him, or Raziel did give Lucifer the book and he killed him to get rid of a witness. If that's the case, if Lucifer has the Key, our world could be destroyed at any moment."

"*Your* world, maybe," Evangeline says, dismissing his rhetoric. "Not mine."

"Evie, look at me." Michael gently takes her by the shoulder, and turns her to face him. She allows herself to be moved. "You're not safe, either."

At this, Evangeline bursts out with a loud snort. "You are mad."

"My father is right, Evie."

"Your father is wrong," she refutes, feeling her anger rekindle. "Tell me, *how* does a book written to create peace among the angels thousands of years ago destroy the Heavens today?"

"I don't know," Michael admits. "There's something inside, some knowledge, some magic maybe."

Evangeline scowls, annoyed. "*Magic*? Magic is for fairy stories. Magic doesn't exist."

Evangeline suddenly stops. Not magic, no . . . but *Slivers*, maybe. She'd forgotten all about it, another legend of the book. Michael wouldn't know about it, nor would Gabriel, since so few people know about the Assembly's book, let alone its alleged contents. But she does, since she learned at Uncle Raziel's feet. Everything he ever researched about the ancient Assembly of Angels, he passed on to her, including an understanding of *Slivers*, a sprinkle of divinity bestowed on certain angels, giving them the slightest fraction of the power of God, the equivalent, her uncle told her, of one grain of sand of all the beaches in all the Heavens. The ability to guide travelers safely through the night, for example, or the capability to divert rain clouds toward dry agricultural lands. No one understands what, exactly, the *Slivers* were, nor how many angels had them, and no one knows when or why they were chosen. Raziel always assumed the answers would be found in the lost book.

Evangeline feels a chill snake down her spine. Had Raziel found the answers? Did he know about the *Slivers*? Did they actually exist?

The Keys to the Kingdom.

The title of the book.

The Keys are the *Slivers* . . .

But how would that destroy the Heavens? If the *Slivers* ever did exist, they don't anymore. There is no recorded evidence of *any* angel ever having a touch of divinity.

Unless the answers are all in the book.

But that's pointless to consider because no one knows the location of the book except Uncle Raziel, assuming he did have it, and she obviously can't ask him.

Evangeline feels a growing sense of frustration, especially toward Uncle Raziel himself. If he had found such a significant manuscript, one that would ultimately cost him his life, why hadn't he told her instead of wasting his last breath on numbers?

Numbers . . .

Something in Evangeline's mind clicks.

Books, she thinks.

"Six, six, six," she says aloud. And there it is, the answer clear in her mind. She turns to Michael. "I know where Uncle Raziel hid the book."

CHAPTER 10

"*Here?*" Michael asks.

Evangeline stares at their old school, Diaga Academy, the Fifth Heaven site of her agony for two years. It's a beautiful setting. The building, castlelike, is made of stone, carved into a lush hillside at the foot of a spectacular mountain. A winding river of fresh, clear glacial water weaves its way downhill, an azure blue ribbon that culminates in a powerful waterfall near the base of the school's grounds. From an outsider's perspective, the scene is idyllic. Evangeline knows better.

"Here," Evangeline confirms, nodding in the direction of the school, on the rise of manicured lawn above them. The sun rises above the castle, splashing a pallet of pastel pinks and purples across the early sky of the fifth morning of the week.

Michael leans back against an ancient willow tree hanging over the river near the waterfall, whose thunderous torrent masks their approach. He shakes his head in obvious disbelief, but Evangeline doesn't know if it's because he distrusts her or because he's amazed at Raziel's audacity.

"Your uncle hid the most powerful book in all the realms, the book that could bring down the Heavens, in a *school* library?"

Evangeline nods, then sighs. If the book was originally hidden in plain sight, in the very archives all the Cherubim have worked in for a millennium, why is it so hard to believe Uncle Raziel would again hide it among books?

"Anyone could have picked it up," Michael cries.

"I'm sorry, did we go to the same school?" Evangeline asks. "I don't recall a stampede of angels begging to borrow library books."

She speaks the truth. Books, the library, weren't disparaged by any means. Angels in all classes held great respect for books, but always from a distance. And especially if they were read and studied by other angels, like the Cherubim.

It's why she hid in the library. It was a quiet sanctuary, blessedly free of potential tormentors. And, she discovered, she had a genuine interest in the history and knowledge contained among the texts and scrolls lining the shelves. That was partly Raziel's influence, but she can't determine whether her interest in scholarly texts came before her meetings with Raziel, and he simply fanned the flames of her passions, or whether her tutoring sessions with Raziel led to her love of ancient texts. No matter. In the end, Evangeline was simply glad the other angels finally started leaving her alone.

"Fine," Michael says, "no one would have picked it up. But how can *you* find it? We don't know what it looks like and there are thousands of volumes."

"My uncle told me where it was," she says.

Her uncle's dying words. His secret, revealed only to her. A location only important to the two of them.

"Yes," Michael says, exasperated. "I know. Six, six, six. But what does that *mean*, already?"

"You'll see." Ally or no ally at the moment, Evangeline isn't about to let Gabriel's soldiers get their hands on the book before she does. Uncle Raziel specifically waited to tell *her*. He wanted *her* to get it, so she intends to be the one to find it.

"God, Evie, you are infuriating," Michael throws up his hands. "You've been saying that for the past day and a half. This is a joke to you, isn't it? This whole time, our travels through Fourth Heaven, is a game to you. You're leading us by the noses on a wild goose chase."

Evangeline's body goes cold. Her beloved uncle dies before her eyes, claiming to be murdered by her own father, and Michael says she's *joking*? During the entire trip here, slowed by her injuries at the hand of a djinni with an uncanny family resemblance, Evangeline felt like she was living on the edge of reality. For most of the journey, accompanied by Michael, Gabriel, and only two of his trusted guards, Evangeline has tried to make sense of the violent turn her life has taken. She hasn't yet succeeded.

Now "six, six, six" drives her forward. She takes heart in Raziel's cryptic message, knowing that whatever he was up to, he believed she could figure it out.

"Fine," Michael says, resigned. He pushes himself off the tree, ready for action. "I have no choice but to follow you. I'll get my father, then we go in. It shouldn't take long, since it's early and the students will still be asleep."

Students. Evangeline feels a surge of resentment. While her home, her lands in the First Heaven and those of the angels in Second Heaven, have been decimated by the war, Fifth Heaven looks untouched by the battles. At home, Commoner children long ago had to abandon their schools, fleeing for their lives from the advancing Archangels out to destroy them, but here, the smug privileged Dominions continue to send their children to school, snug and cozy, far from the fighting. To Evangeline, it's a slap in the face as if the war, *her* war, doesn't exist, as if the life and death battles of her people never happened.

"No," she says, "I go in alone."

Michael turns to her, again with that look of vexation. "That's stupid, Evie," he says.

Evangeline bristles with indignation. No, not stupid. Smart, cunning, strategic. They need her, so *she'll* make the rules. She'll ensure she gets the book—alone—and then she'll flee. She has absolutely no intention of handing this most valuable text over to her archenemy. She'd be mad if she did. Assuming Gabriel and Michael are right, assuming this book truly *is* the Key to the Kingdom, she's not going to let it disappear into the bowels of the Archangel vaults. Because she *knows* Gabriel will never return it to the Archives, no matter how hard the Cherubim protest. In his eyes, the book is a dangerous weapon, and Evangeline fears he will use it against her people, to destroy Commoners for good. She can't let that happen. If her father can't get the Key, the one thing that will win them this war, then *she* will.

She pictures it already, her heroic return. She stands on the stone monolith in Siog Glen, the sacred valley in the Farlands where her father declared victory over the djinn in their *last* war, and she will do the same for this war. With her adoring people gathered below, she lifts her arm in victory, the book, the Key, held high in the air, and the crowd roars in adulation. And then she, Evangeline, a half-breed, will have finally proven her worth. Already she feels the love. Even here, at the edge of the school grounds, far from First Heaven, her skin prickles in delighted anticipation.

"I go alone, or I don't go," Evangeline challenges.

Michael balls his hand in frustration. "We don't have *time* for this, Evie. Your father is still out there; we have to get the book before he does."

"He doesn't *know* where it is," she says. "It's why he killed my uncle, remember?"

She shivers, as if giving voice to the truth finally makes it real. Her father, her protector, her guardian angel . . . a murderer. Her heart constricts. There's *got* to be more to the story. And she'll find out, she will. She'll investigate her uncle's death; she'll learn what her father did and why, but first she has to retrieve the book because she's convinced the answers about her father's plans, about how to win this war, are in those pages. So if she gets it first, *she* can use the Key to reclaim the Commoners' rights in the Heavens. If her quest started out to save her father, she realizes now it's changed. Now her mission is to save her people.

Evangeline marches forward, unwilling to negotiate with Michael any longer. She feels a pang of regret, a sliver of remorse that she'll betray Michael—he has been surprisingly supportive of her, considering their enemy status—but she brushes aside the discomfort.

What's she's doing is for the greater good, to bring peace to the Heavens.

It's a heady thought that *she* could be so valuable, and it propels Evangeline forward. After a lifetime of living with insecurity, she will finally be rid of it.

She follows the riverbank, dotted with trees the color of autumn fire and thick green shrubs that conceal her from the main buildings. A long, stretched shadow catches her eye, and for a moment, Evangeline is pulled back to her first week at Diaga.

Alina caught up to her on the lawn after class, smiling widely. She was flanked by her two friends, nameless to Evangeline. This was before Alina's attack, when Evangeline held out hope she could befriend her roommate.

"Come with us," Alina said and cheerfully linked an arm through Evangeline's before she could answer.

It was the first time Alina showed any hint of kindness since they met; Evangeline had never felt so alone in those first few, long days, so yes, of course she jumped at Alina's offer. The four girls took off toward the waterfall. At the river's edge, Alina and her friends took to the air, heading straight for the thundering water. Evangeline hesitated, but then Alina turned and waved her on, so she leapt into the sky after them. On top of the wind, she could hear Alina's shrill laugh, then her roommate sped off—straight into the mist and froth of the raging falls and disappeared.

Evangeline gasped. She slowed, her heart pounding as she watched Alina's two friends vanish into the water. The force was too great to fly, Evangeline knew, and she looked frantically into the swirling base of the falls, terrified to see if they emerged in the river. She thought about diving after them into the cold water, or flying back to get help, but then she remembered a conversation she'd had with her father. About a cave her mother had told him about long ago, a cave behind the waterfall that was almost impossible to see, almost impossible to navigate into.

Evangeline hovered in the air for a moment, hurt and angry. Alina had obviously brought her here to embarrass her, and Evangeline was furious at herself for being so pathetically desperate to fit in that she bought into Alina's "kindness."

But Evangeline would not let Alina win. Instead, she backtracked to the edge of the river, then, picking up speed, drove herself straight toward the falls. She couldn't see the cave, knew it only by her father's description from his memories long ago, but she was determined. She flew into the mist, beating harder to keep her speed, then abruptly drew in her wings and spun in a horizontal corkscrew. Through the dizzying rotation, she spotted the black speck. Her heart hammering, she aimed for it, sliced through the powerful falls and slid into the hole in the rock.

It was dark as night. Evangeline concentrated on pulling herself back as hard and fast as she could since she had no idea how shallow the cave actually was. She crashed into the wall, but not as hard as she feared. She'd be bruised in the morning, for sure, but no broken bones. Evangeline shook her head and stood, back to the wall, looking into the light of the curtain of water.

She looked into the shocked, outraged expressions of Alina and her friends. Evangeline knew instantly, from the murderous expression on Alina's face, that she would pay for her success. Alina was not one to suffer defeat, especially embarrassment at the hands of a petty *Commoner*, but for that one second of triumph, when Alina looked like a braying donkey with her mouth hanging open, Evangeline felt the momentary victory was worth the later, dire consequences.

The broken wing two weeks later was only one of them.

Evangeline refocuses and winds her way past the falls and up toward the school. She knows where she's going, what she's doing. It's not the first time she's snuck back in the castle this way. Often she would escape her cloistered, claustrophobic room and venture into the woods. Students were allowed as far as the waterfall, normally, but Evangeline always crept further and further away. The willow at which she and Michael had stopped was often where she'd end up, soaking in the pounding waterfall, letting its thundering beat drown out her pulsing misery. And of course, they were never allowed out at night, another rule Evangeline ignored. She was used to slinking across the lawns both in the moonlight and again, like now, at sunrise.

"Evie," Michael hisses, running up beside her. "Come *on*."

Evangeline doesn't answer. She wants to tell him to go; she wants to stick with her resolve to find the book alone—how *else* will she sneak away with it? But—damn, she's so mad at herself—she's scared to do this alone. The school scares her. Always had. The first time she saw it, when she arrived as a fifteen-year-old, she quivered from the tips of her wings to the tops of her toes. She'd come alone; her father would never have been welcome, not even for an innocent trip to drop off his daughter, and what she'd imagined—a beautiful, glowing sanctuary, inhabited by her mother's benevolent spirit—materialized only as a dark, foreboding monstrosity. She'd softened to its beauty over the years—how could she not, in such a gorgeous setting?—but still, her initial terror still resides in her bones. She is glad, therefore, that Michael, her one friend and ally among these walls, is beside her.

"I go alone," she says again, without confidence.

"No," Michael insists. "I'm going with you. We can leave my father out of it, but I'm going with you."

Evangeline feels a rush of relief—because Michael can be useful, she tells herself. He can be a distraction. The son of the revered Archangel returning to his alma matter, even under unusual circumstances, could be valuable indeed when she takes off with the book.

"Fine," she concedes, unwilling to acknowledge how grateful she feels for his presence beside her. "But I lead."

Michael nods.

They snake their way through the underbrush by the river and then they follow the contours of a gentle knoll, its gradual incline enough to shield them from the building's main windows.

Michael stays close behind her. Very close. She feels his breath on her neck, then feels an unnerving and distracting swoop in her stomach. His cheek is beside hers now. He whispers in her ear.

"You remember when we met out here?"

Evangeline closes her eyes, takes a deep breath. Yes, she remembers. It happened only once, when she was sneaking in late at night and Michael was sneaking out. With Penelope. God, she hated Penelope.

"I remember you were soaked to the bone," Michael says. She feels the warmth of his skin next to hers. She holds her breath, and bites her lip.

"I was swimming," she replies.

"Alone, at night?" Michael asks again. It's the same question he asked her that night. "Tell me who were you with. Was it Mark?"

Evangeline catches her breath in a snort. "You think I was with Mark?"

"Well, who then?"

The swoop in Evangeline's stomach dissipates. The memory of that night, the loneliness, the hope, the disappointment, rushes back at her.

"No one," Evangeline answers. "I told you that then."

She's not lying. She'd met no one, although she had intended to. She'd slipped a piece of parchment under Michael's door for him that afternoon. She'd finally found the courage to approach him on her own. They were friends if only in secret, and he'd been so nice to her that she thought maybe they could be . . . more than friends. So she invited him to join her at the waterfall. It had been a full moon; the water sparkling in the dappling moonlight. There, on the rocks in the middle of the river, they'd be free to talk for hours, uninterrupted. No worries about an angel careening around the staircase to where they were hiding or stumbling on them in the far corners of the hall.

But Michael never showed. She'd waited for a long time; the moon was on its way to bed by the time she returned. She felt so stupid, thinking he'd come. He'd always been clear that his father was making him be nice to her; why had she let her imagination run wild? As soon as she realized it, she dove into the falls. It wasn't safe; she remembered its force from plowing through the water toward the cave, but she didn't want to be safe. She hit the water, frigid with

the glacier spring runoff, and plummeted into the river's depths. She
was used to the churning oceans in First Heaven, but the constricted
force of a narrow river surprised her. She was immediately crushed
against the rocks, battered and bruised as she kicked frantically to
the surface. She gulped the crisp night air when she broke through
to the surface.

"Why were you with Penelope that night?" she asks now with a bite
she can't seem to disguise.

"Because she left me a—" Michael starts, then looks at her. "Oh,
God . . . " he says, "Penelope didn't leave me the note, did she?"

Evangeline blushes. She is so stupid. She shouldn't have said
anything.

She lowers her chin and powers ahead across the lawn. Her whole
body aches with embarrassment.

Michael hurries to her, then pulls her behind a copse of thick
maple trees, whose fiery leaves glow in the rising autumn sun.

"My roommate told me Penelope left the note," Michael says, his
voice desperate. You both have long black hair . . . "

"And how was your night with Penelope?" Evangeline's voice is
bright. Too bright. *God*, what is she *doing*? That was years ago. She
has no reason to be mad.

Or hurt.

Michael owes her nothing. Not then, not now.

Michael puts his arms around her and draws her close. She feels
his warm breath on her face and for a moment, time stops. Her father,
her uncle, the war, *his* father, all disappear. She and Michael are students again, alone outside after hours, and he leans into her the way
she wanted him to back then.

The way she wants him to now.

He does.

He touches his lips to hers, and she responds to his kiss, her own mouth tingling with a passion she can't explain. Her whole body trembles. She melts into him, as Michael wraps himself around her. She never wants it to end.

But it does.

Evangeline feels Michael pull back. He's hesitant; Evangeline thinks that he doesn't want to stop, but then, she realizes, rationality prevails. His and hers. They're enemies. They're trying to find a book that will either save their world or destroy it. This is neither the time nor place to *kiss*.

Except she wants it to be. She wants Michael to lean into her again, to kiss her again, to feel his warm lips on hers. And she wants to be bold enough to kiss *him*, to show him how much she wants it.

"You left me the note," Michael says, stating the obvious, and Evangeline chokes back an emotional laugh.

"Your roommate's an ass," she quips, because she doesn't know what else to say. Michael is the son of her father's worst enemy.

Michael is the son of her father's once-best friend.

Michael cups her cheeks in his hand, and she leans into the soft scent of his skin.

"*I* am the ass," he concedes. "Penelope said it was her and I believed her."

The words hurt Evangeline, although she doesn't know why. *She* is the one in front of Michael now, the girl he is kissing, not Penelope, but still . . .

"You wanted it to be her," Evangeline says quietly. She pulls away and takes a deep breath.

"No!" Michael is vehement. "I wanted it to be you."

Evangeline's heart falls, because she so wants to believe him, but all evidence to the contrary suggests otherwise.

"Don't you get it, Evie?" Michael draws his finger under her chin and she allows herself to be turned around. "You were too good for me."

At this, Evangeline laughs bitterly. She can't let this go. "Me? A half-breed, whom everyone could torment? A mongrel your father forced you to befriend?"

"Didn't you ever see yourself?" Michael asks. "You were so confident, so self-assured. You entered a viper's pit willingly, and you kicked ass. I don't know *anyone* stronger than you, Evie. You put yourself through hell and yet you shined the whole time."

Evangeline thinks of the book they're after. She remembers the sessions she had with Uncle Raziel when they would talk about the Assembly of Angels book. *You're so smart, Evangeline,* Uncle Raziel would say, *can't you see that for yourself?*

No, of course she couldn't. She wasn't smart, and she wasn't—isn't—strong. She doesn't know how she managed to fool Michael—or, more precisely, how he fooled himself, but it's all wrong.

"I'm not strong," she murmurs. She wishes it were true. She grew up witnessing the strength of her father, his commitment, his passion. She always admired it, but she never deluded herself into thinking she could emulate it. She was much too weak, much too insecure. Hell, she spent most of her two years here cowering in the library, she was too scared to stand up for herself. And if it weren't for her uncle's prestigious position protecting her, she would have been fed to the wolves long ago.

Michael seems to shake himself loose of their reverie. He straightens, although still with her in his arms. "Okay, we'll agree to disagree. You are everything I admire, but I accept you don't see things the same way."

Evangeline's breath catches. See things the same way? No, they don't see things the same way. He's the son of a privileged, revered soldier; she is the daughter of a demonic, traitorous angel. The thought is enough to pull Evangeline from Michael's magnetic grasp.

"Let's get the book," she says brusquely. She hates herself for her tone.

"Evie . . . " Michael tries to pull her back, and her heart breaks at his voice. It sounds like he's sincere, like he actually meant what he said.

"Our fathers are trying to kill each other," Evangeline reminds him. Someone has to recalibrate his or her reality. "You support your dad and I—"

"Support yours?" Michael jumps in. "Do you support Lucifer's murder of your uncle?"

Evangeline stiffens. That's so not fair. She's cut by his comment, but more, she's angry with herself. She let herself be lulled into a fantasy world that can never be real. Her father always warned her against emotional warfare—how the strongest warrior can be felled by manipulation of the mind. That's what Michael is trying to do—confuse her. He's trying to recruit her to his side, and he's preying on her old emotions and insecurities, and that makes him untrustworthy.

"I'm going," Evangeline storms off, and in her heated state, she forgets stealth is essential. For a reckless moment, she doesn't care if someone sees her or hears her; she wants to get away from Michael, get away from her thoughts of Michael. She's halfway across the lawn, exposed to the guards who would turn her way, but then she sees her uncle's dying face, feels his faint breath on her cheek.

Six, six, six.

She scuttles back into the shadows of the trees lining the path to the dormitories and Michael catches up with her. Evangeline spies two guards patrolling the grounds. One scans the gardens by the terrace outside the dining hall; the other, her wings spread wide, flies up and down from the parapet on the third floor, roving with a bird's eye view.

"Security is tighter now, since the war began," Michael says quietly. "It's not enough to charm the security guard."

Evangeline glares at him. How can he do so much to help her, yet be such an ass at the same time? As if she could have snuck in and out so often simply by sweet-talking whomever was on watch. Maybe Michael, the great and mighty son of Gabriel, could have done that, but not her, a lowly half-status angel. No, she had to rely on her own stealth to slip past the guards. A thrown acorn in one direction, an imitation of a crow's caw in another—anything to momentarily distract the guards. She might have had enough social capital as a Cherubim's niece to evade the dorm monitors, but the guards reported indirectly to the Archangels. There is not a Heaven in which she, Lucifer's daughter, would be able to charm them to look the other way.

But she also feels plain stupid. She never thought about increased security. Of course it makes sense. Pretending a war isn't happening can only be effective if angels around you keep it out of your way. Considering the impact Lucifer and the Commoners have made throughout all of the Heavens during the war, Evangeline shouldn't be surprised that it would take a great deal more effort to anesthetize a whole school population against reality.

"There's a window in the east hallway, whose lock doesn't latch," Evangeline whispers to Michael.

He raises an eyebrow, but there's no skepticism in his expression, only genuine interest in her knowledge. Evangeline closes her eyes, shaking her head. Of course Michael will never get it. He never felt the need to escape the way she did.

"It's close to the library," she says impatiently.

The window leads to a hallway of storage rooms, stacked with old desks, old textbooks, old maps of the Heavens and other forgotten teaching tools. Evangeline had slipped into these rooms many times, as much out of curiosity of their contents as a means of escape from her fellow students. Uncle Raziel encouraged it when she'd first shown him her find.

"Let your curiosity lead you," he told her. "But don't get caught," he added, winking at her.

They wind their way through the trees, using the foliage as cover as long as possible.

"There will be more guards around front," Michael whispers. "You know, it would be easier to get my father to run them off."

"No," Evangeline hisses. "No one can know that *anyone* is anywhere near the school."

Evangeline understands Gabriel fears Lucifer could be lurking anywhere and doesn't want to tip him off. It's why they took so long to slip through Fourth Heaven. But Gabriel's paranoia works in Evangeline's favor. It's going to be much easier to steal the book from the Archangels without the Archangels around.

"If their schedule is the same, there'll be a shift change soon," Evangeline reminds him. "We'll sneak around them when they're distracted."

They don't wait long for another pair of angels to appear, and Evangeline is pleased her knowledge of the school's security isn't outdated. But they're dumb, the angels in charge of security, if they keep the same schedule they've always had. That's not the way to improve security in a time of war. But then she thinks that maybe it's not stupidity, but arrogance. They are so confident nothing will befall their school that they don't need to change. The thought rankles

Evangeline, and makes her want to show them all up when she has successfully stolen the book from right under their noses.

At the moment the guards' backs are turned, Michael and Evangeline sprint across the open space and slip into the shadow of the stone wall not far from the terrace. Their backs against the wall, they shuffle their way around the corner of the building. Two more guards patrol this section, too, and here's where Evangeline worries it'll get tricky.

She points up. "It's the second window on the third floor."

Michael frowns. "Can you fly yet?"

"I'll manage."

She doesn't know how, though. That djinni did real damage to her. While her side from the knife would is healing, her broken left wing still hurts. A mere a flutter sends paroxysms of pain down her back.

"I'll fly you up," Michael offers.

Evangeline shakes her head. "It's better to flatten ourselves against the wall so they don't see us. We need to go one at a time."

"I'll go first and unlatch the window so you don't have to hover," Michael says. He jumps into the air before she can reply, and Evangeline feels grateful. She raises her chin, keeping one eye on the guards and one on Michael as he floats up. Evangeline holds her breath. She hopes the latch on the window is still broken. She reasons that if they didn't change up their security detail too much, they haven't discovered the broken latch.

Michael is at the window. She sees him tugging at it, but it doesn't seem to be moving. *Come on, come on*, she wills the window to open. She glances back at the guard on the lawn. He seems to be scanning the forest beyond the lawns, doesn't seem to be interested in the school itself.

"Got it," she hears Michael's faint whisper float down to her, and then Michael disappears inside.

Evangeline steadies herself, then opens her wings. She winces from the pain, but she bites her tongue. She can do this. She flaps. Her right wing feels stiff from lack of use, but her left wing screams in agony. Hot tears spring to her eyes, and she tries to blink them away. Digging her nails into her palms, Evangeline launches herself into the air, but immediately, she tumbles down, a gasp of surprise escaping her lips. The guard turns, glares at the wall and inches closer, and Evangeline's heart hammers. Then she hears a thump to her right—and the guard hears it, too. She looks up; Michael's arm retreats from the open window. She didn't see what he threw out to distract the guard, but she realizes this is her only chance. With a grimace, Evangeline pushes off. Pain sears through her left wing; she can't use it, so she tries to compensate with her right. She flies up crooked, lopsided. Michael holds out his hand, grasps her wrists and drags her inside. She tumbles to the floor, breathing heavily.

"Hey!" the guard calls.

Evangeline's stomach drops. Michael grips her by the arm, pulls her to her feet, and they pound down the hall. It's too late for stealth; now they have to get to the library before the security teams inside intercept them.

Michael is in front, tugging Evangeline behind him, but she yanks on his hand.

"This way," she says, and runs to a narrow door and wrenches it open. They hurry inside and slam the door behind them.

They're in a storage room piled high with boxes. It's dark, with an old, dusty odor.

"Evie, we can't hide," Michael hisses. "They'll search everywhere; we have to get to the library and get the book."

"I *know*," she snaps. "Help me move these. There's a door to the library back here."

They start shoving stacks of crinkling scrolls out of the way.

"You're a genius," Michael says.

"No," she says. "There's no handle. It only opens from the other side."

Michael runs his fingers along the edge of the door, trying to wedge it open, but he gets no leverage. He pulls out his sword, but the blade is too narrow to pry the whole thing open. Evangeline unsheathes her own sword and wiggles it into the crevice at the bottom. Together, they work their swords, but door remains firmly shut.

Evangeline stands and retracts her sword. "We don't have time for this," she says, "Stand back." She pushes him out of the way, then raises her sword and attacks the door. A clean slice appears in the wood, and Evangeline takes another hack at it, wincing with pain.

"Let me do it," Michael steps forward. "I know you're hurting."

Evangeline steps back and listens at the hallway door as Michael hacks at the door to the library. She hears slow, methodical footsteps, doors opening and closing; the guards are closing in.

"Hurry," she says. Michael lifts the heel of his boot and kicks at the door. It doesn't budge, but the sound reverberates around the room and out into the hall.

She stands up and Michael shuffles over to make room for her. "Together," she says, and then, "One, two . . . *three*."

The force of their combined kick shifts the door slightly in its frame, but they don't break through. Evangeline hears shouts in the hall, a stampede of footsteps.

"Again," Michael says, and this time they don't count. They kick in sync. The wood warps.

The door to the hallway behind them flings open. Evangeline sees the dark silhouette of a guard, hears the staccato of her heart.

Michael launches his whole body at the hidden door and it

splinters under his body weight. Momentum propels him forward; he falls, headfirst into the grand, circular library. Evangeline is a step behind him, scrabbling through the hole in the door. She feels the splinters brush her arm and her wing, but she ignores them. Michael is on his feet, his hand out to her, and she grabs it. They run.

But there's no place to hide. The large, ornate room is round, with carved bookshelves encircling the room on four levels. Evangeline and Michael are on the third floor; an intricate wrought-iron railing is to their right; the bookshelves, flush against the wall, to their left. They careen toward the grand marble staircase that sweeps up from the ground floor, but they don't get to the landing before the guards barrel through the broken door.

"My wing hurts too much, but you can fly down," Evangeline tells Michael as they rush down the stairs.

"I'm not leaving you." Michael grips her hand tighter.

The wide double doors at the entrance to the library on the ground floor crash open; another security guard rushes in. Instinctively, Evangeline dives to the stair, out of the guards' line of sight and Michael follows her.

"Fenial, Rybald!" the guard at the door yells up to her colleagues. "We need you down here *now*. The Dragons are attacking."

Evangeline's eyes widen. Did she hear right? The *Dragons* are attacking?

One of their pursuers objects. "But the intruders—"

"Forget them! We're being overrun. We need reinforcements *now*."

The two guards who were after them hop onto the top of the railing and flutter to the ground. "Where are the Archangels?" one of them asks.

"On their way," the guard at the entrance answers.

Evangeline and Michael listen as the guards run out. Evangeline leans against the stairs, taking in a deep breath and breathing out. How did the Dragons get here? When? *Why?* Evangeline didn't believe in coincidences, but none of her father's generals knew her mission, and none would know she'd be coming here to Diaga. Still, it's strange because she feels like the Dragons are protecting her. How is that *possible*?

Michael rises to his feet. "It's your father," he says. He turns to face Evangeline, his hands grasping her shoulders. "*Don't* give him the book."

"It can't be my father," Evangeline says. "He doesn't know where I am. He doesn't know I came after him."

"Well *somebody* told him."

Evangeline narrows her eyes. "The only angels who know I'm here are you, your father and his minions." She lets her voice drop and Michael doesn't miss the accusation.

"My father is trying to *stop* Lucifer!" he explodes. "And you have the *gall* to accuse him of betrayal?"

"If the shoe fits . . . " Evangeline glowers. She's so mad, but she's not sure why, considering Dragons are helping her. By drawing off the guards, she now has time to find the book.

"Evangeline," Michael demands, "What is six, six, six?"

Evangeline winces at Michael's use of her full name. It sounds wrong, dripping from his lips, like he's spit out something dirty. She feels the sting; he did it on purpose.

Evangeline tries to think of a way to distract Michael so she won't have to divulge the code's meaning, so she can retrieve the book alone, but she's aware he won't fall for any scheme. He'll be glued to her side until the book is in her hands.

So she has to ensure the book stays in her hands.

Evangeline closes her eyes, imagines her uncle here in this room a day or so ago. She pictures his movements; they would have been flustered, but not his mind. No, he's thinking clearly, hiding the book where only Evangeline can find it.

Six. The shelf number.

Six. The row number.

Six. The book number.

Evangeline doesn't speak to Michael, refuses to explain. Instead, she hurries up the stairs to the second floor. There are no numbers on the shelves; only those who often access the library would learn the system. Evangeline skims the bookshelves to the right of the landing, as Michael trails after her.

Here, bookshelf #6.

She counts the rows from the top. Her body trembles. The Assembly of Angels book. The Key to the Kingdom. In another second, she's going to put her hands on a manuscript that's been lost for a thousand years, one that passionate believers have been searching for ever since, one that, until a week ago, she never actually believed existed.

She wonders what her uncle thought when he found it, when he touched it for the first time, and the harsh realization that she'll never know the answer crushes her.

. . . four . . . five . . . six.

She feels Michael's breath on her neck like in the woods, but now it feels hot, stifling. She wants to push him away, make him give her space.

Evangeline raises her hand to the edge of the row. She lets her index finger slide over the worn leather covers. One, two, three . . .

Her eyes jump ahead. She can't wait to see it. Her stomach churns in anticipation.

Fourfivesix.

Evangeline's heart stops.

There's no book.

She's staring at a dark cavity where a book should be.

No, no, *no*! She feels her insides shrink with fear, terror, confusion, bewilderment.

Six, six, six. Shelf, row, book. She was *sure* that was Uncle Raziel's message.

Cold ice runs through her blood. Did her father know? Did Lucifer figure it out before Uncle Raziel died? Is that why the Dragons are here? Because her father already has the book?

She turns to Michael, forgetting for a moment she's angry with him. Her face is white.

"Six, six, six," she whispers. "It should be here."

Evangeline slides her hand into the empty space where the book should have been.

Her fingers knock against something hard.

Evangeline wraps her fingers around it and pulls it out. It's small, the size of her palm, no bigger.

She stares at her hand as she unfolds her fingers. She feels Michael's eyes on her hand, too.

She looks.

On her palm rests a real, old, solid, heavy iron key.

CHAPTER 11

"A key..." Evangeline says, grasping the thick black iron object. It's heavy in her hand—and it burns. The key feels hot on her skin, like it had been seared in flames, but she doesn't drop it. Instead, she's transfixed by the sensation, as if she has no choice but to accept the pain. She looks up at Michael, her eyes wide in surprise. He stares at the key, his expression as uncomprehending as hers.

Her mind whirls in confusion. A key instead of a book? The Key to the Kingdom? She looks at the bookshelf in front of her.

Six, six, six.

Uncle Raziel wanted her to find this key. He put it there, of that she is certain. But if this *is* the Key to the Kingdom, how did he get it? Did he stumble upon it and plan to give it to Lucifer? Or had Lucifer given the Key to Raziel—to pass on to her because he was afraid, maybe, that Gabriel was onto him?

Michael turns back to the bookshelf and starts tearing volumes off the shelves. He's frantic as he rips each book away.

"What are you *doing?*" Evangeline demands.

"Searching for the book." Michael hastens down the aisle, ransacking the shelf. Evangeline holds her hand out to him, the key, still hot to the touch, clearly visible.

"*This* is what Uncle Raziel wanted me to find," she says.

"But it's not the book," Michael replies, not looking up. "The book is the key."

Evangeline shakes her head. "You don't know that."

"Yes, we do," Michael asserts. "Raziel stole it and was bringing it to Lucifer. For some reason, he hid the book before Lucifer could get it, and then told you where it was before he died."

"He told me where this *key* was," Evangeline says. She wants to believe that's the end of it. She wants to believe she holds in her now-hot hand, the Key to the Kingdom, which grants her people the power to reclaim their rights in the Heavens. She wants to believe she now possesses the ability to end this demoralizing and destructive war. It makes sense. She's holding a key obviously hidden by Raziel for an important, secretive reason. Her father left to retrieve a key. All logic, therefore, would assume this *is* the key—and Michael's theory about the key being a book is plain wrong. What evidence does he have? That her uncle snuck out of the Divine Archives with a book? He does that all the time. That's how Evangeline learned so much. That the book had an image of a key on its cover? That's hardly proof it's the Assembly's lost manuscript. And if it were the Assembly's lost manuscript, who's to say the book contains the type of power her father seeks as a way to end this war? No, it's much more logical to assume the simplest explanation is here right now. Her father was searching for a key—a symbol of access to power in the higher Heavens—and she now possesses a key.

In fact, she likes the idea enough that she changes her reverie. She imagines unveiling the key, not the book, to her people in Siog Glen. She'd still hold it up high over her head, still hear the adulation of the crowd below, and her father, beaming at her side, would still glow with admiration.

But the image fades as Michael plunders the shelves. There's one small detail that nags at Evangeline's mind.

Her uncle was all about books.

Not keys.

When he gave her the three numbers in his dying breath, she expected that she would find a *book*. Uncle Raziel wasn't one for games. He felt puzzles were pointless. There were enough mysteries in the world, he would tell her, without artificially adding more.

So why a *key*? Why leave *this* for her to find? If her father had left the six, six, six clue, she might have accepted that the key was the prize, but not Uncle Raziel. She wondered if the key was meant to lead her to the book, locked somewhere in the library, perhaps, in a vault, maybe, or chest, but if so, she had no idea where to begin a search.

Evangeline feels weary. She pockets the key, useless piece of iron that it is, and kicks aside the fallen books Michael has yanked off the shelves. She's tired. Her wing still hurts; her side isn't fully healed and she misses her uncle more than she can bear. She heads down the marble stairs, one slow step at a time.

She's done. She doesn't want to be part of this fight anymore. She doesn't want to find a mythical book and then choose whom to give it to. All she wants is to find her father, confront him about her uncle so she can put to rest her wicked doubts, then return to the way things were before. When everything made sense. When she had a clear vision.

And that vision, she realizes with a flash of welcome certainty, was fighting for the rights of her people. Not traipsing around the Heavens after old stories and legends.

"Where are you going?" Michael calls after her. "We don't have much time before they come back."

Evangeline ignores him. She knows he'll try to coerce her to stay, and while it would be nice to go back with him to the grove of trees where he kissed her, that idea is as much of a fantasy as her mission has been.

No, she needs to refocus. She needs to help her people win the war the traditional way. Train soldiers. Fight battles.

"Evie!" Michael hurries down the stairs after her. He grabs her arm to slow her down. She likes the warmth of his hand on her, but she pulls away.

"I'm going home, Michael."

"No, Evie, we need you," Michael implores.

"You need a librarian. An archivist," she sighs. "I don't know the book you're looking for and I can't find it."

"But your father's looking for it. He's going to find it."

She shakes her head. "Raziel may have been eccentric, but he wasn't stupid. If he thought my father was a threat and hid the book, then he did it to make sure it would never be found. Maybe Uncle Raziel was cursed by finding it and now he's protecting everyone else by taking his secret to the grave."

"It's too much of a risk to leave the book," Michael pleads. "It's too dangerous."

Evangeline sighs, exasperated. She speeds up her pace. "I don't care."

She swings open the door and hears the battle down the hall. It sounds like her people are fighting Michael's people in the atrium. Swords clang against each other, sharp cries of victory and pain. Vaguely, she wonders who's winning. She helped train some of the Dragon soldiers, so she'd like to think they're holding their own. And they had the advantage of surprise; even with Gabriel right outside, the Archangels weren't prepared to defend the school.

Still, this is not her fight. Taking the school will gain them nothing—only greater wrath of their enemies.

She thinks of the momentary peace she felt on top of the cliff in the Farlands, the *thin place* of tranquility. She longs for the same feeling now, and that won't occur here at Diaga Academy. She turns away from the battle. She walks away.

Unexpectedly she hears a deep voice rumble behind her. "Evangeline." It's Zephon, her father's second-in-command. She turns as he thunders down the hall toward her—and Michael, who has slipped out of the library after her. Zephon is flanked by a phalanx of guards, and it seems less like they're retreating from the battle and more like they're closing in on her.

Evangeline stops. She draws herself up as tall as she can, as her stomach flip-flops. She's always been intimidated by him. He's an old warrior, grizzled and mean. He's the cruelty to Lucifer's charm, the heavy to Lucifer's light. No matter her skill with a sword, Zephon has never shown her respect. She understands it's because she hasn't fought in battle; he believes it's her innate cowardice and not Lucifer's orders that keeps her from action. She'll admit that she does often slink away at the sight of his grimacing bulk, happy to let her father leash his beast, but Lucifer isn't here.

And, Michael is standing right there. She can't let him see her as a coward.

She juts her chin higher.

"Zephon," she says, addressing him coldly. For a moment, she forgets they're fighting on the same side.

The giant's eyes slide to Michael, then to Evangeline and back behind her, to the empty hall. He raises an eyebrow, mockingly.

"You flee?" In two syllables he combines contempt with scorn, smugness with conceit.

Evangeline's skin prickles at the insult, but she controls her expression. She will not let him see her discomfort.

"Since when do I owe you any explanation?" Evangeline asks. She tries to lower her voice, but still a squeak slips out, and she's mortified.

She notices a thin veneer of a smile stretch across his face. In it there is malice he seems to enjoy. "Since your father ordered me to confiscate a book from you."

Evangeline feels like she's been walloped. She staggers back—only a step, but it weakens her. Her father sent Zephon in after her. Her father knew she was here. Her father knew about the book.

My God. It's all true. He has been after a book, Raziel's book, and when Raziel didn't hand it over, Lucifer killed him, then followed her. Because he knew Raziel had given her a clue.

She'd been right—Lucifer would never have found it on his own, so he used her.

Evangeline's cheeks flush with shame and bitterness.

It's why the Dragons were here, ready to attack; Lucifer arranged it all, so she could get the book.

And give it to him.

But did he truly believe she'd turn it over to him after what he did to Uncle Raziel—*if* she even *had* it?

Evangeline feels her gut clench in agony as if she's been punched.

"If he wants it, he can come and get it himself," Evangeline says. She's bluffing. She tries to sound strong, confident, tough, but she's trembling and she can't stop.

Zephon steps forward, brushing past Michael like he's a gnat. The other guards hold their swords against him, but he doesn't respond to their threat. Instead, Evangeline notices he keeps his sword firmly sheathed. What option does he have?

"Your lip will cost you, little girl," he taunts. "Papa's not here to save you."

A surge of anger boils up inside Evangeline's chest. How *dare* he . . .

But she can't get any words out; she feels as if her lungs can no longer hold air.

She sees Zephon's eyes again scan Michael, calculating, and Evangeline is now shaking. Zephon may seem like a dumb brute, but he is cunning and smart and vicious. Evangeline has always understood it's a dangerous combination, an effective and an invaluable resource in their war, but now she feels the weight of his wrath directly.

She wants to run but another part of her mind won't let her.

"Cavorting with the enemy now?" Zephon drawls with a sneer directed at Michael.

Evangeline understands he is baiting her, but fury, like lava, roils near the surface. She *hates* him, this angel who has always belittled her, and now he stands here questioning her loyalty?

"You are a disgrace," he spits at her. "I told your father a half-breed like you can't be trusted."

Evangeline explodes. She has her sword unsheathed before she has crossed the distance between them, and she attacks. Her blade is at his throat; she slices a crimson line across his neck before he jerks out of the way. Evangeline feels the same surge of energy, of power, she did when she was fighting the djinni. She feels invulnerable against the giant as he stumbles backward, weak and on the defensive. Adrenaline courses through her veins, the wrath she feels fueling her attack. *No one* questions her loyalty to her people. *No one.* If she's been working with Michael, it's because she doubts her father's tactics, not their cause. She sacrificed her childhood for the Cause. She has—and continues to—dedicate her *life* to fighting for the rights of Commoners. No oaf, no matter how senior in her father's army, will denigrate her devotion.

"Evie!" She hears Michael call to her, as if he is miles away. She hears the blood rush through her head, pumping her full of energy.

She hears the clank of swords. She gauges, vaguely, that Michael has jumped into the fray, that he's fighting off Zephon's cronies.

Evangeline launches herself again at Zephon. He's fallen backward, the mighty giant felled by her sword. She sees blood slowly pool on the stone floor behind his head.

Abruptly, a pair of arms, stronger than an iron bar, wraps around her waist, lifting her off the ground. Under attack, she twists her upper body, her right arm swinging her sword around to slash at her assailant.

And she's good. Although locked in place as she is, she's able to slice her attacker across the lower back—at the kidneys, if she's lucky. The arms fall away with a muffled cry and Evangeline steps back, poised and ready again to strike.

It's then that she sees who was behind her.

Michael.

He collapses to the ground as Zephon's soldiers come after her. She jumps in front of Michael, thinking only of battle strategies because she can't think about what she's done.

Two soldiers, her own people, come at her, as one tends to Zephon. Her hands freeze and she almost drops her sword, but self-preservation kicks in. She duels and parries, and quickly realizes these soldiers are no match for her. Of course. This is a throw-away mission, important only to allow Zephon cover to get the book from Evangeline. The Dragons need only enough strength in battle until Evangeline and the book are extricated, then they won't care if the school falls to the Archangels.

Evangeline feels a bitter resentment toward Lucifer for manipulating her. She won't let it happen again.

Evangeline, sword in one hand, blocks the attacks defensively as she grasps Michael's arm and wrenches him to his feet. He cries out, his pain jarring her every nerve, but she can't think about what she's done to him. She has to get him out of here; if she doesn't, they will kill him.

And maybe her.

She pushes him backward, making him walk despite his agony. She understands the pain; she was stabbed by the djinni two days ago. As Michael saved her then, she will save him now.

Although he wouldn't need saving if she hadn't stabbed him. But she pushes the thought far from her mind. She must divorce herself from emotion in battle.

Only, no training has prepared her for her own people turning on her, at the behest of her own father, while she tries to escape with her enemy.

Michael moans but remains pliant to her unspoken commands. She stays in front of him as they back up toward the library doors. Her aggressors are thick, heavy, like Zephon—leave it to him to choose stooges in his own image—which means they are also slow. Evangeline whirls her sword in a flashing display of acrobatics. It's not that she is stronger than the two of them, but that she is faster, more skilled. Warfare, she learned long ago, isn't a matter of brute violence. It's an intricate dance where the smarter of the opponents will prevail.

And Evangeline, if anything, is smart with her sword.

Her blade flashes in the brightening rays of the sun coming in through the hall windows. She shields Michael as they move backward, toward the library door. Within seconds, she's pushed Michael through the entrance and edged her way inside.

She tries to slam shut the two wooden doors, but Zephon's soldiers push back.

"Help me," she orders Michael. She doesn't care that he's injured;

if they don't barricade this door to buy them time to escape, he'll be dead.

He seems to understand. He leans against the wooden door; Evangeline notices his face is ashen, and he has little strength, but it's enough that she can latch the door with the thick bolt.

For a moment—less than a moment—she leans against the wood, panting. How did she get here? To this? Running from her own people with the son of her father's enemy in tow . . . her world feels opposite, inverted, upside down. What should be one way is—

Oh my God.

Inverted. Upside down.

Six, six, six.

Nine, nine, nine.

Her uncle didn't like puzzles, but he loved symmetry. The idea and its opposite. The image and its mirror. *Find a different perspective*, Raziel would tell her.

Evangeline pulls Michael away from the door. She can hear Zephon's soldiers banging against it, but this door is thicker than the one she and Michael burst through from the storage closet. They don't have long, but maybe it's enough time . . .

"Stay here," she tells Michael, helping him to the floor by the stairs. His skin is clammy to the touch; she has to get him to a healer soon or it won't matter whether the soldiers break through.

She runs up to the marble staircase to the third floor, sprinting past the crushed door of the storeroom, counting the shelves as she goes.

"Seven, eight . . . nine."

Evangeline skims her fingers from the top of the shelf she can barely reach. "One, two three, four, fivesixseveneightnine."

She crouches to the bottom shelf, risen marginally off the floor.

Her hand trembles as she counts from the inside. "One. Two." Her fingers move faster.

Nine.

She balls her fist, hesitant to pull out the book in this slot. She doesn't have time to linger, but what if it *is* the book? It looks no different than the other soft leather bindings; how could this be a thousand-year-old manuscript?

Or maybe it isn't.

Then, before she can force herself to think, she whips her fingers out, like a viper's tongue, and snatches the ninth book.

It feels old and brittle to her touch. Trembling, she looks at the cover.

She looks at the image of a key.

CHAPTER 12

Evangeline whips her head around at the sound of the library's wooden door splintering. Zephon's minions are almost through. Evangeline casts her eyes to the book, aching with curiosity to open it and learn its secrets, but there's no time. She slips the book into her cloak and races down the stairs to Michael. His eyes are closed and he's breathing heavily. He seems to be in greater distress than she was from the djinni's stab wound and panic boils up inside her.

"Get up, Michael," Evangeline says, grasping him under the arms and wrenching him to his feet. He wobbles with the effort, but he manages to stay standing, as his weight rests against her. "Our only way out is through the storage room. We have to fly up. It's faster than the stairs."

Evangeline doesn't know if she can fly herself, let alone help Michael, but she's afraid he can't do it on his own. His eyes are glassy and unfocused and he doesn't respond to her.

So should she leave him here?

She has the book; it's what she came for.

And if Zephon's soldiers capture him, Evangeline is sure that Gabriel won't rest until Michael is rescued—and maybe that's all the better for her. She can use his capture as the distraction she needs to make her own escape. It's all actually perfect except for one thing: she likes Michael too much to risk his life in Zephon's hands.

"Michael, *now*," she hisses into his ear.

She lifts off, her right wing beating double time to compensate for her injured left wing. The pain is intense, but she struggles on, tugging at Michael's collar as she rises, nudging him to do the same.

But he doesn't. He spreads his wings, as if he knows what he's supposed to do, but he stays on his feet. Evangeline is already at the second level, but Michael still hasn't moved.

The door crashes open. Zephon's soldiers swarm in.

"Michael, fly!" she screams. She's almost at the third level. She can get to the storage room, and out into the corridor before they follow her. Or she can go back for Michael and risk being caught.

And risk the book falling into her father's hands.

She can't let that happen. She understands, finally, that her father is the enemy. She looks down at Michael, as if to say goodbye, but then with a strangled cry of frustration, plummets downward. Gravity eases the pain on her wings, but she's aware it will be short-lived, especially if she has to drag Michael up through the air. She thinks, for a fleeting second, that maybe they should take their chances running up the stairs, but the soldiers are nearly at the base of the marble staircase, nearly at Michael.

Evangeline lands behind Michael and leans in to wrap her arms around his waist. She feels the blood from his wound, can smell its metallic tang, and her stomach lurches. She kicks her feet hard off the floor, pulling up Michael with all her strength. Her good wing feels like it's on fire, but she manages to get Michael eight feet in the air and out of the soldiers' immediate grasp.

But the soldiers aren't injured, and there are more of them, so in no way can Evangeline fight them all off. With Michael's near-dead weight and her broken wing, she's slow to rise. Another second, and the soldiers will leap into the air and catch them.

But then Michael swoops his wing around in a wide arc, whipping the closest soldier in the face. Evangeline can hear Michael's ragged breathing; he's hurting, he's struggling, but he seems to have come back to himself. With an enormous flap of his wings, he's immediately airborne. Evangeline feels a swoop of relief. She grasps tighter around Michael's waist, and drags him with her.

The soldiers take a leap into the air, but Evangeline gives one last mighty beat of her wings and she and Michael make it over the railing on the third level. They tumble to the floor, and she immediately jumps to her feet, tugging Michael. She's tired; her injured wing feels like lead, but she pulls herself and Michael through the shattered door and into the storage room. There's no time to block it from Zephon's soldiers, so she keeps pressing forward.

Michael gasps often, in obvious pain, but he keeps up. They race out of the storage room and across the hall to the window through which they entered. It's still open; the crisp morning air floats in on a breeze. She pushes Michael through the window first, then launches herself after him. At first she thinks they should simply fly to the ground and make a run for it—they'd be able to camouflage themselves in the trees, rather than the obvious targets they'd make in the sky—but speed is more important. The soldiers following her don't have bows and arrows; to harm her and Michael, then, they'd need to be within sword's reach. Evangeline is determined to ensure that doesn't happen.

"The waterfall!" Evangeline shouts. She thinks of the cave behind the waterfall; the soldiers obviously wouldn't know about it so it would be the perfect hiding spot. She worries about the book getting wet, but she shoves it deep into her inner pocket. The two-second burst through the falls will soak her cloak, but not her tunic, if she remembers correctly from last time. But it's a tough entry and both she and Michael are injured. As it is, Michael is dropping in the sky, quickly losing altitude. She wants to steady him, the way he helped her after the djinni attack, but she's too weak herself. She gulps at the air, feeling the tightness in her chest, a shortness of breath.

But she presses on because she has no choice. She flies lower, nudges Michael higher, then leads him around the tops of the trees lining the riverbank. They come to the falls where the rush of water, the mighty roar, deafens her. She wonders briefly how close Zephon's soldiers are, but she can't waste her concentration on them. She has to focus on the corkscrew flight through the pounding water and into the cave. She's never returned since the time she showed up Alina, so she worries her one and only success was a fluke. Especially being injured, she fears she'll misjudge the opening and either plunge into the pounding surf, trapped in the dizzying eddies of the river and ruin the thousand-year-old manuscript, or crash into the rocks behind the water. She's heard of both calamities happening to other angels who've tried to brave the cave's entrance.

The other option is to be caught by Zephon's angels.

"Ready?" she calls out to Michael. She's sure he's come here before, a lot more times than she has, but never in such rough shape.

Michael nods.

"You first," she shouts.

She watches, hovering, as the spray of the water weighs down her wings. Michael flies harder, pulls his wings into the spin and punches through the water. Evangeline holds her breath; she sees no shape tumble into the dizzying swirls below her, so she thinks he made it.

Her turn. She flaps her wings, trying to gain enough speed, then folds them into the corkscrew. She's seized with a spasm of pain. Her vision blurs, she feels faint, and she's terrified she'll pass out, but the moment passes and she refocuses as she approaches the opening. She zooms in, but too fast. She slams into the cave wall at the back. She screams in agony as her left wing crumples from the crash.

When the pain finally subsides a little, she shakes the water from her cloak and feels for the book. It's still dry. She looks for Michael. He's beside her, collapsed with exertion, but still conscious. Evangeline can see his chest heaving but can't hear his breathing over the roar of the falls in front of them. They're behind a raging curtain of water, as if on a thunderous stage, hidden from view. They're safe here for the moment, but they can't linger; Michael obviously needs medical attention. So now does she. She tests her left wing; she can't lift it and she's frightened she won't be able to fly out. She wonders how long Zephon's soldiers will take to give up their search, how long until it's safe for them to leave.

And then what? Where do they go from here? She needs to find Gabriel, but she can't venture back into the school.

Evangeline leans against the back wall, her head pounding like the thunder of water.

One thing at a time. Wait out the soldiers, get back to dry land, and then she'll figure out how to help Michael.

She counts out a minute, two minutes. She's itching to leave but forces herself to wait another minute. It's not long, but she's going to guess Zephon's soldiers wouldn't remain in the skies without eyes on their target. It's what the Dragons have been taught: regroup to regain control of the environment so they're not taken in by a surprise ambush.

It's a risk, though. There's no way Evangeline can check outside the cave without going outside. If the angels are near the river, they'll spot her. She weighs the idea of waiting longer against Michael's worsening condition. When he starts to drift toward unconsciousness, Evangeline realizes they have to leave now.

"Michael," she nudges him and he blinks, barely awake. "Let's go."

"I can't," he whispers.

She can barely hear him over the pounding falls, and leans closer, her ear close to his mouth.

"You go," he says. "Be safe."

She feels his hot breath on her cheek; feels his lips brush against her skin. She closes her eyes for a millisecond, savoring the sensation, but then she returns to her senses.

"Don't be ridiculous," she replies, tugging at his arm.

"Evie," he pulls her close again, but Evangeline resists. She is not going to have this conversation. She is not leaving Michael.

"You have a tiny cut, but I have a stab wound from a djinni *and* a broken wing," she retorts. "If I can get out of here, you can."

"A tiny cut . . . " he repeats with a wan smile.

"Come on already."

Michael struggles to sit up and leans heavily on her as he stands. Evangeline can see the rock is slick with blood.

"Going out is easier than going in, remember," she squeezes his arm. "Punch through the falls and fly toward the left bank. I'll follow and help you in the air."

"With a broken wing?" Michael says, his face wan and pale. "No, I'd better support you."

"Hah, hah."

Evangeline helps him to the narrow opening, then gives him a gentle push. He takes off and a second later, Evangeline follows. She presses through the pounding water and emerges into the air, the wind icy against her skin. She can barely move her left wing, but she grimaces through the pain to catch up to Michael and guide him to the riverbank. They land on the edge of school grounds, close to where they were supposed to meet Gabriel. Evangeline wraps her arms around Michael, guiding him to the cover of the trees when she hears a harsh whisper: "Michael!"

A figure appears from behind a thick trunk, sword drawn. It's one of Gabriel's bodyguards who accompanied them from Fourth Heaven. He doesn't acknowledge Evangeline, but immediately rushes to Michael's side, pushing her out of the way.

"The chapel," Michael murmurs.

Of course, Evangeline thinks. The little stone church is nearby. Far removed from the fighting in the main building, it'll be isolated and empty.

"Where is it?" the guard asks Michael, but Evangeline jumps in, irritated he's ignoring her.

"Follow me," she says sharply.

Evangeline leads the way on a stone dust path through the woods. At the edge of the trees, bordering the rolling green lawns sweeping down from the school, sits a charming little chapel. Evangeline steps up and unlatches the door as the guard drags Michael inside.

Bright sunlight streams through the large windows cut into the thick stone walls. It falls in rays across the floor, worn smooth by generations of angels, as smooth as the gleaming mahogany pews. There are only four benches on each side of the aisle, much too small to house the current student population, so it rarely gets used. In fact, Evangeline has only been in it once, when Madame Hariel gave her a tour on her first day. Evangeline vowed then and there that she would never set foot inside here—or any "house of worship"—when its only purpose was to praise a God who allowed for the destruction of her people. Half Dominion or not, Evangeline couldn't bring herself to assimilate with their hypocritical faith. She's always hated this place.

The guard lies Michael down on the cold stone floor in front of the raised alter. He whips off his cloak and covers Michael.

"I'll get Gabriel," he says—again speaking only to Michael—then scuttles away.

Evangeline still bristles at him ignoring her. *She's* the one who saved Michael, she thinks, and then quickly realizes that he only needed saving because of her.

With the rush of adrenaline easing, Evangeline settles into a pew, her wing throbbing, her body aching. She glances at Michael, whose eyes are closed, and who seems unaware of her presence. She can see his face pinched in pain and a wave of guilt washes over her, knowing she's responsible. Evangeline thinks to make a pillow for him out of her own cloak. She slowly removes it and shakes off the water. She pulls out the book, ensuring it's still dry, then tucks it deeply back into her tunic pocket with Uncle Raziel's mysterious key. She balls up the cloak, but then she finds herself hesitating. All of a sudden she doesn't want to lift Michael's head. She doesn't want to rouse him and have to talk to him. She doesn't know what she would say. *Sorry*, she supposes. But that's the problem. She's *not*. She's *not* sorry for what happened. Michael grabbed onto her and she'd defended herself. She would have fought back against anyone attacking her.

Feeling an unexpected surge of resentment, Evangeline throws her cloak back around her shoulders. It's Michael's fault he got injured because it's Michael's fault he got in the way.

She turns and tiptoes toward the door. She's getting out the way she had planned. She has the book, which she's dying to read, and with help on the way for Michael, there's no reason to stay.

"Going somewhere?"

Evangeline is startled by Michael's thin and shaky voice. She turns back, surprised to see Michael sitting up, leaning against the marble alter. His face is wretchedly pale and clammy, his eyes bright. She looks at him for a long minute, but no words get past her lips.

"Not even a goodbye?" There's a bitterness to Michael's tone that unsettles Evangeline, and she finds herself on the defensive.

"You told me to go. To be safe," she counters.

They stare at each other down the aisle, the gap between them wide.

Michael is slumped, his arm wrapped around his midsection, as if he's trying to hold himself together, and he's breathing hard. He takes only quick, shallow breaths, though, which often come out as a wheeze.

"You found the book." It's not a question.

Evangeline feels his eyes boring into her as her stomach flips over. She'd been stupid, careless, to pull the book out with Michael here. She thought he'd been unconscious. But she tells herself not to react. Instead, she stares right back, unblinking.

"Now what?" The coldness in his voice draws fire from hers.

"Now I leave," she says hotly, and this time turns on her heels.

"To run back to your father."

The jab bothers Evangeline more than she wants to let on; Michael makes it seem like she's a child, needing to hide under Papa's wings.

"He's a menace, Evangeline, and he'll turn you into one."

Evangeline bristles—at her full name, and at the implications that she can be so easily coerced by her father.

"I'm my own person," she declares.

"Are you?"

His comment feels like a sharp slap in the face. He'd been so caring, so protective all this time, willing to sacrifice himself in the cave to give her a chance to escape, but now he's discovered her betrayal. Now he's fighting back, lashing out at her by exploiting her greatest fear: that she'll never be enough like her father—that she's not charismatic enough or strong enough or passionate enough. But now Michael is making her see herself for who she truly is. A version of her father.

Violent, brutal, vicious.

Not because she accidentally stabbed Michael or attacked Zephon, but because she *liked* attacking Zephon. She *liked* fighting him. She *liked* winning. She *liked* the rush of power she had over him.

Is that why Lucifer does the things he does? Starve out his own people in First Heaven and the burn down refugee camps in Second Heaven? Kill her uncle . . . does her father trample the boundary of morality simply for the intoxicating rush of power, and not for the greater good of the Commoners, or the righteousness of their cause?

And by attacking Zephon, did she succumb to the same thing?

She tries to rationalize her behavior. Zephon was insulting her—no, not merely insulting her, but calling into question the very core of her being—her commitment to their Cause. Of course he *deserved* to be taken down.

But Evangeline thinks back to her fight with the djinni. She remembers the exhilaration of her anger, the strength of her rage.

She remembers how much she liked it—as much as she liked the surge of power she had over Zephon.

So she is like her father.

Just in ways she had never before fathomed.

"Show me the book, Evie," Michael's voice softens, but she doesn't think it's because he's softened toward her. It's because he's injured; he's exhausted. He's run out of energy.

Evangeline shakes her head. No way is she letting him near the book. If it's as powerful a weapon as Gabriel and her father and Michael think, then *she* needs it. Not to destroy the Heavens the way Gabriel thinks her father will, but to end the war. And more than ever, she realizes it has to be *her*. Zephon may be a rude bastard, but

Evangeline fears his sentiments may not be solely his own. She sees now that other Commoners also view her the same way. That she's a half-breed who can't be trusted. It's true she distanced herself from her people when she came here to Diaga, and maybe they haven't forgiven her for that. Maybe they don't see her as one of them anymore. Maybe they never did. If that's the case, then she needs to prove to her people once and for all that she's on *their* side. Learning the secrets of this ancient text—a text that *she* retrieved—and then using its power to restore the Commoners' rightful place in the Heavens, will do that.

"Evie . . . " Michael pleads.

"I'm not going to give it to my father," she snaps, anticipating his tired old refrain.

Michael lifts his chin. A ray of hope touches his eyes. And for a moment Evangeline thinks she sees mirrored in his eyes the deep faith within his soul, the foundation of his dedication, his determination. For that moment, Evangeline wishes it were her own. But she has to accept that she will never experience the quiet confidence that seems to be at Michael's core; her own soul is much too fragile, much too shattered, so Evangeline barks back in frustration.

"I'm not giving it to *your* father, either."

Michael closes his eyes, the effort of their conversation obviously wearing on him.

"So, what now?" he asks.

Evangeline is half tempted to explain her thinking about becoming the savior her people, to have him validate her plan, but she comes to her senses quickly.

"I leave," she says abruptly.

Michael nods dejectedly, and there's a painful silence that follows.

Finally, Evangeline coughs awkwardly. "Goodbye, Michael."

She doesn't look at him; she can't look at him. Instead, she turns and heads for the door. Her feet feel heavy, as if weighed by anchors, and there's a weight inside her chest, too, but it's for the best. Uncle Raziel wanted *her* to have the book, so that's how it's going to be.

She has her hand on the latch when Michael again calls to her.

"You can have it," he says, "and I won't tell my father. But let me at least see it?"

Evangeline takes her time turning to face him. She doesn't trust him. Retrieving the book for the Archangels has been his sole mission all this time. Why the change of heart?

"So you can snatch it from my hands?" she counters.

"And escape with it, how, Evie?" he asks sardonically. "I can't exactly sprint clean away."

"You have a whole army at your disposal," she replies wryly.

"Whom I could send after you whether I've seen the book or not." Evangeline sucks in her breath, incensed at the threat.

"Show me the book and I won't tell my father. Either about the book or . . . " Here, Michael pauses. " . . . or who stabbed me."

Evangeline's eyes widen in indignation. "Are you *blackmailing* me?"

When Michael answers, he sounds weary. "What do you think my father will do when he learns you almost killed me?"

"It was self-defense!" Evangeline cries. "You came at me from behind. I didn't know it was you."

"Says you."

Evangeline's whole body tenses. Every muscle is tight, every nerve ending quivers.

"Do you *actually* think I tried to kill you?" Evangeline laughs, the idea is so preposterous.

Or is it? She may not have been trying to kill him, but she did think of abandoning him in the library.

Michael seems to see the shadow that crosses her face. He nods in her direction, as if her expression is confirmation.

"You wanted the book. You got the book and I'm injured," he says. "And," he takes a shallow breath, "you *are* Lucifer's daughter."

Evangeline feels like he's thrown a knife into her chest. She's been vilified for being Lucifer's daughter many, many times at this very school, and she's always withstood the taunts because of her unwavering loyalty to her father. But now that the world in which her father is a good guy seems to have vanished, she fears the comparison.

Lucifer's daughter. She doesn't know what that means anymore.

And the comment hurts all the more, coming from Michael. After all they've been through, she managed to fool herself into thinking he was different.

Stupid fool, Evangeline chastises herself.

Michael speaks again, but now his voice is barely a whisper. "It's a good deal. Show me the book and I'll tell my father it was Zephon who stabbed me."

Evangeline seethes at the turn of events. She's angered that, just as she regained control, it's all slipping away. But she doesn't have a choice. Gabriel has always had a soft spot for her, but she's afraid to test his benevolence if he truly does believe she tried to kill his son. He may be a soft-spoken, altruistic angel, but he's also the general of God's army for a reason.

But Michael said she can keep the book; she only has to show him. Maybe it is all he wants. Maybe his curiosity is as vast as hers. And he did rescue her from the djinni when he didn't have to.

"Why do you want to see it?" she asks.

He takes a long moment before answering, and Evangeline is unsure if he can't speak or if he doesn't know what to say.

Finally, he raises his eyes to meet hers. "It's our history," he explains, "Yours and mine, Commoner and Dominion. I want to understand how we once had that unity."

Evangeline feels herself soften at his response. He may be playing her, but he's saying what she wants to hear. She finds herself taking a step toward him but then the door to the chapel bursts open and Gabriel rushes in, cloak flying. Raphael, his uncle the healer, also enters, although his movements are more languid than his brother's.

Evangeline, startled, jumps back against the side of a pew as Gabriel hurries down the aisle. If he notices Evangeline, he doesn't acknowledge her. Instead, his whole focus is his son. Evangeline observes the open love and pain etched into his face as he bends down to Michael, and for a split second she feels a jab of jealousy, wondering if her own father ever looked at her the same way. But no, that's silly. Of course he did. If these past few days have made her question everything else she thought she knew about her father, she shouldn't be questioning his love for her. Lucifer may not be openly affectionate, in the same way Gabriel now cups Michael's pale cheek in his palm, but his actions have always spoken loudly and clearly. He did risk being killed or captured in the Farlands barely a week ago, to see her on her birthday.

But she worries, too, as she hears father and son whisper to each other. She never actually accepted Michael's offer; will he turn her in? Will she lose the book and her freedom and all possibilities of redemption in the eyes of her people because she hesitated too long to agree to Michael's terms?

Raphael nods to Evangeline as he passes, and she again senses a subtle detachment in his bearing. He walks slowly, as if he is simply strolling through the woods, his face smooth and relaxed. She feels a surge of hope, thinking that maybe he's confident his nephew's wounds are no match for his skill. He has the reputation as the Miracle of Medicine for a reason.

"Zephon did this?" Evangeline hears Gabriel's voice rise, and she exhales. Michael is going to cover for her. *Though I did nothing wrong,* she defiantly reminds herself.

Michael murmurs in response, but Evangeline can't make it out. Whatever he said, though, riles up Gabriel, a sight Evangeline has never seen. He slaps the floor beside Michael, palm open, in obvious frustration. He stands and paces, quick little steps, as Raphael moves in to examine his patient. Evangeline is both amazed and a terrified at Gabriel's ire.

An anger that could have been directed at her, if Michael had wanted it.

She feels beholden to Michael now, which adds to her resentment.

But Michael seems to be upholding the bargain they nearly made. When Evangeline hears Gabriel ask about the book, she sees Michael shake his head and a surge of relief, of gratitude, washes over her.

Raphael waves Gabriel away as he helps Michael remove his shirt to examine the stab wound. Evangeline eyes the scene with surprise. Since Raphael has no supplies with him, like cloths or bandages or sutures, she expected they'd move Michael to another location. Yet Raphael has Michael lie flat on his stomach, his back exposed. Evangeline winces; she sees the long, deep wound her sword made, the blood still oozing from it. She reels back from the sight, shaken about how much blood he's lost, and also impressed he was actually able to escape with her. Michael is stronger than she believed.

With energy left over to blackmail her, she reminds herself.

But Raphael, his expression smooth and calm, seems unconcerned about Michael's condition. He tears away Michael's shirt and places his hand to Michael's bloody back. He starts at the shoulders, then, with a soft touch, moves his palms toward the wound. He chants quietly, a strange hum of words Evangeline can't make out. Evangeline doesn't understand his technique, has never seen a healer work with only his hands like that before, but she has to believe he knows what he's doing.

"You didn't find the book, then," Gabriel says, approaching her. He's resumed his regal bearing, the general again in control of himself.

Evangeline's hand involuntarily shifts to her pocket, where the book is hidden, and for a frantic second, she feels like Gabriel noticed her movement and has discerned the truth. She shakes out her hand, trying to cover up the motion, and then shakes her head.

"I was so sure about my uncle's instructions," she says, attempting to add in a whine of disappointment.

Gabriel sighs. "Well, we've run out the Dragons, so we'll scour the library inch by inch."

He seems to forget he's talking to a Commoner, and it rankles Evangeline. She's *not* on his side, but if even Gabriel thinks she's abandoned her people, no wonder Zephon and the others believe she's a traitor.

"Maybe my uncle never had it," Evangeline snaps.

"Oh, he had it all right," Gabriel responds, either oblivious to her attitude or purposely ignoring it. "And your father's attack on the school proves it. Lucifer is smart, strategic. His every action is always precisely planned," Gabriel continues, and Evangeline catches a subtle tone of admiration. "He must have followed us from Fourth Heaven and never once did we suspect." He shakes his head, then looks Evangeline in the eye. "You're not safe here. We've got to get you to the Archangel fortress on the other side of the valley. Then we'll rethink how to find the book. At least we know your father doesn't yet have it, since he's coming after you."

"*Excuse* me?" Evangeline doesn't know *where* to begin contradicting Gabriel's little speech. She's not going *any*where with him, let alone the Archangel fortress—and she's obviously not doing *any*thing to help him find the book, which is tucked ever so snugly in her tunic.

"You're the key now, Evangeline."

Evangeline lets out a loud laugh at the absurdity of his suggestion. She thinks of Uncle Raziel's literal key, plus the book in her pocket. She is no key.

Gabriel cocks his head as if he's surprised at her reaction. "Your uncle gave you a clue to the book's whereabouts and your father knows it. He'll try to get to you, so we have to keep you safe."

She stares at him hard. "You want to keep me safe from my *father*?"

Gabriel doesn't blink. "Lucifer will use you and then kill you," he says bluntly.

"You are *mad*," she says. "My father would never hurt me."

"You saw what he did to your uncle."

"That's my *uncle*. My mother's relative," she says. "Not *me*, his own flesh and blood." She can't believe she's having this conversation. Of course she's been shocked by her father's violence, and yes she has to reevaluate who he is, how she sees him, but Gabriel is crazy if he thinks Lucifer would actually harm her.

"Evangeline," Gabriel begins, with the paternalistic tone of admonishing a child.

"Whose side do you think I'm *on*?" She crosses her arms, feeling the book and the mysterious iron key.

Gabriel blinks, and Evangeline sees a momentary flash of confusion, one Evangeline suspects he's unfamiliar and uncomfortable with.

"I am *not* here to do your bidding," she says sharply.

Gabriel's eyes narrow, and now Evangeline sees a steeliness to his expression.

"You think you're going to stroll out of here?" There is a dangerous warning in his voice, and Evangeline feels her stomach drop with a streak of real fear.

"Yes," she replies, with a defiant confidence she no longer feels. She *has* to get out of here. She has to examine the book and obviously that has to be on her own.

"You will remain our guest," Gabriel says coldly.

"Prisoner, you mean," Evangeline tries to match the ice in his voice, but inside, she's crumbling. How is she going to get out of this?

"Semantics," Gabriel responds, dryly.

"Father, please," Evangeline hears Michael's voice, stronger now.

Both she and Gabriel turn toward the front of the church, where Raphael has Michael sitting up. He looks a million times better; his skin is flushed, his eyes bright. His breathing sounds deeper, regular, and Evangeline feels a rush of relief.

"Hush, Michael," Raphael chides him. "Let me finish."

Gabriel and Evangeline both watch in silence as Raphael again moves his hands over Michael's back and side. He continues his unusual chant.

And then she notices the strangest thing: she sees—*sees*—the skin on Michael's back, the two sides of the wound, knit together. Raphael has no needle in his hand, no sutures over the wound, but still Michael's skin pulls together. Before her eyes, Michael's body visibly heals.

Evangeline's jaw drops. How is this possible?

"There, good as new," Raphael says, pulling Michael to his feet. Michael stands, hesitant for a moment, then twists his torso, slowly, gingerly, then with greater gusto. He turns and stretches, his eyes widening with every movement.

"No pain, I presume?" Raphael asks, bemused.

"None," Michael breathes. "But how—?"

"A magician never reveals his secrets," Raphael jokes.

Magician . . . magician . . . the word sticks with Evangeline, and she doesn't know why. Magicians don't exist, obviously, since there is no such thing as magic but—

There are *Slivers.*

The stories of angels who have been gifted by God with *Slivers,* a slice of divinity, bestowed on them, giving them the slightest fraction of the power of God.

Evangeline is thunderstruck. Raphael has a *Sliver.* They actually exist. Here and now, in her world. That must be why Raphael has such an admirable reputation as a healer. A miracle worker, they say.

Questions whirl though Evangeline's head, so many of them, they crash into each other without logic or order. How did he get his *Sliver?* When did he get it? How long has he known about it? *Does* he know about it? Or does he not understand why he can do what he does? How does he know how to use it? What else can he do? Who else has a *Sliver?* Who else understands what they are? She looks at Gabriel and Michael, both of whom seem relieved, pleased, but unsurprised. Do *they* know why Raphael can do what he does? Do they understand his *Sliver?*

Or is her mind so feverish from all the shocking revelations she's had to process over the past few days that she is imagining things?

But Evangeline knows she's not. As incredible and unbelievable as it sounds, she is absolutely convinced she's right.

Raphael has a sliver of divinity.

He approaches her. "And my dear, will you now let me see your wing?" Raphael approaches her, holding out his hands, palms up.

She looks beyond to Michael and he's beaming like a little boy, nodding his encouragement. She takes a step forward, hesitant, yet curious. She wonders what it'll be like to be touched by a divine hand.

Raphael motions for her to turn, which she does. She can feel his warm hand on her broken wing. He has a light touch, soft and comforting.

But she doesn't feel a surge of power or energy or anything. In fact, she actually feels no different. Her wing still hurts, it still feels broken, she's still in pain. She can't see the back of her wing, of course, doesn't know if it's mending before Michael's eyes the way his skin healed before hers, but she doubts it.

So maybe the *Slivers* thing isn't real after all.

Abruptly, she feels Raphael pull away. Then he touches her wing again. He's chanting, in the same strange language he used with Michael, but his voice sounds strained. There's a tension in his choral tones, like the plucking of a taut string. Raphael's chanting speeds up, and now it sounds desperate. Evangeline tries to twist her head to see what he's doing, but abruptly he stops.

She turns to see him, his brows furrowed, his face puzzled. When her uncle was dying of egregious wounds, Raphael remained uncannily calm. When his own nephew was gravely injured, he stayed serene. But when he confronts a simple broken wing, he looks worried?

"Who is your mother?" Raphael demands.

Evangeline is thrown by the non sequitur. She can see no connection between her broken wing and her mother.

Gabriel takes a step forward, answering for her.

"Seraphina, daughter of Laila," he says, but there's an undertone Evangeline can't make out. She feels like the brothers are involved in a second layer to this conversation that she doesn't understand, and it's unnerving.

"An old family . . . " Raphael mutters.

Evangeline glances at Michael, whose expression is as surprised and confused as hers.

"And her father is Lucifer, a Commoner . . . " Raphael continues.

Evangeline's spine straightens, again feeling defensive whenever her father is mentioned.

"Raphael, what is it?" Gabriel asks.

And as quickly as his frown appeared, it's gone. Raphael's face again relaxes into his contented detachment.

"I'm sorry, my dear." He shakes his head. "I'm a foolish man to believe the stories angels spread about my abilities. I can't cure every injury. But we won't let you suffer. There's medicine in the school infirmary. I'll mix you up a draft and bring it straight away. You two head over to Madame Hariel's quarters. We'll arrange for hot water and you can clean up there."

With that, Raphael nods, as if making up his mind, then sweeps down the aisle and out the door.

Gabriel ushers Michael and Evangeline after him. Evangeline follows—she has no choice right now—but she leaves the chapel with a distinct sense of unease. She doesn't buy Raphael's vapid argument that he overestimated his abilities. Something happened during the healing that surprised him. Something that made him unable to work his magic.

Something about her.

CHAPTER 13

Ｗith her hands folded neatly in front of her, Evangeline sits primly on the edge of Madame Hariel's ornate wooden chair, in her private sitting room in front of a warming fire. There are luxurious cushions at the back of the chair into which Evangeline would love to sink, but though she and Michael are alone in the headmistress's quarters, she feels like she must maintain a formal sense of decorum. It's strange, being here. She's never entered these premises before—no student has, to her knowledge, an opinion Michael seems to support with his own hesitant step across her threshold. It feels wrong, as if they are peeling back a curtain and revealing an element of life to which they have no right to witness.

Evangeline wonders what Madame Hariel must have thought when she was kicked out of her own chambers, knowing her rooms were to be infiltrated by former students, but Evangeline supposes the headmistress had no choice, given the Archangels' takeover of the school.

Michael made her promise not to examine the book until they had cleaned up. She'd been tempted to sneak a peek when she was alone in the wash chamber, but she found herself drawing back from it. She realized she wanted to open it for the first time in Michael's presence. She felt like the book required reverence, that its opening deserved more than a fleeting, stolen glance. Or maybe she wanted to share the experience with someone. With Michael.

Now Michael emerges from the wash chamber, scrubbed clean of all the blood, with fresh clothes and a fresh lavender scent. He looks good; he smells good, and Evangeline feels a burst of irrational jealousy. Despite his injuries and his blood loss, he is now whole, made new with Raphael's *Sliver*, yet she still struggles with the ache of her broken wing and her own knife wound. Raphael's promised draft did nothing. She's thought about it—why Raphael couldn't heal her the way he could with Michael—and can only conclude that it must be her Commoner blood. She'd always thought there were no biological differences between the classes of angels, that the hierarchies were social constructs alone, but what else could it be? Or, maybe, it's the mix of Dominion and Commoner. Maybe if she'd been a full-blooded Commoner, Raphael could have helped.

"Those clothes look good on you," Michael says and smiles, and Evangeline blushes.

The borrowed dress, an unsuitable soft black velvet, most definitely does *not* look good on her. She heard it belongs to a student who's obviously smaller than she is. The cinch of the dress at her waist pinches, and the bodice feels restrictive, but she does admit wearing clean clothes feels good. She wishes Gabriel could have found her riding pants and a loose tunic, but she suspects he provided the dress—and a too-small one, at that—on purpose. If she is to be their "guest," there would be no reason for her to require traveling clothes. She thought at first that she'd refuse the offer, that she'd continue wearing her own clothes, but from her hard journey, her fight with the djinni and her escape with Michael this morning, they are in bloody tatters. Once behind the door of the washroom, she quietly removed the key, the book, and her father's forgotten

Naofa feather, the one he gave her earlier this week on her birthday. At first, she gripped the plume with a vehemently angry intent to rip it to shreds, the betrayal by her father cutting so deep, but she discovered that she couldn't. The black feather held no protection, no safety, not even symbolically anymore, but still, it was the last gift from her father—not Lucifer the monster, but her *father*. So she tucked it safely into the pocket of her new dress along with the book and key.

"Let's have a look at the book," Michael says, much too loudly.

Evangeline whirls toward him, a finger to her lips and shushes him. She points to the door, to the guard outside.

Michael lowers his voice as he sinks into the second chair, his face lit by the crackling flames. "I kept my end of the bargain."

"We made no bargain," Evangeline says. Her logic won't work; Michael can choose, at any moment, to tell Gabriel the truth about his injury and Gabriel will forgive Michael's original lie and turn on her. And then there will be no more hot baths and soft dresses if that's the case.

More importantly, she won't be able to keep the book and the key a secret.

Michael huffs in frustration. "You can keep the goddamn book," he whispers harshly. "I told you that. I only want to see it."

"*Why* let me keep it?"

"Because I trust you."

At this, Evangeline laughs. She wishes it were true, that he trusts her and she trusts him, but that's not their reality.

It's then that she finally realizes Michael's plan, and she feels stupid she didn't see it before. "You're after the information in the book," she says. "You're going to learn about its power and then tell your father. You don't need the book itself if you know what's in it."

"Yes, congratulations, super sleuth," Michael says, sighing. "If I know what you know, we neutralize each other."

Evangeline swallows a lump of irritation. He may be right, but still, if she has the book, she may still gain the advantage.

"Fine, but here?" she asks, again motioning to the door. She's afraid Gabriel or a guard may enter at any moment and catch them with the book.

"If anyone comes in, I'll distract them," Michael assures her.

It's risky, but her own burning curiosity wins out. Shifting so her back is to the door, Evangeline withdraws the book. Her hands shake, cradling the thousand-year-old manuscript. She runs her palm over the leather, soft and cracked, running her fingers along the embossed image of a key, recognizable to her from the pictures she drew years ago based on legends of the book. She feels like she's desecrating the manuscript by touching it with her bare hands. She should be wearing gloves, the way Uncle Raziel taught her how to handle ancient documents, to protect it from the oils on her skin. But she has no time for precautions. Instead, she opens the cover, revealing brittle, fragile parchment.

"Wow," Michael says, exhaling. He reaches for it, and Evangeline has to fight her instinct to withdraw it. She'll let him touch it but she won't let it leave her hands. He hesitates, then runs the tips of his fingers over the thin pages.

Evangeline sees in his eyes a giddiness she remembers experiencing herself when she was first exposed to Uncle Raziel's archives— both his personal collection and the Cherubims'. She's not foolish enough to conflate Michael's interest in this book with an enduring interest in all ancient texts, but it still inspires awe to read the words of angels who lived so long ago they seem to exist only in their imaginations. Evangeline always felt it was like reaching back through the threads of time, connecting the generations in a real, tangible way.

Evangeline enjoys the thrill of anticipation for a moment longer before she reads the text. For so long she believed this book was a fantasy, a creation of myth and legend, yet here, in the palm of her hand, is the weight of history. She's long imagined the Assembly from all of her uncle's stories, but now she'll finally have answers to all her questions.

She opens her eyes and lets her gaze fall on faded ink soaked into crisp, brittle vellum. She knows, she expects, the text will be difficult to decipher—it's *a thousand* years old, after all—but when she strains her eyes, she is startled.

She can't read it.

She holds the book up close to her eyes. No, it's not the print, or the age of the manuscript. While the ink is blurred, yes, the letters are still distinct.

They're simply not letters she can read.

"What is it?" Michael asks.

Evangeline lays the book on the table in front of them, pushing aside the chess board, its pieces ready for play. She flips the page, then another and another. They're all the same. Small, neat, script, line after line of words she can't make out. It's as if it's written in a different language—

Because it is.

Evangeline breathes out, amazed. "It's written in Enochian."

"Enochian?" Michael asks.

"The ancient angelic language," Evangeline explains. "It was the language of scholars. Of Cherubim and Seraphim."

"But you can read it, right?" Michael asks, an edge to his voice. "Your uncle taught you, right?"

Her uncle had taught her.

A word or phrase here and there.

She knew of the language, had seen a few examples in the ancient texts Uncle Raziel had let her see, but no, she can't actually read it.

Which is why she starts laughing, a small, bitter, thin laugh.

"Shhhh," Michael glances at the door, no one enters. "What is so *funny*?" he hisses.

"*This*," Evangeline shakes the useless book at him. "The lost manuscript. The Key to the Kingdom. The answer to all our prayers." She feels the pitch of her tone climb, her voice reedy, thin. After all this, after her search for her father, and the unfathomable encounter with his look-alike djinni, and the monstrous murder of her uncle, and the clues and secrets and codes and keys—she can't *read* the ancient manuscript. It's like a joke. A cruel, sick, sadistic joke.

Someone is messing with her. Her uncle, before he died. Or her father. Maybe he actually *has* the real book, *knows* its mysterious secret and this volume is a mere decoy, a diversion.

But they would never stoop to such petty games. Her uncle was far too serious and her father, far too preoccupied. Neither would waste time planting a fake, then leaving clues for her to find it.

Which means the most obvious solution is the truest: this ancient, lost manuscript is written in a nearly dead language, inaccessible everyone but two angels. Her uncle would have been the third.

She wonders at the irony. If her father did actually kill Uncle Raziel for the book, then he must not have known her uncle's importance.

Evangeline looks at Michael's puzzled, worried face.

"I can't *read* it," she clarifies.

"Well, then, who can?"

Evangeline stares at him, her eyes wide with disbelief.

"Are you crazy? We can't show this to anyone. It'll end up in your father's or my father's hands."

And then all hope of her ending the war, of bringing peace to the Heavens is lost.

Evangeline clutches the book, the useless, pointless manuscript, and now she's enraged by the injustice of it all—her father's secrets, Gabriel's smugness, Michael's righteousness. She wants to hurl the book, the ancient, precious artifact sought after by countless angels for countless years, into the fire. She wants to watch it *burn*. With a cry of anguish, she shoves it hard across the table, away from her, but Michael grasps it before it falls to the floor.

"Hey, careful," he says, placing it gently between them.

Evangeline trembles with anger and then sudden shame that she wished, for her own benefit alone, the destruction of the book.

Evangeline hears the creak of the door and the guard pokes her head inside. Evangeline whirls, so her body blocks the guard's view of the book.

"Michael," the guard says, ignoring Evangeline like all the others. "Everything okay in here?"

Michael quickly strides over to the guard, turning on his wide smile.

"Yeah," he says, leaning his hand across the doorway, effectively barring the guard from the room. He tosses a white carved marble piece in the air. "Simply a heated game of chess. Evangeline tried to jump my sky horse from the back row with her hayyot. I told her it can't be done, right? I'm right, aren't I?"

Evangeline appreciates Michael is covering for her own foolish temper, but still she glowers at his back. He doesn't have to flirt with the guard, Evangeline thinks. Tell her to get out.

The guard laughs. "You're right, Michael. Don't let the little half-breed win."

Before Evangeline can make sense of what's happening, Michael twists the guard into a headlock, his forearm pressing dangerously against her throat.

"*Never* call her that again," Michael growls.

The guard's eyes are wide with surprise and fear, and as much as Evangeline thinks she should tell Michael to let her go, she doesn't. Instead, she thinks, *Good. She deserves it.*

Again she feels the rush of pleasure at the violence, but then immediately is appalled with herself. Good God, what is *happening* to her? How did she turn into such a sadistic creature?

"Evie," Michael commands, nodding to the table. Evangeline slips the book into her pocket next to her uncle's iron key before the guard can notice it. Michael pushes the guard further into the room, then, with an aggressive shove, lets her go.

"Come on," he tells Evangeline.

She keeps her head high as she sweeps past the fallen guard and out into the hall.

"My father will hear of this," Michael says to the guard, then he slams the door, twists the key and locks it.

"What are you *doing?*" Evangeline whispers to him.

"Improvising," he says, taking her by the arm and ushering her down the hall. When they round the corner and see a group of Archangels walking their way, Michael nudges her back into an alcove, his back to the hall, blocking the soldiers' view of her. He moves in close and she understands it's to hide her, but nevertheless, she feels a welcome swoop in her stomach. She can smell the lavender soap on his skin, the mint of his toothpowder on his breath, and she thinks of their kiss outside the school—was that only this *morning?* She wants to kiss him again, wants him to kiss her again, but she has to remind herself that they don't trust each other.

After the soldiers pass, Michael steps back, and Evangeline feels immediately deflated, then embarrassed. Of course he wouldn't waste time trying to kiss her.

"Who can read Enochian?" Michael whispers, all business.

Evangeline stays silent, still upset at Michael's coolness toward her.

"Evie, I *promise* you, we will not let the book fall into my father's or your father's clutches."

Evangeline shakes her head, knowing that's an impossible vow. She's met the two angels who can speak Enochian: Dana, a Cherubim colleague of Raziel, and Dana's brother Camael, a Seraphim, one of only seven angels protecting God. Of course they would never let two young angels, a Commoner and an Archangel, retain control of the most powerful weapon in the Heavens.

Michael crosses the hall and places his hand on the windowsill, obviously frustrated. He stares out at the rolling, manicured grounds. Abruptly, he turns to her, hopeful, excited.

"Maybe you can read more than you think. You're exceptionally brilliant."

Evangeline blushes at the compliment, but it doesn't change her ability. She can read only a few words, none of which she recognized on the page. It's a difficult language, she remembers her uncle telling her, reassuring her when she was struggling with the Enochian alphabet.

"Each symbol, each letter, can represent multiple different sounds," Evangeline explains, feeling like she has to justify her lack of skill. "It's tricky to know which meaning is the right one."

"But you can try?"

"Not without a dictionary," Evangeline replies ruefully. "And none exists," she adds quickly, heading off Michael's next question.

If only one did exist, she thinks. She could, with time, match the symbols with the multiple meanings and then work on deciphering the correct one.

Match the symbols . . .

"That's it! Evangeline spins toward Michael, incredibly buoyed. "Uncle Raziel has other books in Enochian, some of whose contents I already know. If I compare those symbols with what's in this book, maybe I can piece something together."

She's thinking of the *Slivers*, of the knowledge Uncle Raziel has taught her about the Assembly of Angels. Maybe with a little context, she'll be able to decipher parts of it.

Michael smiles, his eyes flashing with elation.

"I told you that you were exceptionally brilliant," Michael says.

Evangeline again feels her cheeks redden. "The chances of me actually discovering the secrets of this book are still incredibly remote, you know that, right?"

Michael shrugs. "One in a million is better than nothing."

Evangeline feels a surge of excitement, but this anticipation feels different than anything she's experienced before. This exhilaration seems to be coming from a sense of power and control. *She* has the book everyone wants and now *she* is going to solve its mysteries. She never realized before how stifled she felt, always doing her father's bidding, always following someone else's orders. Now *she* will decide her own course of action.

It's incredibly liberating.

But she also can't do it alone. "I need to get to my uncle's library in Sixth Heaven," she tells Michael. "You'll cover for me?"

There's an awkward silence and Evangeline feels her face redden. She's both embarrassed and confused because she thought Michael would actually help. Now she feels stupid for believing it.

"Evie," Michael says slowly, "I'm coming with you."

Evangeline's head snaps up. "You can't."

Michael narrows his eyes. "Why not?"

"*I'm* not supposed to be in Sixth Heaven, but at least the Cherubim have seen me there before. If they catch you, the Archangel general's son, you'll create an inter-Heaven incident. No soldiers crossing the border, remember?"

"Then we won't get caught."

"Michael . . . "

"You think you can sneak out of here, undetected, and make it all the way to the gates of Sixth Heaven on a broken wing?"

Evangeline presses her lips together, annoyed.

"You need me to get you out and I need you to get me the information, so it's a win-win for both of us."

"I still get the book," Evangeline negotiates. She needs it, the physical book, the symbol, the *key* to show her people.

"Fine," Michael agrees. "I'll get weapons and supplies. Make your way to the shore across from the waterfall and I'll meet you there." Michael turns to leave, then spins back. He has a wry smile on his face. "You *can* sneak out of the castle without getting caught, right?"

Evangeline feels a tug on her own lips. "I think I can manage."

And she does. Ten minutes later, she's safe beside the falls, hiding behind the trees, rubbing her arms from the nip of the late-afternoon autumn air, wishing she had traveling clothes, hoping Michael gets there soon. They have a long journey ahead if they want to get to the border of Sixth Heaven by nightfall, especially because they'll have to travel on foot, since she can't fly long distances with her broken wing. It was painful enough to fly across the river. She wonders again why Raphael's *Slivers* didn't work on her.

Evangeline hears a whoosh under the thunder of the falls and

Michael swoops beside her, with a rucksack and sword for each of them. Evangeline notes with dismay that it's not Sophia's sword. Still, it's better than nothing, although when she takes it from Michael's outstretched hand, it feels hot and uncomfortable on her skin.

"You couldn't get me my own sword?" Evangeline grimaces at her discomfort.

Michael scowls at her. "Beggars can't be choosers," he snaps.

She glowers at him, but says nothing as she follows him out of the grove of trees and into the nearby glade.

She's shocked to see a sky horse grazing on the tufts of grass along the river.

"Michael, you *stole* a sky horse?" she asks. She stares, awed by the silver-gray animal, larger than its land cousins, with its gorgeous iridescent wings and soft, silky fur. Evangeline has never seen a more beautiful creature. It's as if he shimmers in the weak daylight. "Now for *sure* we'll get caught."

Michael juts his chin out in mock offense. "I did not *steal* him. Icarus happens to be mine. He came with the troops this morning."

"But your father will know you're gone."

"Evie, my father will know I'm gone the second he tries to get into Madame Hariel's quarters. We might as well have some advantages. Besides, Icarus will get us there much faster than walking."

Michael brushes past her, out into the air, and Evangeline follows. She has to admit that her wing does feel better after Raphael's medicine, although it's not healed. She lands beside Icarus as Michael strokes his nose. He helps her up onto Icarus's back, and she clings to his thick mane, trying to hide her nerves. Commoners don't own, don't fly sky horses; they are a luxury of the rich.

Michael mounts easily behind her. She's hyperaware of his proximity, but then decides her reasons are practical; if she falls from

Icarus, she fears her wings won't sustain her and she'll plummet to the ground.

Michael nudges Icarus with the heel of his boot, and with a deft motion as smooth as an eagle, they take to the sky. Michael guides Icarus low on the treetops until they are a good distance downriver. Then, with the school behind them, Michael urges the winged creature high into the sky. Evangeline feels the rush of the sharp wind on her cheeks as they climb, and she loves it. She loves the speed, and Icarus's smoothness and the rhythmic beating of his vast wings. She eases her grip on his mane and settles in for the flight.

They carry on at a good clip, occasionally checking behind them, but no Archangels are on their tail. Evangeline worries about that, thinking Michael has set her up for a trap, but it's too late now. Whatever will happen, will happen.

They take longer to get to the border of Sixth Heaven than normal, because Michael skirts around Fifth Heaven villages and keeps wide of the riverbank. Evangeline thinks the added precautions are worth the extra time, and appreciates Michael's caution. She can't bear the thought of the book falling into the wrong hands.

When they finally land near the border, it is already dusk.

They are in a field of late-season wildflowers, a thick bouquet of glowing amber, goldenrod, and burnt orange stalks bordering a small river. It would seem like an easy task to cross the water and arrive in Sixth Heaven, but the lands and sky are invisibly sealed off with a Divinity Shield. Evangeline isn't sure how the system works—she could never persuade Uncle Raziel to tell her—but now she wonders if some sort of *Sliver* is involved. If Raphael has a spark of divinity, surely there must be others who have it, too?

Regardless, it's not what the barrier is, but getting through it that matters.

"Better we wait till after dark," Evangeline suggests.

"But your father's soldiers have been known to haunt this region; are you sure we're safe here?"

Evangeline is about to answer yes, of course, because even if they see Lucifer's army, she's his daughter—until she remembers that may no longer be enough. Instead she shrugs. "We'll be well-hidden in the rock outcropping."

They make their way to a circle of thick, vertical stones, placed here by unknown angels long before recorded time. They remind Evangeline of Siog Glen in the Farlands, a place sprinkled with the spirit of sacredness. Like the rocks in Evangeline's glen, no one knows why their ancestors arranged the stones in this way, although an abundance of theories abound. Evangeline's favorite is that the circle was home to a species of fairies and the ancient angels were protecting them from the violent djinn, who, at that time, still shared the Heavens. Fairies, of course, don't exist—but then, Evangeline never believed a book with the power to destroy the Heavens was real and yet it sits heavy in her pocket, so maybe there are tiny, winged creatures who live nearby.

Michael and Evangeline settle against the rocks, while Icarus grazes inside the circle. Michael pulls out a loaf of bread and a chunk of cheese, splitting each in half.

"I know all the ways into and out of the kitchens," Michael says, taking a bite.

Evangeline smiles. "You think there have ever been any angels who actually followed all the rules at Diaga?"

"Rules were made to be broken," Michael replies.

They eat in a companionable silence and for the first time in more than a week, Evangeline feels herself relaxing. It's true they're in for a challenge, getting into Sixth Heaven, translating the book, then figuring out what to do with the information, but for the moment, while they wait for nightfall, Evangeline values the breather.

She finds herself leaning into Michael, telling herself it's for warmth, since the air is cooling as the sun drops in the sky, and he wraps his arms around her, pulling her close. For a moment, Evangeline feels it's only the two of them in these vast Heavens, only Evie and Michael, not Lucifer's daughter or Gabriel's son. She wishes they could carry on like this, wishes they could move forward without dragging the past with them. And for a moment, Evangeline imagines how it would be if they could. She'd change all the rules of the Heavens, and open up Sixth Heaven and the Cherubim archives to everyone. She'd live there with Michael in a cottage, as a family, and then she'd finally discover her *thin place*, where a touch of her uncle Raziel's sense of the Divine, the source of his calm tranquility, would break through the veil between God and Evangeline.

"You know you have to renounce him, right?" Michael says softly.

Evangeline tenses and sits up. "What?"

"If you want to save your people, you have to distance yourself from Lucifer."

Evangeline bristles at Michael's gall, and she scoots away from him.

"You know I'm right, Evie," Michael says quietly. "You've seen what he does. He's a monster."

The description may be accurate, Evangeline realizes, but she can't bear to hear it from Michael.

"Your people made him that way," she snaps back at him. "I know his story. You Dominions made it impossible for him to showcase his full talents as an Archangel."

"*My* people?" Michael's voice rises in indignation. "*My* father was the *only* one who stuck his neck out, time and again for *your* father. And *you*," he adds, in a huff of frustration.

"My father is a product of his environment," Evangeline insists. "Simply because everyone else turned their backs on him, doesn't mean I will."

"After everything you've *seen*? How can you be so blind?"

"I'm not blind! In fact, I see more clearly than you, because I *know* there's more to my father than you'll ever see. And if he's taken a dark turn, it's because he was forced to."

"You can't make excuses for him, Evie. He's evil."

But he wasn't always, Evangeline thinks. *He wasn't always this way, violent and cruel.*

Which means that maybe he doesn't have to stay this way . . .

"You're wrong," Evangeline tells Michael in a determined whisper. "And I'll prove it to you."

She doesn't know how and she doesn't know when, but after she learns about the secrets in the book, she'll seek out her father, and then hear him out, and then set him straight. The man she grew up with, the loving, attentive father, must still be a part of him. He's gone down a dark path, yes, she acknowledges, but that doesn't mean he's stuck there. She thinks of the last violet Naofa feather she gave her father that was meant to bestow on him her blessing for deep passion and insight. If she could remind him of how to use that passion for good, then maybe she could redeem him. And if anyone can redeem Lucifer, it's going to be her.

His daughter.

CHAPTER 14

The night is cold. The biting wind swirls through the circle of rocks where Evangeline and Michael hide, chilling Evangeline to the bone. The frigid air is no surprise, given how high in the mountains they are, but Evangeline nonetheless longs for a cozy hearth and a blazing fire.

And an end to this infernal journey.

She remembers the thrill of anticipation she felt flying out of the Farlands and through the rest of First Heaven. She'd nurtured a sense of mission, of moral purpose to find and protect her father. Six days and six heavens later, Evangeline has not only *not* found her father, but no longer aims to protect him. And she doesn't know how this is going to end. Whatever optimism she had—about finding the Key, about redeeming her father—all seems to have dissipated in the cold night air. The book, she now thinks, is just a book. If it does contain magical or mystical powers, she doubts she's the angel to reveal its secrets. Whatever she's led Michael to believe, she now holds out little hope that she'll be able to decipher the Enochian text.

Evangeline digs out of her rucksack the wool blanket Michael snagged from the school and wraps it tightly around her shoulders. As she does, she feels the hard lump of her uncle's mysterious iron key sitting heavy in her pocket. Another reason to dismay. She's no closer to learning what it is or why her uncle planted it among the school's books, and as a result, she feels she's let Raziel down. He sacrificed his *life* to protect this key and entrust her with its existence, yet she is no closer to understanding its importance than she was when she first pulled it off the shelf. She tries to tell herself that she's had little time to contemplate its meaning, but the excuse leaves her little comfort.

Evangeline curls up against a cold rock, trying to stay out of the wind. She's supposed to sleep; she needs to relieve Michael on watch soon, but as exhausted as she is, she can't keep her eyes closed. When she does, her imagination fills her with dread: Gabriel's army descending on them and taking her prisoner, or her father's army descending on them and taking her prisoner . . .

She appreciates that her fate and Michael's have already been set in motion. She and Michael did that the minute they fled the school. It won't be long before one army or the other finds them, and now Evangeline regrets the circuitous route she and Michael took to get to the border. If they'd risked being seen, they could have landed before dark and swum underwater in the river, bypassing the Divinity Shield. Instead, they sit all night, exposed, waiting for the first break of day. If only she knew the waters better, if only she trusted herself to navigate the shallows so they could avoid both the rocks below and the Divinity Shield above, they could have risked it. But she is a coward.

"Not cowardly," Michael assured her when she vented her frustrations deep into the cold night, "Prudent."

"Same thing," she muttered, but was secretly glad Michael didn't push her. As much as she didn't want to sit around, she was more terrified of crossing the border underwater in the pitch black.

Evangeline sighs. She gives up on sleep. She stands and stretches, the freezing wind nipping at her cheeks. She eases her way to the outside of the rock circle, where Michael sits, alert.

"Go rest, Evie," Michael says softly. "I'll get you when I can't keep my eyes open."

"Can't sleep," Evangeline replies. She settles next to Michael, over-looking the plains. The night is thick; there are no stars, as if they were candles long ago extinguished.

She shivers, and Michael pulls her close. She's grateful for his warmth and for a sad moment, she wishes this is how it could always be, sitting close to someone who cares.

He leans his head on her shoulders, and she feels the weight of his fatigue. She doesn't want to, but forces herself to nudge him.

"Get some sleep," she tells Michael.

And despite her insistence, she's disappointed when he disentangles himself from her and fades back into the circle of rocks.

The result is that she feels more alone now than ever. With the thick pall of night, she feels shrouded in darkness as if she is the only angel to exist in all the heavens. There is not a sound, not even Icarus, tucked safely among the rocks. She hears only the whistling of the wind, which adds to her sense of isolation.

But she is lulled by this illusion because when she hears the snap of a twig, she is startled with fear. She strains her eyes, but sees only black, and she strains her ears, but hears only wind. She wonders, for a moment, whether she imagined the crack, but she's far too well trained. Her hand tightens on the hilt of her sword as she presses against the hard rock. Her heart hammers in her chest as her nerves tingle. She thinks to rouse Michael—maybe he heard it? He didn't leave her long ago—but no sound emanates from the inside of the circle.

She waits for a long moment, readying for an attack, but it never comes. After a while, her heart slows; it can't take the adrenaline much longer, and she eases her grip on her sword. She must have imagined it, the sound, the snap. Or maybe she didn't, but it was a scurrying mouse or a jackrabbit hopping across the field. Besides, she tells herself, if it were Gabriel's Archangels or her father's army, there would be a thunder of noise. No, she reasons, she and Michael haven't yet been found.

Snap!

Evangeline's heart leaps into her throat. She whirls toward the sound, but still there is only the night's inky blackness.

"Michael," she croaks, because her fear overrides her pride that she can take care of herself.

"Yes, do let's call for your boyfriend," an ominous disembodied voice speaks.

Evangeline's blood runs cold. She straightens; her every muscle is taut. She can't see the speaker; there is still only a cloak of heavy darkness, but the voice sounds oddly, vaguely, familiar.

A shadow steps out of the black night, close enough to her that she can smell his fermented breath. With a deft swing of utter terror, Evangeline lashes out with her sword, but she catches only air. She hears a cackle, to her left, and she strikes again, but this time, her sword is plucked from her hand. Defenseless, she shrieks in panic as the figure looms over her.

Then she feels Michael by her side, but her relief is short-lived. She hears the clang of swords, a brief, aborted scuffle and Michael's pierced cry of frustration as a sword clatters to the stone. Michael backs into her, protective.

A flick of a flint; the spark of a flame, and a torch comes to life. Behind the fire is a terrifying, grotesque distortion of her father's face.

The djinni.

Michael grips her arm defensively, but Evangeline knows there is no use. They beat the djinni last time with the element of surprise—and swords. Now, they have neither.

"Neecy," the djinni drawls, his voice reed thin and high-pitched. Evangeline shudders, recognizing the same word the djinni had called her before.

"Who—" Evangeline's voice cracks with fear. Who *is* he? She wants to ask. What does he want? And how did he find them?

The djinni's sharp cheekbones cast long shadows over his pale face in the flickering flame of the torch, and against the shadows of the night, his ears, more pointed than an angel's, seem to Evangeline like horns. He is a frightful beast, but something in his movement—a momentary jerk, a too-quick flick of his head—makes Evangeline thinks his gestures are studied.

"Who am I?" the djinni sneers. She catches a hint of her father's inflection in his voice, but it is faint, like an echo.

It's all too much for Evangeline. A djinni who looks like her father and tries to sound like him? A demon from the UnderRealm here in her world who *knows* her?

She lashes out, calculating her surprise. He has not attacked, which means he wants or needs something from her—otherwise she and Michael would be dead. She throws herself at him, but Michael seems to have anticipated her reaction, and holds her back by the waist.

"Impulsive, like your father," the djinni says and laughs.

"How do you know my father?" Evangeline is shaking, from adrenaline, from anger, from fear. *How do you* look *like my father?* That's the question she truly wants to ask.

"Oh, old Lucifer and I go way back." the djinni again cackles.

The djinni is making no sense. Djinn live in the UnderRealm, sealed long ago from the Heavens. Djinn can't come here and angels can't venture into the UnderRealm, so what is this creature playing at?

"I am Balam," the djinni sweeps his arm wide, but if he is attempting gallantry, it rings false to Evangeline. He has no grace to the movement, no flow or smoothness, not like her father, and it dawns on Evangeline that she's watching a stilted version of Lucifer. She's seen this before, angels trying to imitate her father, in vain efforts to impress or intimidate others. She's noticed new recruits and experienced generals both study Lucifer's movements, as if they believed they could unravel the secrets of his charm by simulation alone. Her observations about Balam's behavior embolden her.

"What do you want?" she demands.

"To help you, Neecy." And here, Balam, seems to slip into his fearful natural register.

Evangeline leans back into Michael, grateful he hasn't yet let go.

The djinni slips his hand under his cloak and, with a drawn-out movement—all Balam, no Lucifer, Evangeline notes—reveals a dark leather and metal band.

Evangeline gasps.

Her uncle's Divinity Cuff.

The bracelet that all Cherubims wear to pass through the Divinity Shield into and out of Sixth Heaven.

The ones only the Cherubim are allowed to possess.

And Evangeline recognizes it's her uncle's; each Cherubim cuff has its own distinctive design, reflective of its wearer's personality. Uncle Raziel's has an intricate pattern of crisscrossing ovals, a continuous band of infinity rings.

Evangeline feels as if she's been punched, the pain of seeing her uncle's precious cuff in the hands of this grotesque monster is so great. A rage boils within, like the anger she felt against this djinni the first time or when she attacked Zephon. Her hands clench into a fist, as her body stiffens against Michael's grasp. But as she strains against his hold, he doesn't release her.

"Where did you get that?" she seethes, her body coiled, ready to strike.

And then a thought hits her. Did *he*, this djinni, kill her uncle? He looks like Lucifer, so perhaps in Raziel's excruciating pain he mistook the demon for her father. It would explain how Balam got the cuff. And with the thought that her father couldn't have committed such a heinous crime after all, comes a rush of welcome relief. Her father isn't, can't be, the monster the Archangels have made him out to be.

Or is that only what she hopes? She's desperate to believe in her father again. She's worshipped him as her hero for eighteen years; she's only seen his dark side for the last six days. So is it possible this djinni—and *not* her father—actually killed her uncle? Or is she clinging to false hope?

"How can you help us?" Michael asks.

Balam dismissively twirls the band around his finger. "I believe you need this to cross into Sixth Heaven."

"And you're going to give us a pass," Michael replies, dripping with sarcasm.

The djinni laughs, and to Evangeline it sounds like shards of glass scraping in her ear.

"I'm going to escort you," Balam says, smiling widely in a horrid grimace.

Evangeline frowns. "But djinn don't need cuffs or anything else to pass through barriers," she says, remembering her father's stories. Their ability to dissipate, an ability given to them by God instead of wings on an angel, made the djinn a formidable foe. There are only two barriers through which they cannot pass: the veil between

Heaven and the UnderRealm, and the reinforced cast iron lamps in which they can be imprisoned.

"Need and want are extraordinarily different, little Neecy," he replies.

"Why will you help us?" Evangeline asks. She doesn't trust him, of course she doesn't, but she's thinking of the book. It was always a risk that their waterproofing efforts would fail, trying to cross into Sixth Heaven underwater. It would be much safer to cross on land or in the air and safeguard the book. But is the risk worthwhile if both she and Michael end up dead?

"Our interests align," Balam answers cryptically.

"How?" Michael demands.

"The Commoners," he says.

This surprises Evangeline. The last thing she expected to hear from this demon's lips is the name of her people. She narrows her eyes, distrustful.

"We djinn have a lot in common with you," he says to Evangeline, purposely ignoring Michael.

At this, Evangeline laughs, a derisive snort. The demon djinn whose civil wars almost destroyed the heavens share *nothing* with her persecuted people.

"Are you not being banished to God's new Earth? How is it different than our exile to the UnderRealm?"

At first Evangeline blusters at the comparison—but then she wonders, she fears, is Balam right? Not the reasons for banishment, obviously—Commoners are being persecuted unjustly because of prejudice and hate, whereas the djinn were destructive—but the end result is the same. The thought worries her more than she cares to admit.

"Don't listen to him," Michael pushes himself in front of Evangeline, as if he can guard against the djinni's words.

But words are an insidious weapon, and Balam's poison slips into her head. She knows he is using her in a way she doesn't yet understand, and she knows not to believe him, but she can't help herself. She can't unhear what he's said.

Balam continues, his voice reed thin. "*I* understand you, Neecy, better than this, this . . . " Here he shakes his head at Michael with scorn. " . . . this insolent boy."

"Hey!" Michael cries, and this time he readies for a fight while Evangeline holds him back. She's insulted, too, of course.

But is he right?

The thought terrifies Evangeline, but how can she deny it? Michael has lived in soft comfort his whole life, knowing who he is, where he belongs. Never has he experienced looks filled with daggers and words filled with scorn. But the djinn have, long before their banishment and subsequent war to reclaim their rightful place in the Heavens.

Rightful place in the Heavens . . .

Oh God . . . that's what the Commoners are trying to do.

She looks at Balam, his sharp features shadowing his face in the flickering torchlight, then to Michael, whose face glows with a righteous indignation—one that Evangeline believes he hasn't earned. Who is he to feel all virtuous when *his* people have done nothing but mistreat hers?

"Evangeline," Michael turns to her, "Don't let him get in your head. You know I'm on your side."

Except that's the thing. She doesn't know whose side *she's* on anymore—because she doesn't know which sides there *are* anymore. Her father, who seems to be a demon in his own right? Commoners like Zephon who scorn her because she's different? Gabriel and the Archangels who defend the unjust status quo? Or Balam, a djinni who has appeared inexplicably in their midst for reasons unknown? She preferred the simplicity of her old life: there was one set of good angels—Commoners—and one set of bad angels—everyone else.

But now the lines have blurred. The problem is, she still has to choose.

"We go with him," Evangeline finally decides.

"What?! *No*, Evie," Michael pleads. "He's bad news."

"Who has my uncle's cuff," she replies. It's not an answer, it's an excuse, but it's all she's got right now.

"Evie, we can't trust him," Michael says, staring at Balam, daring him.

"Like we can't trust your father?" Evangeline retorts. "Or trust mine?"

She takes a deep breath, trying to rein in her emotions. She feels she's at her breaking point; her nerves are frayed to the thinnest thread. She is keenly aware that she could be making the biggest mistake—Balam tried to kill her only three days ago—but given their circumstances, she thinks it's the best way forward.

"I'm sticking with my plan, Michael, to get to Uncle Raziel's," she says, expecting Michael to understand she means how important it is to learn the contents of the book. "If Balam takes us through the Divinity Shield, we can fly on Icarus and get there faster."

"*If* we get there—" Michael starts, but he's interrupted by the sound of a low rumble. They all hear it; Evangeline sees both Michael and Balam turn toward the sound. It's off in the distance, like slow-rolling thunder, but it's real.

And it's coming.

Evangeline recognizes it. It is the approaching sound of trampling hooves. She doesn't know which army it is—Gabriel's or Lucifer's—but whoever finds them first is irrelevant. If they are caught, the book disappears along with every hope she has of a resolution—whatever that may be.

"Michael, *now*," she hisses.

Michael looks at her, casts a glance at Balam, then returns his gaze to her face.

"Please, Michael," she whispers. "You say you're on *my* side."

And when Michael finally nods, Evangeline is filled with relief because she was terrified to go alone with Balam although she's convinced that's what they have to do.

"Icarus can only carry two riders," Michael says as he scampers behind the rocks to retrieve the sky horse, who whinnies at the sight of Balam, which does little to reassure Evangeline she made the right decision.

"You and Balam," Evangeline promptly answers. "I'll fly beside you. As long as I'm holding Balam's hand, I'll get through the Shield, too."

She thinks of her uncle's warm hand, the one she wrapped her own fingers around whenever they crossed into Sixth Heaven, and a surge of nausea washes over her at the thought of clinging to this demonic creature. "But your wing—" Michael counters.

"Is more than Balam has," Evangeline interjects, "so he needs to be on the horse, and you know Icarus won't be guided by me, which leaves you."

"Then you can't let go of Balam," Michael warns her, and Evangeline appreciates that he doesn't argue.

"Promise me you won't either," she replies, with a pointed nod to the djinni.

Michael brings his horse outside of the rock circle, and motions—with great reluctance, Evangeline understands—for Balam to mount. The djinni swings his legs expertly over the horse—do they exist in the UnderRealm?—and settles himself with a gentle pat to Icarus's mane. The horse quiets immediately, which Evangeline can see Michael bristle at. She guesses Michael would rather fight a bucking sky horse through the Divinity Shield then have his own beloved horse be so passive toward such an enemy as Balam.

As Michael takes to the air on Icarus, Evangeline flies up beside them. Her wing hurts, but nothing like before Raphael's healing potion. Besides, it won't be long; crossing the border will take only a few seconds. All she has to do is fly up, hold onto Balam as they pass through the invisible barrier, then land on the other side of the river and part ways with the djinni.

She hopes.

The cold night air is still coal-black. She can't see the river below, but she hears the crescendoing sound of trampling hooves, a rolling thunder of horses, gaining on the rocks where they were hiding only a moment ago. She can't see the army, but she takes no comfort in the fact that they also wouldn't be able to see her in the thick cloak of night. Instead, she reaches for Balam, wishing they were already on the other side and she could be rid of him. Still, Evangeline isn't foolish; she's careful not to get too close to Icarus's whomping wings and understands the dangers. She can't take a chance on guessing where the Divinity Shield begins, so when Balam offers his outstretched hand, the one on which her uncle's cuff is securely fastened, Evangeline knows she must take it. Yet still she hesitates before touching him. It feels wrong—it *is* wrong—to ally with this djinni, but she has to do this.

Balam's hand is cold to the touch and his skin is coarse, calloused. Instinctively, she wants to pull away, but she wills herself to hold on. She can barely see Michael in the pall of night, but she imagines his revulsion at placing a hand on the djinni's shoulder.

Evangeline takes a second to look below her. She thinks she can now make out the advancing troops, although she's still unsure whose army it is. She sees that they're closing in hard and fast on the rock circle, and tells herself that she made the right choice.

Then she feels it, a crackle in the air. It's familiar to her, the barely-discernable hum of energy. She's always been wary when she approaches the Divinity Shield, even with her trusted uncle. The thought of a sudden, incapacitating zap always scared her. She'd press closer to Uncle Raziel and he'd wrap a protective arm around her whenever they passed through the barrier. Now, though, she's at the mercy of a demon who once tried to kill her, with her own body an arm's length away from the necessary protection of the cuff.

With the cuff, it's obvious when they're passing through the Divinity Shield. The air around them thins, and for an instant, it is hard to breathe. Evangeline always feels a chill, too, although she doesn't know if that's the actual effect of the shield or her worry. She wonders, too, if crossing in the air the way they are, far from the usual gates, will make the passage worse.

But it's okay. Icarus flies on without missing a beat of his wings, and she hears no screams from Michael, so she assumes he's grasping tight to the djinni.

And then her hand slips down Balam's fingers and her heart rises to her throat. She scrambles to tighten her grip—but she can't.

Because Balam is twisting his hand out of hers.

He's strong; it takes him no more than half a second to release her completely. The betrayal is so fast and so sudden that her scream cannot escape her mouth before she is untethered. A million dis-jointed thoughts crash through her head in an instant. She's going to die, she's going to kill Balam, she's never going to live this down with Michael, she's never going to read the book, she's never going to see her father again.

She tenses, her whole body rigid in anticipation of the shock, but it never comes. Michael and Balam and Icarus beat on, as she scrambles to fly after them. The air is full again; the hum diminishes. They're through the barrier.

Shaking, Evangeline gasps in a full breath. Had she passed through the Divinity Shield *alone*? Without getting zapped?

No, that's impossible. She must have miscalculated. They must have made it through the shield—barely—before Balam shook her off.

"Land here," she shouts to Michael, because she has to get on the ground. Her head is spinning and her wing aches. She needs to stop. She needs to regroup.

Michael complies, and the moment Icarus's hooves skim the ground, Michael pushes Balam off his horse. Evangeline uses the moment of distraction to swipe back her sword and Michael's and she rounds on Balam in the now-graying wane of night, holding the sharp tip to his thick neck. Swords and surprise.

"Get *away* from us," Evangeline says. Her voice is shaky. She tries to steady it; she needs to stay in control.

Balam takes a step back, his hands raised as if in surrender. But his actions, seemingly submissive, sit uneasily with Evangeline. It's the quiet little smile on his face, the glint in his eye that worries her. It's as if he's enjoying this. Like he expected it.

"But of course, milady," Balam gives a false bow. "Off you go."

Michael taps Evangeline on the shoulder, indicating he's covering her as she unsteadily mounts Icarus. She keeps her sword trained in Balam's direction, but he doesn't move. Michael maneuvers the sky horse into the air, where they are safe from their wingless enemy.

"Remember who helped you, Neecy!" the djinni calls after them.

Yes, Evangeline will remember him. She'll remember the twist of his wrist, abandoning her to the killing energy of the Divinity Shield.

Which she did not feel.

Why did she not feel the zap?

And *why* in Heavens' name, Evangeline also wonders, does Balam keep calling her by another name?

"Remember whose side I'm on!" Balam says.

As she and Michael rise into the morning light, Evangeline wants to ignore Balam. But she realizes, with an anxiety-fueled dread, that there is so much more she doesn't yet understand. It's unnerving, being aware of secrets without access to their meaning. All she can hope is that the book will contain answers to all her questions.

CHAPTER 15

The Cherubims' monastery is a vast complex of ancient stone buildings and elaborate courtyards. Evangeline always thought it seemed much too large for the ten Cherubim and their attendants who lived and worked there, but Uncle Raziel had explained how the compound had been designed for dozens more, back when the Cherubim were a formal religious order instead of the Divine Record Keepers they are today. In those days, once an angel was accepted into the Order and entered through the gates, he or she never left.

"But angels aren't meant to live in isolation," he'd say, which is why he said he loved to visit her in Fifth Heaven so much.

Evangeline thought her uncle had it all wrong. She remembered thinking she would never leave these peaceful walls, filled with serene silences, especially not to return to a school where she constantly had to watch her back. The idea of losing herself in either Uncle Raziel's vast personal library or the more massive Cherubim archives was seductive in the extreme. But when she confessed her longing to her uncle one time, he shook his head sadly.

"The monastery is not a place to hide from the world," he said.

"*You* do that," Evangeline said, stung by the gentle rebuke—especially because she knew he was right about her motivation.

Uncle Raziel put his arm around Evangeline and gave her a tight squeeze. "I may live here, but I'm not hiding here," he said.

Now as Evangeline and Michael approach the gates on foot, with Icarus safely hidden in the forest, she wonders what would have happened had she convinced her uncle to let her stay with him. She never would have returned home to the Farlands, never would have joined her father's war efforts, never would have fought for her people—the very people, it seems, who don't want her. Would her uncle still be alive if she'd been allowed to remain? He left to seek out her father, to help her and her family and her people, and he ended up dead. What if he'd never needed to venture out? Would he still be alive?

She's sickened by the thought that Uncle Raziel died because of her. Being here, at his home, brings that truth into stark, painful reality. It's surreal for her to be in these gardens without him. It feels wrong.

That's because it is wrong. This whole situation is wrong. Her uncle's death is wrong, her having the Assembly book is wrong, being here with Michael is wrong. Wrong, wrong, wrong.

And yet here she is.

"How do we get in without being seen?" Michael whispers. They've stopped behind a tall, meticulously sculpted hedge at the edge of an ornate, palatial garden, a labor of love by one of her uncle's Cherubim colleagues. Every Cherubim is impressive in so many more ways than just their superior scholarly skills—it's why she laughed when Uncle Raziel first floated that idea that in the future, she could be chosen a Cherubim. She might be good with a sword, but that skill isn't necessary in a protected Heaven like this.

"We walk through the gate," Evangeline answers.

She can feel Michael stare at her as she keeps her gaze on the wrought-iron gate straight ahead.

"You're kidding. You said yourself I'll cause an inter-Heaven riot if the Cherubim see me here," Michael says.

Evangeline turns to him with a wry smile. "I think you and I already have. Your father's army or my father's army—or both—are on the border of Sixth Heaven as we speak. The book is everything, and everyone thinks it's here. It won't be long before they find a way in."

"But we still need time to translate the Enochian," Michael says.

"That's why we'll wait for the matins," Evangeline explains. "At the toll of the dawn's bell, they'll all head to the chapel for prayer." The Cherubim may no longer be an official religious Order, but traditions die hard. It's one reason why, despite her fantasies of a scholarly life, Evangeline was relieved to know her uncle was wrong about the possibility of her being chosen as a Cherubim. It would never happen, and that's all for the better. She'd hate to live around angels who constantly praise an unjust God who abandons and exiles His people.

It's not long before they hear the melodic chimes of the church bells ring out across the monastery. They wait a few more minutes, time for the Cherubim to make their way to the chapel, then Evangeline beckons Michael forward. She's nervous, being out in the open, but it's less about her fear of getting caught than her fear that getting caught means this saga will never end. It's her last shot—long as it is—to end this conflict. If she can only figure out what power is in the book, then maybe she can put a stop to the war. She's still afraid she won't be able to translate the book, but since it's the only thing she can think of to do, she'd rather not be detained doing it.

Evangeline and Michael walk softly on the flagstone path, alert to suspicious sounds, but she hears only the singsong of a lark, the herald of the morning. She reaches for the heavy gate, always unlocked because there are never intruders in Sixth Heaven, and it squeaks when she pushes, but no Cherubim appear. Evangeline leads Michael through a maze of courtyards and walkways, past the massive dome of the Divine Archives to her uncle's quarters at the far corner of the compound. Evangeline exhales when they reach his door, as her heart flutters with grief. Never again will Raziel walk through these doors; never again will he set his own eyes on his beloved library, and the guilt that Evangeline *can* weighs heavily on her.

She grasps the door latch and opens it. She steps into the airy chamber, large and spacious, albeit sparsely furnished, and stops dead in her tracks.

There, sitting comfortably in her uncle's cushioned chair in the nook that is his library, is her father.

"Ah, my sweet Evangeline," Lucifer says and languidly eases himself off the chair, strolling over as if he were expecting her.

Her limbs freeze and her heart beats double-time. Her mind reels—here is her father, in her uncle's sacred space.

Again, it all seems *wrong*.

And yet, this was her mission, she remembers. To find and protect her father from Michael and Gabriel and their army. She is here, but now she's aligned with Michael against her father.

Lucifer cups her chin in his hands, like he did before they last parted, and kisses her on her cheek.

And she lets him.

Her logical brain cries out in revulsion, but her emotional mind cannot make the connection. In front of her isn't a murderer, a demon, a monster, but her *father*. The angel who scooped her up into his lap and read her bedtime stories, who stroked her hair when she awoke from nightmares, and who brought her brimming cups of hot tea before she had to ask, *that's* her father.

She thinks again of the djinni who resembles Lucifer, again thinking that maybe Raziel was mistaken about the identity of his killer.

"Oh, my sweet daughter, you came all this way to protect me." Lucifer drops his hand from Evangeline's face, and she instantly misses the warmth of his hands on her skin.

Evangeline blinks away, consumed with guilt. How does she respond? *Yes, Father, I was terrified you'd be killed by your archenemy in your quest to retrieve the Key to the Kingdom that will free our people, so I came to warn you, but then I saw evidence of your cruelty, especially when my own uncle, whom you know I loved, revealed on his deathbed that you were his killer, so I then teamed up with the son of your enemy to stop you.*

But she is a child again, an acolyte at the feet of her hero, desperate for his approval, so she nods.

"You are so brave, my dear. A true leader."

It's what Evangeline always wanted to hear, that she could live up to her father's greatness. Living in the magnificent Lucifer's shadow was a privilege she accepted but also a burden she was loathe to admit. She could never compete with his charm, his charisma, his talent, his bravery. By the time he was a bit older than she is now, Lucifer had already single-handedly defeated the djinn; all she's ever done is wield a sword in training. So to hear her father admire her accomplishments—despite defying his orders to remain in the Farlands and rally their people—should have filled Evangeline with a warmth beyond measure.

And yet, she feels hollow. Because she believes the praise is not earned? No, in fact, the title "leader" sits surprisingly well with her. It conveys a sense of confidence she never believed she possessed, and it's true she's not sure what she's doing, but ever since she found the book, *she's* taken control. Right or wrong, she's making decisions. To hide the book from Gabriel, to plan how to translate it, to accept Balam's help in getting here . . .

Because her faith in her father is shaken.

"Michael," Lucifer nods civilly to him. "I hear you've been invaluable to Evangeline. I hear you saved her life. Thank you."

She feels Michael stiffen beside her, and she, too, feels tense. If he is referring to their fight with the djinni, how does her father know about that?

Lucifer, languid in his movements, saunters back to Raziel's chair as if he owns the place, and it rankles Evangeline. She bristles at his conceit. This is her *uncle's* place; whether he's dead or not, her father should show more respect.

Lucifer settles in and waves an arm, inviting them to join him. Evangeline doesn't move, but Lucifer shows no sign of offense.

"I expect you have a lot of questions," he says. He picks up a pipe—*Raziel's* pipe—and twirls it absently in his hands.

Evangeline's head swirls with questions, and has since she left the Farlands a week ago. Every day, every stop, every Heaven added more and more questions. *Why do Sidriel and Christie think you've starved them? What do you know about this djinni Balam? Who is he? How did you learn about the book being the Key to the Kingdom?* But ultimately, there's only one question she needs to know.

"Did you kill Uncle Raziel?" she asks.

Evangeline holds her breath. She understands the next words out of her father's mouth will change everything.

Or maybe everything has already changed.

Lucifer stares at her with a strange, detached curiosity. He cocks his head and she thinks—imagines?—he looks at her as if she is a new creature whom he is sizing up.

Then he answers: "Yes."

There it is. The confession straight from her father's very own mouth. And yet his tone is so benign, as if he is responding to a request for tea. In that one syllable Evangeline hears no remorse or guilt or shame.

But the word has the power of an arrow. It strikes her heart, piercing it with an intensity she fears her heart will not be able to withstand. That one small word steals from her any remaining hope she had about her father, about his innocence, about his character. That one small word strips away Evangeline's dreams of his redemption. And that one small word tears apart her every childhood memory. Who *is* this monster who raised her? And who, then, is *she*, to have been raised by such a demon?

She senses Michael grip her shoulder, but she feels separate from the touch, as if she is disembodied, no longer herself.

"Why?" It's a breath, more than a whisper, but part of her doesn't want an answer. No answer could be sufficient to explain away the cruelty to which her father has only now admitted.

"I'm so sorry, honey, I truly am, but there was no alternative," Lucifer says.

Evangeline's jaw drops—not only because of the outrageous *lie* of that statement, but also because she thinks he actually believes it.

"Raziel found the book," Lucifer explains calmly. He leans against the cushions, his voice low, as if he were recounting a sad storybook tale. "You know the book, don't you, Evangeline? The book that is in fact the Key to the Kingdom? I have you to thank for that. Do you remember the sketch you drew so long ago? The one with the key? You told me it came from Raziel's plethora of legends about the Assembly of Angels's book—and that's when it hit me. The power of the kingdom never had to reside in an *actual* key. I never believed in that." He finishes with an air of smug superiority.

Evangeline listens to this, still at the door, still frozen. She remembers the drawing she brought home in her second year at Diaga. The picture of the key was on the cover of one of Raziel's many books on the myths and legends of the Assembly and its *Slivers*, but it was the image itself that fascinated her, because of its size, its detail, not so much the stories held beneath its cover. She chose to draw the sketch for its artistic merits; never did she ever dream it was the beginning of the end.

"I approached Raziel with my theory," Lucifer continues casually.

But here again, she feels hurt that her father and uncle interacted on their own without her. She feels the sting of betrayal because *she* was the one linking the two of them; *she* should have known what was going on.

"Raziel was utterly intrigued," Lucifer says, and then he adds, wistfully, "It was so nice to have such a valuable ally."

"But you *killed* him." Evangeline marches forward, her shock, her hurt, turning to anger. She grasps the back of a chair, her fingers digging into the hard wood.

"He wouldn't give the book to me, don't you see, Evangeline?" Lucifer sounds mildly exasperated, like he's trying to explain a simple concept to a dense child. "Your Uncle Raziel had recently discovered it and said he would bring it to me. He told me that what the pages seem to reveal would not simply end this war, but forever alter the power in the Seven Heavens. You can imagine, can't you? The significance of this? I had to go—it's why I had to leave you on your birthday. But when Raziel and I met up, he didn't have the book."

For the first time, Evangeline hears frustration in Lucifer's tone, an underlying growl as if *he* had been wronged.

"He refused to reveal its whereabouts, no matter how hard I implored its importance. But then I learned that you were on your way to me, and then my path forward became clear. I'd wait for your approach and then I'd maim him so when you came across him, I knew he'd confide his secret to you—he is so predictable, that angel. Then, I'd simply follow you until you found it."

Evangeline's eyes widen in horror, in disgust. "You killed him to *manipulate* me?"

Lucifer frowns, as if realizing for the first time that Evangeline is not agreeing with his logic. "It was the only option, sweetheart. I couldn't very well put a knife to *your* throat as a way of making Raziel talk." Lucifer laughs, short and sharp.

Evangeline shakes her head. Her stomach turns, her skin prickles; she feels coated in slime. She understands, finally, that it's all true. What Sidriel and Christie said about starving out the Commoners in First Heaven, and the old angel who accused the Dragon army of attacking the refugee camp, the horror of her uncle's final revelation . . . all obscenely true. But how had she never seen this side of her father before?

"But I concede you outsmarted me at Diaga," Lucifer says, with a surprising sprinkle of admiration. "You leading me there was a brilliant strategy, a great bluff. It shows you're your own person, Evangeline. And I'm proud of you."

Evangeline cannot respond.

"And I've learned my lesson," Lucifer continues with a humility that astounds Evangeline. Her father actually believes his mistake was following Evangeline—not the wholesale slaughter of hundreds or maybe thousands of angels. "I should have confided in you in the first place," Lucifer says. "We've never had secrets before, right? But I refused to believe you were growing up. You're my little girl, my sweet angel. I never wanted to burden you with such profound issues. But I admit it. I was wrong," he says, and *bows* to her, a mea culpa Evangeline cannot *begin* to address. "And now that I see how wise and mature of a young angel you are, I come to you with a direct plea: help me find the book. I know he told you where it is."

Evangeline steps around the chair and sinks into it. This is beyond overwhelming. She feels displaced, as if her mind and body are separate. She sees herself at her father's side, listening to his macabre tale as if it is a terrifying horror story. But no, it's her own reality. *How* is that possible?

Lucifer reaches out to cover her hand with his, but this time his touch is like fire, and Evangeline recoils.

Lucifer ignores Evangeline's reaction. "It's here, I know." He sweeps his arm along the tall bookcases built into the wall.

Evangeline considers the weight of the book in her pocket, the one her father *killed* for before knowing its contents. She sees now that Gabriel and Michael were right to keep it out of Lucifer's hands. Whatever information the book contains *must* be kept away from her father.

"I don't know where it is," Evangeline says. She's not good at lying, has had little practice, and she fears her voice isn't steady enough to be convincing.

"Honey," Lucifer drawls out the endearment. "Of course you do. Otherwise you wouldn't be here."

He's wrong and Evangeline would dearly love to tell him why he's so wrong—that she already found the book and she's here only because she needs her uncle's resources to translate it, that she's *better* than what he thought—but obviously she will reveal nothing.

"Come, Evangeline, what did your uncle tell you?"

Evangeline feels the bile rise up her throat as the brutal image of her dying uncle swims before her eyes. She feels as well the sweet anger that powered her attack on the djinni Balam and her father's general Zephon. This time, she doesn't fight fury, doesn't question it. She owns it.

She lunges at her father in a blind rage, pouring out her grief and bewilderment into the strength of her hands as her fingers claw at his face. She feels the skin of his cheek tear under her nails, feels the warm drops of his blood on her hands.

"Evie!" she hears Michael cry, but she doesn't respond. She attacks with abandon for what this monster did to her uncle, to *her*.

But in an instant, she is pulled off her feet, her arms yanked behind her back, and she is trapped in her father's hold.

"Enough now, Evangeline," he says sternly, as if she were a child. "Be a good girl and settle down."

Evangeline heaves in his arms, straining to free herself, her rage still boiling over. *Good girl?* What happened to her being a wise and mature young angel? Evangeline struggles again, but her arms are pinned. A sharp pain races up to her shoulders and she lets out a yelp.

"Let her go!" Michael demands. He has his sword drawn on Lucifer, and she realizes how futile it is—as futile as her own attack. Who did she think she was to go up against a seasoned warrior like Lucifer?

More terrifying to Evangeline, though, is her own reaction. She abandoned herself to her rage, purposely trying to hurt her father, like she'd wanted to hurt Zephon and Balam. And she is ashamed.

Because it's what her father would do. Her father would inflict—has inflicted—violence and pain and now Evangeline fears she understands why.

Because it feels good. *Very* good.

Oh God, she *is* her father's daughter.

Abruptly she goes limp, and after a tense moment where she is a ragdoll in her father's arms and Michael is the picture of a shining warrior, sword held aloft, and Lucifer is a statue of confidence, her father releases her.

She falls to the ground and Michael immediately rushes to help her up.

It is the only moment Lucifer needs and it is one Evangeline fears will haunt her for the rest of her life.

Before she can blink an eye, Lucifer has pulled Michael to his feet, locked his arms around Michael's neck and pointed a sharp dagger at his throat.

Evangeline shrieks in surprise and fear. She scuttles back, terrified about how this situation has spiraled out of control.

"I may not have a knife to your throat, Evangeline," her father sneers, "but you should know that fathers don't like boyfriends."

"No," Evangeline whimpers, and is ashamed of her own squeaking voice.

She sees Michael's eyes wide with fear, and notices he's trying to control his breathing. Lucifer digs the point of his dagger into Michael's skin and draws blood. She sees Michael wince in pain, sees his face blanche, but he doesn't cry out.

"Find the book for me, Evangeline." Lucifer slices a longer line across Michael's throat and a thin red line appears.

Evangeline's stomach knots up. She catches Michael's eye, trying in one glance to convey her regret—if she hadn't attacked her father, if she had played it cool, played it off, they might have been able to stall Lucifer until they could have come up with another plan—and her determination. She'll get him out of this. But Michael's eyes read something different and it cuts her as much as her father's betrayal: defeat. The hope, the confidence she remembers seeing mirrored in his eyes even after she stabbed him, has disappeared. Instead, she sees that he expects to die; it's in his eyes and in his face.

"Don't, Evie," Michael gasps, but the effort only earns him a deeper cut.

"Stop!" she cries. "I'll find the book."

Michael tries to shake his head, but Evangeline ignores him. She will *not* let him die, not at the hands of her father, not like her Uncle Raziel.

Evangeline thinks at first to stall her father, to pretend to look through Raziel's shelves for the book, but she can't think what the delay would buy them. If anything, she fears her father may get impatient and hurt Michael more before she "finds" the book.

No, she's got to work with what she has: more knowledge than her father. She suspects he doesn't know the book is written in Enochian—he wouldn't have killed his guaranteed translator if he had—which means that in his hands, like theirs, it is powerless. And, she's betting on the fact that Lucifer wouldn't know who *does* speak Enochian, so she's hoping they can find a way to take back the book before he figures that out.

Lucifer doesn't move; his knife is still firmly pressed to Michael's throat. Evangeline saw what her father did to her uncle; she knows he's not bluffing.

"You promise you'll let him go after you get the book?" Evangeline asks, though she won't trust any answer. Instead, she's hoping he'll trust her, that she's negotiating in good faith.

"Anything for my daughter," Lucifer smiles and to Evangeline's horror, his expression seems genuine. Does he truly believe he's doing this *for* her?

Evangeline thinks about immediately pulling the book out of her cloak, but then she fears what her father would do if he knew how well she'd tricked him back at the school. She thinks, in the end, it would be better to "find" the book on Raziel's shelves.

She turns her back to her father and Michael, staring at the wall of books.

"What's the clue, Evangeline?" Lucifer says from behind her.

Evangeline draws in a deep breath. She doesn't want to reveal Raziel's last words, doesn't want him to know how Raziel outsmarted him, but her brain whirls in a fog and she can't think of another cryptic message.

"Six, six, six," she replies truthfully, painfully.

"What does that mean?"

Michael's life is on the line. Again she offers up the truth.

"Sixth bookcase, sixth shelf, sixth book," she answers.

Lucifer counts out loud, shuffling his prisoner along with him. " . . . five, six . . . "

He's giddy now, Evangeline thinks. His voice cracks and so does his smile. He thinks he's so close to his prize.

Be careful what you wish for, Father, she thinks ruefully.

Evangeline reaches up to count the shelves, and when she brings her arm down, she plucks the book from her pocket, hiding it the sleeve of her cape as she brings it up to the shelf. She twists her body into the bookshelf so Lucifer can't see the row, can't see her "pull" the book off the shelf. She has the book in her hand now, holding it as if she'd just removed it, but she hesitates. Is her idea too risky? What if Lucifer does know it's in Enochian? What if he does have another reader lined up? Whatever the secrets of the book, Michael is willing to *die* to protect them. In the hands of her father, those secrets could become powerful weapons, so maybe she shouldn't arm him.

But if she doesn't hand over the book, Michael's death is certain, whereas if she does give it to her father, there's still a chance they can pluck it from his hands before he learns, and wields, its power.

Evangeline slowly turns, her heart pounding loudly in her ears.

Please God, let this work, she thinks—then catches herself praying to a God she despises. Regardless, this would still be a good time for Him to come through.

She holds out her hand, the book resting in her palm as if on a throne. It hurts, it hurts with every fiber of her being, to give up to her father the very object her uncle died trying to protect, and she hopes that his soul, now resting in God's Realm, will forgive her.

"Please, Papa, let him go," she begs, her childhood name for him slipping out. She begins to tremble, tears welling up in her eyes at the intensity of this whole surreal situation.

Lucifer grabs the book at the same time he pushes Michael away.

"For you, my sweetness, anything," Lucifer says, and Evangeline honestly cannot make out if he is serious. But he didn't kill Michael, as he easily could have, so Evangeline wonders if there's still hope to reason with him.

Michael collapses to his knees, and Evangeline scrambles over, helping him to his feet. He presses his hand to his neck, but he nods. "I'm okay."

In silent agreement, Evangeline and Michael scurry to the door. They'll find Gabriel, Evangeline thinks, then go after her father. She prays the book will be indecipherable until then.

"Evangeline!" Lucifer's roar is loud, filled with fury.

"Run!" Michael hisses to her, but before they get the door unlatched, she hears the whizz of a blade by her ear. She can feel the displaced air on her cheek, Lucifer's dagger comes so close to her.

She still has her sword, and instantly she has it unsheathed, poised in front of her. Michael has ducked at the commotion and retrieved his own sword.

"What the hell *is* this?" Lucifer thunders, waving the book at her.

Evangeline can hardly breathe. She tells herself to take a breath, trying to slow her racing heart before she answers.

"Uncle Raziel's book," she replies, still ready to attack.

"This is gibberish," Lucifer rages. "You're tricking me!"

Evangeline turns cold. She didn't anticipate this, her father thinking *she* was manipulating him. For the first time, she fears for her life at the hands of her own father.

Evangeline sheaths her sword, and slowly walks toward him, hands held up as if in surrender.

"I swear to you," she says truthfully, "*This* is the book Raziel led me to." She's flustered, her mind whirling. Lucifer has always had a hair-trigger temper, but never before was it life-threatening—at least not toward her. Now she realizes she needs to keep him calm—or he *will* kill her, daughter or not. "Look at the cover, Papa," she pleads. "See the image? The key?"

Lucifer glances at book, then at her, and he seems marginally mollified. "What is this?" he snarls.

Evangeline remembers she's not supposed to have looked in the book, so she eases closer, holding out her hand. "May I see it?"

He strides over to her, and shoves it in front of her nose, but he doesn't release his grip on it.

The page is too close; the faint, spidery script swims before her eyes, but of course she knows what she's looking at.

"It's Enochian, Papa, the ancient language of Angels."

Lucifer roars in frustration, then thrusts it closer to her eyes. "Read it," he demands.

"I—I can't . . . " she admits, slowly backing up.

"Do it *now!*"

Evangeline trembles all over. A part of her wishes she did know how to read it so she could appease her father and escape his wrath. What will he do to her—or Michael—if he can't get his answers?

"It's too hard . . . " Evangeline says. She tries to sound confident, but instead she feels the shame of a student who has failed a simple test—and then she feels shame about that because, of course, she's not expected to know how to read Enochian.

Then in the blink of an eye, Lucifer transforms. His anger dissipates. His warm smile, his charm, return. Gently, he snaps the book closed, and hugs it to his chest.

"Sweetheart," he says, and his voice is honey, the voice he always reserved only for her. The one she always thought was genuine. She wonders now whether that, too, had been a lie. "I cannot overstate how important this is, for all of us—not only me. The answers to our survival are in these pages. With the power of this book, we can not only halt the exodus of our people to Earth, we can *transform* the Seven Heavens."

"What power, Father? What's in the book?" Evangeline worries about how much Raziel told Lucifer about the contents. She's only guessing the book speaks of the *Slivers*, but Raziel would have read the book. Raziel would have known. How much did he tell her father?

"Why, my darling," Lucifer says and smiles again. "In these pages is the secret to destroying God."

CHAPTER 16

The secret to destroying *God*?

Evangeline tries to process her father's words but since it's unfathomable—because God is infallible—she can no more absorb her father's comments than she could accept the world is at an end. The words bounce off her like a stone skipping across a still lake, because it is simply inconceivable that God can be destroyed.

Michael obviously agrees because he breaks into a guffaw. He turns to Lucifer. "You are insane, old angel," he says, and his expression morphs into a lopsided grin, one obviously intended to mock.

To her enormous surprise, Evangeline is incredibly hurt. Michael shouldn't make fun of him. Her father may be speaking nonsense, but he is not a laughing stock. He is ruthless, yes, and monstrous, as she's discovered, but he is *not* an angel to be ridiculed. He is strong and charismatic. He's one to follow or one to fear, not one to scorn.

Lucifer, however, merely gives Michael an indulgent smile, like one bestowed upon a small, simple child who should be pitied.

Evangeline can't imagine that even if what her father says is true (*how* could it be true?), her uncle would have divulged such powerful information to him, so Lucifer must be making it up. Or maybe Uncle Raziel's reading of the text was incorrect—his grasp on the Enochian language was, after all, weak. "Uncle Raziel told you that?" Evangeline asks.

"There are more things in the Heavens, Evangeline, than are dreamt of in our philosophy," he responds cryptically. "And you shall know it." He waves the book at her, like a prize. "Who else understands Enochian?"

"No one," Evangeline tells him, but as she speaks, her eyes shift away from Lucifer's face.

"Honey . . . " Lucifer steps closer to her, and Evangeline stiffens. She always loved her father's closeness, his arm around her shoulders, her head leaning against his chest, but now she cringes, knowing she's been caught out in a lie.

"Who understands Enochian?" His words are slow and menacing, and Evangeline experiences a jolt of fear.

She has the answer. There are only two others: Raziel's Cherubim colleague Dana, who shares her uncle's passion and interest in ancient angelic history, and Dana's brother, a Seraphim, who would often visit his sister and Raziel for what he called "stimulating intellectual discourse." Evangeline would sometimes be in her uncle's quarters when Dana and Camael dropped by. Camael never spoke to her, never acknowledged her presence. By rights, she was not meant to be in Sixth Heaven, and she never knew how Raziel persuaded the others to tolerate her presence, but Camael seemed especially put out that a Commoner was able to flout the strict angelic hierarchy. For her part, Evangeline was sufficiently terrified by the Seraphim—an angel who had stood in the presence of *God!*—that she often hid in the nook of her uncle's library when he'd drop by with Dana. Enochian wasn't the three elders' only topic of conversation, but the challenge of the language excited them enough that they'd often spend long hours poring over the few Enochian texts in the Divine Archives.

"Why do you waste your time, Uncle?" she'd asked after one of Dana and Camael's visits. "Enochian is indecipherable." Evangeline still felt the sting of failure and frustration from an earlier tutoring session on the ancient language.

Uncle Raziel laughed. "All knowledge is indecipherable before it is learned," he reminded her. "Remember how you could not read as a tiny child, yet now the words in a book leap easily off the page at your swiftest glance."

"And Enochian leaps off the page for you?"

"Oh my goodness, no," Raziel chuckled again. "Dana and Camael, yes, I suspect. They have a keen mind for the pattern of language, much more so than me. I muddle through, but they seem to excel at it."

"*Who* understands Enochian?" Lucifer demands again, and Evangeline recognizes the low rumble of his temper. She sees him grip the dagger in his hand, then purposely cast his eyes to Michael. She wonders if they can wrench open the door and escape before Lucifer lets the knife fly, but Evangeline appreciates her father's skill. Either she or Michael may make it out, but not both of them. She imagines already the dagger whirling through the air, embedding itself deeply into one of their backs.

But if she reveals Dana's name? And if Dana does translate the book for him? Once she tells him there *is* no way to destroy God, he will kill her.

But if Evangeline offers up Camael . . . he's in Seventh Heaven, a realm completely inaccessible to any angel but the Seraphim. It's not a Divinity Shield that protects the highest Heaven, but a power beyond all angelic understanding. No one but the Seraphim, the souls of the departed and God Himself can pass through the Pearly Gates—and to Evangeline's knowledge, no angel has ever tried. So if she tells her father truthfully that Camael speaks Enochian, Lucifer's plan stops. Since he cannot gain access to Seventh Heaven, he will never learn the contents of the book.

Evangeline looks at Michael, whose hand lies on the hilt of his sword. He stares at Lucifer, his eyes sharp and focused. He is not laughing at him now.

"The Seraphim Camael," Evangeline turns toward her father. "He speaks Enochian."

Lucifer raises an eyebrow in mild surprise. Evangeline thought he'd be angrier, once he realized his plans are collapsing, and she feels a frisson run down her spine. She's missing something; what is she missing?

"Intriguing," her father says, but then seems to immediately dismisses the information. "But who here in Sixth Heaven?"

Evangeline feels a rush of panic. She glances at Michael.

"Ah, there *is* someone here," Lucifer says and Evangeline curses her unguarded expression. She's never been able to lie to her father; he's always found her out. "But you are having trouble remembering, yes?" There is a terrifying sweetness to his tone. "Then I will help. We will visit every Cherubim, and no doubt being in their presence, face-to-face with each one, will jog your memory."

Evangeline blanches as she hears Michael gasp. Her father will kill each and every one of them until they reach Dana. Now the stakes of her decision shift.

Would you risk one life to save a dozen? It's question her father often poses his troops to test how far they'll truly go. Now Evangeline has to ask herself if Dana's life is worth all the others.

"Say nothing, Evie," Michael urges. "This isn't on you."

But it *is*. It *is* on her. It may be easy for Michael to say that, to have her sacrifice the lives of the other Cherubim, but he doesn't know them, has never met them. They are her uncle's colleagues, his *friends*. How can she stand back while her own father slaughters them if she has the power to save them?

At the price of Dana's life.

A part of her wants to think that her father won't kill Dana—the Cherubim is incredibly valuable to him—but deep down, Evangeline fears Dana's value is limited. One is only valuable to Lucifer, Evangeline is beginning to understand, if one can aid him in his quest for power and domination. When Dana doesn't tell him what he wants to hear—because she can't, because it's impossible to destroy God—Lucifer will kill her.

"Very well, shall we go find our first Cherubim?" Lucifer says.

In one swift stride, he's at her side, gripping her arm so tightly she lets escape a squeal. It's not that he's hurt her, but that he's so aggressive. Evangeline has often witnessed Lucifer's cold hostility with his troops in training, but never has she experienced it herself. A piece of her, the little child inside her, crumbles.

"Michael, do join us," Lucifer says, brushing past him to reach for the door latch.

Evangeline sees the muscles in Michael's face quiver, but also the fear in his eyes. He doesn't move against Lucifer, so Evangeline assumes he also understands they're trapped.

Lucifer hauls her outside onto the stone walkway, and Michael follows.

No, she wants to cry. *Don't do this, Papa.* She wishes she could. She wishes she had the power over him that she'd always imagined. That she was Papa's little angel, that he'd do anything for her.

Another lie from her childhood.

Lucifer spots a Cherubim on the far side of the courtyard, who doesn't yet seem to see them, and yanks Evangeline in his direction. The courtyard is large; Evangeline doesn't recognize him from this distance, but if she allows Lucifer to lead them to the Cherubim, this angel will die.

"Dana," Evangeline blurts out and immediately her stomach drops. *God forgive me*, she thinks, before remembering that she cares nothing for the forgiveness of a God who forgives even the most violent of her enemies. Before she remembers her father was the one who told her to care nothing for the forgiveness of a God who forgives even the most violent of their enemies. Evangeline's head swims with confusion, no longer sure what thoughts are her own and what seeds of hatred had been planted by her father.

Lucifer relaxes his hold on her ever so slightly. "That's a good girl."

Evangeline rankles at his condescension. He never treated her like that as she was growing up. In fact, she always felt special, privileged, that her father would talk to her as if she were one of his generals, asking for her opinion on a battle strategy or what she thought of a new fighting tactic. He'd always respected her opinion, even if he didn't share it, so this new heartless attitude of his cut her deep.

"Lead the way," Lucifer orders her.

Evangeline takes them to Dana's quarters. They are at the far side of the monastery, on the edge of the grounds next to a large glass building. Evangeline had never seen the likes of it before coming to Sixth Heaven for the first time, and Uncle Raziel explained it was Dana's revolutionary design to grow plants and flowers year-round. The greenhouse, as Dana calls it, keeps in the heat and moisture, allowing the plants to flourish all the time. Since horticulture is Dana's ultimate passion, Evangeline suspects this is where the Cherubim will be, now that matins are over.

Evangeline pulls open the door and walks in. Immediately she's encompassed in temperate, humid air. The sensation always reminds Evangeline of being enveloped in a warm blanket. She hears Michael take in a deep breath, and turns to see his eyes widen in surprise. The room is impressive. It's an expansive garden, bursting with greenery.

Thick ivy climbs up the glass walls, creating a shimmering latticework of sunlight on the rows of tables overflowing with a brilliance of colors: rich red roses, golden sunflowers, fiery orange day lilies, velvet-purple irises. It's a haven in here, a sweet-smelling sanctuary, neat and ordered. It's the way Evangeline always imagined the higher Heavens would be— lovely, formal, tasteful—not the wild beauty of the Farlands.

"Hello?" a crisp voice calls out.

Dana appears around the corner, a cloth in hand, wiping dirt from a thin, pointed trowel. She wears a dusty smock over her crimson robe, and a few wisps of hair have escaped her chignon, but still, Evangeline thinks she exudes an elegance befitting the greenhouse gardens. She walks with a regal posture, straight and sure, and she talks with formal assurance. She strikes an impressive figure, one that initially intimidated Evangeline, and although she discovered Dana has a kind heart, Evangeline never truly felt relaxed in her presence. Despite Dana's clipped efforts to engage with Evangeline, asking about her life at school, for example, Evangeline much preferred her uncle's easy chatter and warm comfort.

When Dana sees the three of them at her door, she stops.

"Lucifer, I assume," she says formally. "Your reputation precedes you."

"You must be Dana, the Cherubim my daughter speaks so highly of."

Evangeline flushes with shame at the betrayal Dana doesn't yet know is coming; she drops her eyes, unable to meet Dana's gaze.

"Evangeline is a brilliant young angel," Dana replies.

For a quick second, Evangeline's heart flutters at the unexpected compliment. Does this classy, refined angel actually believe that about her? Uncle Raziel told her that all the time, but that's because he was Uncle Raziel. She never thought it could actually be true.

"But *you* have the knowledge I seek," Lucifer says to Dana. He then opens the book in the palm of his hand and holds it out.

Dana doesn't move.

"It is the Assembly of Angels's book," Lucifer adds.

Dana's lips widen into the shape of an "O" and Evangeline sees a twitch at the corner of her eye, but otherwise, the Cherubim contains her surprise.

"Raziel was a fool to trust you," Dana says.

"Most assuredly," Lucifer agrees. "But that is irrelevant."

Evangeline wants to scream at both of them that Uncle Raziel was no fool, that Lucifer was *family*, that *of course* you trust family—but immediately Evangeline's indignation recedes. They're right, she concedes. Uncle Raziel was a fool, like her, for believing in her father all this time.

"Read it to me," Lucifer demands.

Dana's lips curve into a tight little smile, as if she now understands her power over him.

"No."

"My apologies," Lucifer says. "I did not make myself clear. Read the text or I will kill Michael." Lucifer does not move. He does not step behind Michael or draw his dagger to Michael's neck; he does not unsheathe his sword. Only his words are a menace, but Evangeline can see in Dana's eyes that she understands Lucifer's threat is real.

Dana reaches for the book. She goes to a nearby bench, sits at it and bends her head low over the brittle pages. Evangeline wonders if she is as awed to hold the ancient text in her hands as Evangeline was.

"Out loud, please, Dana," Lucifer says. His voice is honey, even as his words are steel.

"I . . . I can't . . . " Dana says.

"But of course you can." It's an expression Evangeline heard often from her father. Supportive, reassuring, Lucifer always pushed her to do better. Every time she felt inadequate or unprepared for a task, like meeting a new host family on their travels to gather supporters, or learning an effective overhead strike in sword fighting, Lucifer would always encourage her. *But of course you can.*

And he would often be right.

Which means, Evangeline thinks, maybe there *is* a way to save Dana. All she has to do is tell her—without Lucifer hearing—to make something up, something Lucifer will believe, then Dana will be safe.

Slowly, Evangeline eases her way toward the Cherubim. Her father says nothing, so she assumes he's allowing it. As she moves, Dana speaks.

"It . . . it tells of *Slivers*."

For a moment, Evangeline feels elated that she was right, that the power of the book lies in the *Slivers* of angels.

"Explain," Lucifer demands.

"*Slivers* were splinters of divinity granted by God to certain angels," Dana says. "This touch of God gave them abilities beyond a normal angel, but in one area alone. Planting crops, diverting rains, healing wounds . . . the types of skills that would keep angels alive."

At the mention of healers, Evangeline thinks of Raphael, and she casts a sideways glance to Michael, wondering if he'll too, react, but his expression remains stone.

Dana pauses momentarily, studying the words. Evangeline makes her way to Dana's side, her curiosity about the contents of the book almost overriding her idea to save the Cherubim.

"While there were few angels with *Slivers*, angels with the divine touch—God ensured hope would live in all angels," Dana summarizes. She focuses again on the page, and for a long moment, she seems lost in the text.

Evangeline bends over; she listens for a rebuke from her father, but none comes. She lets her hair fall across her face so Lucifer cannot see her lips. Now, she needs only to whisper to Dana, without her father hearing.

"How?" Lucifer demands, and both Evangeline and Dana fling their heads up. "*How* is there hope?"

Dana looks up and meets Evangeline's gaze. Evangeline sees fortitude in her blue-green eyes, and it buoys Evangeline, knowing Dana seems ready to resist, but Dana twists away before Evangeline can say anything to her.

"Everyday angels could temporarily harness the full force of the *Slivers*," Dana explains. "For a moment or two, they could have the same abilities as the *Slivers* angel—enough to see them through a crisis. It gave angels hope."

Evangeline's jaw drops. She is floored. She's never heard this part of the legend, had only ever known that *Slivers* were rumored to have existed, not that ordinary angels could command the power, the *Sliver*. Like Raphael, she thinks. Could anyone harness his ability to heal? Could *she*?

The possibility is dizzying, and Evangeline feels giddy at the thought. Imagine, she thinks, if she could actually channel a portion of Raphael's healing *Sliver*. She could save her people on the battlefield; she could stop her friends from dying.

But then her thoughts turn bitter. If this is true, how many of her people, how many of her friends could she have saved if she had known—if *anyone* had known—this tactic sooner? Evangeline thinks of Sophia, her one true friend who died in battle last year, and a sharp pain pierces her heart, thinking now that there had been a way to save her all along—but in their supreme ignorance, they all let her die.

"*How* does one harness the *Slivers*?" Lucifer demands.

"By invoking the *Sliver's* true, angelic name," Dana answers.

"What is a 'true angelic name'?" Lucifer demands aggressively. "How does that differ from a regular name?"

Dana turns back to the text and Evangeline glances at Lucifer, whose whole attention is on the Cherubim. She still wants to whisper the warning, but she's terrified her father will hear.

Her attention is immediately drawn to Dana's face, swiftly blanching with fear. Lucifer notices, too.

"Speak," he commands.

"It's not possible . . . " Dana murmurs, as if she's forgotten the others are there.

"*What?*" Lucifer demands.

Dana hesitates. Evangeline can see a wash of emotions cross her face, an open, visible struggle about how much to reveal. And as much as Evangeline wants Dana to lie, she feels an irresistible surge of interest. She *has* to know what's in the book.

Finally Dana obliges, and when she speaks, her voice is small and thin.

"It says here that God also has one true name. When spoken aloud, the angel will temporarily harness God's power."

Oh good God. Evangeline shudders, as the calamitous pieces of this sick scenario fall into place. Her father could invoke this name, channel the infinite power of God and then . . .

Destroy God.

And then destroy the Heavens. She imagines her father would rain fire and brimstone down on his enemies, scorching the lands. He would crush God's new Earth, eliminating the nascent humans, their sister species, and then, Evangeline fears, he would reopen the portals to hell, allowing the djinn to terrorize the Heavens. Life for everyday angels, if they survive, would be catastrophic.

"What is God's true name?" Lucifer demands.

Evangeline's stomach lurches as she turns to see Lucifer at her shoulder—the dagger still at Michael's throat.

In a flash, Dana whips around and Evangeline sees the sharp trowel in her hand, then she sees Dana ram it into Lucifer's eye. He howls with rage, with pain, as he drops his dagger, releases Michael and flings his hand to his face.

"Run!" Dana yells at Evangeline and Michael.

Evangeline, shaken by the violent turn, grasps Michael's arm and he leaps to his feet. His stride is longer than hers; he reaches the door first and yanks it open. He stretches out his hand to pull her to him. She reaches out her right arm, when a hand clamps hard onto her left foot. She swivels her head and sees her father's threatening face, blood dripping from his right eye, his left eye wild with fury. With the strength of an uninjured angel, Lucifer drags her toward him. She yelps and claws the air desperately in Michael's direction. At once, he grasps her arm and pulls, but Lucifer's grip is tighter and a second later, she's wrapped in her father's arms.

With a dagger to her own throat.

"*No!*" Michael cries.

Evangeline shivers with shock, with fear, with disbelief. This isn't her father. Her father would never hurt her. She feels the heat of his chest against her cheek and feels the pounding of his heart and tries to imagine he's simply enveloping her in a bear hug and at any moment, he'll let her go with a small squeeze and she'll realize she imagined this whole scenario. But the cold point of the dagger against her skin makes denial impossible. She feels its pressure, feels the first cut, feels the warm blood—*her* warm blood on her neck. Hot tears sting her eyes and cascade down her cheeks, but she's unsure if it's because of the physical pain or her emotional anguish. Because now she understands, with gut-wrenching certainty, with unbearable agony, that not only is her father the devil but that he loves power more than her.

"The *name*, Dana," Lucifer grimaces at the Cherubim who now stands, frozen with fear, in front of them. Dana holds the book in one hand and the bloody garden tool in the other.

"You won't kill her," Dana says, her voice shaking although she tries for calm. "She's your daughter. You love her."

"Then you appreciate the sacrifice I have to make," Lucifer responds, and he pulls Evangeline tighter to him, as if he is truly hugging her.

Evangeline's body wracks with sobs. *Please, Papa!* she pleads in her head, but she can barely get breath to her lungs, let alone her voice.

"It's the last time I will ask, Dana. What is God's true name?"

Evangeline looks at Dana, wants to communicate with her. *Don't tell him,* she wants to shout. *Let me die.* Maybe if she dies at her father's hand, he'll appreciate the gravity of his hubris, that he gave up the only angel he loved for cold, heartless power.

And maybe if she dies, this will all go away. Her pain, her tumult, her confusion. Her soul will travel to God's Realm, where she will be reunited with the mother she barely remembers and her beloved Uncle Raziel. She will never grow old, it's true, and will never be able carve out a life with Michael—a life she realizes she has come to want.

But she begins to think her death would be for the greater good. For her people. If she stops Lucifer, maybe she'll stop the war he started. Maybe the other classes of angels will finally see how close they came to annihilation and finally be ready to accept that Commoners have a place in these Heavens. It's what she's always wanted, to make a difference, and now she can.

She feels the dagger press in harder and cries, "No!" Her theories be damned. She doesn't want to die.

She looks at Dana and is surprised to see peace smoothed over her face. Dana's eyes, reflecting the interior of her soul, are calm, her smile relaxed.

"You know I am the only angel who can give you the answer you seek," Dana tells Lucifer.

Evangeline's stomach flips over, a cold dread spreading through her. What is Dana saying? What is she doing?

And only at the last second does Evangeline realize what is happening.

With a swift stroke, Dana plunges the sharp, pointed garden trowel into her own heart.

Lucifer roars, drops Evangeline, and lunges towards Dana.

Before Evangeline hits the floor, Michael has her in his arms. In a flash, he is dragging her out of the greenhouse as she stares at Dana's slumped figure on the ground.

Her heart bursts with emotions she can't contain. In her terror, she hears something she can't possibly be hearing.

A war drum.

Chapter 17

Evangeline grasps her injured throat, her mind reeling. It must be her imagination, since there are no war drums—there are no *wars*—in Sixth Heaven, but when she turns to Michael, his eyes are as wide as hers. He hears it, too.

Her legs still tremble from the trauma of her father's attack but Evangeline rushes toward the thrumming beat of the drum. She leaps into the air, ignoring the pain in her wing. Her heart constricts with fear as she flies. She doesn't yet understand what's going on, but she senses catastrophe. The Archangels and the Dragons had been coming for them; one army, or both, were at the border when she and Michael crossed with Balam—

All of a sudden, Balam's plan crystallizes in Evangeline's mind. She *did* get through the Divinity Shield unaided. Balam didn't shake her off after they crossed the barrier; he let go in the middle. To prove to her the shield was actually down.

Remember who helped you, the djinni told her.

Evangeline thought only the head Cherubim could shut down the shield, but Balam must have discovered another way, and that allowed the armies to push into Sixth Heaven.

Which must also explain how her father got in . . .

Which confirms that Lucifer is working with the djinni.

Evangeline cannot fathom how it's possible, how Lucifer found a portal and allowed a djinni into their world. Before today she would have thought it inconceivable her father would align with the very enemies he defeated years ago, but after learning about her father's insane plan to destroy God and after his attack on *her*, his own daughter, Evangeline has to accept she's right.

Michael flies faster; his wings cut through the morning air with sharp, powerful flaps. A moment later, he whirls back to her, locks his arm around her and draws her into him. Evangeline feels the rigid tension in his body and thinks how it mirrors her own.

Michael helps Evangeline keep her balance as they land on the monastery's roof overlooking the shallow valley in front of them. The swath of green dell stretches between the compound and the most imposing sight in all the Heavens: the gilded Pearly Gates, the singular entrance to Seventh Heaven. Evangeline stood in awe the first time her uncle showed her this view; she appreciated that she, a lowly Commoner, was fortunate beyond measure to see with her own eyes the gate to God's Realm.

But it is with terror that she views the sight now.

Below and to her left, facing the Pearly Gates, is a battalion of infantry Archangels, in rank formation, their swords raised. A company of cavalry on battle-ready sky horses hovers, in tight configuration, directly above the soldiers on the ground.

To Evangeline's right, she sees her own army, the Dragons, also in strict, disciplined formation. They are much fewer in number, perhaps only a third of the Archangels, and they have no sky horses, but Evangeline knows her father has trained them well to fight against great odds.

What shocks her, though, are not the two armies preparing to fight in Sixth Heaven; what leaves her cold with dread is that neither army faces the other.

Both the Archangels and the Dragons stare ahead at the vast army of djinn.

The wingless soldiers, wearing metal breastplates and horned helmets, stand deep in columns that spread across the valley, but Evangeline sees they have also learned how to take to the skies. Hovering above the djinn are two dragons—*real* dragons!—each muzzled, each with two riders astride the giant creatures. From the beasts' fight against their restraints, as they buck their enormous scaly heads and thrash their long, jagged tails, and from the strain of the reins in the hands of the riders, Evangeline sees the terrifying difficulty of controlling the dragons.

Fear strikes at her core. Her father had always spoken of dragons as if they were real; it's why he named his army after them. But she was certain the beasts were myths, tales of monsters told to frighten children into good behavior. Yet here, in front of them, with an innumerable army of djinn, are two of these fearsome creatures.

The sound of the war drum continues its steady rhythm. Evangeline catches the movement of the drummer, an Archangel in the back row, his arm a pendulum of even swings as his stick hits the drum.

Otherwise, the morning is eerily still. Evangeline understands the discipline it takes to maintain complete silence in the moments leading up to the first attack. She hasn't experienced it, of course, but in practice, the instinct to rush forward with an exploding cry of adrenaline is overwhelming.

"Where did the djinn come from?" Michael whispers to her, his eyes on their common enemy.

"Balam," she breathes out, certain she's right. There is no coincidence that they encounter a djinn entering Sixth Heaven then come upon a djinn army an hour later.

"*How?* There are no portals," Michael replies.

The Heavens had been swept thoroughly after the Djinn War, everyone had been assured, Evangeline remembers her father telling her. With the last portal slammed shut by Lucifer himself, the Heavens were finally safe. Yet here, now, the djinn stand, at the Pearly Gates, ready to attack.

Standing at the Pearly Gates . . .

"They came from *Seventh* Heaven," Evangeline's eyes widen at her guess. "Djinn can pass through any barrier."

Michael looks at her, uncomprehending.

"Including the impenetrable Pearly Gates," Evangeline explains. "No ordinary angel can pass through, but the djinn can dissipate."

Even still, her theory seems absurd. Surely, the Seraphim would never have allowed an UnderRealm portal to remain accessible so close to *God* . . .

Unless they didn't know about it.

But how is *that* possible?

The questions swirl in Evangeline's head as she tries to swat them aside. She and Michael and the entire Heavens are standing on the edge of a knife. At any moment, any second, the insufferable tension will break and there will be blood. Evangeline grips her sword. Her hands feel like ice, but her skin burns at the touch of the hilt. She's confident in her skill, but she's never been in a formal battle like this one.

The drum stops.

The suffocating silence is scarier than a thousand battle cries.

And then into the fray flies her father. Like a regal king, descending among his loyal subjects, he lands in the center of the valley, equidistant from all three armies.

The ringmaster.

Lucifer's right eye still bleeds, but he seems immune to the injury.

"Dragons, unite with your brother and sister djinn!" Lucifer cries.

There is a moment of silent disbelief. From her perch on the roof, Evangeline can see her people, the Commoners who joined her father's Cause to reclaim their rights in the Heavens, shift uneasily. They are confused, she assumes, bewildered by their leader's demand for an allegiance with an enemy they thought had long ago been vanquished. And Evangeline wants to fly down in front of her father and tell her people *no*, don't listen to him. She wants to tell them he's mad, driven by an insatiable thirst for power he can never have. She wants to tell them Lucifer is leading them to their slaughter, and that they must fight *with* the Archangels, because they are *all* angels, and work to defeat their common enemy together.

But before she can move, Zephon, her father's most loyal general who seems to have recovered from Evangeline's beating, steps toward Lucifer. He raises his sword and bellows.

"We are *Dragons!*"

Evangeline's own cry of protest dies in her throat, as the rest of her father's army seizes the moment. They charge at the Archangels, their familiar enemy, and leave their flank vulnerable to the djinn, their ally only because of the word of their leader. Evangeline wonders how they can be so *stupid*, so *careless* to immediately trust Lucifer about the djinn—but then she realizes that she herself worked tirelessly with her father over the years to indoctrinate them. They were all duped by Lucifer's skillful manipulation.

Evangeline sees Gabriel, on a sky horse at the front of his troops. With a holler of righteous conviction, Gabriel unleashes his Archangels. They rush at the Dragons, both on the ground and in their air, in intricate maneuvers, a deadly dance.

The first swords clang in a discordant harmony as the battle begins. Michael is in the air and at his father's side before Evangeline can blink, but for her, she is lost. A week ago, she'd have made it faster to her father's side than Michael to Gabriel. But now, alone, on top of defiled sanctuary, Evangeline can no longer figure out whose side is right. She believes in the Commoner's Cause—the one she thought she was fighting for all these years—but the rights of Commoners are no longer why Lucifer battles. Yet how can she support the Archangels who continue to repress her people? The very people who themselves don't accept her.

Then she spots Balam striding purposely toward Lucifer. He raises his arm and crooks his elbow, an obvious signal to the djinn army to wait. As the Dragons and Archangels clash in bloody strokes, Lucifer falls back to speak with Balam as if there were no deadly battle surrounding them. She cannot hear what they are saying, but she's seen enough of her father's grand gestures to know he's enraged. She takes this as proof of their collusion, and while she doesn't understand the details of their plot, she suspects that Lucifer didn't get what he wanted. She feels a twinge of glee at the thought, pleased that he will never succeed. Not only will Lucifer never find out God's true name because he can't get to the Seraphim Camael in Seventh Heaven to translate the book, but now his dominance in his own world is also being challenged.

Evangeline is aware of the battle below her; she hears the clang of steel, the cries of death, and she's aware she must act. But for another minute, she fixates on her father and the look-alike djinni. The resemblance is uncanny, even from this distance. They look like brothers, she thinks.

And the air disappears from her lungs.

Unite with your brother and sister djinn!

Brothers.

My mother was wild, Lucifer once told her, *and my father hated me.*

It was the only information she'd ever heard her father speak of his parents, and only when she'd pressed him about their deaths. They'd died in a fire in their cottage not long after Evangeline's own mother was also killed by fire. Evangeline had been curious—her father's parents were the reason she and Lucifer were in First Heaven when her mother died, and Evangeline suspects Lucifer never forgave himself for being with his parents, whom he hated, instead of with the wife he loved.

So is *this* why he hated his parents? Because, unfathomably, Lucifer's mother had been with a *djinni*? Evangeline tries to remember her history. Forty-five years ago, the djinn had already been expelled, but there were portals to the UnderRealm. It's how, twenty years later, the Djinn War began. Could it have been possible for djinn to regularly come into the Heavens and seduce wild young angels?

Evangeline feels as if she's been struck by a bolt of lightning. Her head is light, her skin tingles. The implications, the ramifications if her father were actually half djinn . . .

Evangeline wavers on her feet. That would make *her* a quarter djinn . . .

A thunderous roar rents the air and Evangeline snaps up her head. She sees the djinn dragon riders snap off the muzzles and the mighty beasts scream in response. One djinn rider works the reins while the other sits backward, sword in hand, the defender. For a split second, the battlefield freezes. Archangels and Lucifer's army alike look up at the snarling beasts. Then, to Evangeline's horror, the lead dragon breathes fire, scorching the earth and all the angels in its narrow path. Cries of anguish pierce the air as angels burn.

Evangeline dives off the roof and heads toward the flames, her only thought to pull the victims out of the fire. But she doesn't get close. She feels a sword whip by the tips of her wings and, on instinct,

Evangeline whirls around and attacks. Her sword is met with another, the clang of metal lost in the din of war, but she is quick and she is strategic, and her enemy, an Archangel, is heavy. Evangeline zips higher in the air; the soldier follows, but he takes an extra second, and it's all Evangeline needs to tuck and roll and stretch out of her summersault with a hard kick to his chest. Evangeline can hear the air escape his lips, a balloon deflating as he drops, and she zooms away.

But she feels herself slowing. Her wing, never fully healed from Balam's attack three days ago, pains her. If she tries to keep fighting in the air, she'll lose.

Weaving in and around dueling angels, Evangeline drops out of the sky. The battle is fierce on the ground, too. Angel wings are fragile in war, the first casualties in aerial combat. Few soldiers can remain airborne for a whole battle; it's why they train as much for footwork as they do for acrobatics.

Evangeline sees the djinn army advance. If the Archangels are graceful and elegant in their fighting style and Evangeline's own Dragon army are quick and swift, the djinn are cutthroat. Evangeline notices they bear their swords with a heavy hand, but the power with which they yield them is frightening. Evangeline watches one young angel, a Commoner, slashed through the belly before he could raise his sword against his "ally." The djinn, as Evangeline feared, care nothing for the distinction between angel ally and angel enemy.

Evangeline fights off another Archangel. Her sword flashes with skill and prowess, but revulsion grows in her stomach as she sees the blade glow red with blood. The rank odor of charred flesh, of metallic blood, nauseates her; she knew of a battlefield's wretched stench, but she's never before had to fight in one. It takes all her willpower to push the sights and smells of carnage out of her mind so she can stay alive.

A djinn soldier attacks. She is strong, but Evangeline is agile. Evangeline glides out of the djinni's path as a heavy blow rains down where her head had been a split-second before. The djinni's sword remains, for a heartbeat too long, mired in the grass, and Evangeline presses her advantage. Instead of winding up for an overhead blow, which may be more deadly, Evangeline doesn't waste time. She whips her sword in an arc around her hips—and by all rights, she should have sliced her enemy. But as the point of Evangeline's sword is about to strike her, the djinn soldier dissipates. A moment later, she reappears behind Evangeline. Evangeline hears the *pop* of the djinni before she sees her, and has her sword raised in defense as the soldier rains down another blow. Their swords clash, each blade pressed against the other, each fighter pressing in against the other.

They are at a stalemate, neither gaining ground nor ceding it, but Evangeline worries she cannot hold much longer. She wonders, fleetingly, how Michael is faring. He's stronger, so she expects—she hopes—he'll prevail, but for her, she feels her arms weaken against the power of the djinni. She'll have to outsmart the soldier instead. If she can hold on for a moment while she strategizes . . .

"Neecy, how pleasant to see you again." Balam's voice is right by her ear.

Neecy.

She hears it now. Niece.

The thought rattles her; she feels her sword droop, but instead of the cold slice of steel from the djinni's blade, she feels only air. Evangeline twists her head as she regains her defensive position, but the djinni dissipates and Balam takes her place. With a grip on

Evangeline's upper arm, Balam drags her to the edge of the battlefield. She tries to wrench free, but Balam holds her as tight as a vice.

"*Now* you don't let go?" Evangeline snaps. She is frightened, but not for her safety because she's keenly aware he could have already killed her.

"You understand now, do you, Neecy?"

"I understand nothing, *Uncle*," Evangeline spits at him. The word burns in her mouth, a self-rebuke for hijacking her beloved Raziel's moniker.

Balam doesn't look at her, but instead stares at the bloodshed in front. Evangeline notices a wicked smile creep over his lips.

"So you accept the truth," Balam says. "Your father and I share a father, Iblis, the great djinn prince."

The confirmation of the truth slams her hard. Djinn. *Prince*. If her whole world was shaken before with the revelation of Lucifer's evil, the whole core of her being is destroyed with her revised family tree. If she felt like a fraud as half-class before, how can she identify as a Commoner now that she's learned she's only a *quarter* Commoner? She feels chilled, like a sensation of ice runs through her veins.

And her father knew. He knew and never told her.

Like he never told her his diabolical plans to destroy God.

"Why are you here?" she asks Balam, but before he responds, she answers for him. "My father sent for you. Somehow."

She sees Balam visibly bristle.

"I am *not* Lucifer's minion," Balam decries. "*I* am in charge of this army, not big brother, no matter what he thinks."

Evangeline hears the childish whine in his tone and recognizes it as that of a jealous sibling, but she can't understand it. Her father is here in the Heavens—an angel with wings—not in the UnderRealm with the djinn.

"*You* did this?" Evangeline asks, repulsed. She stares out at the battlefield, the bloody mayhem this djinni unleashed. The angels, Dragons and Archangels alike, are being decimated. She sees the two djinn dragons rampaging through the valley, blasting narrow spurts of fire and death at every turn. With the djinn's ability to dissipate, Evangeline fears it won't be long before the angels are wiped out.

"Your papa dearest expected me to wait," Balam sneers. "Find his precious key first and then attack, he said, but I will *not* bow before such an insolent half-breed. *I* am the rightful heir to Iblis's throne."

Evangeline understands nothing of djinn royalty or politics, but she suspects that since Lucifer has designs on *God's* throne, he'd easily allow his younger half-brother to have Iblis's seat of power in the UnderRealm.

"How did you let them in?" Evangeline asks. If she learns how they arrived, could there be a clue to their destruction?

Balam's chest puffs out and Evangeline recognizes the path she needs to follow is one of flattery.

"There are but two remaining portals," he explains. "The house in Third Heaven upon which you so serendipitously stumbled," he says, and here Evangeline gasps, as all the pieces fall into place. That dark, dank house is a portal . . . "It's much too small for an army, but then your father discovered the yawning gap in the Seventh Heaven—which can only be opened from your side. Obviously Lucifer couldn't get one of his minions to do the job, since no angel can pass through the Pearly Gates, so he recruited me. The damn fool." Balam chuckles. "But I take orders from nobody. *I* decided the time was right to reclaim the Heavens for my own kind. *I* released them from our world and into yours."

"Is that why you lowered the Divinity Shield?" Evangeline asks. "To ensure an immediate battle?"

Balam seems momentarily startled. "I had no need to lower the shield. That was your Cherubim, when they saw us swarming through the Pearly Gates."

Evangeline again feels like her world has tilted. "But when you and I crossed the Shield, there *was* no Shield. You let go of me, and I was fine."

Balam laughs. "The Divinity Shield was firmly intact, I assure you."

"But . . . " Evangeline feels again as if she's been thunderstruck. Since she's part-djinn, does that mean—?

"You can pass through all silly angelic barriers, of course," Balam smiles.

Evangeline's mind reels. All those times she held tightly to Uncle Raziel, terrified she'd be zapped as they entered Sixth Heaven, and all this time she could have let go? Evangeline feels as if her whole history is writing itself in front of her eyes. It's too much, too much . . .

"Which is why I brought you here, Neecy," Balam continues, and holds out his hand. "Join me."

"*What*?" Evangeline must have heard wrong.

"Your father is unstable, I think we can all agree on that," he says, again with a tinny laugh.

And while Balam has her firmly trapped in his grip, and his army seems set to destroy all of the angels on the battlefield, for a brief moment, Evangeline actually feels sorry for this fool. If there's one thing she is certain to be true, regardless—or maybe because of—the revelations about her father this past week, it's that one should *never* underestimate him.

"We need an ambassador," Balam says. "The angels will find life under my djinn rule . . . uncomfortable . . . at first, but, well, you, Evangeline, belong to both of us. Djinn and angel. Who better to bridge the gap?"

Evangeline goggles at this demon. "Are you *crazy*?"

She sees in his eyes a flicker of insecurity, a splinter of hurt, a trait she *never* observed in her father. If Lucifer felt doubt, he never revealed it. And that's when it hits Evangeline—the power of her father's charm is, in part, in his confidence. He was steadfast in his beliefs—at least how he presented them to his followers—and he never cared about their approval.

Balam, by contrast, seems on edge, driven by personal emotions. Jealousy, fear, insecurity. Evangeline tucks this all away, wondering if and how she might use her new insight to defeat him. But she is getting nowhere right now. He keeps his hand on her arm, digs his talonlike fingers deeper into her skin, with a pain as sharp as needles.

"It is in your best interest to reconsider, Neecy," Balam sneers.

Evangeline can barely process her newfound pedigree, but she is certain that she cannot let Balam take control—uncle or no uncle. Balam doesn't know these lands, hasn't grown up here, lived here. He doesn't understand their people and their needs, not like her.

Evangeline feels a frisson course down her spine.

She *does* know the Commoners. She knows their lands and how they live and what they want. She may not share their blood—and less of it than she ever imagined—but she shares their cause. She shares their hopes. She shares their fears.

She shares their identity.

And she always has, regardless of whether she was born part djinn or half Dominion. Evangeline finally recognizes that she is, and will always remain, at heart, a Commoner.

"Go hang yourself, Balam," she spits at him.

She means to pull away, if only symbolically, but without warning, Balam punches her in the head. Her brain explodes; she sees stars, but she fights the blackness, willing her mind, her body, her spirit to stay strong. But another punch comes, and another to her face, and then a kick to her stomach, and Evangeline doubles over, collapsing to the ground. Balam continues his assault as she curls into a ball to protect herself, and Evangeline understands in the dim haze of consciousness left to her that he means it to hurt. He could have stabbed her instantly; she could have been yet another sad casualty, another body on the heap of destruction in the battle. But this is personal and vindictive, and Evangeline, in her foggy mind, wants to laugh. Did Balam think she could be so easily won over? That her loyalties would shift immediately from her people when she learned of her true heritage?

She readies herself for another blow and she accepts it might be fatal. She is too weak to fight back, that without Michael to fight off Balam, like the last time, in Third Heaven, she expects to die. She's sad about that because she would have loved to say goodbye to Michael.

And Papa. She wants to say goodbye to Papa. The Papa from her dreams, from her childhood, from her memories. The one who sang her to sleep and held her close. She wishes he existed, the loving, dedicated soul who raised her, but she has to accept that angel, that Lucifer, turned out to be an illusion. Still, it was nice to believe it at the time.

Another blow. Evangeline's eyes grow dim.

Goodbye, Papa.

Evangeline hears a roar, and at first she thinks it's a dragon, the animal, but this dragon sounds like her father. "Get away from my daughter!"

And then the blows stop.

Evangeline tries to open her eyes, but they are heavy, like iron, and she cannot raise her eyelids. But she hears a soft whisper in her ear, a puff of breath.

"You'll be okay, Evangeline."

She feels her body swaying and realizes that she's been picked up off the ground. The movement, the steps, the motion feel quick and harsh and jerky, but the hands that wrap around her feel gentle. She squeezes her eyes and then with a will of concentration, she forces them open.

She sees Papa. His rugged face is lined with age, with worry, with blood—his right eye a jagged wound—but also with ardent determination.

Lucifer roars his way through the battle, and everyone—the djinn, his own Dragon army, even the Archangels, cut him a wide swath. Evangeline doesn't know, can't see, where they are, but the immediate cacophony of the fighting fades. Her father lowers her to the ground, gently wiping her matted hair from her face.

"Papa," she says, and for an instant, one mystical, magical moment, the Heavens exist only for the two of them.

"It will all be better soon, my darling," Lucifer tells her. "You'll see. It will all be worth it."

"Father?" She feels a kiss on her cheek, a leathery, sandpaper kiss, a typical Lucifer kiss.

Evangeline tries to sit up, and when she manages it, he is gone. She sees him in the air, among the soldiers, flying away.

She tries to understand what happened. Her father saved her. Yet only this morning, her father threatened to kill her. And he killed Uncle Raziel. He's evil, a demon—she can't deny that.

But he loves her.

And he always has. The papa of her childhood *was* real. Lucifer did sing to her and hold her close. He did teach her how to fight and asked her opinion on battle tactics. He did support her wishes to go to Diaga and he did teach her how to be resilient.

Evangeline realizes now, with a heart full of swirling emotions, that her father made her who she is today.

And who she is, she now understands with startling clarity, is *not* her father.

She sees the carnage on the battlefield in front of her, the culmination of a war her father started for his own gains. Evangeline doesn't know how or why her father chose the path he did but she will not follow.

She will forge her own path.

Helping her own people without Lucifer.

"Evie!"

Evangeline shakes her head, tries to focus on the face swimming in front of her.

"Evie, we need you," Michael wraps his arms around her shoulders and pulls her to her feet. "The djinn are killing us—all of us, all the angels. We need to fight together."

Evangeline's head pounds and her body aches with bruises. She hears what Michael is saying, but she doesn't know how she can fight anymore.

"Lucifer's gone," Michael tells her. "This is your chance. Take charge of the Dragons and order them to fight with us. They'll listen to you because you're Lucifer's daughter."

"Wait, what?" Evangeline takes in a deep breath, trying to clear the fog from her head. "Where's my father?"

"He retreated to the Pearly Gates," Michael says.

Evangeline's stomach lurches. She spins around toward the gilded gate, her eyes frantically scanning the valley.

"He's not retreating," Evangeline explains with a growing horror. "He's going to find Camael and learn the true name of God."

Evangeline tries to spread her wings, but she can't move them. She cries out in pain, in frustration.

"That's impossible," Michael reaches for her, helps steady her. "He can't get through to Seventh Heaven."

"He *can*," Evangeline insists. "He's half djinn."

"*What?*" Michael narrows his eyes. Then a pause, a beat Evangeline knew would be coming. "But that would make you . . . "

"Part djinn," Evangeline finishes for him. "That's why I'm the only one who can stop him. I'm the only one who can get into Seventh Heaven to go after him."

"Evie, no, it's too dangerous to face him alone."

"I face him alone or Lucifer destroys God."

"Camael won't tell him anything," Michael reasons. "Like Dana."

But Evangeline has met the Seraphim Camael, and he is nothing like his sister. Evangeline fears that leaving the fate of the Heavens up to a self-serving, arrogant angel like Camael will ruin them all.

"Please, Michael, help me to the Pearly Gates."

Michael shakes his head. "He'll kill you, Evie. I can't let that happen."

Evangeline feels a pang of love, a pang of sadness. She reaches up and puts her palm to Michael's bloodied, war-torn face. "I love that you want to protect me," she says. "But it's not your choice to make."

CHAPTER 18

Evangeline's first challenge is to get to the Pearly Gates. At first Michael thinks he can fly her over to the gates, but the war in the air with the sky horses and dragons is as dangerous as the fighting on the ground. They decide instead on a small guard of Archangels who will shield them on their push to the other side. One of whom, Evangeline is surprised to see, is Michael's sister Danielle. She nods to Evangeline, with an easy familiarity, a reminder Danielle knew all along who she was back in Second Heaven. And now she stands, ready to fight by Evangeline's side. Evangeline shakes her head in wonder at all that has happened, then picks up a fallen sword—her own was lost when Balam attacked. She's startled to notice how cool the hilt is in her hand. In the heat of the dragons' fire and the intensity of battle, the last thing Evangeline expected was for a weapon to feel cool to the touch.

Her guards advance, plunging into the thick of the fighting. It would make more sense to curve around the edge of the valley, instead of pushing right through the middle, but Evangeline can't afford to waste time. As it is, she fears her father has already worn down Camael, that Lucifer has already learned God's true name, and every second she cringes with dreaded anticipation that the Heavens will crumble and reveal she is too late to stop her father.

With the guard in front of her, Evangeline parries and thrusts as the djinn soldiers descend on them. A few Commoners see the concentration of Archangels and attack, but Evangeline bellows at them to desist.

To her great surprise, they do.

"Fight *against* the djinn!" she cries. "My father was wrong. The *djinn* are not our brothers and sisters; the Archangels are."

To her greater surprise, the Commoners, her father's followers, fall in line with her. Perhaps, she reasons, they could never understand his order to align with an old enemy. Or perhaps they now see how their "allies" do not protect them. Either way, Evangeline is glad for their support.

She feels the whoosh of air and whirls to see a djinni behind her, but before she can react, Danielle slashes first. She gets a nick on the djinni, but the djinni dissipates before she can kill the enemy. The djinn soldiers are simply too fast.

Evangeline remembers her father's stories about the first Djinn War and how he conquered them.

"Since the djinn were fast, we slowed them down," Lucifer explained. The answer made sense to Evangeline as a young angel; she never thought to question the actual tactics.

Now, though, she needs the details, and she wishes she could ask her father, but he has obviously chosen his side.

Yet *Gabriel* . . . Gabriel was there all those years ago. *He* must know . . .

Evangeline scans the valley, but she can't see the Archangel general. She and Michael are almost at the gate now. Their guard, Evangeline notices, has grown as they've crossed the battlefield. More Archangels as well as Dragons work together to protect her and Michael.

From above, Evangeline hears the deafening screech of a dragon;

she looks up, sees the dragon spit flames, and immediately leaps to the side. She can feel the wave of heat ripple through the air, can feel its power scorch her skin. The grass around her sparks into flames, scattering their guard as the angels race to escape the fire. Evangeline finds Michael and they run. From overhead, she hears another roar, but it is strangled this time, and when again Evangeline lifts her head, she sees Gabriel on his sky horse, challenging the dragon. He is tiny next to the massive creature, and that, Evangeline notices, is Gabriel's advantage. The Archangel flits in and around the dragon's face, as irritating as a nagging fly, and it drives the large beast to distraction. The djinn riders try to control the jerk of the dragon's head, but it's strong. When the dragon seems most distracted, Gabriel shoots forward on his sky horse and with his sword, and stabs the dragon in the eye. The creature emits a howl that shakes the earth, and then tumbles from the sky.

Michael and Evangeline sprint to the edge of the Pearly Gates. They have to squint against the brilliance of the light radiating from the poles and Evangeline fears that her djinn-ness won't be sufficient to propel her through the gates and into Seventh Heaven. She is, after all, mostly angel.

Gabriel lands his sky horse beside them. "What are you *doing*?"

"Lucifer is half djinn," Michael explains quickly. "He can get into Seventh Heaven."

Gabriel exhales. "A djinni . . . "

Evangeline sees his mind calculating, reprocessing, recalibrating everything he ever knew about her father. She understands, more than anyone, how painful it is.

"It explains everything . . . " Gabriel breathes.

He shakes his head and refocuses. "In the Djinn War, Lucifer knew where all the portals were. He also suggested we use smaller weapons. It seemed counterintuitive, to fight with shorter swords, but it worked. He must have known something about those swords . . . "

Evangeline feels the heft of the pilfered sword in her hand. It remains cool and comfortable, like the ones her father would make her. But the one Michael gave her to use, the one stolen from the school, stung her hands. Evangeline assumed it was merely the shape, a poor design, but . . .

"Give me your sword, Michael," Evangeline demands.

He offers it to her, and the second she places her hand on its blade, her skin burns.

Like when she picked up the key her uncle left her in the school library . . .

"Hold this," she says to Michael, giving him her own sword. She then digs into her tunic for the thick, iron key.

The Key to the Kingdom, she had thought, but it wasn't.

Yet Uncle Raziel had left it for her as a message. He must have learned about the djinn. And how to defeat them.

"Take the key, Michael," she orders. "What do you feel?"

Michael grasps the old key from her and shakes it on his palm. "It's heavy?"

"That's it? Nothing else? It doesn't feel hot to the touch?"

Michael frowns. "Hot? Why would a key feel hot?"

Gabriel abruptly grabs Michael's sword and studies it. "It's made of iron, like the key."

"It burns my hand," Evangeline explains, "and I'm only part-djinn."

"The swords Lucifer had us use . . . " Gabriel recalls. "They must have been *iron*."

Slow them down . . .

"I think the djinn can't dissipate quickly if they're injured," Evangeline surmises. She remembers the nick Danielle gave the djinni on their way across the battlefield. If that had been with an iron sword, would that have prevented the djinni from dissipating? Could her soldier have then won? "And iron burns them."

She thinks back to her own father, her own swords. They've always been steel; Lucifer is an expert blacksmith, has always made his own weapons. She merely assumed her swords were different from the rest because her father saved the best for her. He was protecting her, protecting himself.

"How are we going to get an armory of iron swords, though?" Evangeline scans the battlefield. Obviously there are a few, like Michael's, but it hasn't been enough so far.

She and Michael and Gabriel are silent. Evangeline knows she has to get to her father, but she's loath to leave Sixth Heaven without a plan to defeat the djinn. With the angel casualties mounting, she is terrified that even if she stops her father, she won't stop Balam.

Which means she may lose Michael.

And she can't lose Michael. With her father gone from her, Michael is all she has left. And, she finally admits to herself, he's the one she wants to be with.

Their protective guards abruptly dash out to drive off a mass of djinn. She, Michael, and Gabriel are running out of time.

Michael then slaps his hand to his forehead. "We don't need *swords*. We need *iron*."

Evangeline frowns. "We don't have iron."

"No, but we have iron *ore*," Michael responds. He points to the thick limestone buildings of the monastery.

"For which to extract the iron we need a *blast* furnace," Evangeline points out.

Michael grins. "We have one."

He draws their attention to the fire-breathing dragon Gabriel maimed. It lays injured on the ground, its djinn riders having abandoned it for the melee of battle.

"You're crazy," Evangeline's eyes widen. "You can't control a *dragon.*"

"You're only saying that because I never have," Michael grins cockily.

Gabriel weighs in. "Fire and limestone do *not* make iron."

"We don't need iron to manipulate into swords," Michael argues. "I think we only need the iron ore in the stone. Launch the heated stones at the djinn, and then see how quickly they dissipate."

Evangeline is skeptical. She remembers, from her early years watching her father in his blacksmith shop, that smelting is a much more complicated process.

"What choice do we have, Evie?" Michael asks, and she knows he's right. She thinks, for a moment, she should stay with him; she understands more about metalwork than he does, but the Pearly Gates shimmer in the corner of her eye. While Michael and Gabriel may be able to come up with iron-type weapons, primitive as they may be, she understands she's the only one who can go after her father.

"I'll form a squad to take control of the dragon," Gabriel says. In an instant, he is airborne.

"Dragons are dangerous," Evangeline tells Michael. She's stalling, but she's afraid. For him, for herself.

"Don't I know it," Michael smiles. "Ever since I met one, she's stabbed me and then saved me and has now dragged me into battle."

Evangeline swats him. "Funny."

"I've got this, Evie," Michael says softly. "You go." He nods his head toward the Pearly Gates behind him.

Evangeline stares at the gleaming gates, shimmering and iridescent in the midday sun. The battles still rages behind her, but the din seems muffled, as if cries of anguish travel to her over a great distance, as if the battle itself between angel and djinn has dimmed. Instead, she focuses only on the gate. Through it, she can see only haze; what is on the other side is a mystery no common angel was ever meant to discover. But she isn't common, she reminds herself. She is Commoner and Dominion and djinn. Still, she's frightened. It's possible Balam lied about her ability to pass through the Pearly Gates. It's possible he tricked her into thinking she'd slipped through the Sixth Heaven Divinity Shield on her own. And if she's wrong, she doesn't know what will happen to her. No living angel except the Seraphim has ever tried to gain access to Seventh Heaven.

She clutches her fingers together to hide her trembling, but Michael grasps her hands in his.

"You've got this, Evie," he says, and then he lets go, drawn back into the battle he must win.

Evangeline takes a deep breath. She takes one hesitant step forward, and then another, and now she is committed. She reaches out her arm, unable to control her shaking, and taps the golden rods on gate. Her hand feels warm, like it touches the glow of a candle, and so she moves closer. The gates don't shift in their hinges; they are not like conventional openings, but she feels her hand slide through as if she were swimming in a balmy sea. Now her body is in line with the Pearly Gates and now she passes through the barrier to Seventh Heaven. She smells the sweetness of honey as she glides through the gate.

And she is on the other side. She is in Seventh Heaven.

She looks behind her first, at the opposite side of the Gates, fearful to move on from everything she's familiar with. But like the glimpse into Seventh Heaven was hazy, so too is the view back into Sixth Heaven. She sees nothing but white, and Evangeline feels like she has entered on a cloud.

Slowly Evangeline turns around. She doesn't know what to expect, despite her proximity to Camael over the years. He never spoke of Seventh Heaven and she was much too shy, much too afraid, to ask.

In front of her is a beauty she has never seen, a splendor that does not exist in the other Heavens. She sees a meadow of wildflowers and a babbling brook, and, nearby, an expansive manor on a hill. Each of these exists in her world—the wildflowers, the brook, the manor— but these all seem infused with a radiance that is at once imposing and welcoming. Evangeline climbs the slope, slowly at first, as if to absorb magnificence around her, until she remembers the urgency of her mission: find her father, stop her father.

Evangeline quickens her pace, now on the lookout for some sort of hole, the portal through which the djinn army arrived. She sees nothing in this pristine landscape to indicate the hell that was unleashed here, but then again, she has no idea how large Seventh Heaven actually is. She knows only there is the home of the Seraphim and a separate entrance, through a veil, to God's Realm. She cannot imagine penetrating into such sacred space, but she assumes her visit will never come to that. Lucifer is here for Camael, a Seraphim, so the Seraphim's manor is where she expects to find him.

Evangeline's legs shake as she approaches the front entrance of the manor. She wonders how best to get inside—sneak in or announce her presence? Which would throw off her father the most?

The decision becomes moot. As Evangeline approaches, she notices the heavy front door is open, kicked and splintered. Her father.

Evangeline draws her sword, and walks up the stone steps, alert to danger, but she hears nothing.

The entrance foyer is a massive round stone room, off of which lead two wings. A doorway, an arch, is across from her and opens onto a courtyard. When she hears the murmur of voices, she slides toward it, her heart racing. She doesn't have a plan; she doesn't know how she's going to stop Lucifer.

You'll help me, right, God? Since I'm trying to help you.

And for a second, Evangeline freezes. It's the first time she's thought about her motivation in those terms. She is risking everything to save God, yet she grew up believing He had long ago deserted her. *Why?* Why would she try to protect Him? Because her father would be a worse violent and evil deity? It's hard to argue God has a better record, given the persecution of Commoners He's allowed over the centuries.

Yet here she is.

She thinks of her uncle, of his peace and tranquility, of his unshakable faith in God, of his fervent belief in a *thin place*, a place among the Heavens where even mortal angels can experience the touch of the Divine, and she thinks of her own longing for the hopeful world her uncle inhabited. Since everything about her father turned out to be such a monumental lie, perhaps everything he taught her about God was false, too.

So perhaps that's why she fights now for God. She fights for her uncle's version of God, for the hope, the peace, the love he assured her exists in God.

"It is about believing that we belong to something larger than ourselves," Raziel told her. "We are, all of us, connected."

Evangeline isn't yet convinced of her uncle's spiritual beliefs, she's not sure she can commit fully to the goodness of God, but if there is a chance—if there is *hope*—that Raziel is right, then she will fight. The alternative is to let her father's profound darkness and bleak despair reign.

The choice, to Evangeline, is now blindingly obvious.

She eases to the doorframe and peeks out. Her stomach lurches at what she sees.

Around a large stone table, on smoothed cobblestone, lie six bodies, all dressed in royal purple Seraphim robes.

Evangeline stifles a sob at the carnage. Angels of God, struck down in their own house.

The seventh Seraphim, Camael, sits at the table with her father, the book open between them as if they are in a scholarly study session. Camael shows no sign of fear; his hand lays flat next to the pages, calm and still. His wrinkled face gleams with interest, his eyes bright with excitement. Lucifer, beside him, leans back in his chair, a small smile playing at his lips.

No, Evangeline thinks. Camael wouldn't *voluntarily* translate the book. He is God's messenger, His protector, not His usurper. Camael's own sister gave up her life to protect the secrets; would he dishonor her sacrifice?

Beyond the two angels at the table, at the edge of the courtyard, Evangeline finally sees the portal to the UnderRealm. It is a jagged fissure, a wide, deep trench the length of the vast garden. To Evangeline, it seems like a ragged scar slicing the smooth beauty of the Heaven. It is newly ruptured, that is obvious from the torn shrubbery and turned soil, but there are trees that perfectly line the furrow. It makes Evangeline wonder how much the Seraphim knew of the portal.

"Ah, Evangeline, you are brilliant to discover a way in," Lucifer calls out to her.

Evangeline's heart stops at being found out, but she will play along. She has no choice.

"My uncle told me," Evangeline walks toward the table. The sight of the slain Seraphim nauseates her, but she swallows her rising bile.

"An insecure creature," Lucifer laughs off Balam dismissively. "He simply had to forge ahead with the battle before we were ready," Lucifer throws his head back carelessly toward the trench, the portal.

Evangeline feels a sharp sting in her eyes, tears that betray her illusion of control. How can her father joke about such a profound revelation of who she is?

"You never mentioned him before," Evangeline lets the bitter comment slip out. She realizes she is here to stop her father and save the Heavens, but she can't help focusing on her own pain.

"It was a family secret," Lucifer replies easily.

"*I* am family," Evangeline says, unable to hide her hurt.

"Yes," Lucifer says softly in the voice he always reserved for her alone. "But your heart is too pure, like your mother's."

Evangeline feels a rush of pleasure at the welcome comparison, an intangible link to the mother she barely remembers.

"Did she know who you were?"

"A djinni, you mean?" The word is sour in Lucifer's mouth. He looks at Evangeline with a flash of disappointment. "No, Seraphina did not know I am half djinn, but yes, she knew who I was."

Evangeline feels the sting of his rebuke, because she hears the truth in her father's meaning, that the blood in their veins does not define them.

"And she would want you to seize power from God?" Evangeline is scared she's on shaky ground, using her mother against Lucifer. Seraphina, in all of Evangeline's childhood stories, was an angel of perfection.

But Lucifer seems unoffended, and only smiles wryly. "Seraphina was the feistiest angel I've met. She understood power. So, yes, when I seize control and can speak to her spirit on the other side of the veil, she *will* smile with me in victory."

Evangeline's eyes widen at this first hint of darkness she's ever heard about her mother. But then she reminds herself that Lucifer is delusional. He may think Seraphina would be pleased, but only because he wants to believe it.

Except Lucifer isn't delusional. He may be demonic, but he is far from insane. Throughout his quest for God's power, he has proven himself to be smart, strategic, and exceptionally cunning.

Evangeline's skin grows cold, realizing now that she knows so little about her mother. Lucifer just acknowledged Seraphina understood him; would her mother *actually* have supported Lucifer's hubristic plan to dethrone God?

Evangeline shudders at yet another scale dropping from her eyes, her history again being rewritten, her perspective again being revised. The revelation that her mother wasn't perfect seems trivial compared to what she's learned about her father, but the effect is nonetheless monumental. Seeing her parents for who they truly are sharpens her clarity of purpose. It sharpens her identity. Even if Seraphina would support her father's monstrous ambition, *she* does not.

Which means she is not her mother. She is choosing not to be like her mother.

Which means she is choosing to be herself.

"Camael, please," Evangeline turns to the intimidating Seraphim. "Say nothing." Camael casts his eyes upon her and to her great shock, she sees in them only pity.

"My child, I am alive because I know Enochian," he replies, with a sweep of his arms toward his slain brethren. "If your father requests a translation, then I shall oblige."

"But your sister—" Evangeline starts.

"Was a fool," Camael interjects, "to throw away her life for nothing."

Evangeline gapes at the Seraphim, a chosen messenger, one of only seven angels honored to stand in the presence of God. How can he so carelessly dismiss his sister's sacrifice? And how can he so easily dismiss the threat from which Dana was protecting God?

"The name, if you please, Camael," Lucifer says. "And do remember I will know if you are lying."

Camael runs his finger over the brittle page, his eyes scanning the text.

Evangeline's heart races; adrenaline courses her body, her muscles taut, like an animal ready to pounce.

"*Shem—*" Camael begins to utter the powerful name.

Evangeline lunges. She hurls herself across the table, knocking the book to the cobblestones. Camael topples over on his chair, but he is agile, quicker than Evangeline would have assumed, and he's scooped up the book before she can get to her feet.

Abruptly, she feels a hand at her collar, dragging her back, but she's not surprised, nor is she unprepared. Evangeline twists in a figure-eight pattern to escape her father's hold and jumps back, her sword raised in defense.

No, not defense. It's what her father will expect.

Instead, Evangeline attacks.

She thrusts the sword at her father, but with a clang of metal, Lucifer blocks his daughter's blow. Evangeline eases off, pivots, and comes at her father from his side. But he spins with her and again clashes with her sword, and Evangeline sees her mistake. Lucifer trained her; he anticipates her moves, her strategy, her tactics too well.

"The *name*, Camael," Lucifer calls out to the Seraphim, as he keeps his focus firmly on Evangeline.

She hears the rustle of pages, the croak of Camael's voice.

"No!" she screeches, and continues to yell. If her father cannot *hear* the name, he cannot utter it.

But abruptly she feels a wallop across her face, the hot, hard hand of her father's stinging her cheek. It's enough to startle her into silence and in that second of stillness, Camael utters one word.

"*Shemhamphorae.*"

The ineffable name of God.

Lucifer laughs, but Evangeline is filled with rage. *No!* She will not let her father win. For all that is good and holy in these Heavens, for all that is just and right, for all of the angels dead because of her father's manufactured war, Evangeline will not let Lucifer win.

For Uncle Raziel, Evangeline will not let evil win.

And Lucifer cannot win, cannot pronounce the name himself, if he is dead.

Evangeline comes at her father with a fury greater than any anger she's felt before. The rage that powered her attack on Balam and again on Zephon flows through her body now, stronger, tougher than ever.

She can see surprise in her father's eyes, but he is a warrior, and he responds immediately with his own attack. She fights and parries, and he thrusts and cuts. Lucifer is more skillful, has the advantage of intricate flourishes that confuse Evangeline's defense, but even with her injuries Evangeline is more agile, better able to bend and sway out of harm's reach at the same time as she strikes.

As they fight, Lucifer presses his advantage, pushing Evangeline to the rim of the portal, but then Evangeline rallies and swings her sword to her father's throat. He bucks her off, and again their blades clang together, proving father and daughter are matched in power and skill.

It takes all of Evangeline's concentration to match her father, but she is pleased. Lucifer is the ultimate sword fighter in all the Heavens, yet he cannot beat her. The master has taught the student well. If she kills him now, *she* can claim dominance.

But then Evangeline is awash in revulsion. What is she thinking? What is she *doing*? Not long ago, on the cusp of life after Balam's vicious beating during the battle in Sixth Heaven, Evangeline concluded that she is *not* her father.

Evangeline abruptly raises her sword.

She will not kill out of anger. She will not hurt out of revenge.

She is *not* her father's daughter.

Lucifer, startled by the unexpected end to the duel, relaxes his grip, but he does not hesitate to speak.

"In the names of the *Slivers*, in the names secret and divine, I call on Shemhamphorae!"

Evangeline cringes at the incantation.

Her father now has the power of God.

The Heavens will burn.

She hears Camael moan behind her. "He knew the first part of the incantation," Camael mutters, and Evangeline now understands Camael's ploy: in his arrogance, he believed Lucifer did not have the incantation, and would not realize the name alone was insufficient.

But Evangeline has learned through observation and experience never to underestimate Lucifer.

Her father is now only a breath away from his goal to destroy God and take His place. In this one minute that Lucifer now wields God's power, he needs only to command God to relinquish His supremacy and bestow it upon Lucifer permanently.

Evangeline remembers her father's edict, that passivity would always be their gravest threat. She realizes how right he is, so it is in that minute, before the words can escape Lucifer's lips, that Evangeline acts.

She cannot kill her father; she loves him too much. She will not seek revenge; she has too pure of a heart.

But she will banish him, as the Commoners were meant to be banished to the new Earth.

In the second her father—vainly, arrogantly, hubristically—believes he has won, Evangeline reaches out with both hands. For a flicker, she thinks her father believes she has come to join him to rule the Heavens, father and daughter together, but instead of folding herself into his arms as she so desperately wishes, she places her hands on his chest and shoves him towards the jagged portal.

She cries into the still air as her father, shocked, is knocked off balance. He flails for an instant, and then he falls.

Deep into the djinn portal.

Evangeline hears his scream.

Then she hears her own.

CHAPTER 19

A minute passes, then two. The Heaven remains silent. No sound emerges from the portal, no scrape of hands against the rocks from inside the crevice.

Lucifer does not appear.

Evangeline kneels at the edge, staring into the void. Her stomach clenches in a pain she never believed could be real. She felt profound grief at her uncle's death, but this loss of her father is laced with guilt and anger and a terrible, plaintive, desperate wish that she could get him back. She sees in her mind's eye not the ruthless tyrant who tried to destroy God, but the loving father who'd been her only family.

And *she* destroyed *him*.

Evangeline wraps her arms around her midsection and clenches her sides, desperate to control the pain. She remembers thinking, on her birthday last week when Lucifer unexpectedly appeared, how she couldn't bear to be responsible for her father's capture or death. She remembers her constant fear, her terrorizing nightmares, watching her father die over and over and over, but never could she have imagined his death would be literally at her hands.

She spies near her on the ground a clutch of black and violet feathers, remnants of their battle. She grasps one of her father's, bent and broken, its plumes rough to her touch. She pulls out from her pocket the Naofa feather Lucifer gave her on her birthday just six days ago.

A lifetime ago.

In her right hand, she holds the Naofa feather, the feather meant to symbolize safety and protection, which remains soft and silky, so vastly different from the broken, battle-scarred one in her left hand.

Each came from Lucifer. The loving father, the monstrous devil.

Evangeline closes her hand around the soft Naofa feather and slips it gently back in her pocket. She lets the second, damaged feather drop to the ground and turns away.

Camael approaches. Evangeline watches as he walks the length of the portal, chanting. He waves his hand over the trench and to Evangeline's amazement the ground starts to shift, as the sides of the hole slide toward each other. In a moment, the jagged wound in the earth is healed; the ground whole and firm again; the portal is sealed.

"Divine intervention," Camael explains. "Lucifer can never again return."

A sprig of hope nestles its way into Evangeline's heart. "He's not dead?"

"No, I suspect not. Since he is djinn, he can survive in the UnderRealm."

Evangeline exhales with relief, but the bright spark of knowing he's alive quickly flares out. Her father is never coming back.

"What will happen to him?"

Camael gives a wry smile. "Evangeline, I have learned, at my great peril, to never underestimate your father. He will no doubt rise in his new home."

I'm the rightful heir to Iblis's throne, she remembers Balam vehemently telling her.

But Balam is here and Lucifer is there . . . a small smile plays at Evangeline's lips as she imagines her father, crowned, wielding his power in the UnderRealm.

Evangeline runs her eyes along the grass. Not even a scar is visible where the portal, like a maw, had burst open.

"Why was this not sealed like the other portals?" Evangeline asks Camael. She hears a note of accusation in her own voice. If the Seraphim had blocked the portal the way all the others had been stopped after the Djinn War, then none of this would have happened.

"God is a being of hope," Camael replies gently. "He left open for the djinn a path of reconciliation. We, the Seraphim, were thought to be the only ones who could open it, should God dictate."

"So God was willing to allow the violent, destructive djinn to return to the Heavens all the while kicking out the Commoners?" Evangeline refuses to hide her bitterness.

Camael sighs, then slides down to the stone patio beside her. It's disconcerting, Evangeline thinks, to see this proper Seraphim sit so informally.

"God never banished your people," Camael says.

Evangeline stares at him, open-mouthed. "Are you *kidding*? We have been hunted for a *year* since God's decree came down. From you." Evangeline feels herself shaking with the familiar rage, and she breathes heavily to keep herself under control.

Camael shakes his head. "No, our message from God was one of hope. He chose the Commoners to be his new creations, the humans' guardians, because of your unshakeable honor and integrity. He believed your people would guide the humans along the right path."

Evangeline snorts in disgust. "Disguise the motives with any sweet words you want," she says. "Then end result is our banishment."

Camael shakes his head. "You misunderstand. It was never meant to be exile; God wanted to give Commoners the choice. He wanted to offer you a chance at a new life, free from the vitriol of hatred and persecution at the hands of the other classes of angels, but never did he plan to force you."

Again, Evangeline laughs bitterly. "Then I guess his plan backfired." Her old hatred for God bubbles up.

"No," Camael answers quietly. "It was not God's plan. It was ours."

Evangeline stares at him, uncomprehending.

Camael drops his head, his eyes downcast. Evangeline feels as if he is aging before her eyes. The lines etched into his face seem to deepen and the color of his skin seems to turn sallow.

"We, the Seraphim, ordered the Archangels to round you up. Lucifer's rebellion was growing; we feared he would destabilize the whole Heavens, so we thought it best for the peace and security of the Heavens to evacuate you all." He pauses for a beat. "Like with the djinn."

Evangeline feels as if she's been walloped. She can barely appreciate what he's saying. That it wasn't God's will to tear her people from their homes.

For a moment she thinks of Uncle Raziel's faith in God and his confidence in God's goodness. Could he have been right all this time? Is it possible to believe in peace, to believe in hope, by believing in a benevolent God?

But she cannot yet go that far, as much as she yearns for Raziel's divinely inspired tranquility.

"God did nothing to stop you," she throws back at Camael.

Camael rubs his hands over his old face. "God offers all of us free will."

The excuse of the faithful, Evangeline thinks ruefully. Can she accept such a reason? Could God truly be as good as her uncle argued when He allows such sustained cruelty to flourish in his Heavens?

Would a parent allow such deplorable behavior from a child to continue without repercussions?

"God allows you to wipe out an entire class of angels?" Evangeline demands. She feels her chest tighten, the tension in her body acute.

"God does not approve," Camael replies meekly, "But he allows us to learn from our mistakes."

"*Mistakes*?" Evangeline is shaking, she is so angry. "The annihilation of a whole class of angels is a *mistake*?"

"Annihilation was *never* our intent," Camael shoots back, but his words are heavy with the weight of his guilt.

Evangeline jumps to her feet, unable to listen to him anymore. She thinks of Sophia, her best friend who died in battle, of all the Dragons who died in battle. Did the Seraphim's *intent* help them?

She has half a mind to return to Sixth Heaven and tell Michael and Gabriel to give up, to let Balam and the djinn win. She thinks, for a moment, that having the djinn in charge would be less cruel than the Seraphim.

But then she amends her thought. She doesn't want Balam to rule—nor Camael, the last of the Seraphim. She doesn't know how God will select his next messengers, but she does know, with a certainty bred in her bones, that she will not acquiesce to their command either. Never again will she allow herself to be subjugated by the power-hungry whims of others.

Evangeline spins back toward Camael. "You will order the Archangels to desist." She doesn't know if she's in a position to demand such concessions, but she feels like she is. She saved the Heavens from Lucifer. Camael—and *God*—owe her.

Camael, too, gets to his feet. He straightens his shoulders, the bearing of an angel used to power. "Then you must order the Dragon army to stand down."

Evangeline starts. "Me? I'm not—"

The leader, she thinks.

But she hears Michael's words from the battlefield echo in her head. *They'll listen to you because you're Lucifer's daughter.*

She thinks of what she's been fighting for all these years, the restitution of the Commoners' rights in the Heavens. She believed her father would lead them to victory; the Cause was him and he was the Cause.

Yet it wasn't, she now understands. He wasn't the Cause—or, more accurately, he was his own Cause, using his people to gain ultimate power. The food blockade in First Heaven, the torched refugee camp in Second Heaven . . . all to manipulate the Commoners. Evangeline wonders, suddenly, how much of their misery was actually her father's making. The thought terrifies her. She feels like she can no longer parse truth from her own reality.

But her father is gone now and she realizes that if she cannot change their past, maybe she can alter their future. Lucifer always meant for her to step into his role; it's why he expected her to rally their people six days ago. Of course, he meant her to follow his lead, but she won't. She'll lead in her own way.

"The war ends," Evangeline tells Camael, "but the world changes. Life for the Commoners will change."

Camael looks at her with a hint of pity. "I cannot dictate the minds of angels," he says sadly. "Prejudices run deep."

"Only because they're taught it's okay to hate," Evangeline shoots back.

Camael says nothing, although his expression remains tired, wary.

Finally, he speaks. "I can only promise you open dialogue."

Evangeline considers his words. He is offering no concessions, no assurances. She expects many of her people, the likes of Zephon, for example, would never accept such vague terms—and her father, she is certain, would never agree. For too long, the Commoners have been fighting for equality; can she instead settle for merely the possibility of it?

"You guarantee the exile of Commoners will stop," Evangeline counters. She has to have something to offer her people in exchange for the end of the war.

"Agreed," Camael says, "but you must explain their choice to live on Earth."

Evangeline nods. It's an easy compromise; she can't imagine any of the Commoners wanting to leave the Heavens for a strange new world that will be shared with a strange new kind of creature.

Camael continues, but with a heavy sigh. "These are but proposals. I can do nothing for you if the Heavens are no longer . . . my responsibility."

"You mean the djinni Balam," she says. "Michael and Gabriel have a plan."

Still, Camael's expression remains grim.

"They brought dragons," Camael says ruefully.

"We are Dragons," Evangeline replies fiercely.

Camael looks deflated. He sinks into his chair at the stone table, the book still in front of him. Slowly he closes it, with an air of defeat. But Evangeline wonders whether it's truly because of the djinn that he feels conquered.

After all, he's the one who said that prejudices run deep.

Evangeline strides to the table and swipes the book from him. He looks up, and Evangeline catches a flash of wicked animosity in his eyes. It fades quickly, but Evangeline is wary.

"I cannot let you have the book," he declares, though the brittle volume rests in her hands.

"My uncle left it to me," she replies, holding it tight.

"Yet you are Lucifer's daughter," Camael says, and in his voice, she hears a trace of a sneer.

"I *am* Lucifer's daughter," she says. "*Not* Lucifer."

"You could take control. You know the secret name of God."

"Which I heard only because you told my father," Evangeline shoots back.

Camael doesn't respond, and a long silence elapses, in which Evangeline feels the ebb and flow of hostility and resignation. Finally she pockets the book and turns her back on Camael. Maybe the Heavens are already no longer his responsibility.

She walks up the stone steps toward the manor, planning to retrace her steps to the Pearly Gates.

"Evangeline," Camael calls to her.

She wants to keep walking, to not turn back, but she shoves down her petulance and spins slowly to face him.

"The meaning of your name, do you know it?"

Confused at the unexpected shift in topic, Evangeline shakes her head.

"It means 'the bearer of good news,'" he says.

Evangeline smiles and keeps on walking.

The sweet smell of honey lingers as Evangeline again glides through the Pearly Gates. She comes out into a cloud of mist, one that slowly dissipates, revealing before her the battlefield in Sixth Heaven. The scent of honey changes to acrid smoke, the air thick and full with it. She scans her surroundings, assessing. The valley is littered with smoldering boulders, chunks hewed from the monastery's walls. She sees no djinn. She hopes that means Michael and Gabriel's plan—her plan—worked, but she's worried, because she doesn't know where the djinn could be safely held. She can't imagine the Cherubim have a plethora of iron lamp prisons.

What she does see, though, dismays her. A battle still rages.

Between her Dragons and the Archangels.

The fighters are tiring, Evangeline can see. There is little fervor in their movements, less malice than she witnessed earlier. She wonders if the two armies of angels worked together to defeat the djinn, or if only the Archangels routed them. Lucifer's army has had no leader, not since she left them.

No, not true . . . Evangeline sees Zephon, her father's loyal general, on the front lines. Of course. Where there is a vacuum of leadership . . .

Well, Evangeline is here now, and she will stop this fighting. Sword at the ready, she flies through the battle, toward Zephon.

"Hold!" she cries and for an instant, the Dragons and the Archangels pause. But the moment ends almost before it begins, and Zephon returns to his command.

Evangeline grabs his shoulder as he's blocking a blade from an Archangel.

"Stop," she tells him. "The war is over."

Zephon spares a fleeting glance at her, laughs harshly, and resumes his battle. The other Dragons do the same.

Evangeline is momentarily lost. They listened to her when she was crossing to the Pearly Gates; why are they ignoring her now?

She thinks. At that time, they were fighting a common enemy, the djinn.

Now, they are back to fighting each other.

Evangeline retreats, ignoring Zephon's sneer, to find Gabriel. She doesn't know how Camael will communicate his orders to the Archangels, which is why she must get Gabriel to stop his army.

Again, Evangeline scans the valley, her anxiety rising. Where *are* Michael and Gabriel?

There. By the wall of the chapel, a familiar figure, the silhouette of thick wings.

She darts around the fighting, the useless, senseless fighting, and rushes toward the complex.

"Michael!" she calls.

His head shoots up and he immediately flies to her. He envelops her in a bear hug and Evangeline never wants him to let go. She succumbs to the warmth of his embrace, blocking out, for a moment, at least, the drama unfolding around them.

Michael breaks the spell, pulling her gently away to see her face. "Lucifer?" he asks.

"Gone," Evangeline says, but when she sees the worry in Michael's eyes, she adds, "to the UnderRealm. Banished. Forever. By me," she adds quietly.

Michael's expression softens. "You stopped him."

Evangeline can't talk, the pain in her heart rising up to her throat.

"The djinn are also gone," Michael says with a smile of pride. "The iron ore in the limestone worked."

"Where are they?" Evangeline asked. "You know only an iron lamp will detain them."

"Not to worry," Michael says. "They are in iron chains in the monastery's dungeon."

"The monastery has a dungeon?" Evangeline asks, surprised.

Michael nods, smiling.

"Then why the battle?" Evangeline points behind her, to the fight between the Dragons and the Archangels.

"Zephon refuses to stand down. We worked together to defeat the djinn, but as soon as I caught Balam, Zephon turned on us."

Evangeline understands that's true, but still feels like Michael betrayed her. "We were supposed to end this," she says. "Camael promised to call off the Archangels."

"But we have to defend ourselves," Michael protested, and as much as Evangeline wants to blame him, she realizes he's right. She'd do the same thing. If someone came at her with a blade, she'd fight, regardless of her orders from Lucifer.

"*You* can get them to stop, though," Michael insists.

"I tried," she admits, her cheeks reddening.

"Well, *make* them listen."

"*How*? The Dragons aren't under my control—"

Evangeline stops.

"What?" Michael presses.

"Where's your dragon? The one you used to blast apart the limestone?"

Michael cocks his head. "Why?" he asks, his eyes narrowing.

"I need it. And the key. Uncle Raziel's key. Do you still have it?"

Michael pulls out of his pocket the thick iron key, the clue to the djinn's defeat, and hands it to her. He leads her to the field behind Dana's greenhouse. There, tethered to a thick iron peg in the ground, is the dark gray, scaly dragon.

"You rode him? Like the djinn did?" Evangeline asks Michael, impressed.

Michael nods, beaming.

She sees the glint of excitement in Michael's eyes, a welcome surprise given the heavy darkness they've had to endure this past week.

A soul cannot lie and the eyes are its only mirror.

She finds herself smiling at the enthusiasm she sees behind Michael's eyes, the strength she sees in his soul, and feels a strange surge of . . .

Hope.

It's the same unguarded optimism with which her uncle lived.

Evangeline feels, too, an unexpected sense of love and trust and connection to something larger than herself. She's still not sure she can yet accept Raziel's version of a benevolent God, but she does feel like she is on the brink of a whole new uncertain, scary, and exhilarating world.

The rush of emotions propels her into Michael's arms. She cups her hands to his dirt-caked cheek and pulls his head close to hers. Without hesitation, she kisses him, and his only reaction is to draw her in tighter and kiss her harder. She's elated by his passion and she responds in kind.

Finally, she draws back, her smile wide. She looks at the beast of a dragon beside her and hears the thunder of battle behind her, but she feels no fear. Apprehension, yes, anticipation, of course, and possibly a sprinkle of agitation, but no longer anxiety, no longer desperation.

"We've got this, Michael," she says.

He grins in reply. "Never doubted it."

He runs his hand along her arm, turning her palm outward toward the dragon's snout, then nudges her closer as he takes a step back.

"Let him smell you first, like a sky horse," Michael instructs.

"He'll roast me!" Evangeline counters.

Michael shrugs. "You want to ride him or not?"

Evangeline looks at the massive dragon's head. She'd never wanted to go anywhere near his cavernous, fire-spewing mouth, but now she has no choice. She flies slowly toward him, afraid with every wing flap that she'll awaken the dormant giant. Evangeline approaches the beast. He seems docile, with his great reptilian eyes closed, but Evangeline remembers his fiery fury in the skies not long ago. She swallows, and swallows again, but it does no good because her mouth is so dry.

"Hover by his nostril," Michael calls to her.

Out of which smoke bellows when he breathes fire, Evangeline thinks. But she hovers by his nostril because she has to. Because she wants to. Because it's the only way to end this war.

The dragon lifts his massive head, sniffs, as if he is about to sneeze, and Evangeline zips away. She can hear Michael chuckle, but she expects he wasn't chuckling earlier this morning when he was trying to ride the dragon. She moves closer and this time the dragon breathes in her scent. The rush of air sucks her to his scales, but Evangeline flaps hard to keep herself steady. The dragon snorts, then lays down its head.

"Now sit behind his shoulder, and grab the scale on his spine," Michael yells. "I'll untie him."

Evangeline's heart is pounding. She flies to his back, then lowers herself gently. His scales are like armor; she feels like she's sitting on breastplates or shields. But through a joint in his neck, she sees his soft flesh. A creature like any other. She grabs onto the ridge of his spine, and at that touch, the dragon rears its head, spreads its wings and takes to the air.

The movement is fast, swift, and smooth. Quickly, she grabs the reins, still in his mouth, and pulls to her right. The dragon resists at first, so she tugs harder. This time he responds. Evangeline guides him toward the valley, aiming straight for Zephon. She's terrified he'll breathe fire all over her people—she has no idea how to control that.

The angels in battle stagger back as she approaches. She pulls on the reins, hoping the dragon will stop, and he does. His heavy wings flap with a regular beat. Evangeline has to speak up to be heard over the sound.

"Hold!" she cries to her father's—no, *her*—army.

This time, as they look up at her on the back of the massive dragon, they listen. She thinks of her reverie of standing on the rock in Siog Glen with the key, with victory in hand. She's glad that it didn't turn out that way because she realizes that their sacred land in First Heaven is now also tainted with Lucifer's deception and lies. She recognizes there is so, so much she'll need to learn about her father, about his legacy. And she understands it will be her responsibility not to inspire, as she once assumed she'd have to, but to educate. Just as she's had to accept the reality of her own life is altered, so, too, will her people. Evangeline will now have to rewrite history.

And that starts now.

Evangeline dares to hold the reins in one hand and retrieve the key in the other.

Her father was a showman. He knew how to keep a crowd. He knew the importance of winning hearts and minds. He knew the importance of symbols.

Six days ago, Lucifer set out to find the Key to the Kingdom, the possession of which, his people believed, would allow them to reclaim their rights in the Heavens. It would be the end of the war.

Well, Evangeline, not Lucifer, found the key—the book—and she negotiated with Camael to reclaim their rights and end the war.

All she needs now is for her people to believe it.

"We are *Dragons!*" she cries from the top of her ferocious beast.

Then, for all to see, she holds up the key.

And is met with a deafening roar of unity.

ABOUT THE AUTHOR

© Annemarie Grudën

J en Braaksma is a writer and book coach from Ottawa, Canada. She started her career as a journalist, then veered into the classroom as a high school English teacher for almost two decades. Now she helps other writers develop and share their stories. She lives with her husband and two teen daughters. And cats. Four of them. *Evangeline's Heaven* is her first published novel, though it's not the first one she's written. That one still lives in her drawer.

SELECTED TITLES FROM SPARKPRESS

SparkPress is an independent boutique publisher delivering high-quality, entertaining, and engaging content that enhances readers' lives, with a special focus on female-driven work. www.gosparkpress.com

Eye of Zeus: Legends of Olympus Book 1, Alane Adams
$12.95, 978-1-68463-028-8. Finding out she's the daughter of Zeus is not what a foster kid like Phoebe Katz expected to hear from a talking statue of Athena. But when her beloved social worker is kidnapped, Phoebe and her two friends must travel back to ancient Greece and rescue him before she accidentally destroys Olympus.

The Medusa Quest: The Legends of Olympus, Book 2, Alane Adams
$12.95, 9781684630752. Phoebe Katz is back on a new mission to save Olympus—this time to undo the fallout from her last visit, which changed the outcomes of several important myths, including the trials of Hercules and her brother Perseus's quest to slay Medusa. Can Phoebe collect the items she needs to stop Olympus from crumbling?

The Goddess Twins: A Novel, Yodassa Williams. $16.95, 978-1-68463-032-5
Days before their eighteenth birthday, Arden and Aurora's mother goes missing and they discover they belong to a family of Caribbean deities. Can these goddess twins uncover their evil grandfather's plot in time to save their mother, themselves, and the free world?

The Thorn Queen: A Novel, Elise Holland. $16.95, 978-1-943006-79-3
Twelve-year-old Meylyne longs to impress her brilliant, sorceress mother—but when she accidentally breaks one of Glendoch's First Rules, she accomplishes the opposite of that. Forced to flee, the only way she may return home is with a cure for Glendoch's diseased prince.

Red Sun: The Legends of Orkney, Book 1, Alane Adams
$17, 978-1-940716-24-4. After learning that his mom is a witch and his missing father is a true Son of Odin, 12-year-old Sam Baron must travel through a stonefire to the magical realm of Orkney on a quest to find his missing friends and stop an ancient curse.